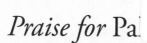

*Praise for Pa...*

"A timely, page-turning ride through Civil War history, *Pale Blue Light* is full of derring-do, romantic twists, and memorable characters."

— KENDAL WEAVER, state editor, Associated Press (ret.)

"I liked this action hero, Rabe Canon, from the outset, but I didn't know he was going to turn into James Bond. This novel will leave you stirred, and parts of it might leave you a little shaken, too."

— TOM WRIGHT, editor, *Decatur Daily* (ret.)

"Climb into a murder plot in this visual thrill ride of a novel that sweeps us through the Civil War with guns blazing and ends with—of all things—an aerial episode and a flight not easily forgotten."

— TIM PRINCE, publisher, *Clanton Advertiser*

"Writing a work set during the most tumultuous period of American history is a dauntingly ambitious task . . . Tucker puts *Pale Blue Light* onto the pages with amazing grace."

— CARROLL DALE SHORT, author, *The Shining Shining Path*

"*Pale Blue Light* is a compelling story that blends history with fiction in a way that puts you right in the middle of the Civil War-era South.

— JAMES PHILLIPS, editor, Jasper (Ala.)
*Daily Mountain Eagle*

"Skip Tucker's novel of the Civil War South is a time machine to the gritty nineteenth century."

— BILL PERKINS, editor, *Dothan Eagle*

"Skip Tucker can flat-out tell a story. His characters are colorful, his facts are straight, and his writing is engaging."

— FRANCES COLEMAN, editor, Mobile *Press-Register*

"*Pale Blue Light* is a book anyone who has an interest in Southern history should read."

— WAYNE CLARK, Valley *Times-News*

# PALE BLUE LIGHT

A Novel By

## Skip Tucker

NewSouth Books
Montgomery

NewSouth Books
105 South Court Street
Montgomery, AL 36104

ISBN 978-1-60306-310-4 (paperback)
ISBN 978-1-60306-206-0 (ebook)

Library of Congress Cataloging-in-Publication Data (for hardcover edition)

Tucker, Skip.
Pale blue light : a novel / by Skip Tucker.

p. cm.

ISBN: 978-1-60306-205-3 (hardcover)

1. United States—History—Civil War, 1861–1865—Fiction.  I. Title.
PS3620.U329P35 2012
813'.6—dc23
2012013105

Design by Brian Seidman

Printed in the United States of America
by Versa Press

*I dedicate this book, foremost, to my wife Lissa and my son Jeb.
Having saved my life, they became it.*

*And in memory of John Hamilton Elliott.*

And we are here as on a darkling plain
Swept with confused alarms of struggle and flight,
Where ignorant armies clash by night.

— MATTHEW ARNOLD, "DOVER BEACH"


Hush now, or Stonewall will get you.

— WASHINGTON CITY MOTHER TO HER FRETFUL CHILD


We see him now,—the old slouched hat
Cocked o'er his eye askew;
The shrewd, dry smile, the speech so pat,
So calm, so blunt, so true.
The "Blue-Light Elder" knows 'em well;
Says he, "That's Banks,—he's fond of shell;
Lord save his soul! we'll give him hell,"
That's "Stonewall Jackson's way."

Silence! ground arms! kneel all! caps off!
Old "Blue Light's" going to pray.
Strangle the fool that dares to scoff!
Attention! it's his way.
Appealing from his native sod,
"Hear us, hear us Almighty God,
Lay bare Thine arm; stretch forth Thy rod!"
That's "Stonewall Jackson's way."

— JOHN WILLIAMSON PALMER, "STONEWALL JACKSON'S WAY"

# Contents

# Preface

This is not a history book, but historical fiction. While I have described battles as accurately as possible, there are inconsistencies in the interest of storyline and movement. I own them.

It is also likely that I have wronged one of history's great generals, A. P. Hill. There is possibility, however small, that I am right.

There is authentic intrigue. I found once, in a tenth grade literature book published in the twenties, an account of that night in Chancellorsville by someone in the reconnaissance party who described "a shadowy presence" bent over the stricken Stonewall. I never relocated it.

Finally, this is not about the Civil War. It is an espionage, spy thriller set in the War Between The States. Importantly, one of my goals is to humanize the legendary Jackson and to provide a fun, thrilling read and ride. I hope folks enjoy it.

# Acknowledgments

With appreciation: the late, great John Hamilton Elliott, a Renaissance Man if ever one lived; my sister and brother, Beth and Tuck, and Penelope and Sarah and contingent; my in-laws, Fernando and Lourdes Astilla, and sisters Kristy and Lena and their crews, and to Danny, who came into our family at just the right time; to absent friends and family: Claude and Frances Tucker, Chuck Tucker, Shelton Prince, and Trevor Armbrister, who believed; and to J. B. and Ann and all the Beatys, a second family.

For their help and assistance also, thanks to Kerry Kelley, my friend since the eleventh grade, and his Beverly; Tom and Judy Camp, beloved buds who gave aid and comfort; Bobby Horton, for the Stonewall drawing and for being Bobby Horton; Mike Kilgore, for the read; Coach L. C. Fowler, for two years of football practice hell and twenty great games, and my Carbon Hill Bulldogs; the *Daily Mountain Eagle* in Jasper, Ala., present incarnation and past, where I learned; George Deavours and the Ranch House crew and posse; Brian Seidman and the staff of NewSouth Books, for excellent work; and Kendal Weaver, for encouragement and kind words about the novel for me and to others.

# PART I

## 1

# *Rabe Canon*

Rabe Canon launched his long body from the saddle even before the shrill whine of the ricochet faded into the moonlit midnight mist.

Leaving the saddle, he shouted the code that would cause his huge stallion to execute a wide left circle and return to him. From that point, Canon was no more conscious of thought than was the cordial autumn night that embraced bleak California hills.

He did not recall how he dove, left hand outstretched to break his fall, while one of his twin custom-made .50 caliber Krupp revolvers snicked automatically into his right hand. And if some cosmic referee had stopped the proceedings long enough to ask Canon how he had gotten from the saddle to his position behind a boulder, pistol in hand, he could not have said.

Nor did he remember the way he rolled, first on his left shoulder, then his right. The shoulder rolls added a zig-zag effect to his course, and the initial roll on his left shoulder absorbed the greater impact of the dive from his saddle, protecting the newly drawn pistol.

Canon was not aware the shoulder rolls had taken him behind the one boulder, equidistant of three, that afforded the best cover and best view of the landscape. From the moment Canon heard the bullet's dark song, grown too familiar, he became the machine that three years of war had taught him to be. His instinct shifted from defense to offense. Person or persons unknown had tried to kill him, had failed. Now it was his turn. And he would not fail. After all, Canon thought with a wolfish grin, he was in the business.

Had the three men atop the adjacent hill seen that grin, they might have nodded silently to each other and gotten the hell out of there. Perhaps not. They had killed before. They were three to one, were being paid to do a job.

They had no more compunction about killing than about eating supper, though they probably enjoyed killing just a little bit better.

Nor had Canon compunction about killing. Not this feral Canon. The pampered plantation creature he had been before the war had died even before Mulberry Manor died, with comrades blown to pieces around him and enemy who fell before his guns.

As he checked the loads in his twin pistols, Canon cleared his mind in preparation for the mental drill taught him by the Indian war chief who was friend to his father and companion of Canon's youth.

The sense of smell was important, Mountain Eagle taught him, and the sense most often ignored by white men. Its importance was critical. In the dark, Canon brought in a deep draught of cool air, first with mouth open, then closed. It bore the smell of dust and light dew; there was the loamy aroma of sere grasses and a faintly tasteable tang of gunsmoke mingled with woodsmoke.

Woodsmoke. Canon cast his mind back to the instant of the shooting, calling on his mind's eye to reconstruct the scene. He imaged the craggy hillock which bordered the right side of the narrow trail, saw the muzzle flash cut the darkness, but there was no evidence of firelight in the scene.

That meant at least two of them up there; one to tend a covered fire and one to watch the trail. Canon added sound to his recall, mentally deleting his horse's hoofbeats and the creaking of the saddle rig. He concentrated on the rifle shot, yes, it was a rifle. The muzzle flash and rolling report indicated so. And it was a Sharps, he was sure, though oddly flat for the sound of a Sharps. Could it be . . . yes! It was the new seven-shot repeating rifle supplied only to Union troops besieging Petersburg. The Rebels disparagingly called them "Sunday guns" that could be loaded on Sunday and fired all through the week—one shot per day. But Canon had tried out a captured piece and recognized that it would elevate the death rate in this war and any wars to come.

He no longer had doubts about what awaited him in San Francisco. There would be much death this day, very likely his among them. That was all right, too, so long as he could do what he came to do. He did not mind dying. He felt he deserved it.

What the hell, wondered Canon, is a seven-shot Sharps doing in an ambush ten miles from San Francisco? The answer suddenly snapped into his mind, and with it came the solution to a puzzle that had baffled him for more than a year. The answer filled him with rage. His long-held suspicions were suddenly confirmed, and now he felt a blood lust so strong that a coppery taste tingled on his tongue. The urge to kill was so fierce that he wanted to charge the hill with a Rebel yell that would freeze his enemies to their marrow. He wanted to fight hand-to-hand. He wanted his hands on the throats of any and all who stood in the way of his mission.

The mission. Yes. Must remember the mission. The thought curbed Canon. His blood lust became anger, and he mentally iced it into a cold killing rage.

He thought of the way Indian warriors greeted dawn on the day of battle: It is a good day to die. Canon had greeted many dawns with those words during the past three years, and he silently mouthed them. It is a good day to die. A very good day to die.

Canon sensed movement behind him, dropped and spun to one knee as he brought up the gun barrel, then he grinned again. The horse had returned for him. He signaled the animal to be still, then turned his attention to the top of the hill fifty yards away. The enemy had made a mistake. The moon, though shrouded by the mist, was in front of him. It would offer an outline, however faint, of those who tried to kill him. Like a lion leaving his lair on the veldt, Canon slipped softly into the night.

Atop the hill, the three would-be assassins were hotly engaged in whispered debate.

"Gawddammit, you shoulda let us shoot, too," said the leader in an injured tone.

"Hell," replied the rifleman, "they wasn't no time. He was on us too damn quick. 'Sides, I got him, didn't I? Ya'll seen him pitch outa the saddle. Say, ain't that sumbitch big, or what?"

"He cain't be big as he looked, but I barely seen anything," said the third. "It's too damn dark and it was too damn quick, but I'll tell you one thing; you better get yore ass down there and make sure of him."

"Awright, awright, I'll go," complained the first outlaw. "But seeing as how I do all the work, I claim the hoss."

"So that's it!" hissed the leader. "You took it on yourself 'cause you want the hoss. Well, it ain't gonna work. We sell the hoss and split the money even."

"Right," declared the leader. "But the hoss ain't no problem. Here he come up the hill. And it be a beauty."

"First, go see if the sumbitch is dead," said the third, wearily, "then catch the horse, if it's still in the territory, then let's decide who gets what."

"Gawd, but you said it right," agreed the rifleman. "Look at the size of 'im. Come here, horsie," and he stretched out his hand.

Canon, hanging onto the saddle horn and his handcrafted slings on the opposite side of the horse, reached his right hand under the horse's neck, across the brisket, and fired three big rounds from the Krupp revolver.

The first bullet passed through the rifleman's outstretched hand and tore into his heart. The leader, too, died with a bullet in his breast. The third outlaw had time only to gape, then he flapped backwards with a bullet through his sternum.

Canon dropped from the slings and walked toward the moaning outlaw, gun ready. He took the holstered pistol, flung it away.

"I think I know who sent you," Canon said, "but I want to make sure. Tell me the name." The outlaw only groaned. "Look," Canon said, "we can do this the hard way or the easy way. Your choice." The outlaw said nothing, then screamed as Canon kicked him in the ribs.

"Give me the name, or I'll shoot you," Canon said.

"Go ahead, mister. Finish me off. I'm done for anyways."

Canon shot the man in the leg. When the screams died to a whimper, Canon glared down at him. "I didn't say I'd kill you, I said I'd shoot you," Canon said. "Now tell me who hired you or I'll shoot you again." The outlaw quickly, whimperingly, complied, then again begged Canon to finish him.

"Well," said Canon, "I guess you'd do the same thing for me." The .50 roared.

Riding away, he wondered how things were at the plantation, now that the manor house was gone. If he knew his father—and Canon felt he knew

Buck Canon better than anyone else, with the possible exception of Mountain Eagle—then Buck and the Eagle had not stood idly by and watched the Yankees burn it. Yet he was certain the two men most important in his life were alive. It would take more than a couple of Yankee regiments to stop those two.

Canon would like to have seen Mulberry once more, to have his memories made real again. He had thought himself so worldly then, before the war. Now he knew he had been an innocent twenty-three-year-old who leisured at hunting game and pursuing the belles around Montgomery.

But Canon had rarely boasted of his prowess or paramours as did many of the young bloods in Montgomery. For one thing, it was dangerous to do so. He had seen too many of his contemporaries shot, married or run out of town for their boasting. Rightly, too, he thought. He considered such actions beneath the dignity of a gentleman.

Life on the central Alabama plantation had been gentle and sweet. Many a pampered, powered pretty had fallen willing victim to Canon's philistine physique, family wealth and the hint of cruelty that lurked in his gray eyes.

Canon considered the word. Gentleman. Gentle man. Strange that nearly every male in the South, high born or low, would cheerfully call for a duel to the death with anyone who disputed his right to be called a gentle man.

## 2

# *Broken Hearts*

Canon prized his palomino, Hammer. The stallion stood eighteen hands tall at the withers. He was "much hoss" as old Buck Canon was wont to say, and Canon meant to have him on the spring day he first saw him. It was a warm Friday afternoon, the kind of day that made the twenty miles from Mulberry Manor to Montgomery a pleasure ride through white honeysuckle and apple blossom.

Hammer was tied to the hitching post outside Canon's favorite Montgomery emporium, Hospitality House. Even as a two-year-old, Hammer dwarfed the horses hitched beside him. Canon, approaching his twenty-first birthday, found the present he wanted. He took one look and went in search of the owner.

The wiry Texan, Bill Kelley, would not even discuss selling the horse. After hours of coaxing by Canon, he finally agreed to play five-card stud poker for him, his two thousand dollars in chips representing the horse. They played for a day and a night, then Canon found the momentum and ultimately a club flush.

Hospitality House was well appointed. The gaming room chandelier lit the furthermost corners and set the brass and cut glass asparkle. The house drink, Planter's Punch, was known statewide.

Kelley tried the punch as the two men chose a green baize table and called for cards. He pronounced the drink deserving of its excellent reputation. But poker, he declared, called for bourbon whiskey. He looked inquiringly at Canon, who nodded and then found himself in a drinking match as well as the toughest card game of his life. If Canon won, it would not be right for his genial companion ever to regret his own conviviality. By midnight, Canon was ahead on drinks but down a thousand dollars.

He had rarely been happier than when Kelley called a rest break and headed out back. Canon chose the front door, marveling at the man's capacity for bourbon and branch water. But as the cool wind off the river began to thin the cobwebs thrumming in his head, Canon looked at the hitching post to which Hammer had been tied Friday. He's mine!, thought Canon, suddenly certain he was going to win.

Close on the heels of that thought came another. It was a stern warning to himself that there is no such thing as a person drinking himself sober. Canon determined to open up a bit but at the same time to do nothing foolish. Poker was sometimes nothing more than pouncing on another's mistake.

By daylight, Canon had won back his thousand and fifteen hundred more, thanks to an outside straight he drew against two pair showing. He refused to fall for the bluff that he was facing a full house. Kelley congratulated him good-naturedly.

By noon, word had gotten round about the game. Spectators were lined three deep around the table. Cigar smoke billowed about the players and each hand was played to applause for the winner. More and more often, it was for Canon.

After eighteen hours, Canon was up thirty-five hundred dollars and clearly owned the momentum. It was over soon after. Canon dealt the cards, one down and four up, with bets made after each new card was dealt. Canon held four clubs, Kelley had four hearts. Each man used a thumb to lift a corner of his hole card, peered at it. The fifth fleur-de-lis sat pat under Canon's hand. He had hit the flush!

Canon showed calm, but his heart was racing. If Kelley had also hit his flush, Canon was in trouble. Kelley's hand showed an ace up, which would outrank Canon's hand. His was only to the queen. Kelley smiled as he pushed his remaining chips to the middle of the table.

"Fifteen hundred, Rabe," he said.

A thin film of sweat gathered on Canon's brow. He knew that, under strict rules of the game, he could raise the bet and that Kelley would not have enough chips to call. Kelley would have to withdraw his bet.

Canon slowly pushed his chips to the middle of the table. "Fifteen hundred, Bill. I call," he said. The room, which had been filled with a low murmur, fell quiet. This was perhaps the deciding hand of the game. Should Canon lose, the momentum would shift in a big way.

Kelley grinned widely, grabbed the deck and slipped his cards into it.

"Broken hearts, son," he said. "No flush, no pair, no nothing. If you have another puppy's paw, you also got you a damned fine horse."

Canon flipped over the fifth club, and Hospitality House went wild.

Later, after the crowd finished back slapping, hat throwing and drink buying, Canon walked Kelley to the Texan's upstairs room.

"Why did you do it, Bill?" said Canon. Kelley looked at him quizzically.

"Don't play dumb," Canon continued. "I looked at the deck while everybody was buying you drinks. Canon pulled six cards from his pocket, spread them into a fan. "You not only held a heart flush to begin with, you threw one of them away and then drew another heart. You threw away a winning hand, then you folded a winning hand. Why, Bill?"

The big man blushed.

"I made up my mind at midnight that I wanted you to have the horse, Rabe. I'm getting on in years, you know, and I care more about that animal than most anything I've got, with the possible exception of the old lady that's waiting for me back at the house.

"It's just me and her and a few ranch hands. Apaches got my boy years ago. He'd be about the same age as you. So I decided last night to leave Hammer to you in my will. But it's a long way to Dallas and mayhap a few more years before I pass on. A lot can happen.

"So I set you a test with that flush hand. If you had raised the bet and made me withdraw, I would have probably found an excuse to get out and left Hammer to you in the will. But you showed me you deserve that hoss. He's yours, quick as I can fill out the papers. You get the saddle, too. Ain't no Alabama saddle fitten for that palomino."

Canon had noticed the saddle's horn, something that most saddles did not have. Mexicans devised it. It was used to anchor the rope when working with tough range cattle. Western cowboys had copied the invention. Canon had heard of the saddle horn, but had never seen one. He doubted he'd have much use for it, but thanked Bill profusely.

Kelley took the horse Canon had ridden to town, for a memento, he said. But he refused any extra payment for Hammer and also refused to see Hammer to say goodbye.

"Couldn't stand it," he said with an embarrassed chuckle. Kelley gave orders for Hammer to be saddled and brought around. Canon took leave of the rancher amidst promises to write and to visit one day. He was home with Hammer by dark.

He was up and working with him by dawn, and for many successive dawns.

CANON'S FATHER AND HIS FATHER-FRIEND, Mountain Eagle, were as taken by the stallion as Canon and promised to help train Hammer. They made a formidable team. Canon had traveled, and learned much about European horse training methods. Buck was a pioneer to whom the horse had been the most important equipment he could possess. Mountain Eagle had been a war chief for the Cherokee. Horses, to them, were simply life and death.

Buck Canon carved the sprawling plantation from wilderness bordering the Alabama River, named it Mulberry because of the huge broadleaf berry trees which surrounded and cooled the manor house. He was a pioneer who helped settle the area and usher in statehood. And he paid fair value to the Cherokees for the land, but Buck could not shake a feeling of guilt that he had gotten rich off lands the red man had tended for generations. Worse was the death march the dispossessed Indians were sent on that became known as the Trail of Tears. He also felt some guilt that he "owned" two hundred human beings. Rabe Canon opposed slavery and wanted them freed. His father refused, saying they would be shunned by the other plantation owners. The slaves became the single source of conflict between father and son, as the land had originally been a source of conflict between Buck and Mountain Eagle. The latter conflict had been so severe that it lived on in legend.

MOUNTAIN EAGLE HAD BEEN a leader on the Trail of Tears as the Cherokees were pushed from Alabama. He watched his people die on that torturous journey to Oklahoma and vowed revenge on the best known settler in Alabama, whoever he might be. He turned out to be Buck Canon. Mountain Eagle did not know that Buck had favored Indian rights. The Eagle only knew his vow.

Once the limping remainder of his tribe was settled in the West, the Eagle returned. He found Buck clearing land. For long minutes, Mountain Eagle watched his enemy. It was early morning in early summer. The woods were singing with sounds of nature even as the axe rang and fire crackled. The pioneer was stripped to the waist, his long sandy hair swinging wildly as he put all his two hundred pounds into each swing of the blade. Slabbed muscles on his sweating six-foot frame rippled and shone in the morning sun.

As the Indian watched, he also took in aromas born of this beautiful land. The sharp, fruity tang of pine nettles blended with perfumes of wildflower and honeysuckle. Eagle identified the songs of thrush, robin and mockingbird. This land of my forefathers, he thought, taken from me forever. Hatred awoke in him. Three inches shorter than the white man, thirty pounds lighter, he would need rage to win open combat. He would have to be quick, quick, quick. He must kill this white devil.

But should he risk his own life in open combat? This was the choice he had to make. He could strike from his hidden position—there was no shame in it against a sworn enemy—or face death for the greater glory of hand-to-hand fighting.

Spurning ambush, the Indian stepped forward and called out a warning. Buck whirled, reached, and brought up a long rifle. He guessed the Indian's identity, though he said nothing. Buck had heard that a dangerous Cherokee was on his way back from the west, intending to kill a white leader. Buck knew there was no time to explain, though he spoke some Cherokee and knew most Cherokees spoke English. This Eagle would not believe him, would think him a coward. He also realized the Indian could have probably ambushed him, rather than stepping out as he now did with nothing but breechclout, war hatchet and knife.

The Indian wore paint, and the single Eagle's feather in his hair announced his name and status. Nodding his compliments to the Indian, Buck set the rifle aside, drew his knife and picked up his axe.

Eagle had heard stories of the ferocity and fighting ability of this white man. He began to chant his death song as the men closed.

The story of their struggle was still told over campfires. The doctor who treated the men passed the tale through white ranks, and Indians who had been allowed to stay temporarily behind took the story with them when they traveled west. The fight took place a year before Rabe Canon was born, but he prevailed on the men to re-enact the battle at the spot where it occurred. He stood mesmerized as the aging warriors perfectly recalled the scene, and demonstrated tremendous blows exchanged and sustained.

They fought almost an hour, as recollected. Canon chilled at the description of terrible wounds each had inflicted on the other. Anyone would have doubted the veracity of the story. Anyone, thought Canon, not there now to see the scars the men displayed as they told the way of the wounds that caused them.

Finally, Mountain Eagle said, his journey from the west, coupled with loss of blood, weakened him until he began to fail. Neither man had strength to stand, so they continued on their knees to slash at each other. The axes were gone. They stabbed and grappled.

Mountain Eagle said he could feel his spirit begin to leave him, but that he was proud because he knew his enemy could not live out the day. Finally, Eagle said, he was exhausted. He toppled onto his back and called out for the Great Spirit to accept him.

"Your father reached down and took the knife from my hand, and I awaited the thrust of his blade in my breast," Eagle said. "But this man beside me, he I named Lion Heart, for he threw away the knives and took my hand. He said we would journey together as brothers to the Great Spirit.

"My spirit had darkened so that I could no longer see. The last thing I remembered was the sound of your father's body falling next to mine."

Canon knew what had happened then. His mother, worried because her husband had not come home for the noon meal, rode out and found the two men. She stanched their wounds and rigged a travois on which she moved them back to the house. She patched them best she could though she expected neither to live through the night and then fired signal shots until neighbors came. She sent them to Montgomery for a doctor. By the time he arrived, the men had returned to semi-consciousness. The doctor stayed long enough to get the story, patch them somewhat better, and pronounce them both goners. Then he left to spread the story.

"She said we both lived just so's she'd have to wait on us hand and foot for a month," the elder Canon winked at Rabe. "Said it was nothing but pure cussedness on both our parts. Might be so. Your mother was a great seeker, knower and teller of the truth, boy. But you watch this here lyin' redskin bastid. He was fit as a fiddle when he jumped me. Weren't tired a bit from that trip."

Mountain Eagle gave a rare smile, clutched Buck by the shoulder, looked at Rabe and shook his head in comic resignation.

A GREAT REGRET IN CANON'S LIFE was that he never knew his mother. Her blue blood went back to the English cavaliers. Her hair was like spun gold.

She died at Canon's birth. Died holding him, Mountain Eagle said, gazing at him as the light left her eyes. Buck grieved mightily. He had at first, against his will, blamed the infant for his wife's death. But the Eagle convinced Buck that the baby was Evalena's last and greatest gift to him. Father, son and Indian friend became inseparable companions.

FROM HIS YOUTH, CANON learned love for the hunt and the skills of a master woodsman. Hunting bear taught Rabe courage and coolness. These things were required when a cornered three-hundred-pound black bear turned to fight. Riding to hounds tested Canon's horsemanship. Long chases on foot for deer built up legs and wind, and hunting the wily raccoon honed his skills of moving quickly and quietly through woods at night.

Buck Canon's marksmanship was heralded, but Rabe was his equal at age sixteen. Hunts for dove and quail elevated the young man's snap shot to deadly accuracy.

Their favorite hunt was for wild turkey, an elusive and crafty bird. Alabama enjoyed one of the largest concentrations of the bird Ben Franklin wanted for America's national symbol.

The domestic turkey is so stupid it will tilt back its head during a rainstorm, open its beak and drown. A wild turkey is its opposite, so cunning that an accomplished outdoorsman might never see one in a state with a wild turkey population of two hundred fifty thousand.

Every turkey hunter has at least one story of a "character turkey" that tricked him, using what seems like supernatural intelligence. These stories are for the most part true. Eagle likened turkey hunting to a game of chess. There are moves and countermoves, thrusts and parries. Stalking a wild turkey is more than just hunting a prey outdoors.

The expert hunter must be able to move through dawn's half-light without snapping a twig. His patience must be such that he can sit immobile for hours. He must be a dead shot, for one shot is all anyone gets. To be an expert turkey hunter, one must be expert at many things.

All this Mountain Eagle explained to Canon. One of the initiation rites into the Eagle's band of Cherokees was to catch a wild turkey with bare hands. It took Canon two months to accomplish the feat. By the time he was nineteen, Canon enjoyed a statewide reputation among turkey hunters. At twenty-three, his fame had reached regional status. And it was that fame that brought about Canon's meeting with Professor Tom Jackson.

A LETTER FOR CANON arrived on a bleak Monday afternoon in the winter of 1860. The weather, which had been low and threatening for several days, unleashed itself the previous night. Winds lashed and moaned, filling the gutters with debris and terrifying the house servants. Finally the storm passed, but the skies were still gray and black, and occasional showers of sleet pelted down.

Canon's mood, as he received the letter, matched the weather. He puzzled over the return address: Major Tom Jackson, Virginia Military Institute, Lexington. The name rang no bells, yet Canon felt somehow hesitant to open the letter. It felt heavy to him, much heavier than it was possible for so thin an envelope to be. There is portent here, he thought.

Seconds later, Canon was laughing at his own timidity. It was as straightforward and innocuous a note as he had ever received.

Dear Mr. Canon:

I make so bold as to write to ask you, whom I have yet to meet, a favor. My sole justification in doing so is that I have it on good authority that you and I are afflicted by the same pernicious disease, namely, the American Wild Turkey.

We also share a mutual friend, whose name I shall not divulge for fear of getting him in trouble with you. It is from him I learned your address.

He tells me you are the perfect turkey stalker and often succeed where others fail. That is why I am inviting you to visit me in Virginia. There is a veritable demon of a gobbler here that has proved totally beyond me. I enjoyed a reputation similar to yours until I ran across Old Scratch. Both my reputation and mind are now largely gone.

If you have any plans to be in Virginia in the near future, please plan to spend a few days with me and we shall pursue this demon. All I can promise you is a good hunt, a decent larder and an excellent cook.

Our friend also told me you are a student of military history. If this is so, we have more common ground as I am a professor here at Virginia Military Institute. We can talk turkey and also discuss the noble profession of making war.

    Please come if you can.

Sincerely,

MAJOR TOM JACKSON (RETIRED)

Canon smiled again at his misapprehension. He looked at the gray day outside and was suddenly bored with the sameness of his life. Though pleasant, the distractions he normally enjoyed were beginning to pale. Even the finest of routines, he decided, can become jaded.

The second reading of the letter decided him. A turkey that roamed in winter, while not rare, was unusual. And Canon for some time had wanted to visit the South's new war college. War both fascinated and repelled him. He was sick of hearing about the Confederacy, sick of hearing about the Union. But mostly he was sick of being trapped indoors. He rang for pen and paper. A week later he was on a train to Virginia.

The train ride from Montgomery to Virginia was grand. Flat from Montgomery to Atlanta, the dirt rich and red, the land begins to give way to the loamy soil of the Appalachian chain.

Gentle hills roll higher and higher until, near the North Carolina border, peaks loom in the distance. Past that point, the skyline is dominated by the beauty of the Blue Ridge Mountains.

Canon had made the run before, in spring and in the fall. Each trip seemed to overshadow the previous. Spring brought myriad shades of green from mountain glades, offset by high meadows with varicolored wildflowers. In autumn, the slopes fairly shouted with a cacophony of color, flaming and bursting within the brilliance of dying leaves.

But Canon had never seen the Blue Ridge in winter. He realized that spring's beauty and autumn's majesty had hidden, or at least disguised, the mighty grandeur of forbidding mountain peaks. Now, denuded, as if a prize fighter had thrown off his velvet cape, the mountains were barren, stark and awesome. They awaited their covering of snow.

Canon drowsed. But he finally gave up the notion of real, restful slumber.

The pullman chamber beds were not adequate for his frame, and the hard passenger car benches were almost as cramping.

The bit of thin sleep Canon managed was interspersed with nightmare images and alarms, staccato glimpses of gray men mingling wildly with blue men, of shouting and the screams of dying horses.

Shortly before dawn, the conductor announced the Lexington stop. Canon gathered his gear and made arrangements for the unloading of his luggage, then returned to his seat.

Through the window, as the train slowed, he could see a few blurred lights twinkling through night and mist. The train stopped. Canon stepped out into the dark and fog.

# 3

# *Old Scratch*

A phantom awaited Canon on the depot platform. At least it seemed a phantom, tall and shadowy in the cold December mist. Canon's sense of foreboding increased as the shadow moved toward him.

"Hello, Mr. Canon," said the man, extending a welcoming hand, "welcome to the halls of war."

Canon thought the remark unusual but appropriate. The man taught at a military college and, after all, they were meeting to make war, if only on a turkey. They made polite conversation as they walked toward a line of carriages for hire.

The professor was average size, average complexion, and had thinning dark brown hair. His booted feet were huge, but his hands small, almost girlish. Canon's hand enclosed the other man's like a cocoon. Jackson's broad, full face carried a brush beard. Above the beard projected a Roman nose, above the nose a high domed forehead, between them a pair of pale blue eyes.

The voice was a teacher's voice, rather high pitched but not loud, and firm in tone and timbre. Modulated. They climbed into the closed gig as a porter loaded Canon's bags and hunting gear. The driver spoke up his horse. Gauzy outlines of Lexington buildings were visible through the thinning fog as they rolled toward the VMI campus. The professor, for Canon could think of him in no other terms, gave a brief background of town and college as they bumped along.

Canon's apprehensions vanished with the fog. There appeared nothing unusual about this man. He was the epitome of a scholarly Southern gentleman and most likely a very ordinary fellow.

Canon was beginning to silently chide himself for his wild imaginings when the professor reached into the pocket of his black broadcloth suit, produced two large lemons and matter-of-factly offered one to him.

It was not yet seven A.M. Canon had never considered lemon a particularly desirable fruit, except in the odd bowl of punch, and certainly not for breakfast. He declined, he hoped, graciously.

The professor was nonchalant. "I am of unfortunate physical disposition," he said, "and stomach disorders are a constant trouble to me. I have found that fruits and vegetables, scientifically consumed, aid the body and mind. The acidic property of the lemon is of particular assistance to my digestive tract. I recommend it to you. No? You must try it sometime."

He bit off one end of the lemon and noisily sucked its juice.

The fog burned away during the half-hour ride to campus, where students scurrying to class stopped to wave a salute at the professor as the carriage passed.

By the time the driver pulled to a stop in front of a neat white frame house, the two men were engaged in a spirited discussion of astronomy and artillery, the diverse subjects the professor taught at VMI.

Canon warmed to the man. Though certainly a bit unusual in some of his beliefs, the professor at times displayed intensity which Canon found engaging. Most of the talk had been small, but Canon learned the professor was graduated from West Point and had earned the rank of major fighting in the brief Mexican War.

His second wife—the first had died soon after their marriage—was daughter of the school president. They had one daughter, born six summers ago. Jackson's young nephew lived with them.

If Canon was intrigued by the professor, he was enchanted by his wife. Mary Anna was a model of what Canon considered a Southern lady. She was slight, and her fine light brown hair was pulled back into a bit of a bun, with loosely rolled curls at her temples. She wore a simple but stylish gray day frock.

Graceful and gracious, she was concerned but not patronizing, friendly without a hint of coquettishness. Canon despised the coquette.

She settled Canon in his room while the professor, who had walked to the train station, set out on another constitutional. His frail health, he said, did not allow him to miss his constitutional, rain or shine.

Canon completed his morning toilet with a wash and change of clothes about the time the professor returned to call him to breakfast. Given the episode with the lemon and Mary Anna's own diminutive frame, he feared there would be light going at table.

Instead, the breakfast board almost groaned in the middle. Everything was in triplicate. There were breakfast meats of ham, bacon and sausage; three gravies; eggs fried, eggs scrambled, eggs poached; pancakes, hoecakes, biscuits. There were fruits, melons, preserves.

Canon willed his stomach not to rumble as he waited through a lengthy and fervent prayer offered by his host. Then he watched in surprise as the professor took one poached egg and a small bowl of preserved figs and Mary Anna took a biscuit and a bowl of hominy grits. The children had apparently been fed in the kitchen and packed off to school.

For the first time since they met, the professor smiled at Canon. Canon would come to learn that smiles were rare to the man because he was of serious demeanor. But the professor smiled over the feast.

"Frankly," he said, "I was doubtful in regard to reports of your physical stature. But I am happy to know that in this world there are some reports which do not exaggerate. In any event, I believe in being prepared.

"We have a difficulty in our home. My wife loves to cook, though we eat but little. It is rare that she has the opportunity to display her culinary skill. So cook prepares most of our simple meals. When I told Mary Anna about the reports of your size, she was delighted at the prospect of cooking for someone who would appreciate it. This breakfast is for you, sir."

Canon thanked them and dug in. A half-hour later, it was he who was groaning in the middle and the professor who was amazed. A mouse would make a poor living off what remained on the table.

"Sir," said the professor, "that was one of the grandest sights I have seen." Turning to Mary Anna in mock concern, he said, "Mother, alert the tradesmen."

After breakfast, Canon accepted the professor's invitation to attend his classes. He needed some exercise after the cramped train ride and huge meal. The brisk fifteen-minute walk to the professor's building pumped Canon's circulation and lifted his spirits. He had been looking forward to this.

VMI was a dozen serviceable brick and frame mainbuildings that resembled medieval castles. Various outbuildings and service structures completed the functional campus.

The professor's schoolroom was well lit and airy. Several windows were partly open even though a coal stove in the corner glowed red in the middle. Canon had enjoyed his own two years of university education and looked forward to learned discussion.

By the end of the day, he was both heartened and dismayed. He was pleased to learn the professor shared his own view of the pervasive war talk in the South. He was dismayed to find VMI Cadets even more rabidly anticipating war than were the gentry back home.

Canon had hoped to find cadets at a war college more enlightened. Instead, they talked as if economics and guns and troop strength were of little consequence in a war with the North. Yankees, by definition, were not gentlemen, they argued. And everyone knew that common Northern rabble could not stand in front of Southern nobility. Consensus was that one Southerner was worth ten Yankees.

The professor listened with patience for a while. He stood beside his desk in front of the blackboard as a score of young men sneered at the prospects of invasion from the north. The professor held up a hand and began to speak. At the start, he was cool and polite. Then a change came over him. The watery blue eyes took on gleam, then flash, until a pale blue light seemed to emanate from them. Without raising his voice, the professor lashed the would-be warriors.

"In Mexico," he said, "they have a little hairless dog called the Chihuahua. I found it to be a most miserable creature. It is tiny and to my eye misshapen. Yet it appears to be the bravest of creatures, barking and snarling and threatening any and everything around it. It will make as if to set upon someone who only wishes to pet it. It will run at dogs ten times its size.

"But if attacked, even the merest touch in anger will send it yipping and yowling in terror. This animal fills no useful function that I am able to realize."

The implication was not wasted on the students. A low grumble rose in the room. It was not safe in the South for anyone, be he teacher or preacher, to suggest cowardice. Duels were fought over far less. The professor's glare never wavered.

"You think I have slandered you," he said. "That is not my intention. What I point out to you is that the wretched Chihuahua has little choice in running away. Otherwise, it would be chewed to dollrags.

"It is to be despised because of its false bravado. It has no bravery, it has no honor, except in its own light. I do not doubt the bravery or honor of any of you. I only point out to you that it is easy to speak of bravery and honor in war before the fight. But is it seemly? Is it manly?"

No one spoke.

"I have been at war. It is a business which requires bravery and honor. I cannot think it so, but the day may come when your wishes of war are granted. Then you will be called to the test.

"If that day comes, some of you may be faced with the Chihuahua's choice: Run or be chewed to dollrags.

"You speak of war as if it were all glory and honor. There is glory and honor, but a fractional amount compared to pain, misery and death. You speak of killing Yankees as if they would stand in awe before your aristocracy and be willingly shot down.

"Gentlemen, I will give you the main tenet of war. If you are willing to kill, you had better be willing to die. A bullet owes but one allegiance, and that is to death. And that's what war is."

During Canon's stay in Lexington, which ultimately stretched to January, he attended many of the professor's lectures. Never again did he hear an idle boast in any of his classes.

It was a while, though, before he heard another lecture. This was the last day of classes before the holiday break. Testing had been finished for the term and students were walking around campus to receive good news and bad as scores were posted.

After dinner that evening, where Canon had been called to consume another huge meal, he and the professor prepared gear for their hunting trip. Sitting in the small, comfortable parlor, a wood fire and snug walls standing proof against the winter, the possibility of war seemed remote indeed to Canon.

The professor agreed. He took an orange from a huge fruit bowl on a sidetable.

"There will be no war, Rabe," he said. "It would be madness. Wars are economic, almost without exception. This one would benefit neither side. Northern industry cannot afford the loss of our cotton and we cannot rely on total export. The industry is interdependent.

"The problem between North and South is political, economic and sociological. Is this nation to be basically an agricultural nation or an industrial one? Will there be slaves?

"I oppose slavery. We hire freed men and women for our help. I preach at a Negro church and, to the horror of many, teach reading and writing to colored people in night classes. I have heard the term 'nigger lover' directed at me more than once. Slavery is sinfully wrong and we must work toward ending it.

"But as to the first question, and the crux of the matter, I see merit in disunion. But I do not want it. And I believe true leaders, Northern and Southern, will find a way to make equitable the trade and transportation tariffs which help create bases for the dispute.

"If not, the South will leave the Union and be allowed to go in peace. Politicians on both sides gesture and posture to remain in favor. But no one is so insane as to start shooting.

"Now let us get some sleep. We have our own shooting to do tomorrow and we must leave at first light if we are to take that damnable bird."

Canon was surprised to hear the professor so vehemently use a word that even approached being crude. It's just a turkey, thought Canon, heading for bed.

THAT DAMNABLE BIRD, THOUGHT CANON, striding angrily back to camp next evening. He had never known such a one.

The two men had started early that morning. Canon learned that first light, to the professor, meant an hour before dawn.

Two fine horses and a pack mule had been brought from the professor's small farm outside town. Canon rode a big bay, and the professor a favorite small sorrel named Fancy. They rode in silence, swathed against the near freezing temperature. Canon was amused that the professor appeared to be a poor horseman, though he claimed to have been a jockey in his youth.

He felt a warm friendship for the eccentric professor and enjoyed his eccentricities. After they set out, the man had raised his left hand. Canon stopped, thinking it a signal, until it was explained that riding in such manner reduced the jolting on the internal organs and kept the body in better balance.

Mary Anna had told him with maternal fondness that the professor had many "little humors" that amused rather than frustrated. Most had to do with careful maintenance of the professor's inner organs.

He was a strict vegetarian, eating only the blandest boiled vegetables. He could not swallow pepper because, he said, it invariably caused his left leg to go numb. Canon had cautiously pursued the subject of eating pepper to the professor.

Was it any kind of pepper? he asked. The professor nodded sadly. Any and all kinds, he solemnly replied.

The night before, as Canon enjoyed several glasses of excellent brandy, the professor declined to join him.

"You enjoy a drink, Rabe," he said, "but not so much as I. In that, I am different from most men. To me, the rawest liquor is as tasty as others find a cup of the most expensive coffee or the finest cordial. I do not drink because I love it too well. If I allowed myself, I would be the greatest drunkard in Virginia."

He also learned from Mary Anna that the professor felt he could not survive on less than ten hours sleep. Ten was required. Twelve preferred. Internal organs require rest.

Although the professor enjoyed reading popular magazines and novels, he had given them up because he believed such reading interfered with the highest functioning of the brain. All considered, the professor was the most compulsive man Canon had met.

His overriding passion now was for the destruction of Old Scratch, the demon turkey from hell that Canon had been called in to kill. For five years the professor had hunted him. Now his compulsion had become obsession. The bird, said the professor, must be taken.

Before daylight, they quietly rode into the domain of Old Scratch.

LIKE ALL LESSER BEINGS, turkeys in Old Scratch's territory knew not of men's naming of names. Had they, though, each would have considered the synonym for Satan appropriate for the big bird that dominated their territory. His territory.

Scratch had been patriarch and overlord in five acres of virgin forest for a decade. His venerable beard was graying, his gobble gone guttural. But he was king. Scratch's harem reveled in the old bird's prowess as leader and lover.

Envious rivals feared the twenty-five pounds of winged fury, his carrot-colored legs boasting long thorny spurs. They had long since pledged fealty or fled.

Scratch possessed no reasoning ability, as humans know it, but genes and experience had given him skills and senses so sharp and special that they appeared to be innate intelligence.

This morning, as Scratch rolled like thunder from his roost, he sensed signals which had the old Tom on alert before he touched earth. There was a stillness among the other animals, ground dwellers and tree dwellers. An undercurrent of alarm rippled through the forest like wind through fields of wheat.

Squirrels had stopped their silly chatter and stayed still among protective boughs. Rabbits hugged their hidey holes. Birds were a-wing and a-twitter.

Something had invaded Old Scratch's kingdom. It was his duty to learn whether it threatened his flock. If it was a predator bigger than Scratch, it was to be watched so it didn't surprise his brood before he could bustle the family into hiding.

And if it were his size or smaller, a rival turkey, perhaps, then it was time for Scratch to add another victim to his list. With a furious beating of wings, Scratch swept toward and through the lesser birds coming toward him.

As the object of their hunt sped at them through limbs and evergreen boughs, Canon and the professor quietly set up a cold camp. It was a quarter-mile yet to the heart of what the professor knew to be Scratch's territory, but that distance had to be covered with stealth if they were to have any chance of even sighting the bird. They had to forego a fire and hot coffee until after the morning's hunt. The professor sucked a lemon. Canon tried it, couldn't do it, reached instead into the pack of biscuits and meats Mary Anna had prepared.

When everything was unpacked and placed, the professor leaned over to whisper, his breath frosting out like dandelion down.

"Rabe," he said, "I feel badly about asking this, since I invited you, but I would like one more opportunity at Old Scratch before you hunt him. If you do not mind, I will hunt in the direction of his roost," he pointed east, "while you go after game in the other direction. If I do not get him this morning, then you hunt him this afternoon."

Turkey hunters don't stalk the same turkey at the same time, and Canon as the invited party should have had first rights. But he understood the professor's feelings.

"Professor," he said. "I insist that you go after the demon, and I hope you bring him back over your shoulder."

Nodding thanks, the professor took his shotgun and stepped out of the clearing toward the woods. Agreeing to return to camp for noon lunch, Canon shouldered his gun and walked west. When the professor walked wearily into sight again, Canon was sitting amidst a freshly made camp, tents up and coffee boiling above a hickory fire. It was two P.M.

Whistling a tuneless ditty and trying not to look at the dejected hunter, Canon continued to pluck a fat quail while another roasted on a spit. The professor knelt by the fire and warmed his hands. Finally he looked at Canon.

"I am no gentleman, sir," he said. "Two hours behind my time and nothing to show. Except these," he pulled up a woolly pants leg to reveal two long blood crusted furrows up his calf.

"I am not normally profane, Rabe, but this damned bird has confounded me to a point past caring. The bird is from hell. It is an agent of the devil. I know it is from hell because I have just visited there. The beast gave me a guided tour.

"I have been up trees and through underbrush a hog wouldn't have. I am mud all over. There are three acres of briars in my backside that I hope will kill the red ants which set up a fort in my breeches.

"He took me into a hornet's nest, Rabe. I am as lumpy as a bride's biscuits. I crossed the creek twice, falling through the ice each time. No spot on my body is dry or without wound. My internal organs will never be right again. I saw him three times, all out of range, of course. Go kill him, Rabe. I have been in hell."

"Then the heat of that place is greatly exaggerated, professor," said Canon with a smile. "You have ice in your beard."

Canon laughed, but he noticed as the professor stripped off his gear that his gunpowder was still dry. Not bad for going twice into the creek, thought Canon. He hoisted his shotgun and stepped away in the direction from which the professor had returned.

Three hours later, a chagrinned Canon stepped back into camp as sunset washed the woods in red gold. He was not so jaunty now. He was disgusted. Canon did not think he would kill the bird the first day. But he had thought to learn the bird's parameters and weaknesses. He found neither.

The professor attempted to put on an air of disappointment. "I heard no shot, sir," he said. "I fear it did not go well for you. Tell me about it." Then he let go one of his rare smiles.

"Professor, that is one bad bird," said Canon. And the two men began to commiserate.

For three days, they took lessons in humility from a twenty-five pound fowl. Though each killed game when he walked west, the eastern province belonged to Old Scratch. When feathers flew there, they all flew in the same direction.

Scratch knew what he was doing, though all was by instinct. He had lived through many a close call, from predators with weapons ranging from fangs, claws and talons to shotguns. There were numerous scars on the skin under his feathers, some shotgun pellets under that skin. But for each narrow escape there had been a lesson learned.

If it were possible to watch Old Scratch dismay a hunter, it would be easy to believe the bird possessed a genius intellect. Sometimes circling, sometimes moving parallel, sometimes showing himself at a safe distance, Scratch always led the hunter, be it man or mountain lion, away from his brood and into terrain of his choosing.

He had watched the tall white animals since the first morning. Scratch knew these were the most dangerous of predators. They possessed a thunderous roar that belched smoke and flame. And their invisible claws were able to reach incredible distances. In his younger days, he had twice been clutched by those deadly claws. Had been knocked spinning by them, horribly hurt, and had only escaped by limping into thick underbrush that was luckily near. The claws were poison, too, for he had lain weak and sick for long periods, barely able to forage.

But he had learned to judge safe distance from the white animals, just as he knew the safe distance from things that flew, slithered or pounced. Always he drew predators away from his brood. Now, even after three roosts, the strange creatures had still not admitted Scratch's mastery over them. Strutting proudly, Scratch gobbled a challenge into the winter dawn for the fools to come after him once more.

The professor flung his tin camp coffee cup at wakening dawn. "Rabe," he said, "today's our last hunting day. One of us must kill that bird."

"Professor, I'm not happy about failing, either. But let's give that wily bastard credit. You'll get him next year."

"No. No, I won't, Rabe. He won't be around next year." The professor took a long, slender salt-and-pepper checked feather from his coat pocket and handed it over. "This is one of his feathers. I saw him lose it first hunt this year when he flew away from me," he said.

Canon studied the feather, then nodded grimly.

"He's sick," he said.

"Old age, more than anything," said the professor. "Some sort of infection in his internal organs, I reckon, from old wounds. But he'll weaken quickly. And I don't want him to end his days as a meal for a skunk, or defenseless against a young Tom that couldn't even look at him today."

"If I have to, I'll shoot him off the roost."

Normally, no self-respecting hunter would shoot a sleeping quarry. But Canon nodded agreement. "From what I know of the disease, it doesn't transmit," he said, "but I agree, professor. Scratch ought to go out the easy way.

"If one of us doesn't get him today, I'll take him in the morning, off the roost."

It was part of the hunt to know the general area in which a turkey roosted, just like it was permissible to use a turkey call to open the stalk. Turkeys usually respond to a gobble call, but only the youngest and most foolish Toms would fly or run up to a call without first investigating from safe distance. It was part of the sport.

But the sport had turned serious for the two men. The professor walked into the woods. He returned at noon, looked at Canon, shook his head. Without a word, Canon began the last honorable hunt for Old Scratch.

The woods smelled of winter. Deep inside gigantic oak and hickory, slumbering sap emitted the thinnest of odors, thin as the sunlight filtering down through skeletal limbs from a high, cloudless gray-blue sky.

Canon's waning determination to take the bird resurged. He had felt a conflict of emotions on the previous day. Though he had wanted to kill the bird to demonstrate his skill to the professor, a part of him had been reluctant. He wasn't sure if he wanted to deprive the man of a hunt that so frustrated him but that he obviously relished.

He realized the professor would not have sent for him if old Scratch was not dying. Canon also knew none of it mattered much insofar as taking Old Scratch. Canon had done the things that had brought down other turkeys which had reputations similar to that of Scratch. But the damned old bird was far better than anything Canon had sought with a gun.

There was no pattern to his movements, no weakness to be exploited. At the end of the previous day, Canon realized that he probably wasn't going to be able to outsmart Old Scratch. He still felt so. But he had to try.

Four hundred paces into the forest, Canon found a monstrous, lightning-blasted oak. It had to be a hundred feet tall, he thought. A huge rent had been torn in it years ago by the savage strike. A man on a horse could fit inside it. Canon sat just inside one edge of the opening. Eyes closed, he took deep breaths, tasting the air. He was rewarded only with the lightly lingering malodorous spoor of skunk, hours old. Disgusted, he spat.

He pulled from his pocket his wooden gobbler call. Chopping the hinged lid sideways across the resonator, he produced the garbled yelping challenge of a young Tom. As expected, from the distance came Scratch's answering war call. "Come on and fight," said Scratch. "Come on."

Silently as a wraith, Canon moved left on moccasined feet. Papery leaves rustled no more than if rattled by a small wind. It took him fifteen minutes to travel seventy yards. Kneeling ever so gently in swampy underbrush, Canon barked a low gobble from the box.

Directly behind him, possibly twenty yards, possibly fifty, Scratch loosed a gobble that caused Canon to whirl, gritting his teeth. Where was the blasted bird? In the tangled brambles? In the huckleberry bushes, thick as hedge?

Canon moved to his right, sacrificing some silence for swiftness. Still, a red Indian might not have heard him. But Scratch did and went trotting away. Canon could hear him plainly and could discern the general direction. Out of frustration, he almost risked a shot but immediately stifled the impulse. Chances of a hit were minimal, of a kill, nonexistent. Slowly, Canon moved through muck and stunted shrub, up a gentle hill. He chopped the box. Scratch replied, a hundred yards to the right. Canon sat down, shaking his head in frustration. It was going to be a long afternoon.

Four hours later, Canon had exhausted every device he knew. The day before he had sat motionless for five hours, save for an occasional call. Scratch had circled him all afternoon. Canon never saw him. Had not seen him these three days. Canon had tried mating calls, battle calls, calls for help. Scratch responded almost every time, but never showed a feather.

Only once on the previous day had Canon sensed a nearness. It was near dusk, probably too late for a decent shot, but Canon had barked out love call after plaintive love call. For no real reason he could think of, Canon felt Scratch was nearby. He had tried to get inside the turkey's head, had offered the half-frightened love call of a young hen. Scratch had fallen strangely silent, not responding at all.

On this alone, Canon pinned his last hopes. He whined out a call of the frightened young hen, half in love and half afraid. Again, Scratch hesitantly answered twice, then was silent. Canon called his heart out. At sundown, he knew it was useless. There was nothing left to try. Cursing to himself, he headed toward camp. He wouldn't be happy facing the morning task he set himself.

Shotgun hanging from his shoulder by a sling, Canon trudged through the darkening woods. Half in salute, half in frustration, he chopped a fluttering female call as he walked. Scratch mocked him from a distance with the call of a gobbler ready to mate. Enjoy it, old boy, thought Canon, walking along. In honor of Scratch, he made the box imitate the sound of a young hen terrified by the approach of a horny old male.

Old Scratch heard a sound he had not heard in years and it filled him with excitement. It made him strut, spread his tailfeathers in a magnificent fan. Scratch loved a conquest by siege, and it had been a long time. He used to chase down his ladies and dominate them with his power and style until they became his submissives forever.

Now they all chased him or cooed to him until he called on them. It had been a long time since he went winging away to take a maiden by royal prerogative. Any female that wandered into his territory belonged to him. But they came willingly to him now. All the young hens were of his own brood. It had been a long time since he flew out of his territory to take a new maid.

Frankly, he just didn't feel up to it any more. And deep down, something told him that he might not be able to handle a strapping young Tom as easily as he had done. So he had contented himself by staying home and protecting his property.

He was content, anyhow, until he heard this new girl who had wandered into his territory and was so afraid of his love. She was running away! How delicious. "Wait, dear," Scratch called to her. "Don't be afraid. It will be all right." Still she ran, calling out her terrified passion.

Scratch ran after her.

Canon couldn't believe it when he heard Scratch follow him with lovesick calls. He ran a few steps and called again. Much nearer, Scratch answered.

Canon ran a hundred yards, gobbling the call madly, then threw himself quietly as possible behind a clump of bushes at the top of a small rise. He dropped the turkey call and pulled his shotgun around.

Scratch was having the time of his old life. He had chased this new honey to ground. Slowing only a bit, he quickly surveyed the hill where his sweetheart waited, no longer calling, but cowering in heat and fear.

"Ho, ho," gobbled Scratch. He charged the hill. Canon watched the huge turkey lope straight toward him. He waited until the gobbler was twenty-five yards away, then thumbed back the ears of the muzzleloader's twin hammers. At the click, Scratch gathered himself to fly. He looked at the long snout suddenly pointing at him from the bushes. "Dammit," was Old Scratch's last gobble.

In camp, not two hundred yards away, the professor heard the shotgun blast and smiled. In the woods, Canon slung Old Scratch over his shoulder.

"Don't worry, old fella," he said. "You're not the first horny old goat who got it for chasing the young ones. You won't be the last."

When they returned to Lexington next day, the professor began a round of victory celebrations for Canon that continued into and finally merged with those at Christmas and then New Year's.

The professor took Scratch to a taxidermist and stood over the man for two days until the bird was mounted. Then Canon and Scratch were taken for display to every hunter in Lexington, novice and adept, who had joined the professor on an expedition for Old Scratch. The number included practically all the town's gentility.

Canon sent a letter detailing the adventure to Mulberry and received in return from Mountain Eagle, who had been educated at white schools, a congratulatory letter and newspaper clippings.

Reporters had come from the Lexington daily paper and even from the

*Dispatch* in Richmond, ninety miles away, to do stories about the hunt. Photographs, the country's new sensation, were made. Party invitations poured in and Canon was rarely seen without one of a half-dozen of the town's most beautiful belles on his arm.

The annual Christmas Ball at VMI was considered the fete of the year. Canon had intended to be home for Christmas, but gave in to entreaties to stay from the professor and Mary Anna. He sent presents home and received handsome presents in return.

The gift he most wanted to present was for the professor, and the VMI ball would be the perfect place.

It snowed all night Christmas Eve which added to the festivity at VMI. The ball began in late afternoon. Full dress uniforms of black, gold and gray were highlighted by afternoon frocks of diverse color and then in the evening by gorgeous ball gowns of every hue.

The huge ballroom was done up in school colors and gaily bedecked by bright crepe and pine boughs. An orchestra played traditional songs of the season and interspersed them with light airs for the dances of the day.

Old Scratch, at the professor's insistence, was perched on a table laden with gifts for the school faculty. Canon had grown tired of telling the story, which suited the professor just fine. He gained relish with each recounting of the tale and was more than happy to take over the telling.

After the roast turkey dinner, which was not diminished by the sight of Scratch overlooking the proceeding, the professor rose at the head table with glass of punch in hand.

"Gentlemen and officers of the school, beautiful ladies, I give you compliments of the season," he said, and was rewarded with cries of "Hear, hear." "I also present my compliments to my guest, Mr. Rabbarian Canon of Montgomery, who has rid the countryside of a noble but pernicious creature.

"Word has come to me that this bird," he pointed to Scratch, "is the world record turkey and I add congratulations to my compliments."

Canon and his chosen lady for the night sat at the guest table next to the professor's. "Excuse me, lovey," Canon said to his date as he rose amidst cheers and applause. He was surprised at the information the professor had withheld and said so, then he thanked his host and acknowledged the hospitality he had received from the people of Lexington. Then he sprang his own surprise when he made a present of the stuffed Scratch to the professor, who flushed at the announcement. But Canon wondered at the sly grin which the professor displayed as he accepted the gift.

That grin was explained toward the end of the evening when the professor called for quiet. The school commandant had just ended a short speech of compliments of the season from the stage and a crafty call for more funding from college patrons.

He announced the last dance of the evening and left the stage when the professor mounted it and called for quiet.

"One good scratch deserves another," he said, and invited the crowd outside. Canon had no idea what was going on but joined the throng as it moved to the exit indicated by the professor.

Outside there stood a magnificent black Arabian charger, saddled and stamping, reins held by a groom. The horse gleamed blueblack in the silvery snow, which was lit by lamps and a lowering half-moon. Twin spumes of smokey breath steamed from its nostrils as it impatiently shook its head.

The professor took the reins from the groom and led the horse to Canon. He handed over the lines.

"I am not surprised by your generosity, sir," he said, "but I am greatly pleased. This horse is for you. His name is Old Scratch."

It was Canon's turn to be flustered. Spurred by the gift and several secret juleps, Canon did his best in a short speech to be as gracious as he had found the people of Lexington.

He refused to believe the professor, who claimed ever after that Canon said he looked forward to riding the turkey and was glad he was able to shoot the horse.

*4*

# *Tom Fool*

On the second day of the new year 1861, Canon took in one last gigantic example of what Mary Anna called a "Canon breakfast." Classes were about to resume at VMI, and Mountain Eagle had written that preparations were under way for spring planting. It was time to return to the plantation, though Canon was reluctant to leave.

The professor walked Canon to the train station. The train for Montgomery was not scheduled for departure until noon, but the two wanted a long stroll and a talk. They had spoken rarely of the prospects of war and they were sick of hearing braggarts yearn for it.

In November, the lanky compromise Republican candidate from Illinois, Abraham Lincoln, had been elected president of the United States. He was to take office in March. Until then, said the professor, no one would know what the man really stood for. Earlier in his political life, Lincoln had spoken in favor of the abolition of slavery. Now he had moderated his views. Let slave states remain slave states if it will keep the union together, Lincoln said. Let there be more power in state's rights. But he said the union must remain inviolate.

James Buchanan, the lame duck president, had in early December argued against secession but expressed doubt of the constitutional power of Congress to make war upon a state.

South Carolina took him at his word and on December 20 became the first state to secede from the Union. The professor felt that all Southern states would secede, then use their secession as bargaining power to re-enter the Union on a basis of stronger state's rights. Still he believed there could be no war.

"War is a great and terrible thing, Rabe," he said. "I'm glad mine is behind me. It is my belief and my greatest wish that there is not one awaiting you."

"What if there is war, professor?"

"There will be no war."

"But what if war comes?"

"There will be no war."

A light snow had dusted the ground New Year's Day but evaporated with only a bit of mud left in its wake. The day was dry and chill. A west wind scudded high white clouds across a background of blue. Against it, both men wore heavy wool coats.

The black Arabian stallion named for the professor's late nemesis had already been taken to the stable car by a groom.

Canon shook hands with the professor, who thanked Canon for the visit and wished him well. Promising to write, and extracting a promise from Canon to return in the summer for another visit, the professor bid him farewell.

He had been home five days when news flashed across the nation that Confederates had fired on the Union ship *Star of the West* as it tried to slip soldiers and supplies to relieve Fort Sumter.

Canon attempted to downplay the incident. He told Buck and Mountain Eagle of the professor's doubts on the possibility of war. But the two men had shaken their heads, unconvinced.

Canon slipped easily back into the rituals of preparing for spring cotton planting. Gear was mended. Equipment was checked. Plow animals were put on rich feed and exercise. Old Scratch was enrolled in the Mountain Eagle school of obedience.

It was a dicey moment when Scratch came into the corral with Hammer. Canon and Mountain Eagle had tried to familiarize the huge horses with each other, holding them under rein as they sniffed and snorted. But sooner or later the two had to be by themselves in the big corral.

That day, had their natures ruled, the horses would have fought until one was defeated, likely dead. But the palomino had learned to love and trust his master, just as Scratch would learn. They faced each other, nostrils flaring, flanks quivering. Stamping and pawing, the gold and the black pealed out war cries to each other as the men cooed soothing words to them.

Love for the humans triumphed over Hammer's nature. The horse spurned millennia of instinct when he turned his back on Scratch and trotted away. It took weeks for the animals to truly accept one another, but love and patience finally led the stallions into a friendship as fast as those developed by draught horses that pull side by side for years.

Scratch would learn from Hammer, as well as his trainers, and Hammer's training was as complete as the three men could make it.

As a youth, Canon had seen circus horses perform tricks and feats of apparent intelligence he could hardly believe. He saw what animals could accomplish, and the idea was reinforced by the cunning of the Old Scratch turkey.

Mountain Eagle told tales of his time on the plains where he had seen Indian ponies perform in an almost magical manner.

An Indian's war pony would on command stand stone still for hours at a time, refusing food or water, until released by his owner. At a touch, or even a signal, a war pony would drop to the ground either to hide or to act as a shield for his master. Like circus ponies, they would prance, rear, buck or circle on command.

All this and more had been taught Hammer. Hour upon hour, since Canon had brought the horse home, Hammer learned through a system of reward and withholding of rewards. He learned to respond only to commands from his masters. For the sheer joy of it, he had also been taught to respond to hand signals, code words and pressure signals transmitted by his rider through knee or hand.

But if given a certain code word or signal by any of his trio of trainers, Hammer would perform for anyone who gave commands. He would allow only the three on his back unless another code word or signal gave permission for another rider.

When the men thought Hammer ready, they gave a summer barbecue at Mulberry so they could put the big horse through his paces. The Canons and Mountain Eagle delighted in remembrances of the day.

Canon had walked through the crowd on the manicured back lawn, a rigless Hammer heeling like a hunting dog. On command, he pranced, danced, rolled over, reared. He counted for the crowd, pawing the tended lawn to the precise number of strokes called out by Canon. He fetched a lady her bonnet, then took the same bonnet from her head and circled the crowd left, then right, before returning it. He knelt to allow Canon easy access to his broad back, then rose so gently that a reclining Canon was never in danger of falling.

After that day, Hammer and Canon became the highlight of many a barbecue and rodeo.

On his return to Mulberry from Lexington, Canon set out to give Scratch the same training. But he was surprised by the intensity that Buck and Mountain Eagle put into it. Where they had worked three hours with Hammer, they worked six with Scratch. Canon put in his time, too, but Buck let plantation duties go in order to spend more time training Scratch.

He wondered about it, but the explanation came on the evening of the day they learned shots were fired on the *Star of the West*.

Canon knew at dinner that something was going on. Buck and Mountain Eagle, his two fathers, were strangely silent and preoccupied throughout the meal. When Buck invited Canon into the library for a drink, he knew by the grave demeanor of the men that he was about to learn whatever it was that troubled them.

In the library, on a corner study table, were two large wrapped packages. Buck sat in an easy chair near the window and motioned for Canon to take the seat next to the study table. Mountain Eagle poured brandy into three snifters then stationed himself stoically by the door, as if daring anyone to try to enter.

Canon was struck by the depth of the moment. What a strange family they were, but a wonderful one. The dusky Indian was dressed as usual, in a pullover linen shirt open at the neck and denim trousers. He was lean as the day he stepped out of the woods to challenge Buck. The elder Canon had grown broader, stocky as the stump of an oak. He wore as usual a short open coat, cotton shirt dyed gray and black cotton trousers. Canon was in his dinner dress of white planter's suit.

He knew the three of them conversed less than other more conventional families, but it was a comfortable silence born of understanding and trust.

Buck motioned to the packages on the table.

"Belated Christmas gifts from me and the Eagle, Rabe," he said. Canon rose, hefted one package, then the other. He chose the larger, lighter one. It was bulky. Under the wrapping was a hand-tooled gunbelt with twin cutaway holsters and cartridge loops. Each holster had a leather thong to slip snugly onto a pistol hammer to keep the weapon tied down. Leather thongs descended from the bottoms of the holsters so they could be strapped to the legs.

Its buckle was turquoise and carried the emblem, in silhouette, of a hawk's head. The leather was light and supple and of an unusual color that looked liked muddy milk.

"It is made from the skin of a white buffalo," said the Eagle simply. Canon could only nod. He knew what had to be inside the smaller, heavier package. A mahogany case gleamed, reflecting the lamplight, as he removed the paper wrapping.

The case was two feet by two. In the polished wood of the hinged lid was a lock, in the lock a key. Canon turned it, lifted the lid and swallowed hard. The twin pistols, lying barrel over barrel, were unlike anything he had seen.

Nestled in crushed red velvet, they gleamed as if with inner light. But as the metal of the pistols reflected light, so the handles absorbed it. They were of teak, Canon later learned, with luster deep enough to smell. Each grip bore the hawk silhouette.

The metal was too rich for iron. It beamed as if white hot. Canon lifted one of the huge guns out almost with reverence and, lo, it was part of his hand. There was weight, but no heaviness. That made sense, thought Canon. How could his own hand feel heavy?

"They are made of steel," Buck said, "from Herr Krupp in Germany. I sent him a pair of your gloves. He wrote me that it took two weeks for him to find someone whose hands fit the gloves exactly. Then it took six men six months to make them."

Canon knew his father's statement wasn't a boast or grandstand. He was simply explaining the reason for the wonderment in Canon's eyes. He recalled telling Buck of the Krupp steel factory in Germany. He visited it during his time at Heidelberg. The pistols must have cost a fortune.

"They're machined to .50 calibre," said Buck. Canon lifted the pistol's twin from the case, noticed that each revolver held seven rounds rather than the usual six. He put them aside and buckled on the gunbelt. Then he picked up the pistols and dropped them into the holsters, withdrew them. The holsters seemed to grab the pistols down, then spring them back into Canon's hands, and the hawk heads kept the grips from being too smooth.

He looked to the two men.

"No one has ever gotten such a gift," he said. "I thank my fathers."

"The hawk is your war totem, my son," said Mountain Eagle. "It is the hunting hawk, and I now so name you."

"War?" said Canon hollowly.

"Listen to me, Rabe," said Buck, "and please let me have my say before you speak. It's time we settle this thing. Now it used to be I was pretty certain in my mind on most things. A thing was right or wrong, and no room in the middle.

"But the Eagle here showed me different. I've learned from him there are few absolutes, as he calls them, in the world. There's no absolute guarantee that the sun will rise in the morning or that the mountains won't shake themselves to pieces before tomorrow night.

"But I absolutely guarantee you that there will be war in this country, and it won't be long in coming. And I reckon you'll decide to fight, and you'd best be ready as you can be for it.

"There will be war, because wars are fought for gain, and not principles, and there's gain to be had," he said. Canon was surprised to hear Buck echo the professor's sentiments, if in different terms. He paid attention. Entranced by his thoughts, Buck slipped back into the rugged speech pattern of the early frontier.

"From the time a' the first ambush, when Cain picked up that rock, all fights and battles and wars have been for profit. Cain wanted Abel out of the way so he would gain the Lord's attention.

"The Romans, Celts, Goths, Persians—all them tribes and peoples—they knew the more people they had under their rule the more tribute, which is another word for taxes, they could take. And they could use that money to build bigger and better armies.

"The Crusades and the Eastern wars are claimed to be fought because of religious differences. Religion wasn't nothing but paint over a ugly fact. Whoever controlled the souls of the inhabitants of an area also controlled their wealth and lands.

"The Mongol armies was at least honest about it. One a them raiders even wrote a little poem about it and they took it as their rule. It's the only poem I know:

> I do not have a mill
> with willow trees,
> I have a horse and a whip,
> I will kill you and go.

"Right on up to British rule, whether it was rule over America or India or the open sea, if they called the tune, they also set the fee. That's the way it is.

"Now this country is split just like Cain and Abel. One is industry and one is agriculture. I want high prices for my cotton and I don't want to pay much to ship it North. And when it comes back to me in the form of a pair a long johns, well, I don't want to pay much for them.

"The people who run the factories up there want it just the other way. They want me to sell my cotton cheap, and also pay to have it shipped and also pay dear for that pair a long johns.

"Some want me to free our slaves, the labor of which is the only way I can grow cotton cheap. But they want me to give up my labor and sell cheap cotton. Can't be did."

Canon held his peace in deference to his father. They had long ago agreed to disagree on the slavery question. "Slavery ain't the only issue in the troubles between North and South, Rabe, but it can certainly be the fuse to the dynamite. And we all agree that any state or nation which allows a man to imprison or put to the lash any other man without due process of law is in the wrong.

"If the damned Yankee would come in here and talk sense instead of trying to heavy hand their way, this war might could be avoided. But nobody is even offering to pay us back the money we paid the Northern slave traders when they brought 'em here to sell. Not the Washington congress, not the abolitionists. Just wants us to free 'em. But it ain't those who are behind the war, Rabe. It's the man in the North who runs the factory. He wants Southern cotton to be cheap and stay cheap, meaning he wants to set the price. If the South separates from the Union, he ain't gonna get it. And that's why we ain't gonna be allowed to go in peace. There will be war."

"Then the South will lose," said Canon heavily. "We don't have the means or men to fight a war. We can't whip the North. In the long run, we'll lose."

"You right about the long run, son. We can't afford a long war. We got to whup 'em quick and whup 'em good, and we can do it. Because what little we have got in the way of men and equipment is ready and waiting.

"Southern units been drilling for war nearly a year. We ready for the thing and the Yankee ain't. They don't want to fight and don't believe we will fight. But we will. We want to. And that's the three main words which have been spoke here today. We want to. And a ounce of want to is worth a pound of anything else.

"I reckon England and France will jump in on our side, too, Rabe. They ought to, quick. They got a stake in this. They got between them every bit as much equipment and supply as the North. The only thing England and France ain't got is the one thing we have got, by the field full, and that's cotton. Let's hope our friends won't stand idly by. But even if they do, we can win, if we win quick."

"Sir, you told me once that the South would win a long war."

"Not a regular war, with regular armies, the way this one is shaping up to be. We could win a hit and run war, like we did the Revolutionary War. Any invaded country, and history will approve me on this, can outlast the invader if they wait long enough. And it will be us who gets invaded.

"I believe the South can and will win a war with the North if it lasts ten months or ten years. Anything much longer or much shorter, and we'll be in trouble.

"One of the problems we got is this notion of Southern chivalry. All you young bloods want uniforms and yessir and nosir and face-to-face fights, more's the pity. I don't trust it.

"I tell you, if we could find a buyer who would run this plantation the way we run it, I would be in favor a' selling and heading out to see the world.

"Two things are wrong with the idea. One is faith. Like I say, the South has got the want to, and want to ain't nothing but faith. If we sell Mulberry, then some folks will think we ain't got faith and it might shake their own faith a little bit. And it might be that little bit that might be needed to end this war quick, afore we get a lot of our boys killed and kill a lot of Yankee boys who probably ain't so bad if you could get them to take a bath every now and again.

"The other thing is that I reckon you'll feel like you got to fight, and nothing me or Mountain Eagle could do would stop you.

"You study tonight on what I say, Rabe, and you'll see I'm right. And then you get some sleep a'cause you'll need your rest.

"As of tomorrow daybreak, this here plantation goes on a war footing. Now let's all have one more taste of brandy, and turn in."

Buck and Mountain Eagle soon headed for their beds, but Canon stayed in the library until rooster's hours. He found pen and paper. Next day, he mailed his letter to Bill Kelley.

Five weeks later, three hundred black horses ended a long trail drive from Houston when they were herded into a series of new corrals at Mulberry. Kelley had not been able to make the trip, though he had hoped to come so he could attend a ceremony held in Montgomery.

It was there, on February 18, 1861, that Jefferson Davis was sworn in as president of the Confederate States of America.

The Canons were present for the oath. Mountain Eagle stayed at Mulberry to continue the care and training of the new horses and the men who would ride them. Canon had advertised in newspapers throughout Alabama for skilled riders to comprise a light brigade of cavalry.

Within two weeks, he picked three hundred of more than five hundred applicants. The morning of the inauguration, having been elected captain of the unit, Canon enrolled his and three hundred other names on the muster list of the Confederate Army.

He had reported to the makeshift garrison in Montgomery. There, he was told to return to Mulberry following the day's ceremony and continue training until such time as needed.

That evening, he and Buck attended the Inaugural Ball. Buck was uncomfortable in tail coat; Canon was resplendent in his dove gray captain's uniform.

Going through the receiving line, he saluted his new commander-in-chief. To his surprise, President Davis leaned over as he shook Canon's hand and invited him to a meeting in his office.

Buck was not surprised, and said anybody who lays out the cash for three hundred horses and equipment ought to be in line for a word of thanks from the president of the Confederacy.

At the named hour of eleven P.M., Canon approached the door of the president's office and was admitted by one of two burly guards standing sentry.

Inside, a coal fire tried to cast light throughout the large, well furnished office. Two lowered lanterns assisted the effort, but the room remained dimly lit. Davis greeted him warmly and drew him into the room.

The president was a small man, dwarfed by Canon's huge frame. As is the nature of many smaller but successful men, he exhibited an air of confidence that bordered on arrogance.

Cigar smoke hung heavily in the room. In the feeble light, Canon could make out dim profiles of two men who sat in armchairs facing the fire. One of the men rose, and Canon recognized Robert E. Lee.

Lee, of late the commandant at West Point, had refused the position of leader of the Union Army in order to accept leadership of the South's Army of Northern Virginia. He was under the command of General Albert Sydney Johnston, who as general of the armies was to remain in the deep South to command defense of the Western Theater.

He saluted Lee, then shook his hand.

"Captain Canon," said President Davis, "there is someone else here I think you already know."

"Forgive me for not rising, Captain," came a familiar voice from the armchair in front of the fire. "I inadvertently took some black pepper in the president's otherwise excellent vegetable salad, and my left leg is numb as cork."

"Professor!" said a delighted Canon, hurrying to shake his hand. He stopped abruptly and had the forethought to stand at attention and salute. The professor wore colonel's insignia on the sleeve of his gray coat.

"Merely a formality, sir," said the professor genially. "The lads at VMI insisted I lead their unit. I doubt we see action. General Lee disagrees."

Lee took it up as he, Davis and Canon took the other armchairs.

"Oh, I don't pretend to far sight," Lee said, "especially with so little to go on. But it appears we must prepare for the worst. That way we shall be ready for anything. If war is thrust upon us, there will certainly be battles. But I wish those people," he pointed in the general direction of Washington, "would just leave us alone."

"Neither do I pretend to far sight," said Davis. Canon, as had the professor, refused the proffered humidor of Cuban cigars to which Davis was addicted. "We have little to go on as to how serious is the Northern threat of invasion," Davis resumed. "But it appears to me we must prepare the best we can for the worst to happen. That way we will be ready for anything. There is, after all, the matter of the *Star of the West*."

Canon wondered how the professor would respond to one of the hot issues of the day. On January 9, Confederates at Charleston had fired on the merchant vessel *Star of the West* as it approached Fort Sumter.

South Carolina had seceded in December and claimed Fort Sumter as its own. The Union garrison refused to leave. When the Confederacy laid siege to the fort, *Star of the West* attempted to secretly reinforce Sumter. Soldiers and supplies were concealed in the merchant steamer.

Many Southerners believed that President-elect Lincoln had intentionally leaked information about the attempted reinforcement, forcing the Confederacy's hand.

"It was an astute political move by the North," said the professor. "The Confederacy is perceived to have committed an overt act of war. But it made little real difference to the situation. It would still be madness for the North to attempt to invade the South, and vice versa.

"I fully agree that preparation for war is necessary, and we must protect our borders. But I maintain that war with the North is a preposterous notion. Yet we will play our part and set our bluff. And I will pray to God that neither side is so foolish as to start shooting."

Discussion of strategies and tactics continued until midnight. Davis had been graduated through West Point as had Jackson. Canon, who was out of his depth and knew it, sat silently in rapt attention for most of the evening.

As midnight approached, Canon learned the reason for his being included.

"I have thoroughly enjoyed the companionship of you two this evening," said Davis. "Now let us end the night by setting plans—contingencies, if you will.

"Colonel, on your return to the Institute, you will continue to drill and train your artillerymen, but on a more pressing basis. We must have expert artillery if we are to be an army.

"Captain Canon, you will return on the morrow to your home and also step up the training of your cavalry unit. If war comes, Southern cavalry will be the one facet in which we far outstrip the enemy.

"Artillery needs scouts. I am assigning you, Captain, on a tentative basis to the Virginia brigade. If the national crisis worsens, you will join your friend the professor in Virginia. You will prepare yourself and your troop and remain in readiness for my call.

"We will not be invaders, gentlemen, but neither will we allow ourselves to be invaded. We will, as noted, defend our borders."

Davis showed the two friends to the door, shook their hands warmly and bade them goodnight. The professor took his leave from Canon.

"I am happy to know, Rabe," he said, "that in the unlikely case of war, you will be with my Virginians. But I doubt we will see a shot fired in anger, and that is my hope and prayer."

Canon raised his hand to salute Davis goodnight.

CANON DROPPED HIS HAND, and three hundred grayclad horsemen streamed screaming with him down the hill toward the blue coated soldiers on the road below.

Canon was confident of his men. They had trained hard the past six months. When he left President Davis and the professor and returned to

Mulberry, he found that Mountain Eagle had the plantation on a war footing. Campsites dotted the plantation fields like a village of Indian tepees.

Throughout February and March, the men of Mulberry had driven their three hundred volunteers mercilessly. When Fort Sumter finally fell on April 14, 1861, the call from Montgomery came. Canon's cavalry was to join the Southern troop build up in Virginia.

Next morning, Captain Canon took his three hundred cavalrymen, every man on a sleek black horse, down the river road leading away from his home. He looked back once at the splendidly shining manor house, before the winding way hid it from view.

He could see miniature figures of Buck, Mountain Eagle and the house servants waving until they passed from his sight. He wondered if the other riders felt as he did as they left their own homes. Canon thought he would never see his home again.

Entraining in Montgomery, the light brigade detrained a day later at Harper's Ferry. The Federal arsenal there was abandoned four days after Sumter surrendered. Professor Tom Jackson had been placed in charge of it, and Harper's Ferry was now a training ground for the Confederacy.

Canon found that the professor had been given a nickname by the raw Rebel volunteers he trained. The men, for the most part, were illiterate but willing. However, they did not understand such things as feints and forced marches. The professor, used to autocracy in the classroom and having a penchant for secrecy, did not deign to explain these things to the recruits. He merely gave orders and expected them to be carried out.

After a few weeks of having men march five miles in one direction, then turning them back on their tracks to send them ten miles the opposite way, the professor came to be a sort of bad joke to the boys he trained.

They called him "Fool Tom" or "Tom Fool."

But Canon watched the professor engineer a great coup that had earned him fame in Montgomery. The Baltimore and Ohio Railroad ran through Harper's Ferry. The South had little rolling railroad stock, and coveted the locomotives which passed through the town every day. Davis hoped that Maryland would join the Confederacy and forbade interference with the trains.

When it became clear that Maryland would not join the secession, the professor was given leeway to act. He sent a telegram to the owner of the B and O. The trains passing through his camp disrupted the routine of his men, he said. Would the railroad please restrict its schedule to one day per week?

A very accommodating railroad president returned word that he would be happy to do so. For a month, trains ran through Harper's Ferry only on Wednesdays. Then the railroad president, happy that his trains were safe, received another telegram.

It would be an inconvenience, the professor said, but the trains passing at all hours on Wednesday still disrupted his men. Would it be possible for them to run only during a four-hour period on Wednesdays? The railroad complied again, and for a couple of weeks, the B and O railroad was the busiest in the world for four hours Wednesday afternoons.

On the third Wednesday, the professor sent troops twenty miles down the tracks in each direction, cut the track and captured twelve locomotives. Each was loaded on a specially built flat bed and pulled ten miles by horse to the nearest Southern line.

The professor was a hero in Montgomery, but still "Fool Tom" to his men.

Early in the evening of June third, Canon was called to the professor's headquarters. Union General George McClellan had that day attacked and routed a Confederate stronghold at Philippi in western Virginia. It was a small victory, but one which cast the South in a bad light.

As his friend outlined the day's dreary event, Canon's excitement grew. The South would retaliate: Canon's cavalry had been chosen for the attack.

Word had come from agents in Washington that a Union detachment which had captured Fort McHenry, at the head of Chesapeake Bay, was about to attack a nearby Confederate camp. The raid, as reported, was to take place within the week. Canon would take his cavalry and stop the Northerners. When he took the word to his men, the surrounding woods echoed with their Rebel yells.

But time passed with no orders to ride. For five days, Canon fidgeted. On the sixth, it was reported that there was troop activity at the fort. Canon called for his bugler to blow boots and saddles. Fifteen minutes later, riding Old Scratch, he led his men out to war.

By late afternoon, Canon had chosen the site for his ambush. It was an open plain on the road from Fort McHenry to the Confederate camp, near Old Bethel Church. A rolling hill lay five hundred yards to the eastern side of the road, the church house on the other.

As the Confederates made cold camp in thick fog on the far side of the hill, Canon walked apart, and whispered a prayer that he be granted war weather for next morning, that the fog hold.

Canon wanted the element of surprise, but he desired even more the element of fear.

Mountain Eagle told him years before of the White Horse Band of plains Indians. Twenty braves had each obtained a white horse, a signal of their totem. When they raided the villages of other tribes, the band always attacked at dawn, out of fog or mist when possible.

The band's reputation soon grew to the point of myth. It became so that when the pale ponies thundered in, enemy braves ran or huddled in wigwams as often as they fought.

Canon also appreciated the use of fog or mist as ground cover. He had learned at Heidelberg how ancient Celts used fear and fog as allies. He studied the fierce strike troops of the Celts known as the Black Watch.

There was little in the way of strategy and tactics in those wild days. Invading armies marched in, the home guard marched out. Wherever place the two armies came together became the battleground.

The Celtic Black Watch changed all that.

Members of the Watch, in black tartan kilts, were berserk bagpipers who led the Celts into battle. Berserk, the Norse word for bear, was the term for warriors who became so charged with energy they went into frenzy in battle.

Wearing bearskins, the berserkers would fight on with wounds that would have killed most people. Greatly feared, the berserkers led the old Norse Viking into battle.

So it was with the Black Watch.

When the Celts went out to meet an invading force, they marched to within a mile of the aggressor and set up camp. They always arrived at dusk. They were always certain there would be a heavy ground fog the following morning.

Once battle fires were lit to announce their presence to the invaders, the Black Watch brought out bagpipes. The skirling of a single pipe, floating eerily out of the mist-shrouded night, reached the ears of the invaders.

Then the one pipe was joined by another, and another and another until, by midnight, the air for miles was charged with a keening cacophony that sounded as if God had stepped on the tail of Satan's cat.

All night, hundreds of pipers played their war pipes. An hour before daylight, the piping would swell, then cease. Ireland's mists would have covered the land like a pall. No birds twittered, no foxes barked. All living things were silenced by the shattering wail of the pipes.

White silence wrapped the invaders in the wraithy mist like a giant spectral spider web. After an hour of that oppressive nothingness, the nervous invaders would be half wild. Then the bagpipe music would burst like a pent-up flood and the army would begin to move, and the invaders knew the pipers were coming, and were coming for them.

Just as the morning mist began to lift, the Black Watch would lead the Celts screaming onto the enemy ground.

On most occasions, the unnerved enemy simply fled.

This effect Canon desired. Hence the three hundred coal black horses. Hence the prayer for ground fog.

Canon awaked at four A.M. the morning of June 10 to the ground fog he wanted. He sent out scouts, then had each man in the unit check harness and weapons. And he made sure each man took at least a mouthful of food. He wanted no hunger, no weakness.

The scouts returned a little after five A.M. with word that five hundred Federal infantrymen were on the road toward Bethel. An hour later, the cavalry was strung out side by side behind Canon, who lay on the ground just beneath the rise of the hill.

By seven A.M., the fog had begun to lift. Where the hell are they? Canon had fumed to himself, checking the Krupp fifties for the fiftieth time. I need this fog, dammit, he thought, going up against a force almost double our own.

The thrumping stamp of a marching troop came so fast on the heels of his silent plea that Canon could hardly believe it. Yet here they came, blue coats with brass buttons gleaming in the misty air.

Within ten minutes, the Yankee infantry column was arrayed in front of him. He back-crawled down the hill, turned and mounted Old Scratch. Canon drew his saber, held it high in his right hand. He felt, rather than saw, the men stiffen behind him. Of a sudden, battle lust of the ages was on him, in him, filling him with a blood rage.

But inside Canon's head, sweet music he had never heard began to thrum. That it was ancient, he knew. It sounded of thousands of voices and orchestras of strange anachronistic instruments. It stirred him in a way he never felt. His mind seemed to take on a new dimension of clarity. He saw, heard, thought with crystal clearness.

"Reins in teeth, pistols in each hand, and scream like the devil, lads," Canon shouted. "Send the Yankees to hell!" He rose high in the stirrups. The Black Horse Cavalry, as the unit came to be known, charged over the crest and down the hill with a shriek.

The yell had frozen and confused the Federal troop. The Union soldiers looked up and saw black horses, ridden by gray men through a gray fog, crashing down on them. Hear the roar of it! The sight was terrible to them. So numb were they that not a single musket was lifted before the Confederate cavalry was upon them.

Canon segued Scratch down the hill. The Black Horse scythed into the shocked Union column. The Northerners lost a third of their men on the first pass. Canon's sword swept through a neck, with his other hand, he fired a bullet into the brain of a Yankee sergeant.

Into and through the blue column rode the cavalry, then it wheeled as one and pounded into the enemy again. The slaughter was over in minutes. Canon doubted that fifty shots were fired by the Union column. Most had thrown down their guns in surrender, many had bolted, not a few had fallen trembling to the ground.

It was not that the men weren't brave. It was simply that they were unnerved and in a state of true shock from the suddenness and ferocity of the attack.

More than a hundred Union soldiers died, one-hundred fifty were wounded and the rest were taken prisoner. Canon did not lose a man.

Some survivors were so terrified by Canon's cavalry that the professor released them to return to their army. In Richmond, in Montgomery, in Washington, word was spread of the terrible Black Horse Cavalry. He wanted the word spread. It was.

The rejoicing lasted only a month

On July 11, Union General George McClellan smashed a force of four thousand Rebels at the Battle of Rich Mountain. A week later, the real war got set to begin.

Twenty miles from Washington, in a picturesque valley cut here and there by small streams known to the locals as "runs," a Jewish merchant named Manassa had in the early 1800s opened a general store. It sat at a crossroad, a junction, of two main thoroughfares. And though, by 1861, both the store and its owner had long since disappeared, the area still bore his name: Manassa's Junction. It became known simply as Manassas.

Through the area ran the shallow stream, the run known as the Bull. Bull Run.

Manassas was now an important railroad junction, one that both North and South considered important. Both sides considered the junction their own.

The morning of July twenty-first, Canon and the professor sat on their horses, atop Henry House hill, and through field glasses watched the Union Army move this way and that, preparatory to attack.

Finally, at ten A.M., the blue army massed and thrust toward the Confederate middle. The gray line tightened to receive the charge.

"No, no," muttered Fool Tom, under his breath, as if to himself. "It is a feint. Our troops must not concentrate so." Again the Union troops began a charge, and again broke it off. More grayback soldiers rushed to support the center of the line.

"It is a feint, it is a feint," said the professor. "Anyone could see that it is a feint."

Canon, who could see nothing of the sort, remained silent, but the professor became more and more agitated. Canon, knowing not else what to do, said, "Professor, are you sure?"

Pale blue eyes, cold as ice, turned on Canon. "I am as sure," came the reply, "as I am known as 'Fool Tom.'"

# 5
# *Standing Like a Stone Wall*

"It is a feint," said the professor yet again. "There," he said urgently, "is the real attack." Through his telescope lens, at the top of his field of vision, Canon saw a mass of blue troops burst from the woods toward the left flank of the gray line.

"The flank will never hold," said the professor, reining his little sorrel away and spurring back toward the line of woods. With mounting fear, then horror, Canon saw the Confederate left flank stand, waver, then break before the onrushing Union troops.

Canon knew enough military strategy and tactics to know the Union was "rolling up" the Confederate line. It was disaster. If the attack continued unchecked, the Northern newspapers would be proved right. The war would likely be over this day, the South defeated.

For weeks, since the Confederate Army occupied this land near a vital Northern railroad link, both President Lincoln and the Northern press had called for action. Pro-Union editorial writers promised the rag-tag Southern army would melt under Union attack like ice melts under a summer sun. It became clear that a battle loomed. When commanding Union general Irwin McDowell finally marched to the attack, there was little secrecy involved.

McDowell left Washington with bands playing and forty-two thousand Union soldiers under his command. He knew that twenty-eight thousand Southern troops, under feisty General Pierre Gustave Toutant Beauregard, were entrenched behind a little creek called Bull Run. Facing an entrenched army, McDowell counted on superior numbers to overcome the Rebel tactical advantage.

But it took the untrained Union Army four days to march the fifty miles from Washington. McDowell fumed as the blue column straggled and stretched out along the way. Union commanders cursed as raw recruits fell out of formation to pick blackberries and search for water. When he finally reached Bull Run, McDowell had to delay another precious day to get his army together.

Those few days provided time enough for word to reach Richmond that Beauregard was badly outnumbered. And for Confederate general Joe Johnston, who was guarding an important gap with ten thousand men, to reach and reinforce Beauregard. The gap became unimportant now that the Confederacy knew where the main attack was to be launched.

But the reinforcements were of little use in the face of McDowell's successful maneuver. When a forest fire rages out of control, it does not matter how many trees are to burn. And the Union attack was raging out of Confederate control.

Canon swung Scratch around and rode after the professor. Hammer was Canon's traveling horse, the black Arabian his war horse. Robert E. Lee had attached the Black Horse to the professor's Virginia brigade that morning, following the skirmish. With the professor directing artillery fire from the hill, and Canon assigned to a scouting role, it appeared that any real action would bypass them. When he reached the woodsline, Canon found the professor calling together the Virginians and the dismounted Black Horse. The professor's pale blue eyes were strikingly vivid. His jaw was set as he paced through the Virginia troops, rallying men who had yet to see a shot fired in anger.

At the crest of the hill, Confederate soldiers were falling back as their comrades wilted before the growing Union momentum. Scarcely three hours had passed since the Union flank attack began, but an increasing stream of gray clad men flowed up the hill.

General Bernard Bee of South Carolina, who had been placed in charge of Alabama troops, had seen his men fight bravely for a while and then join the retreat. It was turning into a rout.

So convinced was Irwin McDowell that he had won a great victory, if not the war, he had already telegraphed Lincoln that the day was his.

General Bee, too, saw defeat looming. Riding up to the professor, Bee said, "I am afraid they are beating us back."

"Then, sir," replied the aroused professor, "we will give them the bayonet."

Turning to the Virginians, the professor cried in a shrill voice, "Men of Virginia, the South is losing the war right here, right now. It is up to us, and only us, to act. If you love your home and your land, you must decide right here, right now that you will die for them. But not until you kill the enemy. If you are willing, we will hold this hill for the South until we lie dead on it, or have whipped the enemy."

With a shout, the Virginians rose and fixed bayonets. Just over the rise, Rebel soldiers were running toward them. Some stopped to fire, but many had thrown down their guns and were fleeing fast as they could fly. Then the blue wave topped the hill, sweeping all before it. General Bee rode back and forth among the retreating Rebels, trying to regroup them.

Canon saw the professor draw his sword. "For Virginia and the South," yelled the professor, and he pointed his sword for the charge.

Canon, now on foot, called for the dismounted Black Horse and they grouped to him. Canon knew there was no time to waste on preliminaries. With a wild scream he scarce identified as his own, Canon took his men into battle.

The charging blue line smashed into the Virginians. Each side reeled from the shock, then closed once more. Fighting was hand-to-hand. Inexorably, the victorious Union troops pressed harder. But they had fought uphill for more than a mile. Many were exhausted. Some were discouraged at running into more fresh troops.

The Northern charge slowed, stopped as men in blue and gray were engulfed in wild melee. Horses and men screamed in anger, fear and pain. Smoke and the crackle of musket fire filled the air.

Confederate units to each side of the Virginians continued to fall back past them, but more slowly. Bee, still trying to stop the retreat, saw the Virginians hold their ground. He saw the professor, atop Little Sorrel, hold the horse steady as the battle surged around him.

Pointing at him, Bee shouted, "See! There is Jackson, standing like a stone wall. Rally, men! Rally to the Virginians."

Bee, having bestowed one of the great *noms de guerre* in military history, took a mortal wound moments later. But the backbone had been removed from the Union attack. Having stalled, it wavered and wavering, broke.

Two Union batteries had gained the hill and began pouring a deadly fire into the Confederate position. But after firing only a couple of rounds, the guns fell suddenly quiet. Then they reopened fire, but this time the heavy shot slashed into Union troops, already beginning to fall back. When the grape shot ripped into them, the blue troops turned to run.

A mounted Union lieutenant who had taken part in the charge up the hill rode furiously to the gun emplacement. "You fools," he yelled as he dismounted and grabbed the extraordinarily tall gunner, "this is a Union cannon and those are Union troops you're firing into."

"Actually," replied Canon with a grim smile, "I'm a Confederate Canon." He pulled back the blue coat he had taken from a captured Yankee to reveal his own gray uniform underneath. Then Canon produced quite the largest pistol the lieutenant was sure he had ever seen. When the lieutenant was directed to sit, he complied.

"These boys," Canon pointed to a half-dozen similarly blue coated members of the Black Horse, "tried to tell me that anything that has a mouth big as the one on this gun had to be Yankee."

Then he pointed to a stack of cannonballs. "But I convinced them that anything with balls this big needed to be Confederate."

Canon had been fighting near Jackson when he saw the two Union batteries rolling into place. As the Union attack crumpled against the Virginians, the lead Northern units surrendered. Canon stripped a few Yankees of their coats and, gathering several of his men, took them through the woods as they donned the blue coats.

Emerging from the woods no more than fifty yards from the big guns, they looked like reinforcing infantry to the Yankee gunners. The Yankee gun crew was happy to see them until a volley from the disguised Rebels drove them away.

The crumpling Union charge collapsed in the face of point blank artillery fire from Canon's men. Blue troops getting ready to charge the hill looked up in surprise to see their comrades suddenly run back toward them.

At the worst possible moment for the Union and the best possible for the Confederacy, some of Joe Johnston's fresh Rebel troops arrived on top of the hill after a march through the woods. With a yell, they joined in the assault on the reeling Yankees.

McDowell saw the fortunes of war undergo a sudden change. He felt dismay but was far from disheartened. He had still won a great victory. All he had to do was reorganize his disordered troops, halt the retreat, reform his lines. He would fight again tomorrow.

This plan would have worked had not so many Washington civilians believed the opinion of the Northern press that the battle would be a quick and decisive rout of the Southern troops by the Union. Much of the pro-Northern gentry in Washington turned out for the battle as if it were an attraction staged for their benefit. It was a soft July Sunday. And soft July Sundays were days for picnics and rides through the country in fancy carriages.

They turned out to witness the battle. They were dressed in finery, in fine carriages, with picnic baskets and bottles of champagne.

Canon had seen through his field glasses the festive way with which the onlookers viewed the battle. He realized these feckless fools had little idea of the horrors they witnessed with aplomb from afar. They saw men jump and fall as bullets struck, and lie where they had fallen, but the watchers could not smell the gore or the foul odors from dying men. They could not hear the groans. The watchers thought it clean and amusing. Canon thought them ghouls, as they enjoyed delicacies and sweetmeats while good men on each side lay screaming out their dying breaths on the horrible field.

As the tide of battle turned, Canon sent word to Jackson—replacement crews were needed for the captured Yankee artillery. The Black Horse would be ready when called for. As he and his men stripped off the borrowed blue coats, he sent word for the horses to be brought up and for the bugler to blow the signal for the cavalry to mount.

Canon knew what Jackson would want, that being what Napoleon would have wanted. The professor carried a volume of Napoleon's maxims in his saddlebags, and one maxim to which Jackson strongly adhered was that cavalry should always be sent to scourge a fleeing enemy.

The horses were standing by and the brigade bugler was blowing cavalry call when Jackson rode up to the gun emplacement. His left hand was loosely wrapped with a bloody handkerchief. A bullet had clipped the top off his left index finger. It was on the hand Jackson habitually held high to "help keep his body in better balance." Neither man mentioned the wound.

"My compliments, Captain," said Jackson in the ritual military manner of greeting on the field. "Are you ready to ride?"

"On your order, sir," replied Canon.

"They have hit us their best blow, I believe," said Jackson, "and we have withstood it. Now it is our turn. Ride after them, chase them back to Washington."

"It will be my pleasure."

Calling his leaders around him, Canon said, "Pass the word. We will pursue the enemy, paroling those who surrender, shooting those who do not. We may encounter unarmed citizens along the way. We are not here to make war on civilians. Do not harm them. But if the opportunity presents itself, you have permission to scare the hell out of them."

Swinging into the saddle, Canon looked over to the artillery crew which had taken over the captured Yankee gun emplacement. "Corporal," he called to a baby-faced teenager who proudly carried two chevrons on his sleeve, "try to put a shell on that stone bridge for me." The young man saluted as he nodded, then turned back to the gun. Canon rode to the front of his troop, drew his saber, and turned to the bugler. "Sound the charge," he called.

At the bridge, civilian party-goers began to notice more and more Union soldiers stream past on their way to the rear. Many picnickers still lolled about, unaware of any change in fortune, but the more perceptive realized something had gone horribly wrong. Among these, thoughts of holiday vanished like wisps of battlesmoke.

Thrumming conversation lessened, palled. Gaily bedecked bonnets, which had been nodding in time with animated discourse, turned south and grew still. Some spectators had field glasses. One man in a carriage, wearing a black stovepipe hat after the fashion of Mr. Lincoln, suddenly leaned forward, peering intently through his lens.

"My God," he muttered to himself, "it is the Black Horse."

Practically all the spectators had read highly fictionalized accounts in the Northern press of depredations and cruelty by the now infamous southern Black Horse cavalry. They believed every word. Another man, standing near the first, overheard.

"The Black Horse? Where?" he said, and brought his own glass to his eye. Then, "My God."

Canon, swinging Old Scratch down the steep hill, deplored coquetry and false modesty with equal intensity. He would have been gratified by the honesty of the first man's lady friend.

Fairly ripping the field glasses from his eyes, she said, "Get me the hell out of here, right this damned second," and essayed a quick glance through the glass as she climbed in the carriage.

It was nearing three P.M. when McDowell gave the general order to retire from the field. His young soldiers were falling back in disarray, but a semblance of order remained. There was confusion and dismay, but no panic. Retreating men were crossing Stone Bridge with purpose but without flight.

As word swept through the Union forces that the dread Black Horse was coming, the retreat became boisterous and unruly. Yankee soldiers, too, had believed the Northern press.

Then the young gunner to whom Canon had spoken loosed the finest artillery shot of the day. Stone Bridge over Cub Run represented the only quick, convenient and dry method of crossing the stream. The corporal's third round exploded in the middle of the bridge, killing several horses and overturning a huge supply wagon. It blocked the way just when an open way was what the retreating army needed most.

Consternation grew as soldiers and civilians tried to force their way through. Then someone looked back and screamed. An account of the battle read: "In the midst of the turmoil, there were shouts that the dreaded Confederate 'Black Horse Cavalry' was riding down on the mob. Newspapers and magazines had carried many stories about the horsemen, and now their name was enough to stir up fear. The raw recruits, who had fought so well, dropped their guns and ran. The army fell apart."

Those who witnessed the charge of the Black Horse did not wonder that the army fell apart. For those who had read the inflammatory stories, seeing the charge thundering down on them must have seemed something from their worst nightmare.

Through clearing coils and ropes of black gunpowder smoke, three hundred glossy steeds of the same intense hue came galloping. They moved as one, veering left or right like an ebony arrow. At the forefront rode a huge figure wielding a sword as long as a small man's body. Soldiers and civilians abandoned the bridge and dove into the water.

Though cleared of people, the bridge was still blocked by the overturned wagon. Without hesitation, Canon took Scratch onto the bridge and effortlessly over the wagon. The Black Horse followed without question or pause.

Those who witnessed it remembered it as one of the most spectacular sights of the Civil War. All three hundred horses cleared the wagon, often three abreast. Men who thought themselves safe on the other side of the bridge were stunned by the display. As these men watched the black horses fly over the wagon, they felt panic descending on them. In mindless terror, soldiers ripped the reins of horses and carriages from their civilian owners. Rushing pell-mell down the road to Washington, they scattered and dismayed other soldiers, still marching in good order, with shouts for them to run for their lives.

It had taken McDowell's army four days to make the fifty miles from Washington. It made the return trip in forty-eight hours.

Night had fallen by the time Canon returned to Jackson's field headquarters on Henry House Hill. Approaching darkness and the delaying necessity of rounding up prisoners had finally ended the Black Horse pursuit.

Canon found the South's new hero in a humor black as the moonless night. "I fear that our army is making a terrible mistake," Jackson said. Although Jackson maintained a controlled tone, Canon could see how affected he was. Eyes glittering, voice straining with emotion, Jackson continued, "General Beauregard has convinced General Lee and President Davis that our army is too tired and scattered to march on to Washington tonight. "If it were up to me, I would take the city before daylight if it killed me and half our army, but I cannot convince them."

Canon knew the words passing between them were from friend to friend and that Jackson would never refer to the matter again. Even now, the man's tone was one of disconsolation and disappointment, not bitterness.

They talked until midnight about the events of the day. Jackson was proud of the way his Virginians had stopped the brunt of the Union attack, but he doubted his brigade would receive the credit it was due. As the evening waned, Canon began to believe that in this, Jackson was mistaken. For, as the victorious Rebels celebrated around the camp, Canon began to hear a chant that would sweep the South.

"Stonewall . . . Stonewall . . . Stonewall!"

When Canon finally left to seek his own tent, Jackson had reconciled his mind to the failure to follow-up the day's victory.

"Perhaps it will serve to bring the leaders of the Union to listen to reason," he said. But he added, "I wish I could believe it."

Many times Canon would think back on that humid July night when the Confederate Army stood at the door of unprotected Washington. But he never heard Jackson mention it again.

The battle of Bull Run/Manassas became little more than a skirmish in retrospect. A total of seventy thousand men had fought for a day; each side lost about two thousand men. Coming battles would see armies of fifty to seventy-five thousand on each side battle for days. Casualties in these conflicts would often reach twenty percent of each army.

After the first battle, many Southerners thought the war was finished and simply left for home without word to anyone. The Union rallied like an eagle whose young are threatened. Washington became a fortress. Mountains of food and material began to rise in warehouses. A call for volunteers went out. Within two months of Bull Run, Union muster lists swelled to one hundred and sixty-eight thousand names.

Out of crisis, the real American Army was born.

6

# The World's Largest General Store

Stonewall Jackson reclined against a pile of lichen-covered rocks that in some prior day was part of a fence or perhaps a fortification. He leaned back against, well, a stone wall, thought Canon.

A year had passed since Jackson earned his war name on the plains of Manassas. Since then, his fame and that of the Stonewall Brigade, as the Virginians were now known, increased in direct proportion to the number of battles they fought. The battles had been many and Jackson's name was great.

It was only seven A.M., but even this cool shade high on Cedar Mountain could not dispel the certainty of brutal heat later that day in Shenandoah Valley. By nine, the early August heat would be a visible shimmering wave like the clouds of rolling dust that marked General John Pope's retreating Union soldiers.

Pope, with sixty-two thousand men, had come to the Shenandoah Valley to lure Lee and his army out of Richmond. When the battle joined, General George McClellan was to close on Lee from the opposite direction with eighty-seven thousand more Federals, catching Lee in a pincer movement.

On paper, the plan looked flawless. But when Abraham Lincoln learned of it, he immediately issued an order for the Union Army to reunite quickly as possible. From what he had seen of past performances, he feared Lee would come out of Richmond, whip one army then hurry on to whip the other. He ordered a recall.

Too late.

Lee sent out Stonewall Jackson and his twenty-five thousand men with orders to hold Pope while Lee took the remaining forty thousand men to confront McClellan. Canon knew little of these machinations. He only knew that yesterday morning, August 9, 1862, Stonewall's Virginians had whaled into the left flank of Pope's army and whipped hell out of the entire outfit. By last evening, they had driven Pope back twenty miles into a defensive position on the banks of the Rappahannock. This morning, Jackson's wiretappers had intercepted panicked cables from Pope to McClellan that Pope's army was badly outnumbered and faced annihilation if McClellan did not hurry to the rescue.

And now Jackson watched as Pope's rear guard retreated to join the Union commander on the Rappahannock. Jackson, his left side in profile as spots of the shaded sun filtered down on him, had lain in quiet thought for an hour.

Canon had decided Jackson was quite mystic. He had become the bane of Northern troops, two steps ahead of any Yankee general's plans. More dread even than Lee, Jackson was known throughout the civilized world.

The cause of Pope's plight serenely sucked on a lemon and gazed thoughtfully at roiling dust produced by a fleeing army. Canon wasn't sure what was going on beneath the kepi forage cap Jackson wore. But he was sure of one thing. Whatever was going on would not translate into good news for John Pope.

In the quiet of the morning, Canon considered the rising of Stonewall Jackson's star. Six months after the battle of Bull Run, Jackson made major general and was given command of the Shenandoah Valley. And to his gratification and delight, Canon was made colonel and permanently attached to the Stonewall Army.

Since then, Jackson had literally become the new Napoleon. In its first three months of operation, the Stonewall Army had marched more than two thousand miles, whipped three separate Union armies and had taken twenty thousand prisoners. Since May, Stonewall Jackson had won seven consecutive victories, including the one yesterday. And at no time had Jackson's army numbered more than twenty-five thousand men, though Yankee reports often credited him with three times the number.

Here's the strange thing, Canon thought: Although Stonewall Jackson was presently responsible for the death and capture of more American soldiers than any other man in history, he was fawned over by the Northern press. Every Yankee, from Abraham Lincoln to the lowest private, spoke of him in terms of respect and admiration, even awe. In the South, the admiration bordered on worship. Whenever Jackson rode into a town, guards had to be posted for his horse, Fancy, or that little sorrel would not have had a hair left in mane or tail.

Yet the man seemed genuinely unaffected by this, except for an occasional display of unfeigned embarrassment. Jackson truly shunned publicity, normally the sweetest of sops to generals. He fled from interviews as if they were Yankee interrogations and adoring crowds caused him to blush and stammer.

Nor was Jackson's heralded piety any sort of affectation. Jackson had always been devout and was neither more nor less so than when Canon first met him. He announced each victory to Richmond with a telegram which opened with the same laconic line—God had once again blessed the Southern cause. Jackson's piety, Canon suspected, helped him deal with the fame.

Jackson's uniforms were almost as tattered as those of his troops. His uniforms were clean, just awfully ragged. Although correct to the button, Jackson's uniforms usually looked as if he had been caught in a shell burst, a direct hit that somehow had penetrated only his clothing.

Canon had seen Yankees, captured in large lots by the Stonewall Army, literally fight for position in the front ranks just to get a glimpse of Jackson riding by. One story had it that two Yankees in a captured throng saw Jackson ride past in his tattered uniform.

"Don't look like much, do he?" said one. "No, he don't," said the other, "but if he was ours we wouldn't be captured, neither."

Canon captured a Yankee colonel who asked to have the honor to surrender himself personally to Stonewall Jackson. Canon had obliged.

The tattered uniforms, Canon thought, might be Jackson's sole affectation, and, if that, it was only in order to identify himself with his ragged soldiers. That identification with his men, apart from Jackson's military skills, was another facet of the Stonewall genius. He does not hold himself above his men, as do so many generals, Canon thought.

General officers usually sought out the most comfortable houses for their headquarters. Jackson often slept in his tent, as did Lee, even if comfortable houses were near. Canon recalled a particularly stormy night, with Jackson suffering a minor cough, when the general had decided to sleep indoors and had taken his entire staff inside. It was not unusual for two or even three fully uniformed soldiers to occupy one mattress.

Canon and a scouting party arrived at the house at three A.M., having spent twelve hours in the saddle without rest. Jackson got up from his bed and threw members of his personal staff out of their beds so they could be given to the Black Horse.

On another of the rare occasions when he stayed inside, Jackson had been asleep in bed when a messenger, who had ridden almost all night, came into the house. Seeing only one man on the bed, and not knowing the man was Jackson, the exhausted captain crawled in beside the general and was soon asleep. Next morning the horrified captain learned he had not only thrown himself down next to Stonewall Jackson, but had pulled all the bedcovers to himself. He sought out Jackson to apologize, but before he could begin, Jackson fixed him a baleful glare.

"Captain," said Jackson, "if that ever happens again I must insist that you remove your spurs before retiring for the evening."

Remembering the episode, Canon also recalled the first nickname given Jackson by the raw Rebel recruits at Harper's Ferry. They called him Fool Tom. They had despised Jackson's penchant for secrecy and the endless training marches that now stood them in such good stead. Fool Tom cum Stonewall. How they hated Fool Tom Jackson. How they love Stonewall Jackson. Shaking himself from reverie, Canon looked over at Fool Tom.

Horrible! Horrible! Jackson still reclined in the same position, but his eyes were closed and his face was pale as chalk. And his left coat sleeve, Jackson's entire left side was drenched with blood. So much blood! How could it have happened? Canon had heard no shot, and no one could have sneaked that close with a knife.

"General!" called Canon, hurrying to him.

Jackson stirred, stretched. The blood danced about on his sleeve, then disappeared.

Canon saw to his relief that it had been simply shade from an oak branch, falling on Jackson's left side.

"Forgive me, Colonel," said Jackson, sitting up. "I decided what we must do, and fell asleep in the planning of it." Rising to his feet, Jackson tossed into the grass the spent lemon he still had held.

Noticing the strange look on Canon's face, Jackson said, "Rabe, all you all right?"

Canon could not quite shake the effects of the apparition, but he nodded.

"I guess so, General," he said. "But the shade struck on you very strangely. I thought for a moment that you had been wounded somehow and I have to admit it gave me a turn.

"I didn't notice you dropping off and you seemed awfully still, and pale as, uh . . .," Canon trailed off the sentence in embarrassment.

"As death," finished Jackson. "Don't be afraid of the word, or of the event, for my sake. The Lord has already fixed the time and place of my death. I assure you that it does not bother me one bit."

Canon nodded again. But a chill shook him all the same.

Riding across the ridge back to headquarters, Canon asked Jackson what he had decided to do. Jackson's secrecy, especially with his own leaders, could be infuriating. Sometimes he would answer a question like Canon's; usually he pretended not to hear.

Obstinately, Canon decided that he had to have an answer.

"What are we going to do, General?" he prodded Jackson.

"Very well, I will tell you," said Jackson, as the horses stepped along side by side. "I will suggest to General Lee that he remain in Richmond for the time being. I believe that we have John Pope and his men under cower. If they are cowed as I believe they are, then we are blessed with a strategic opportunity which General Lee will grasp and appreciate.

"Pope will not move until help from McClellan arrives. But that help will be almighty slow in coming. Little Mac has little love for the man who has replaced him as commanding general of the Army of the Potomac.

"So we will gesture and demonstrate against Pope for a couple of weeks until we are sure he is convinced we plan to assault him full scale. When that happens, we will leave enough men here to keep him occupied and the rest of us will have a game of fox and hounds with the Union Army."

"And we will be the sly fox?" suggested Canon.

"We had better be," said Jackson, "or we shall be the dead fox."

"Where will this fox find a hiding hole?" persisted Canon.

"Colonel, can you keep a secret?" said Jackson.

"Yes, sir."

"Good. So can I," said Jackson, and spurred his horse.

THE MORNING OF AUGUST 26 dawned dark and drear. A soft rain drummed lightly on tin roofed warehouses stretched across the plains of Manassas. The area looked far different from a year ago when the plain had hosted the war's first battle.

Soon after the victorious Southern troops had withdrawn, the Union had fortified the railhead there and created one of the largest supply depots in the world.

Lincoln wanted the supply depot impregnable and the army worked to make it so. It lay in the middle of a triangle of Union armies. Seventy-file miles to the left was McClellan with eighty-seven thousand troops, behind Manassas lay Washington with its home guard of fifty thousand. To the right was the beleaguered Pope and his entrenched army of sixty-two thousand.

Here at Manassas, trainload after trainload of materials and supply were dumped, waiting to be waggoned to troops in the field. The railhead was a solid square mile of clustered warehouses and boxcars filled to bursting with everything from cigars to caviar.

Two supply sergeants were sitting in rocking chairs on the front porch of one of the warehouses, cursing the rain and the boredom of army life.

"Believe it's starting to slack," said one, speaking tiredly of the rain.

"Naw," was the laconic reply. "Thunder coming from the South."

Louder and louder grew the thunder, and with it came wild yells. The two men rose and peered intently up the street. They turned and ran. Inside, the men had barely bolted the door when clattering hoofbeats drowned the sound of rain and all other sound outside.

A little lieutenant came out of his office in a flurry, cursing at the noise and trying to make sense of the jabberings from his sergeants.

All three quieted when a gray rider on a black horse came crashing through the large warehouse window. One of the sergeants panicked and reached for his holster before the young lieutenant had time to surrender. He fell with a bullet in his brain. Surrender was quickly tendered.

Almost in a panic himself, the lieutenant had trouble forming words.

"Wh-wh-who are you?" he said.

Canon pointed to the dual patch on his gray sleeve. "We are the Black Horse Cavalry of the Stonewall Brigade," he said, keeping a tight rein on a quivering Scratch. "And sitting right up at the top of the hill outside is Stonewall Jackson."

Only three days earlier, the lieutenant had seen an official dispatch which assured Washington that Jackson and his army were a hundred miles away, whipping the pants off John Pope each time he tried to lift his head.

"Just what is there to your Stonewall Goddamn Jackson," cried the perplexed lieutenant, "and do his men have wheels or wings?" It was a question which echoed across the North, when reports of the capture of the Union supply depot spread. One year earlier, it had taken Irwin McDowell four days to march the Federal army fifty miles. Stonewall Jackson had marched his army sixty-two miles in forty-eight hours. It was an accomplishment unheard of at the time.

"The feat of the feet" earned yet another nickname for the Stonewall Army: "Jackson's Foot Cavalry."

Two hours after Canon crashed through the warehouse window, twenty thousand tattered and bone-weary rebel soldiers streamed into a foretaste of paradise. Jackson had captured what amounted to the world's largest general store.

A starving, shoeless, half naked mob found itself surrounded by literally tons of things that had filled the hungry dreams of each of its members.

Shoes during the march practically melted off the feet of those few who had shoes. Never mind. Here are boxcars full of boots! Cigars were scarce in the Southern army. Here are crates full of Havanas!

Sugar and coffee had been nonexistent. Just open the door to this warehouse! Have a fifty-pound sack of each. Only the liquor is forbidden. Have hams, smoked oysters, all the fresh fruit you want.

Fresh fruit!

Stonewall Jackson sat on the steps of a warehouse porch, an orange in each hand. Forage cap low over his eyes to deflect the setting sun, knee high brown cavalry boots crossed leg over leg, stained gray coat open to the evening breeze, Jackson held his left hand high to better balance his internal organs.

Canon and two or three other officers were stretched out on the porch. Canon had made a sandwich which required a loaf of bread and most of a small ham. One of the officers lounging near him remarked that just a photograph of the sandwich would weigh a pound, at least. Canon smiled and continued to munch happily.

Feasting continued far into the night.

Next morning, latrine lines were long as rich, plentiful food took its toll on bodies used to privation. Between visits to the line, men were filling knapsacks with sugar and coffee and still gorging themselves with delicacies. Departure, when it came time, would be rapid, yet Jackson waved away any worries brought to him concerning their precarious position.

Finally, one of his staff said, "General, we are in grave danger. What are we to do?"

For once, Jackson was expansive: "Danger? On the contrary, sir. We presently control the board. In fact, we dictate Northern strategy.

"They won't send Washington troops after us because they justifiably fear we would flank them and fall on the city. We have whipped Pope, so they cannot send him after us alone.

"McClellan must be worried to find he is between our army and that of General Lee."

"No. We are in no danger. At least no immediate danger. Generals McClellan and Pope will try to unite and seek us, but they are a couple of days away. We have yet this day of rest and feast.

"Tonight we will have a bonfire. Tomorrow, be ready to move at first light."

IT WAS A SLOW, bitter day for John Pope as his men trudged warily toward Manassas.

Toward evening, Pope saw the first huge billows of smoke rise from the supply depot yet ten miles away. Millions of dollars worth of supplies were going up with the smoke as the world's largest general store burned and burned and burned.

Next morning, a fuming Pope neared Manassas. His scouts had told him that Jackson, like the supply depot, was gone. It was hot, dusty and dry on the Groveton Road. Pope lifted his canteen to his mouth, rinsed, spat. He wished he could rid the bitter taste of humiliation from his mouth as easily as he could rid the dust.

Jackson had whipped him, eluded him, made him a laughingstock. To make it worse, Union soldiers Jackson had paroled reported that Jackson had but thirty thousand men with him. If only I had known that, thought Pope. If only I could catch him. Earnestly, Pope prayed for the opportunity to redeem himself.

Someone far wiser than Pope had many years ago warned that people should be careful about what they pray for, because they might get it. Rifle fire rattled out of the wooded hillside, cutting into the leading Union ranks. The Federals returned fire and began to dig in, preparing for the screaming Rebel attack. But to Pope's surprise, Jackson was already falling back.

It set the pattern for the entire day. The Rebels would stand, fire, fall back in ordered retreat. By late evening, Confederate forces had been driven almost five miles and were entrenched along an abandoned railroad cut on the plains of Manassas.

Pope was exultant. Jackson had backed himself into a trap from which there was no way out. The Rebels had no further room for retreat and Pope's humiliated army was in front of them, thirsty for revenge. Here was far more than a chance for redemption. Jackson would surrender or die. The Union commander should have paused to wonder why Jackson, who had never made a military blunder, should so cheaply reveal his position and then dig himself so deeply into a hole. But Pope was too intent on destroying Jackson to let doubt enter his mind.

On the morning of August 29, Pope hurled sixty-two thousand men at the Rebel line. The charge was met by a withering fire which broke the Union attack. But the Federals charged again and again. Each attack was beaten back, but each drove nearer and nearer to the thin gray line. By early afternoon, it was clear to Pope that Jackson could never hold. He sent a gleeful telegram to Washington that Jackson was bottled up and weakening.

If McClellan would join forces with him now, promised Pope, the Union would have Stonewall Jackson's head on a platter soon. As Union forces threw the day's final assault at the exhausted Rebel line, Pope received a telegram which he knew signaled Jackson's end. McClellan was on the march and would join him early next morning.

Jackson's line still held, but each repulse of a Federal charge had grown feebler. Satisfied, Pope pulled back to await the arrival of McClellan's troops. Jackson was trapped. Escape was impossible. Pope had planned for every contingency. Except one. Intent on destroying Jackson, Pope had forgotten Robert E. Lee, who was on the march toward him. During the night, Lee arrived with his other lieutenant general, James Longstreet, and thirty thousand fresh Confederates.

Silent as stalking gray wolves, Longstreet's men moved masked cannon within two hundred yards of the Union left flank. And ever so quietly, thirty thousand men in gray moved into position for a flank attack.

In the railroad cut, with midnight long past, Canon summoned his will to fight off exhaustion. He tried, too, to think of words of encouragement he could give to his men as he rode along the half-mile long defensive position. It had been the worst day of fighting he had known. The Black Horse fought dismounted this day, in the thick of it, and he had seen death wrought on a scale he had thought impossible. Southern casualties must be fifteen percent, he thought, and the Yankee number of dead and wounded must be three times as great. And still they kept coming. The final Union charge of the day almost broke them. The attackers finally gained the trench. Hand to hand fighting lasted almost a half-hour before the Yankees were driven back.

Worse, a Union trooper discovered a breach in the wall of the trench where a run-off stream had washed a deep ditch into the earth. Jackson had given defense of the ditch to the Stonewall Brigade and the Black Horse, and had placed Canon in charge. Now it would bear the brunt of the next attack.

Both of Canon's back-up commanders in the Black Horse had gone down in the fight, though one would likely recover. And Canon had felt bullets tear his clothing twice, one at his right sleeve and another at his right shoulder. He was unsure how many times he heard the dark hum of bullets past his head. Five? Six?

No matter. He was alive and there was work to do.

The night following a battle was worse than the battle itself. During the heat of the fight, there was no time for the mind to grasp the wicked wet whooshing sound made by a man who takes a bullet in the guts. In war, night is the time for pity. Out in the night, dying men were calling for water and comfort. Some, delirious, called for their father or mother. But even if someone braved the risk of sniper bullets in the dark field, chances were slim that the wounded man could be found amidst all the bodies—hundreds upon hundreds—that lay in the field like crumpled scarecrows.

It was almost two A.M. Men slept on their rifles, and would awake to fresh horrors of the new morning on the field of battle. Those who could waken. But a few small campfires burned in the cut where a soldier or two could not sleep. Canon saw one of the fires in the near distance, approached it with dread.

"Any word, suh? Any word from Genrul Lee?" said one of the two men. In the feeble light, Canon could make out feeble features. Both men were ragged, dirty, with scraggly beards. Feeling at the dirt caked on his face, and checking his uniform in the firelight, Canon realized that he must look much the same as the two men. They were boiling coffee in a coffeepot that wasn't new at Manassas a year ago.

"Still enjoying that Yankee coffee from the supply depot, eh?" said Canon.

"Yessuh," said the bold one, while the other looked into the fire, either angry or embarrassed to have an officer at their fire. "Me and Billy here wouldn't mind stopping by another one like that after we get through with these here Yanks, would we, Billy?"

Billy finally looked at Canon, smiled a shy smile and shook his head. Canon doubted the boy was sixteen. "Would ye jine us in a cup, Colonel?" mumbled Billy, looking back at the fire.

"Have to ride on down to the flank right now, fellows, but I'll be back this way directly," said Canon. "If I'm back this way in time and the offer holds, I'd be much obliged." Canon realized he wanted a cup of hot coffee more than he could remember wanting anything, and he wanted the companionship of these two men who managed to be cordial in the midst of horror.

"And word from Genrul Lee, suh?" said the first, again.

"Help is on the way," said Canon, convincingly as possible.

"Yessuh. Good to hear it," said the man, totally unconvinced.

Canon touched his cap in return to their salutes, rode on. How could he tell them that there was indeed word from General Lee, and that the word meant death? Canon was returning from a midnight meeting at Jackson's headquarters. Lee, Longstreet and Jackson agreed the Yankees must not be made aware of Lee's arrival, and therefore the Confederates in the cut must not be told. Because they could not be reinforced.

"Pope and McClellan must be totally convinced that we are helpless," said Jackson. "General Longstreet will wait until McClellan has committed all reserves to the battle. We must hold until that time."

The atmosphere in the tent was grim as the news.

But here, Canon understood, was an opportunity that must be exploited, regardless of cost. The Confederate Army of Northern Virginia, fifty thousand men under Robert E. Lee, now had a real chance to completely destroy the Union Army of the Potomac, one hundred fifty thousand men under John Pope.

But the Stonewall Army would be at sacrifice. "We must make sure that Pope and McClellan have committed their entire force before we counterattack," reiterated the plump, intellectual Longstreet, fingers twining his long brown beard. Jackson nodded. Lee looked unhappy. Canon still couldn't believe his ears.

General A. P. Hill, who commanded one wing of Jackson's infantry, said incredulously, "Sir, we probably have no more than fifteen thousand effectives fighting in the cut. We will be outnumbered ten to one. What do you expect us to do?"

"You will hold, sir," said Jackson. "At all cost."

"We will try, General Jackson," replied Hill, stiffly, "but it might interest the generals to know that we are also almost out of ammunition. Right now, we have men out removing cartridge boxes from the dead. But we are almost out of bullets."

"Then, sir," said Jackson, "give them the bayonet."

Canon, riding to the Black Horse encampment, understood the situation perfectly. Even if Pope and McClellan held only a quarter of their men in reserve, they would still have superior numbers to drop on Longstreet's counterattack. Canon knew it was all or nothing. What he didn't know was how to explain it to soldiers like the two he had left at the campfire.

He didn't know how to tell these men that help had arrived but, whoops—we're sorry, it's unavailable at the moment. Didn't know how to tell them that yes, there's plenty of ammunition just back up the road a piece, but there's only so much time to get the men in position for a counterattack, you see, and so only a few crates of ammunition can be gotten here tonight. Reinforcements? Sure. You'll be reinforced just prior to the counterattack, which will come whenever Pope and McClellan send Union Soldier Number One Hundred Fifty Thousand at you. You'll get help, just exactly when it's too late.

Back at the breach in the cut, Canon found most men asleep. Exhausted sentries challenged him in the dark. As he unsaddled Hammer, Canon tried to be hearty with the small group who clustered around him seeking news. Yes, Canon said, yes, help is on the way. Drained soldiers had searched out every stone in the area to try to fortify the forty-yard wide ravine. Corpses in blue and in gray lay where they had fallen. The men had put what remained of their exhausted energies in attempts to make the position defensible. The living tried to take care of the living. There was no time for the dead.

Canon called an aide to take Hammer back to the horse line and return with Scratch. Removing holster, pistols and saber, Canon used them for a pillow as he stretched out on the ground. Just before sleep took him, Canon recalled a story from ancient Greece, from the time of the warrior Spartans.

Defending their border at Thermopylae against an imminent invasion, the Spartans sent one small band under Leonides from the main force to guard a hidden gap in the hilly terrain. It was unlikely the gap would be discovered, they were told. But if so, they must hold at all cost. Through luck or treachery, the invaders learned of the gap and threw the brunt of their force against it.

The little band held, but the fighting was so fierce that even the survivors died from their wounds. The Spartan commander was found at the foot of a rocky wall. On it, he had chalked a final message: "Traveler, go tell the Spartans that here, in accordance to their rules, we lie."

Canon awoke after two hours of sleep. He expected an attack at dawn and was accordingly up and moving, readying the forces. All along the line, commanders were rallying the men for the fray. Jackson commanded the right, Hill the middle, Canon the left.

Adrenaline began to pump through the worn bodies as the gray line braced for the assault. Nothing happened. Hour after hour passed, but no shells rained on them, no infantry rushed.

In the Union camp, men on the staffs of McClellan and Pope listened as the two men railed at each other. Pope wanted an all out assault. The ever cautious Little Mac was holding out a quarter of his men. Little heed had been given a scouting report that Confederate reinforcements had arrived.

Noon approached, arrived, passed. Finally, agreement was reached. McClellan would withhold twenty thousand men through the first assault. If it failed, and there was no Rebel counterattack, then the full army would be thrown against Jackson.

Movement was detected in the Union camp at one P.M. Word raced up and down the trench. Get ready! Here they come!

At two P.M., Pope renewed his attack, driving against Jackson with a line two miles long. But it was a thousand yards down the ridge from the Union camp, then another five hundred across the open plain to the railroad cut.

In the Rebel line, battle was a welcome relief from the tension which had steadily increased since dawn. At the ravine, Canon led a foray out to meet the onrushing Union troops. They were to absorb the shock, then fall back to a perimeter set up around the edges of the ravine. Grunts, shouts and shots rang around Canon as the fever of battle gripped him.

Face flushed from heat, eyes red from smoke and strain and lack of sleep, Canon used a pistol with his right hand, the saber with his left. He hacked and stabbed and shot and slew.

Men in his own command were afraid to get too near Canon when blood lust was on him. They tried to stay close enough to offer some help and protection as he ranged among the blue troops.

The blue army's vast number had one drawback. The Federals were forced to bunch as they neared the shortened Rebel line. Only the leading units could get a clear shot. And the massed Union attack presented a target that no Confederate would miss. But the weight of numbers was inexorable. Slowly, Canon fell back, shouting and shooting and slashing. Relentlessly the Union troops pushed Canon and his men back to the cut. But the retreat also opened new fields of fire for the Rebel troops on each side of Canon's men. They poured a galling volley into the advancing blue sea, pushing it back across the plain.

The Federal attack did not break, but fell back and reformed, ready to surge again. McClellan ordered in his reserve. In the respite, Canon checked his pistols. His cartridge belt was empty, as was one of his pistols. He had three loads remaining. Breathing heavily, Canon allowed an orderly to bind a slight bullet wound that furrowed his side. He also bled from a cut to his cheek where a Union bayonet nicked him as Canon sabered its wielder. Another bullet had torn a furrow in his calf.

In the ravine, men were using bodies of the slain to construct a ghastly wall. Brushing aside the orderly, Canon went to lend a hand. He wondered what had happened to the low wall of rocks that had been piled in the ravine during the night. He received the answer from Billy, the young boy he had seen at the campfire during the night.

Standing in the breach with a rock in each hand, Billy handed one to Canon. "Here, Colonel," Billy said with a grim smile. "Have some ammunition." Five hundred yards away, a wild shout marked the beginning of the renewed Union attack. This time, it surged into the ravine, up and over the wall of the parapet. "Yanks in the cut! Yanks in the cut!" came cries up and down the writhing battle line. Sensing a movement behind him, Canon ducked, spinning as he reached for his right hand pistol. He heard the deadly hiss of a bullet passing over his head as his answering shot took the Federal soldier in the throat. The man fell on his back, then rolled down the hill, almost reaching Canon's leg before he stopped. Canon reached for the rifle the man held, even in death, and grabbed for the cartridge box.

Along the wall, all was turmoil. Empty rifles were used as clubs. Bayonets rasped against each other. Rocks rained down on advancing Yankees. Again, Canon ran to the melee. The Federal soldiers finally withdrew, but gaps were torn in the Rebel line. There were no longer enough men to fill them. Frantically, Canon called for the troops to shorten the line, fill the deadly gaps.

We can take one more assault, thought Canon, but not two. The Federal soldiers knew it as well as Canon knew it. They bunched. And here it came, blue men screaming in rage and victory. The Rebel line braced. But the attack never reached it.

From no more than two hundred yards away, Longstreet's hidden artillery opened on the Federal troops. The cannons were loaded with canister, and the iron balls ripped into the charging Union soldiers with horrible effect. Canon could actually see trails and swaths cut through the blue troops.

Atop the ridge, Pope and McClellan watched in shock as the counterattack shook the Federal onslaught like a rag doll. There were no Union troops left to deal with it. Thirty thousand fresh Confederates crashed into the Union flank and decimated it. When the Federal commanders turned to meet the assault, the Stonewall Army, finally reinforced, charged out of the railroad cut howling for revenge.

Calling for the horses to be brought up, Canon began to gather his cavalry. Just as he was about to mount Scratch, Jackson rode up. "My compliments, Colonel," said Jackson, saluting him. "The men who held this ravine are heroes, and you may be assured that Richmond will know it. You're ready to chase the enemy, then? Excellent. Ride on. But tell me, first, how close did they get to the breach?"

"They came within a stone's throw, sir," said Canon, with a straight face.

"Yes," said Jackson. "I see. Very good, Colonel. Very good. Ride on. Ride on."

It was past four P.M. when Longstreet broke the Union attack. But Southern hopes of destroying the Federal Army of the Potomac were shattered against the Union's Iron Brigade, which set up, ironically, on Henry House Hill and refused to be dislodged. It was much the same stand that Jackson had made the previous summer, but it failed to turn to the tide of battle as did Jackson. It did serve to save the Army of the Potomac.

The second battle of Manassas/Bull Run was another great victory for Jackson and Lee. When it was over, the North had lost sixteen thousand men, almost twice the number of the South. And the mere mention of Stonewall Jackson's name made John Pope color with conflicting feelings of envy, rage, dread and shame.

<br>

7

# *Three Cigars*

Hubert Hillary despised himself. In this, he shared the sole opinion he held in common with everyone who ever knew him. Hillary despised practically everything and everyone.

His parents had displayed what he considered the decency and good sense to die from smallpox when he was away at boarding school. More importantly, they left him sufficient means for a thorough business education at a small but social college. Hillary was diminutive, plump, clean shaven and myopic. His lank brown hair, which had begun seriously to thin during his final year at school, was now but a fringe.

It was in that final year of college that Hillary's true character began to manifest itself. He despised his college nickname, Mole, which came to him only partly because of an unfortunate resemblance to the creature, incredibly enhanced by the thick glasses he had to wear.

The name had fallen to him also because he burrowed tirelessly into schoolbooks. He enjoyed obtuse cryptograms, statistics, logistics. A long list of numbers which set his schoolmates (whom he despised) groaning would set off rare feelings of real delight in Hillary.

Last and most, the nickname was derived from Hillary's nocturnal ramblings, the nature of which were suspected but never proven. They were thought to include an unusual interest in whips and prostitutes. But so circumspect was Hillary that no proof was ever evidenced.

Now in his thirtieth year, Hillary was set in character. He was petty, petulant, arrogant, silly and morose by turns. He was sly, shallow, vain, vengeful, dishonorable and dishonest. He took snuff up the nose. He connived, intrigued, backstabbed, mongered rumors and young whores. He dilettanted.

And he could lie, artfully and comfortably, like an expensive rug. He possessed a flawed but massive intellect. Cancer was no more malignant than he. In short, Hubert Hillary was a very dangerous little flower. He ruined people for fun, people he didn't even know, if saw no possibility of getting caught. It was his hobby.

Hillary was also the Confederate Assistant Undersecretary of War. And he harbored a great secret hate for Stonewall Jackson. Hatred was something in which Hillary gloried. Aside from fear, hatred was the only genuine emotion with which Hillary had experience.

Hillary rarely allowed himself this luxury but when he did, he took it to his breast and nurtured it as a loving mother suckles her first born babe. To protect his hate for Jackson, he cloaked it under a guise of ardent admiration. He had met Jackson but once. He would never forget it.

Though he despised everyone in the war department, Hillary was considered to be one of the few people who were practically indispensable. Because of his genius at logistics and handling the supplies remaining to the South, Hillary held almost autonomous power where such things were concerned. He was privy to every scrap of information related to his bailiwick.

The captured stores at Manassas was the muddy point over which he ran afoul of Jackson. Hillary cared not a fig for Jackson's lightning march from Cedar Mountain to Manassas, didn't care that Jackson had astounded the world with the victory there. Hubert Hillary didn't give a damn who won the war, except that he intended to have plenty of power and money. Being firmly imbedded in the Southern bureaucracy, it would serve him best for the South to win. Although he secretly despised Southern aristocracy for not letting him run amok in it.

But no matter to him, really, who won. His secret bank account in France grew a little each month or two. After all, he dealt with the black market and the blockade runners, and he picked a tiny plum or crumb here and there. Nothing big, though he did not lack greed. He was greedy as a pig. But he was also smart. And scared.

A small skimming off a big shipment could double his account. And there had been too few of those lately. When word came that the Federal supply dump in Manassas was taken, Hillary developed a tiny erection which later that evening translated itself into some cane marks on himself and a mulatto girl at a special house ten miles out of town.

When he learned next day that Jackson had not only burned most of the stores, but was keeping the rest for his own use, Hillary lost control and fell into a general keening fit at his office in Richmond. Truth to tell, Hillary had immediately come up with a plan that would not have hampered Jackson to any degree and would have secured much of the needed supplies Jackson destroyed. But Hillary had not been consulted. Not only his bank account, but his very authority had been undermined by the mad Jackson. In a snit which completely compromised his common sense, Hillary on his own authority whipped off a telegram ordering Jackson from now on to put captured supplies under the care and maintenance of himself, Hubert Hillary.

So thoroughly did Hillary inveigh against Jackson that he was taken along, again against his better judgment, to a meeting in the Shenandoah Valley of Davis, Lee and Jackson. Jackson believed Lee's only fault as a commander was that he paid too much attention to politics and orders from Richmond, even if Davis and commanding General Braxton Bragg were graduates of West Point. Since taking over the Shenandoah and recording his great successes there, Jackson had been alert to any attempts at political intervention. It would compromise his effectiveness. For as much as Jackson demanded strict obedience from his own men, he brooked no interference from those in authority over him. He trusted only Robert E. Lee, of whom Jackson said that here was the only man he would follow blindfold.

By the time Davis and Hillary reached Jackson's camp, Jackson's friends in Richmond had seen to it that Southern newspapers somehow received copies of Hillary's telegram. Hard on its heels, they had also received copies of an even more powerful document. Jackson had tendered his resignation, "regretfully," it said. He could not lead if he did not enjoy Richmond's confidence. He would return to VMI.

Jackson had anticipated an attempt by someone in the war department to limit his parameters and he would not have it. The resignation was both polite and real. Between the lines, Jackson said that if anyone tries to impose his will on me, I will quit.

The storm in the press was predictable. Hillary was pilloried, threatened, castigated, ridiculed and called a traitor. By the time he arrived at camp, had his presence there been known, he would not have lived an hour. Even the newspaper correspondents would have helped string him up. That evening, in his tent, Hillary was trying to think of some way to evade the storm and if possible throw it back on Jackson. It was unthinkable that a brute like a common field commander could make him into a pariah. By the morning's meeting, Hillary was sure, he would think of some way to put the matter right.

When the tent entrance flapped back, without so much as a polite knock being given, Hillary raised himself to his full five feet five inches and prepared to give the offender a shrill tongue lashing.

To his dismay, Hillary recognized the craggy features of Stonewall Jackson. Quickly putting on a smile and holding out his hand, Hillary began to mumble placating remarks in the vein that he couldn't think how such misunderstandings occur but that he was sure . . .

"I did not come here to pass amenities or civilities with you," interrupted Jackson, ignoring Hillary's outstretched hand. "I came here to tell you that you are a scoundrel and a damned liar. You have conspired against me and I will not have it. If you were any part of a man, I would slap your face and force you to resent it. And I tell you right here, right now, that if you ever interfere with me again, or cross my path in any way, you will do so at the peril of your life."

Jackson's eyes, those pale blue lights, seemed to strike into Hillary's dark soul. Hillary could only gulp and nod, his heart beating wildly. Jackson turned on his heel and stamped out of the tent.

Hillary's lily white hands fluttered about like trained doves, fanning his face, feeling his heart, grasping his constricted throat, taking his pulse. It was some moments before he was able to speak loudly enough to have his orderly bring him water, then brandy, then whiskey.

Throughout his sleepless night, Hillary suffered alternating bouts of fear and loathing. In the morning, he sent a note to the meeting that he was indisposed and not only withdrew any remarks which General Jackson might have found offensive, but seconded any plans which the hero of the Confederacy might have. He only wished to serve, Hillary added, and regretted that his fervor may well have been misplaced and misunderstood.

Back in Richmond, where the press still sent storms crashing over his balding, jowly head, he bravely appeared before them, impeccably but foppishly dressed, and read a strongly worded statement of self condemnation.

Hillary had groped for the proper verbal hair shirt, then donned it articulately for the public prints. He would never presume to order the gallant hero Jackson, he said, but in his zeal to serve the Confederacy he had been too emphatic in suggesting a plan for Jackson's consideration. Said plan was now withdrawn. Long live Stonewall Jackson.

Since the day Hillary was, as he thought it, crucified by the press, he became on the surface the South's most vociferous admirer of Stonewall Jackson. One mention of Stonewall and Hillary commenced to coo. It was hero worship, long and loud. Inwardly, he seethed.

Suddenly, somehow, shipments of supplies to Jackson began to go awry.

And Hillary began to research reports for a weakness in Jackson, a flaw in Jackson's personality. He found it. Unfortunately, it was a flaw ready made for exploitation by a schemer and would-be demagogue. For the taciturn Jackson not only expected too much of his own officers, he demanded it of them. He would have them be like him. And though they tried their best to live up to his expectations, it was simply beyond them.

SINCE BOYHOOD, JACKSON HAD LIVED HIS LIFE by one cardinal rule; he could be whatever he willed himself to be. He could not learn that he could not will other men, no matter how hard they tried, to become what he was.

At one time or other, every general officer under Jackson was under court-martial. On one occasion, every officer on his staff was under court-martial at the same time. Few of the courts-martial ever came to trial. Usually, whoever had fallen into disfavor with Jackson accepted punishment, which normally was nothing more than having to trail the marching columns for a day or two, eating the dust of twenty-five thousand men stepping doubletime. Canon swallowed his share. But it galled.

Most of the time, such punishment was given when a commander failed to depart on time with his troops, or arrive at destination on time. Canon understood the importance of such timing, especially in light of Jackson's hit-and-run tactics. But still it galled. Stonewall Jackson's men loved him. With his officers, the relationship was often love-hate.

Following the Battle of Second Bull Run/Manassas, though, all was well in camp and in Richmond. The Army of Northern Virginia basked in the glow created by long laudatory articles in Southern newspapers. They reveled as Northern newspapers cried out for leaders like Lee and Jackson, or at least for leaders who might give these men a decent fight.

The continued successes of Lee and Jackson were having worldwide impact. England and France seemed on the verge of pledging allegiance to Richmond, but proponents of the Southern cause, in debates in their houses of government, could not quite swing the required support.

While foreign backers pointed to Lee and Jackson, their adversaries pointed to generals U. S. Grant and William Sherman. They were winning in Mississippi and Tennessee—much like Lee and Jackson were winning in the east.

The South needed to do something truly dramatic to bring on much needed aid, and it was up to Lee and Jackson to come up with the idea. During the first three days of September, following the victory at Manassas, senior commanders spent hours in Lee's tent. The Southern army had once again abandoned the plains of Manassas and taken to the cool mountainsides for rest and recovery. Still, commanders both North and South knew Lee was poised near the Potomac. Practically everyone knew a Southern invasion of the North was being discussed, if not planned.

The morning of September 4, Canon was called to Jackson's tent. Canon felt wonderful, invigorated. The air was cool and bracing, pure as spring water. Smells of rich pine firesmoke mingled with the aromas of boiling coffee and bacon being fried. Banjoes and mouth harps twanged happy tunes.

The whole army was happy. Happy to be alive. Canon knew it was natural for survivors of such a holocaust as Manassas to celebrate life and victory. Word had gone around camp that the army might be about to invade the North, and that meant fighting nearly every day. Bullets would be flying again soon enough. But today they were alive and were heroes. It was a happy time.

At Jackson's tent, Canon rapped twice on the tent pole and pushed inside the flap. Jackson had tied back one corner of the tent roof, and it was light and airy inside. Fully uniformed, sitting bolt upright on his cot so as not to compress his inner organs, Jackson held in his hands the brigadier general's collar star he had worn as commander of the Virginia Brigade.

Jackson looked up at him, and Canon thought the look somehow different from the casual Jackson glance. The pale eyes never looked more vivid.

"Colonel," said Jackson, "let us assume for a moment, and this is between you and me, that I have been promoted." Canon was surprised. Jackson already held the rank of lieutenant general, which was the highest rank attainable. Canon could only assume that Lee was about to be returned to Richmond and that Jackson was going to take full command of the Army of Northern Virginia. He said nothing.

"You have a way with words. If you were going to pin my new badges of rank on me in front of the men, what would you say on my behalf?" asked Jackson.

Canon was nonplussed, then irritated. So it happens to us all, he thought. Even Jackson. Perhaps he is human after all. Jackson had never sought flattery, even shunned it. Now he apparently wished it. Disappointing. But if anyone deserved praise, Canon thought, it was Jackson. Still, he was uneasy. It was so out of character for Jackson that he couldn't fathom it. Oh, well, thought Canon.

A bit coldly, Canon said, "General, you are a true hero. Not a man or woman, hardly a child in the South goes to bed at night without saying a prayer for your safety." He paused a moment, decided he would not let

Jackson's newly displayed ego get by without a little barb.

"Yet you have not sought fame or flattery. All you have asked for in return for your service is confidence from your men and a great battle to fight. A grateful nation salutes you."

"Excellent, Colonel," said Jackson. "Please call the men of the Black Horse and the Stonewall Brigade around." So the old man wants a public ceremony, thought Canon, leaving the tent. He signaled for a bugler to blow company call. The men came running.

"Attend the general," Canon shouted, and Jackson stepped out of the tent. Jackson walked up to Canon, turned and faced the gathered men.

"Rabe Canon," he called out, "you are a true hero. Neither a man nor woman, hardly a child in the South goes to bed at night without saying a prayer for your safety. Yet you have asked for little in return. All you have asked for is the confidence of your men and a great battle to fight.

"For bravery and leadership in the field at Manassas, you are hereby brevetted brigadier general and are forthwith commander of the Stonewall Brigade and the Black Horse Cavalry. A grateful nation salutes you.

"Congratulations, General Canon."

With a mischievous twinkle in his eye, and a step slightly more jaunty than usual, Stonewall Jackson pinned his own brigadier star on the collar of a startled Canon, then walked back to his tent, leaving a new general to the roaring shouts of his men. The celebration that night was considerable, but the South's youngest general officer had no time to dwell on it. Early next morning, Canon was given orders for the part his troops were to play in the invasion of the North.

An invasion into the North was a thing no knowledgeable officer looked forward to attempting. Better to be looked on as victims of invasion, and fight on home turf, than become the invader. Canon understood the need. He knew time was beginning to slip away for the South. Win though it did, there had never been another real chance to take Washington.

Canon heard that one crippled veteran of the Stonewall Brigade, at a fundraiser in Richmond, was asked to demonstrate the Rebel yell. The soldier replied that an authentic replication was impossible. A true Rebel yell, he said, could only be given when cold, hungry, barefoot, out of ammunition and charging up a hill in the face of enemy cannon fire.

Canon knew that Southern victories were becoming more and more pyrrhic. In more than a year of fighting, the South had not lost a battle in the Eastern Theater. But each bloody victory hurt it more than it hurt the North. In the Western Theater, in the Deep South states, Grant and Sherman were winning battles. Nashville had been under Union control since February. Raids into Mississippi were routine.

Jefferson Davis believed a serious threat to Washington might lead to an armistice and a negotiated truce. It was time to go north.

The sixth of September dawned chilly and clear as Canon led his three hundred horsemen up to the bank of a narrow ford on a shallow river. Most of the black horses were the same which Canon's unit had brought from Alabama, but nearly fifty of the men riding them were new, brought in to replace those wounded and slain at Manassas.

The Black Horse had lost forty-seven men at Manassas, the Stonewall Brigade more than twice that number.

Canon warned the new men before leaving camp that strict silence was to be maintained throughout the morning's reconnaissance and the first man who loosed a Rebel yell would be sent back to camp.

He nudged his knees into Old Scratch and the black stallion nimbly stepped from the low bank into the sluggish stream. Three hundred horsemen soon began to emerge on the far side, the Northern side, of the Potomac River into Maryland.

Two hours later, Canon sent back word that all was clear. By day's end, Lee and Jackson had crossed the river with fifty-five thousand men and set up camp a couple of miles from Sharpsburg. Panic soon spread through the Northern states.

In Washington, Abraham Lincoln reluctantly turned again to George McClellan to lead the Federal army. McClellan had fallen into disfavor after Second Manassas, but wrote his wife that he was proud to resume command. She sensed a different tone in his words. McClellan was always cautious. Now he had begun to sound fearful.

Following one aborted attempt to lay siege to Richmond much earlier in the war, where Lee had mangled his army, Little Mac had not displayed any willingness to attack the Southern Army. He preferred to defend, and for once Lincoln agreed.

Under no circumstance, Lincoln told McClellan, can you let Lee get between the army and Washington. McClellan couldn't have been happier. He could sit back, dig in, and defend the city, the Union and his honor without fear of the Southern counterattack that had greeted every Northern sally.

Robert E. Lee was happy, too. Little Mac was doing exactly what Lee and Jackson hoped, expected, gambled he would do. At the approach of McClellan's army, Lee fell back two miles to the other side of a deep, unfordable stream called Antietam Creek.

He believed McClellan would not attack but would stay there, across the Antietam, to keep an eye on the Southern Army. And while McClellan sat there, waiting, Lee would once again split his army and play havoc with Federal posts in Maryland.

The night before Lee withdrew across the Antietam, he sent general orders to Jackson and to A. P. Hill. Jackson would take fifteen thousand men and fall on the Federal arsenal at Harper's Ferry, twenty miles South, while Hill would march with ten thousand men to hold the gap at South Mountain, twenty miles North.

Jefferson Davis and his contingent were in camp for this historic invasion. Davis said little at the meetings, which was unusual. But, always willing to display his authority, he insisted on reading over the general orders for planned troop movement. Against the unspoken but evident displeasure of Lee, Davis took the document to his tent.

It was no more than two hours later that he sent it back to Lee, along with a note of approval. Davis also took a fleeting, forgotten pleasure in the fact that he chose to demean his fawning little assistant undersecretary of war by making him serve as messenger boy.

Hillary, who had kept to his tent to avoid any possibility of meeting Jackson, had committed the document to memory before he had taken fifty steps in the direction of Lee's tent. And the aide de camp, who accepted the document from Hillary, died quickly in the coming battle. It never dawned on him to remark to anyone that he had never seen such a huge smile of pleasure on the face of the assistant undersecretary of war.

Hillary had decided to get even with Stonewall Jackson. And the instrument for his revenge now lay within his grasp. One of Hillary's pet mischiefs was a facility for forgery. Having once seen someone's handwriting, Hillary could within hours offer a most perfect copy.

It afforded him a wonderful avenue of revenge, or even just entertainment. Occasionally, someone who had unknowingly incurred the little flower's displeasure would weeks later be confronted with a love letter, wielded by wife, husband or jealous lover, in his own hand. Denials were useless in front of the damning document.

It was fate, Hillary thought. Delicious, rewarding fate that he had been chosen as the president's courier. Hillary had seen Lee's handwriting many times and even practiced at copying it, just on the off chance it prove useful some day. In his tent, Hillary went to work. By midnight, Lee would have been hard pressed to choose his document or Hillary's copy as the real one.

Next morning, as the army departed for the crossing at Antietam and Davis left with his entourage for Richmond, Jackson found outside his tent a box of fine Havana cigars from an anonymous donor. Jackson rarely smoked, but he kept them to hand out to his men. If he had looked inside the box, he would have likely noticed that three of the fragrant tubes of tobacco were missing. He didn't look. He left them by the officers' mess. And soon, by twos and threes, the cigars were gone.

Two DAYS LATER, GEORGE MITCHELL was lazing on a grassy knoll beside his tent, warming in the soporific fall sun. He had just finished a fine lunch of beans and salt pork. Only a couple of days ago, he had gotten new boots, a new uniform and a new Sharps rifle. And his sergeant had only this morning congratulated him on how quickly he had learned to drill.

Mitchell had mentioned to a passing friend moments earlier that if he just had a good cigar he would consider himself content with army life. Incredibly, he realized he was gazing at a rolled paper no more than five yards from his nose from which extended the butt ends of three cigars.

Almost fearful of having so specific a wish come immediately true,

Mitchell crabbed on hands and knees to the paper. Sitting back down, he unrolled the paper and sure enough, three very fine looking cigars sat awaiting his pleasure.

Mitchell had placed one in his mouth, the others in his pocket, when he noticed writing on the paper. He read the document twice before it dawned on him exactly what he held in his now trembling hand. Taking the cigars from mouth and pocket, he rewrapped the package as near as he could to the way it was when found. Then he went running and shouting in search of his sergeant.

The sergeant looked at the document and went running for his lieutenant, who looked and went running for his colonel, who looked and went straight to the tent of General George McClellan.

For the Federal army now camped on the same soil from which the Confederate army had departed two days earlier. It was normal for an army to take over a prepared campsite left by another army. It was not normal for the departing army to be so kind as to leave a copy of its marching orders behind.

McClellan stared for a long moment at the fateful paper, then said to the men around him, "If I can't take the information on this paper and whip Bobby Lee, then I'll be ready to go back to Washington for good."

No one ever learned exactly what happened to the cigars. Neither Mitchell nor his sergeant nor his lieutenant nor his colonel got one. But it didn't matter. Four days later, they were dead, killed in the Battle of Antietam/Sharpsburg, which saw the bloodiest single day of the war.

"I'M BEGINNING TO HATE RIVERS," Canon muttered, surprising himself and the lieutenant who rode beside him as they neared the Antietam. The lieutenant looked at him but Canon could only shake his head in embarrassment. He had no idea what had originated the thought.

It was Thursday, September 15, 1862, and the Black Horse Cavalry was on the road early. Jackson and the Stonewall Brigade had departed the previous morning for Harper's Ferry and had by now, Canon was certain, reached their destination.

Lee kept Canon and the Black Horse behind for a day. A most disturbing report had come from an itinerant actor who plied his trade at various army camps, North and South, offering soliloquies from Shakespeare in return for contributions.

The man had professed strong Southern sympathies. He said he had been in McClellan's camp on Tuesday and had picked up rumors concerning a "lost order" which Union troops believed compromised the integrity of Lee's war plans. Some of Lee's advisors felt the story had the ring of truth, but Lee did not trust spies, feeling they were often bringers of incorrect information, whether by accident or design.

But the day before, on Wednesday, McClellan displayed uncharacteristic zeal. He attacked A. P. Hill at South Mountain and whipped him badly. Activity in McClellan's camp across the Antietam had the appearance of an army getting ready for a major assault.

Lee was concerned. If the spy's report was true, his army was in dire peril. Lee had thirty thousand men, McClellan eighty thousand. If Little Mac launched an all out assault, the Army of Northern Virginia would be fragmented and likely destroyed.

Lee sent word to Hill and Jackson: Hurry back.

Canon was on his way to Jackson. He and the Black Horse would defend the lower of four stone bridges which crossed the unfordable Antietam. They had stopped to water their horses at a small creek that emptied into the Antietam when Canon made the surprising remark concerning his dislike for rivers.

Canon rode Scratch up the creek to the spot where it emptied into the larger stream. There was a light frost on the variegated leaves and a soft mist rising from the water. He loosened his grip on the reins, allowing Scratch to dip his head to the water.

Canon was gazing, half dozing, into the swirling water as Scratch took great slurping gulps. Gradually, a realization solidified in Canon's mind that something in the stream was rising from the murky depths. Perhaps it is a huge carp, Canon thought, as he focussed on the shadowy object which continued to grow as it neared the surface.

Suddenly, Canon started back so violently that Scratch reared and almost unseated him. Horse and man crashed into horses and men around them.

Canon's attention was riveted to the awful thing which had floated up as if to claim him. It was not a carp, but a corpse which surfaced into view. First emerged a horribly bloated face, grinning in rictus and seeming to glare accusingly at Canon. Fish had been at it. One socket was eyeless, the other held a clouded orb which though sightless seemed to peer directly at him. Now the shoulders slowly rolled up into sight. And then, impossibly, the dead right arm slowly came out of the water and pointed a boney, bleached finger at Canon.

Corpses were surfacing all up and down the stream, hundreds of them, thousands of them. The very water was red with their seeping blood. A red mist swam before Canon's eyes. The entire landscape had turned red. Scratch continued to rear and plunge as Canon, gone numb, held tight to the reins.

The lieutenant saw Canon's features set, saw him stare at the stream. "Genral, what's wrong?!" called the lieutenant, leaping off his horse and tugging to slacken the reins Canon held tightly in his fist.

What's wrong? Canon thought. How can the man ask what's wrong? He loosened the reins; Scratch quieted, and Canon pointed in mute horror at the huge bloated face in the river.

"It's just a turkle, genral," said the lieutenant, quietly. "Just a big ole snapper turkle."

By God, Canon thought, rubbing his hands over his eyes, it is a turtle. The red mist disappeared. The corpses in the river became stumps and logs and clumps of debris. The pointing finger became a flipper which the turtle flicked, disappearing into the depths.

"It's all right. I'm all right," Canon said in answer to the looks of concern around him. "Just a moment of dizziness. I guess I ate too much supper last night."

The joke was poor humor, but it served to relieve the men. They knew Canon had eaten exactly what they had eaten, which was a piece of cold pone and some beans. The supplies from Manassas had not lasted long.

"Let's go see what the commissary at Harper's Ferry is serving for lunch," Canon said, and the men around him shouted their approval. A shaken Canon wheeled Scratch and set his cavalry at a trot. What could the apparition have meant? Canon wondered as he rode. It had been much too real and too sustained to dismiss without thought. Mountain Eagle said such things could be an omen, but could also be nothing more than the result of bad food, of which Canon had his share.

In retrospect, the thing now seemed not to have pointed directly at Canon, although its cloudy dead eye had gazed at his own gray ones. It had pointed at his boot or stirrup or saddle cinch. Later, when Canon called for a break to rest the horses, he checked all these things, though he had already checked them before setting out. He found nothing amiss. Wishing he had Mountain Eagle there to analyze it, Canon put the apparition to the back of his mind.

It was mid-afternoon as the Black Horse approached strategic Harper's Ferry. Canon's concern for Jackson grew with each passing mile. They were well within earshot, now, of battle. An ominous silence wrapped the mountainous terrain.

Already, Northern newspapers had made much of a statement by the arsenal's commander, Colonel Miles. Yes, he said, he was well aware that Lee and Jackson were in the vicinity, but the fortress at Harper's Ferry was impregnable. Surrounded by crags, its overlook commanding any approach by water, the fort bristled with artillery. "We will die here rather than surrender," Miles had said.

Canon signaled his men to kick their lathered horses into a gallop. A half-hour later, they rode into a quiet Rebel camp. Canon dismounted and hurried to Jackson's command tent. He was shown in immediately.

Jackson looked up from the portable desk at which he sat.

"Good afternoon, General," Jackson said, returning Canon's salute with equanimity. "If you have ridden all the way from Sharpsburg today, then you have come at speed. I am glad you are here. Perhaps you can help me with this eternal paperwork and allow me to finish a letter to Mary Anna. I will give her your regards."

Canon looked down at the documents on the table. One was indeed the beginning of a letter to Mary Anna. To his surprise, Canon saw the other was the draft of a telegram to Richmond.

It began: "God has again blessed our cause with victory . . ."

Puzzled, Canon said, "Excuse me, General, isn't this a little premature?"

"Yes, I expect so," replied Jackson. "I sent the request for surrender into the fort an hour ago, and they have asked for a couple of hours to consider it. I do not believe they will surrender until tomorrow morning. We may even be forced to fire on the fort before Colonel Miles will admit his mistake.

"It was difficult for me to believe he left the heights around the fort undefended, and now it is difficult for him to believe it, too. We hoist our artillery up the mountainsides rather easily and that should convince him. It has been in place about an hour and the 'impregnable fortress' commanded by the colonel is now totally indefensible.

"Now, what news of you may I send to Mary Anna?"

Canon gave news instead of the possibility of McClellan's impending attack at Sharpsburg and Lee's concern about the intercepted battle plan. Jackson received the news gravely. He had already heard of Hill's defeat at South Mountain.

"If they really do have our plans of battle, we are in trouble indeed," Jackson said. "That is why I do not like to rely on written orders. But there is no time for recrimination.

"Take your cavalry back to General Lee as soon as you can. Tell him that I do not think we should give up the arsenal, which is ready to fall, but that I will march back to Sharpsburg as soon as Colonel Miles has surrendered."

Two hours later, Canon and the Black Horse set out for Lee's camp on the Antietam. The Ferry had barely passed from view when Canon heard Jackson's artillery open fire on the Federal position. Its thunder grew fainter as the Black Horse pressed on, and finally they heard it no longer. Canon thought the cavalry had ridden out of hearing range. In reality, the Ferry and twelve thousand Union troops had surrendered to Jackson with hardly another shot fired.

Plenty of shots had been fired near Antietam. McClellan attacked soon after the Black Horse departed. Fighting had been sharp but desultory between Jeb Stuart's cavalry and Union horsemen.

When Canon returned to camp shortly after midnight, he found the Confederate army already up and preparing for Friday's battle. Thursday's probes by McClellan had ended in a short Federal advance along Sharpsburg road. Canon reported in, and was told to rest while he could. Friday would be a busy day.

McClellan missed another opportunity. The Union army, like a ponderous heavyweight boxer, threw slow, feeler punches which were parried by the quick Confederate troops. Late in the day, Union General Joe Hooker moved the Federal right wing across the stream and dug in. Just before nightfall, and cessation of hostilities for the day, Hooker drove the Confederate left, under General John B. Hood and his Texans, back several miles toward Sharpsburg.

Only the dramatic last-second arrival of A. P. Hill and a feeble but adequate counterattack by his exhausted men had saved the Confederate left wing from total collapse.

The wounded Hood, en route to a field hospital, was carried past Lee on a stretcher.

"General," said Lee sympathetically, "who did you leave in charge of your Texans?"

"No one."

"No one?" said Lee. "Where are your men?"

"Dead on the field of battle."

"What? All?"

"All," said Hood.

"Those poor, valiant men," said Lee. "Rest now, Hood. Everything will be all right."

With the arrival of Hill, and with Jackson on the way, Lee knew that now he had a fighting chance. By the morning of Saturday, September 17, both armies were in position. The slaughter began.

## 8

# Bad Day for the Black Horse

French Captain Claude Etienne Minie was forty-eight years old when the Battle of Antietam was fought. Minie was not there, but he sent a namesake representative. Many of them. Perhaps a million.

Captain Minie invented the destructive instrument of preference used during the Civil War. It bore his name. The Minie ball, it was called. But it was not a ball, it was a bullet, a conical lead projectile with a hollow base which expanded when fired to fill the grooves inside a gun barrel.

Those grooves were called rifflein in Old Germanic, rifler in Old French. Rifles. The original purpose of those grooves was to allow the residue from gunpowder to sink into them so it would not build up inside the barrel— the bore—finally fouling it.

That was because the black powder of the day smoked awfully. Each discharge from a gun was followed by a thick issue of greasy black smoke, like an inky spray from a small steel octopus. That gunsmoke was so thick it soon obscured vision on the battlefield and covered fighting men with a soot-like coating.

It coated the inside of the gun barrel. After five or six shots were fired, the bore of a smooth barrel musket became so packed with residue it had to be swabbed out before it could be fired again. It delayed the soldier's ability to kill. Rifling lessened the delay, and Captain Minie's ball went far toward eliminating it.

Together, the rifling and the bullet produced an unforeseen effect that perfected man's ability to kill from a distance. The conical bullet cut the air much more cleanly than a ball, which often veered once it left the barrel, especially if fired from a non-rifled gun.

The Minie ball sometimes tumbled, limiting accuracy. Rifling put a stop to that. It put a spin on the conical bullet, greatly increasing its range and accuracy. A round ball fired from a smoothbore musket might be fairly accurate at one hundred yards, if the bore were clean. A Minie ball fired from a rifle was deadly accurate at eight hundred yards and could kill at three-quarters of a mile.

Moreover, accuracy of guns having become pretty much established by rifling and the conical bullet, attention could be turned to size and range. Smoothbore cannons which could lob a ball a few hundred yards were being replaced by rifled artillery which accurately threw an explosive shell for miles.

The Civil War brought man's genius for destroying himself into rarified heights. Machine guns, aerial balloons, submarines, land mines, hand grenades, and repeating rifles were in use or development when Antietam raged.

Problem was, while weapons in the Civil War had increased in destructive capacity, battle tactics and strategy were basically the same as in the American Revolution. In those days, when round musket balls were as likely to veer as to go toward the target, it was best for soldiers to attack in close formation. Since it took so much time to reload, and to clean a fouled weapon, it was best to charge straight at the enemy without pause. Since speed was essential against the time it took for an enemy to load and fire, a cavalry charge against infantry was the most awesome tactic of the day.

Rifling and Messr. Minie turned such charges into attempted suicide on a mass scale.

Antietam became the example of what happens when modern weapons are used against archaic tactics. The slaughter started early that day.

In the Union camp, two hours before sunrise, some of the North's most colorful soldiers sat around the table in George McClellan's command tent. It was a meeting of nicknames.

Little Mac, handlebar mustache freshly waxed, stood at the head of the table. He assumed the pose, one hand thrust inside the breast of his uniform coat and other behind his back, consistent with the nickname given him by the Northern press—The Young Napoleon.

To his right sat corpulent General Ambrose Burnside. The balding Burnside's bushy sidewhiskers were beginning to be copied by soldiers in his command and would soon come into fashion, but the name would be corrupted. Sideburns, they would come to be called.

To the left of Little Mac sat General "Fighting Joe" Hooker. Hooker was touchy about his nickname, at least with those who knew its origin. His picture had appeared in a newspaper earlier in the war, showing him sending his troops off to battle. The caption underneath was to read "Fighting, Joe Hooker." But a careless typesetter omitted the comma, giving Hooker a nickname that was sometimes used in derision, though Hooker was a brave soldier.

Hooker's other contribution to Americanese was also a corruption, and one of which he was not proud. Hooker's fondness for ladies of the evening was well known. A bevy of prostitutes followed his army from camp to camp. These camp followers came to be known as "Hooker's Women" and, finally, simply as hookers.

The other officer in the tent was General George Armstrong Custer, youngest of all Union generals and a staunch McClellan supporter. The red-haired Custer, though a bold, even impetuous fighter, was somewhat dandified. His nickname was "Cinnamon," due to his frequent applications of that spice to his drooping mustache and long, curly beard.

Debate among the Union command ran hot and cold for an hour. McClellan was a general who listened to the advice of his staff officers, though most made sure to give advice that would reinforce his own well-known sentiments.

This morning, opinions differed and McClellan was slowly giving ground to Hooker's argument.

Little Mac was determined to hold twenty thousand of his ninety thousand men in reserve, along with five batteries of artillery. He had no intention of risking a defeat like Pope received at Second Manassas. He would not allow himself to be taken in flank by one of the deadly Southern counterattacks.

Hooker was still flushed with success from the way his men crushed the Confederates the previous afternoon. The Rebels were reeling when they left the field, and Hooker wanted an all-out assault that would end Lee's army.

He was adamant. He would rather his arm wither than see the Union not take advantage of the intercepted battle plan. The Rebel Jackson, said

Hooker, was still at Harper's Ferry. The Rebel Hill and his forces had been mangled at South Mountain on Wednesday. Hooker was certain Hill was licking his wounds and recuperating his men.

McClellan thought Hooker's arguments impressive and was about to give the order for a total assault when a low keening noise reached his ears.

It began to grow in volume.

RABE CANON AWOKE INSTANTLY, fully alert, at the touch on his arm. It was cold inside his tent, and dark, but he recognized the orderly from Jackson's staff in the glow from the lantern the man carried.

Canon figured he was being called to Lee's pre-dawn staff meeting. He knew such a meeting would be underway across the river in the Union command tent. Sometimes Lee held such meetings, sometimes Canon was called to them. Jackson did not like staff meetings and held them rarely.

"Compliments from General Jackson, General," the orderly said. "It appears the Yankees are going to attack this morning early. General Jackson wants to see you."

"What?" said Canon, sitting up. "Jackson here already?"

"Jackson is, sir, but only with an escort. The Stonewall Army is expected to arrive from Harper's Ferry this morning about nine o'clock. It's going on five o'clock now.

"The general says you and the Black Horse will be held in reserve until the rest of the army arrives. He asks that you join him at your convenience."

"My compliments to the general," said Canon. "Tell him I will be there in ten minutes."

The orderly withdrew, throwing a salute. Having slept in his uniform, Canon needed only his boots. He grabbed them, shook them out before drawing them on. He had acquired the habit of checking his boots from Buck while they were on hunting trips. In the wild, creatures like spiders and snakes, some of them venomous, crawled into boots and gave the unsuspecting wearer a nasty surprise. Best to be safe.

Outside, Canon stepped behind the tent to relieve himself, taking in deep draughts of fresh air. The stars were still out, though beginning to dim. The Milky Way's great blanket of stars twinkled the heavens, just as it did over peaceful Mulberry, Canon thought.

Bladder emptied, he walked on toward Jackson's tent, thinking now of home and his two mentors. Mountain Eagle had taught him the Indian trick of early rising. Just drink a lot of water before going to bed, the Eagle said. Works every time.

The army was awakening. Throughout the camp rang sounds of men preparing for battle. It was much the same noise every morning, battle or no. Frying pans clanged, tin cups rattled. Sleepy voices called out jokes and imprecations. Grease sizzled around frying fatback, the smell of boiling coffee wafted on the light wind.

Canon also detected the burnt bitter smell of acorn coffee. It was a sure sign of a hungry army when men were reduced to grinding up dried acorns for coffee substitute.

But underneath the sounds of muttered conversation and muted morning mess, somehow amplifying all other sound rather than drowning it, as sometimes the crickets' chirp seems to amplify other sounds, was the background noise which both thrilled and repelled Canon.

Surrounding him, permeating the atmosphere, providing the true ambience of an army preparing for battle came the steady rasping rhythm of steel on stone. Jackson had a predilection for the use of cold steel. At every campfire, underscoring all conversation and sounds of cooking and morning ablutions, bayonets were being sharpened.

Although the men seemed cheerful, perhaps unusually so, everyone knew that today's work would be close and wet. The grinding sound was lethal and grim as the jokes which passed through it, men laughing at horrible death in order to screw their courage to the sticking place.

Nothing, said Jackson, put fear into a wavering enemy like a bayonet charge. And Jackson possessed an uncanny knack for the precisely correct moment to order a bayonet sweep of the field. Canon had seen many a pocket of enemy resistance melt before a bayonet charge.

Although Canon's insides tightened at the thin grating sound, he responded cheerfully to the good natured kidding of men who recognized him as he passed among them on the way to Jackson. As usual, the kidding was about his size.

"Hide the fatback, boys, or else heat up another pan, for here comes either a bear or General Canon." Canon smiled and waved, his movements lit by the glow of myriad campfires.

"Hey, General, come on down out of that big coat. We know you're in there and it ain't no use to try to hide." Canon joined the banter, pausing here and there to say a word of encouragement or sass. Such men, he thought. Such men.

As Canon neared Jackson's tent, members of the Stonewall escort noticed him. The dark had begun to scatter. Dim outlines of trees and tents were visible in the distance.

Suddenly, one of the Stonewall men throated out a Rebel yell: "Yip, yip, yip, yaaahooooo." The cry was taken up in the next campsite, then the next and the next. In seconds, the fierce scream swept through the entire Rebel army and the terrible, beautiful Southern battle cry became a howling ululation, as if tens of thousands of banshees haunted the night.

Canon arrived at the command tent just as Jackson stepped out, face flushed, eyes flashing. He looked at Canon. "That is the most beautiful music I have ever heard," said Jackson. On seeing their leader, men in the escort redoubled their efforts, and the sound screamed through the wakening dawn.

A mile away, George McClellan stopped speaking as the eerie wail reached him. Louder it grew, and louder still, until it seemed that some mad djinn had sprung from a magic lamp and awaited them, howling, outside.

But McClellan recognized it for what it was, and it shook him.

"No," said McClellan, through the keening cry, "we will not risk a total assault. I will hold out reserves. We attack at sunrise." He dismissed the meeting.

THE LITTLE SORREL HORSE, Fancy, and the black Arabian, Scratch, stood side by side on a hill overlooking the Antietam. On their backs sat an animated Jackson and an impatient Canon.

It was almost three P.M.

The battle, which renewed at sunrise with Hooker's attack on the Confederate left, raged all day. Through field glasses, Canon watched in near disbelief the most savage fighting of the war.

A slight but steady wind blew most of the day, dispersing the thick battlesmoke and allowing the mile-long front to be observed from the hill. Jackson had been moving troops like chess pieces while the Yankee infantry advanced.

General Burnside had been ordered by McClellan to take the lower and most important of the four bridges across Antietam Creek, cross it and attack. But Burnside learned it was A. P. Hill and part of the Stonewall Army holding the bridge. Hill's troops were famously veteran and deadly, some of the South's finest.

He had made tentative thrusts at the bridge and was thrown back with loss each time. Once, Jackson had allowed Union troops over the bridge and then had hidden troops pour in such a deadly fire that scarcely any of the Federals made it back to their lines.

Canon had seen through his glass two regiments, one in blue and one in gray, wheel in from opposite sides of the field until they were on one another so quickly that neither had time to do anything but fire.

The troops could have been no more than thirty yards apart when they opened fire. Men fell like stalks of wheat before a scythe. Each regiment lost half its men before both sides simultaneously began to fall back.

On top of the hill, near the main field hospital, the wounded streamed by Canon in ever growing numbers. He had never seen its like. Yet more and more men were being pushed into the fray. More and more men. But not the Stonewall Army from Harper's Ferry. They were five hours late.

"Where are they?" Jackson muttered to himself again, the third time in the past two hours. Canon had never heard him speak so to himself.

It was likely that McClellan had kept reserves. Although Jackson had bluffed Burnside back from the bridge, Jackson knew reinforcements anywhere along the Federal line would make it necessary for Lee to reinforce the opposite Confederate line.

If that happened, some of the reinforcements would come from Hill. There would not be enough left to continue to hold Burnside back from the bridge.

Hell, thought Canon, there's already not enough to hold off Burnside if he makes a full-scale attack. Through his glass, Canon could see movement in the Burnside troops. And it won't be long in coming, he told himself.

Behind him, the Black Horse cavalrymen stood beside their horses, waiting. Canon knew they were as impatient as he to join the battle, terrible as it was. They had seen too many of their friends carried past them on stretchers.

And that's where it is, Canon thought. Finally, after the flags are waved and speeches made, men fight hardest when they fight for fallen friends.

Canon lowered his field glasses to check, for the hundredth time that day, the Black Horse line. He was looking it over when Jackson said, "General, mount your men. It appears that General Burnside has finally decided to become serious about that bridge."

Canon swung the glasses up. Sure enough, a quarter-mile away, Burnside's division was bunching, getting ready to rush the bridge.

"If he makes it across, and he probably will, it is up to you to check him and break the charge," Jackson said. "Then you will push him back across the bridge."

This ought to be pleasant, Canon thought. Three hundred on horseback against two thousand riflemen, but he only said, "Yes, sir." He motioned for the Black Horse to come up, and was in the process of riding back to them, when he heard Jackson shout.

He had never heard Jackson truly shout before. Jackson never had to shout to get something done. Those cold blue eyes and the soft voice were somehow far more menacing than any screaming fit he had heard from any other general.

But amid the shots and shouts of roaring war, he heard a raw sound that froze him to the marrow. Canon had once, in a stream-driven sawmill, been present when the huge circular saw hit a large spike inside a tree. The spike must have been driven in years before and the tree grew around it, totally absorbing it. No way to know it was there.

The sound had been at once hoarse and shrill as steel bit into steel. It lasted but a moment. The saw cut through the spike and was ruined in doing so. The sound had wrenched Canon's insides like a fist closing on them. Men had doubled over, their hands to their ears.

The scream had not the intensity of that sound, but Canon was reminded of it, and he knew as he turned that the scream had come from Stonewall Jackson himself.

Jackson was pointing. Burnside's men had crossed the bridge and were beating back Hill's division. At first, Canon thought it was the reason for the scream. Then he saw the real reason, running raggedly onto the battlefield.

The rest of the Stonewall Army had arrived. Lead units were already raking the Union troops with countering fire, but more blue troops were crossing the bridge as the rest of the exhausted Stonewall men came up. Canon knew it would take at least a half-hour for the brunt of the fighting to commence and for Burnside's Federals to realize they were under a major counterattack.

Yes, the timing would be perfect. Canon looked back toward the Black Horse. All was in readiness. The horses, veterans of battle, were twitching and prancing, ready to carry on into the thick of it.

Canon raised his arm, dropped it. They charged.

Downhill they raced, through rows of Southern artillery, past powder-blackened faces which looked up at the thunder of hooves pounding the earth.

Dimly, Canon heard exultant cries, swept away by the very wind created by his own swift passage. "The Black Horse! The Black Horse!" came the cries.

On they rode, through the sunny September afternoon, past clusters of wounded men, past decimated platoons and companies brought back from the fight, past men milling around as they waited for orders. They rode through sounds of men at war, through curses and shouts, through groans and sobs. But as they swept past, always the cry went up in their wake: "The Black Horse! The Black Horse!"

The cries filled Canon with pride, but with it came an ineffable sadness, creeping quietly out of one small room in his mind. Deep sorrow welled up within him, along with a sense of pity for those who would die this day. He fought the feelings down. Pity has no place in war, sorrow no place in battle.

They rode onto the plain, now, at speed, wind tearing at hat and clothing. Artillery shells blossomed white, red and black around them. Canon bent low over Scratch, could feel the horse's great muscles flex. Scratch was straining at every nerve. They were forced to slow as they reached the uneven ground near the creek, and Canon absently noticed they were approaching the exact spot where they had watered the horses only two days ago as they rode off to Harper's Ferry.

They were slowed to a walk here, for a few hundred yards, as the horses picked their way across the rough terrain. Without wanting to, but unable to stop himself, Canon looked over at the spot where he had stopped before.

Jesus! thought Canon. The little stream of Antietam Creek had streaks of red in it. Corpses hung from the bank into the water. Bodies bobbed at the surface. Hundreds and hundreds of bodies. And this time Canon knew it was no apparition. Antietam Creek was actually running red with blood.

And even as he watched, face drawn with horror, Canon knew what was about to happen. Skin on his neck and arms prickled as the body broke the surface of the water. It was a Yankee, one who had probably died the day before and sank into the water. Bloating body gases had brought his remains to the top. And the dead arm, which had lain on the corpse's chest, flopped weakly over as it broke the top of the water.

And pointed at him, just the way it had before. Pointed at his boot, or knee, or stirrup. Canon wasn't sure. He had checked all his gear prior to the battle, as he always did. Whatever the meaning, and it had to have meaning, Canon was now sure, was something he would find out.

If it is death, thought Canon, well, everyone has to die sometime: It is a good day to die.

Canon stood in the stirrups and slid his saber smoothly from its scabbard. The Black Horse Cavalry was only a few hundred yards downstream from the bridge and about to ride into the open. Once into the sunlight, Canon stopped and whirled the saber around his head four, five, six times, making sure the polished steel caught flashes of fire from the sun. If you want me, Canon thought, his challenge going both to the Yankees and to death, then here I come, you bastards.

The charge of Burnside's men had carried through Hill's division and was forcing the Confederate right back toward Sharpsburg. Having broken through Hill, the Federal troop commanders felt they could push on for a while, then turn and fall on the Confederate center.

Just as they neared the strategic position they sought, however, the brunt of the Stonewall Army with wild Rebel yells came boiling out of the woods into their flanks. At the same time, Canon and the Black Horse tore into their unprotected rear. The Federals didn't know where to turn.

The Black Horse had plowed into them like a ship's prow breaks ocean waves. Clumps of men gathered, backs to each other, to fend off the assaults. Valiantly though they fought, no men could stand up to this punishment.

At last, the Black Horse and the lead Stonewall unit converged in the middle of the milling mass of men. The Federals cut off from retreat surrendered, while the remainder pulled back toward Antietam creel and its bridge.

Canon, with the reins in his teeth, flailed with the saber in his right hand, fired the pistol in his left. So packed were the now panicked Union soldiers that it was difficult for them to get off a clear shot, even at so huge a target.

Canon was so busy making sure the cut-off companies of Yankees didn't break through and escape, it was long minutes before he realized the roar behind him had lessened. When he looked around, he saw the remaining Union troops retreating to the bridge, leaving a determined rear guard to delay pursuit.

A thousand yards on the far side of the bridge, Union artillery was being rushed up to defend the captured ground. Hurriedly, Canon began to gather the cavalry. The artillery had to be dispersed or the Stonewall troops would be slaughtered.

The artillery crews could see, too. They recognized the dread black horses, and they knew why they were bunching. It became a race to see who would get ready first. It seemed to Canon it was taking forever to mass the horsemen, while he had never seen an artillery battery work so fast. Already they were unlimbering the guns from the caissons.

Finally, though only a third of the cavalry had massed, Canon knew he had to charge. With a shout, Canon spoke spurs to Scratch and the black horses flew toward the bridge. The Federal rear guard had been much too busy exchanging fire with the Stonewall brigade to notice the Black Horse bunching.

Coming out of a different quadrant, Canon was on them before they had time to draw beads, but Canon wasn't concerned with the rear guard. The Black Horse rode over and through the blue coats, scarcely a shot fired by either side, and onto the bridge. Too late.

Canon saw black smoke belch from one of the rifled Parrott guns and then, beside it, a smoothbore cannon shot smoke, flame and ball. The Black Horse was galloping headlong into a meat grinder, and there was no way out. A retreat would take them right back into the Union rear guard. There was nothing but clear field to the right and left. Ahead of them were five Parrott guns and cannon, with assorted riflemen around them. The dark guitar began to play as bullets whipsonged past him.

The joy of battle arose in Canon, rippled through him like chain lightning, but with it came the feeling of sorrow which earlier engulfed him. He felt an unexplainable sense of loss, though he felt no fear.

For no reason he could account for, Canon gave a slight check on the reins and sawed Scratch to the right. It slowed them momentarily, just long enough for the rider behind him to gallop into the place where Canon had been heading. The horse and rider simply vanished into a roaring cloud of smoke and flame. An artillery shell had hit them. They were atomized.

Canon took a quick look around and behind him. The battery had fired its first salvo, but most of the horsemen were still up and charging, though with seven hundred yards to go.

For a moment, Canon believed they would make it. The wall of fire which had marked the Union line became less a blur. He could pick out individual men behind the muzzle blasts, then faces. Jigging this way and that, Canon rode on toward the battery.

But there were just too many of them. Canon heard a sickening wet slap and felt Scratch falter a step, then regain pace. The horse had been hit. Upon Scratch's neck a red flower appeared, blood welled in it, then flowed from it. Sorry, old boy, thought Canon. He stuck his finger in the hole to staunch the blood.

They were three hundred yards away, but Scratch was weakening with every step. The rest of the Black Horse was pulling even with him. Canon felt an awful, deep thrumming thrill deep inside, and time suddenly slowed. It was as if everything slipped slowly into half speed. Canon's senses seemed to sharpen past the point of possibility.

Three of the half-dozen field pieces honed in on him and Scratch. Their muzzles flashed. Three shells were on their way. One, even two of them, could have been evaded if Scratch weren't wounded. But Scratch was wounded, and there were three shells coming.

"Sorry, boy," Canon said, then a giant fist closed around him, shook him the way a small boy shakes a bug in a jar. The world cartwheeled back into normal time, and he heard Scratch's scream of rage and pain. Everything merged into a blur of green and black and red, and terrible blows buffeted him. His breath bleated from him, as he hit the ground and for a moment all was silent.

Dazed, sick to his stomach, confused, Canon managed a sitting position. He was covered with blood. A dozen yards away, Scratch lay still, his muzzle pointed toward Canon. The big horse was too still. Then Canon saw the horrible rip in his stomach, saw the entrails spilled on the ground.

Sitting up became too big a chore for Canon. The earth began to spin softly, like a slow carousel. He slipped back to the earth, felt his face press against the browning grass. He had never felt so peculiar, he thought. It was as if he were weightless, his head felt so light. But when he tried to pull himself toward Scratch, his arms were so weak and his body so heavy that he could not do it.

Then he saw Old Scratch try to lift his head, fail. Canon pulled himself along the ground, clutching handsful of grass, then others as the first ones tore away. But Scratch had seen him and nickered softly to him. The realization formed dully in Canon's brain that he could not make it to the horse, but that he must give Scratch the only help he could.

He reached back and drew one of the pistols. He thumbed back the hammer and steadied the barrel, training the sights on Old Scratch's head.

Consciousness began to leave him, but he could not go and leave Old Scratch in pain. He closed his eyes, then after a moment opened them. "Sorry, old boy, so sorry," he said yet again. Because Canon knew he had not the courage to pull the trigger. Light faded to dim, then dim to dark.

SAFE AND WARM, CANON THOUGHT. So safe and warm. This is what the babe must feel as it rests inside its mother's womb. He was so comfortable, so content. He wanted to feel like this always. But there was damp pressure on his head, then it was gone, then back again. It was taking the contentment away.

Angrily, Canon sought to move his head away from the intruding dampness. A thousand bolts of pain forked through his brain, and he wanted to scream. But he knew if he did, the thousand bolts would turn into a million. With the thought, he realized the truth. If he could think, he must be alive. With that thought, Canon opened his eyes.

Through a haze of pain, Canon saw the rock-hewn features of Stonewall Jackson. It was late afternoon, for Canon saw the setting sun through the open flap of what he knew must be a hospital tent. Jackson was standing over him, a small smile on his face. A young nurse stood next to him, occasionally pressing a cool wet cloth to Canon's temples.

"Rabe, it is good to see you see me," Jackson said. Canon's mind was scrambled as breakfast eggs. He knew only that something terrible had happened. Something in the battle. The battle. The battle! He tried to form the words, though he scarcely recognized the croaking sound as his own voice.

"Is the battle over, General?" he said. "How is Scratch?"

"Both sides left the field last evening," Jackson said. "All is well."

"Scratch?"

Jackson shook his head. It was barely a movement, but it carried an awful finality. Canon could not believe the good horse was dead. But Jackson was speaking again. "General Lee sends his compliments and best wishes, General," he said to Canon. "You have a severe concussion, but no permanent damage was done. You'll be back with the Black Horse before you know it."

"We failed."

"To the contrary. Your charge so unnerved the Federal gun battery, and your wounding so enraged the men, that the Union rear guard was overwhelmed and the guns forced back.

"This morning, we occupy the same ground we occupied yesterday."

Something in Jackson's tone made Canon apprehensive.

"What of our losses? Did we take much loss?"

Jackson said nothing for a moment, then he said, "Losses are the nature of war. There is plenty of time to speak of it later. Rest now, General. That is what is called for. I will send you some fruit."

With that, Jackson withdrew. The young woman gently applied the compress to Canon's head. It finally occurred to Canon that female nurses were so rare at the front that he had never before seen one. She was not pretty, and on the thin side, but her courage and gentle manner made her as lovely a woman as he had seen. Then Canon saw that tears were coursing down her cheeks.

"What's wrong, lovey?" he asked, wanting rather to ask what the hell a nice lady was doing in a hell-hole like this battlefront.

"We are not at the front, General. Or at least the front has moved with us. You were unconscious through the night and day while you were in the wagon."

"Where are we?"

"Virginia. General Lee brought most of the army back across the Potomac and the rest is soon to follow. The invasion failed."

Lee had indeed withdrawn the shattered Southern army. Although the battle was viewed as a draw, each draw was to the Confederacy the equivalent of defeat. Lee had hoped the people of Maryland would rise up on behalf of the cause, but it did not occur.

And though the Federal army lost ten thousand men at Antietam, General Lee had lost twenty-five thousand in just the last month. Almost half his army. It was a blow from which the South could never recover.

That night, Canon lay alone in the hospital tent, mulling over a horrible fact. Jackson had ordered the tent set up especially for the Black Horse, but so terrible was the fighting no others in the Black Horse needed it. Either their wounds were minor, or they were dead.

He had lost almost thirty percent of the Black Horse, but casualties in some companies had run sixty percent and higher.

Canon closed his eyes, and pictures clear as oil paintings presented themselves to his mind's eye. They moved like a story book, where picture pages flip faster and faster, until the pictures on them move as if in real life. He saw the apparition in the river again, pointing at him.

Well, not so much to me, he thought, as Scratch. Scratch! The thing had pointed at Scratch. Not Canon's knee, not boot, not stirrup, not cinch. The thing had pointed directly at the spot on Scratch's stomach where the shell had burst into him.

Hard on that realization came another remembrance, arcane as the first. Canon had known where the shells were going to land. It was perfect now in his memory. He had tried to maneuver around the area where the rounds would land, but Scratch was wounded and, anyway, there were too many rounds.

But he had known. There was no doubt about it. No, no doubts at all. But there were questions about it. Many questions. Spooked, Canon tried for sleep, tried to put off the questions until the following day. He might as well have tried to fly. He did not sleep. Not for hours.

The army surgeon had told Canon not to sleep, if he could keep from it. The surgeon had seen too many men with head wounds slip from sleep into coma, and never wake again. The doctor need not have worried, with this new thing buzzing in Canon's brain. Canon, on the other hand, would have given practically anything to slide into soft slumber.

But he lay there, hour upon hour, with only occasional visits from the nurse or an orderly to interrupt his cloudy thinking. He was in too much pain to move, too deeply in thought to sleep.

He reflected on incidents in his life when he knew what was going to happen. They had been rare but real. Sometimes hunting, sometimes gambling, sometimes doing little or nothing, Canon had known what was about to happen. It was rare, but it was there, and true. Everyone had premonitions, or practically everyone. Nearly everyone, at some time or other, felt they knew what was going to happen.

The difference, Canon realized, is that others had feelings. But, sometimes, Canon simply knew.

# 9
# *A Mutually Beneficial Arrangement*

Clumps of dirt and turf were spewed in the air by the newly shod bay horse as it raced past cheering men. George B. McClellan was one of the finest horsemen in the Federal army and his soldiers took joy and pride in it.

Little Mac knew only two speeds on horseback: full out and dead stop. When Little Mac was joyous, someone in his staff had noticed, he rode upright in the saddle, projecting his Napoleonic image to the troops. But when he was unhappy or angry, he rode low over the mane, as if he wanted no one to recognize him.

Today, on his return from Washington, the Young Napoleon was lying so low over the mane that he appeared almost as part of the horse's neck.

What did Lincoln expect of him? McClellan wondered about it for the eighth or eightieth time that day. He dined at the White House—people had taken to calling it that since Mrs. Lincoln had insisted on new paint— last evening and had expected to be afforded the recognition and gratitude he earned two weeks ago at the Battle of Antietam.

What had he gotten? Threats, by God. Veiled and honeyed, draped with words of concern, but threats no less. The Ape, as McClellan called Lincoln in private, had deceived him again. Before the battle was fought, all The Ape wanted was what McClellan promised. The Federal army would remain between Washington and the Southern Army so there was no threat to the capital.

But I did better than that, McClellan fumed to himself. I attacked and drove Lee back into Virginia. But was The Ape happy? Hell, no. The Ape said the powers that be were unhappy because McClellan had not pursued and destroyed Lee. But, dammit, he had pursued. Little Mac wished The

Ape and the naysayers around him had been in the lead units of pursuit, three days after the battle, when the Goddamned demon Jackson had fallen on them out of nowhere and cut them to pieces.

McClellan slewed his lathered horse to a stop in front of his command tent and strode inside, barely stopping to acknowledge with a wave of his hat the cheers from the soldiers camping around his headquarters. Thinking better of it, he stepped back outside and waved his hat around his head, letting the applause wash over him. Best to keep his men happy, he thought, walking back inside.

Once the flap closed behind him, however, McClellan slammed the hat down on his portable desk and racked down in his chair.

"He has threatened to take away my command," he said to the gathered officers of his staff, who had awaited his arrival for the past hour. The ride from Washington had taken all morning but, though he had forsaken breakfast with his beautiful wife, he waved away the plate of lunch offered him by an orderly.

"He says if I don't attack Lee again within the month, he thinks he can no longer hold off our enemies in Washington"—McClellan placed ironic emphasis on "our"—"who want to see me replaced.

"He reminded me that I am a Democrat serving a Republican administration, in order to try to convince me that he is putting himself on the line for me. But he doesn't understand what I am up against. He is not only an ape, but a fool. I can whip Lee, and I can whip Jackson, but it is a dangerous business to try to take them on when they are together.

"Oh, it can be done. I can do it. But it will take months and the process of siege and attrition to do it. They simply do not make mistakes."

Little Mac had managed to quietly put behind him the fact that the southerners' lost order had been a catastrophic mistake, and that he had failed to take full advantage of it.

But his staff, emboldened by McClellan's pet euphemism for Lincoln, looked to one another to see if anyone had the courage to broach a most delicate subject.

Custer did.

"They are fools indeed in Washington if they try to take command of the army away from you again," he said. After a pause, which he held until he was sure McClellan was not going to reply, Custer said, "They may learn that the army will not let you be taken from it."

It was a thick moment. All in the room knew it. Some of the most powerful men in Washington, including cabinet members and big businessmen, had let it be known in that they favored a negotiated peace if McClellan would negotiate it.

But Lincoln had already cashiered General John Fremont for making such an unauthorized attempt. The only way such a thing could be accomplished would be if McClellan were in a position to insist on it.

That could only be done if Little Mac were to declare the army to be under his complete command. It amounted to establishing a military dictatorship. In a word, it amounted to treason.

Each man in the room had at some time hinted in favor of such a move to Little Mac, who had always equivocated. He would not say yes, but he had never said no.

Now, for the first time, the question had been placed out in the open. A thrill ran through each man in the tent as McClellan clearly deliberated the matter.

"Yes," said McClellan in a low voice, "there is that possibility."

"There is, perhaps, another," came an even lower voice from the circle of half-dozen men who were on the verge of becoming conspirators.

Part of the circle widened as men automatically stepped away from the speaker. The squat man, bulldog features clearly visible through a short beard and mustache, was Major Allan Pinkerton, head of the Federal Secret Service.

Pinkerton with McClellan's patronage created the Secret Service. The dark little detective was in charge of spying and counterspying for the Union. Known in some circles as "McClellan's ferret," he scurried to and fro for Little Mac, digging up bits of information here, planting other bits there. Swarthy, brown haired, big nosed, Pinkerton was rarely seen without the stump of a cigar clenched tightly between white teeth, as if he feared someone might suddenly try to jerk it away.

Nor was he seen in anything but one of four three-piece suits he owned.

They were usually rumpled. His white shirt, collarless and tieless, was buttoned up to the neck.

Always he spoke in a quick whisper, usually with one hand placed over or in the vicinity of his mouth. Difficult as it already was to hear his undertone, the cigar and the covering hand further hampered it until the conversation from Pinkerton's listener usually consisted of nothing more than What? or Excuse me?

Pinkerton insisted that everyone, even in private, address him by his code name: Mr. Allan. His movements, which he considered stealthy, were thought furtive. He could be effective, however. Although he had no military training, he had finagled the rank of major.

McClellan trusted him, and Pinkerton, for all his paranoia and sometimes artless connivance among administration members, appeared totally loyal. Whether bulldog or ferret, Pinkerton served McClellan.

It was he who convinced McClellan, and most everyone else, that Lee had come to Maryland with perhaps as many as two hundred thousand men. Most now believed the figure was grossly inflated, but McClellan and Pinkerton stuck to it.

If defeated, best to be defeated by superior numbers and, if victorious, so much the better.

Regardless of how the other members of McClellan's staff felt about "Mr. Allan," they listened to him because Little Mac listened to him.

"What did you say, Major?" McClellan enquired.

Pinkerton took the cigar from his teeth, but left the right hand, which clutched the cigar between middle finger and forefinger, resting against his upper lip.

"You have heard, no doubt, that Lincoln is considering some sort of emancipation document which would free all slaves?" Pinkerton said.

This was no news to McClellan. Lincoln had said to several cabinet members that he would free the slaves if he thought it would save the Union, or that he would continue slavery if he thought it would save the Union. But what Lincoln really wanted was to free the slaves, then ship them all to Panama, removing their threat to the employed American work force.

Pampering the detective's ego, McClellan merely said, "Please tell me about it. I think it would be a mistake for him to do it."

"Yes, yes it would," Pinkerton said, moved almost to an audible voice by the thought that he was imparting new, secret and vital information. "If the slaves are declared free, the South will have no cause for negotiation. The war will be set as the only course, and the Rebels will be able to use the threat of a million Negroes turned loose on their women and their economy."

"It would be a powerful political tool for them," said McClellan. "What do you propose?"

"Secret negotiations. Fremont had the right idea, but he went about it wrongly. I believe I have the wherewithal," Pinkerton took two dramatic puffs from the stumpy cigar, "to meet in with someone in their war department in order to set up this type of negotiation."

"When?"

"Soon."

"It would have to be very soon, I think, Major, and very, very secret."

Taking McClellan's reply as approval, Pinkerton saluted smartly and left.

A discontented Custer watched him go. "And if the negotiation does not prove successful?" he prodded Little Mac.

"Then we may have a surprise in store for The Ape," said George McClellan.


THE CANE THRUMMED THROUGH the air, landed with a flat thin sound on the startlingly white upturned buttocks of Hubert Hillary as he lay genuflect on the couch.

"Harder, damn you," hissed Hillary, through clenched teeth. "Leave a mark." Nodding, though the nod was unseen, the sweating young prostitute put her weight into the swing. "Ah!" sighed Hillary sharply, simultaneous with the smack of the cane on his skin.

He considered it a danger to let himself be marked, even if they faded in three or four days. There was always the remote possibility of his being in a carriage accident or some sort of mishap which would necessitate the removal of his britches. And there was also the even more remote possibility of an emergency trip to the latrine and an intrusion.

But Hillary was so tense that he decided to indulge himself this night. He would be extra careful for the next few days.

He knew he had to be. He thought surely the bumbling damn Yankees could at least cut off Jackson at Harper's Ferry if they knew the battle plans, and now the insufferable boor was an even greater hero than before.

But I certainly killed a lot of people, Hillary giggled to himself. The papers were full of the carnage which had taken place two weeks ago, and of the "lost order" which McClellan had found. No way could it be traced to him, Hillary thought, wincing happily as the cane ripped into him again, but it would not do for him to fall under suspicion.

Following the battle, Hillary had done the only thing he could to ensure his appearance of loyalty, he had again lengthened his working day. When he assumed his vendetta against Jackson, Hillary began putting in ten hours a day, six days a week, instead of ten hours for five days. Now he had upped his work day to twelve hours, and even Jefferson Davis had come by and personally thanked him. Hillary despised the strutting rooster, Davis.

The work load was a successful screen, but it was beginning to tell on Hillary, as was the constant fear that his role in Antietam might be discovered. It would be ironic, he thought, if he worked himself to death in order to disguise his hate for his superiors. And he did hate them. Davis and Jackson and Bragg—what a fitting name for that pompous little bastard, Hillary thought. He hated them all, except for Lee. Lee was always polite to him, always remembered his name, even shook his hand and thanked him for his work. He couldn't help but like Lee.

But not so much as he liked this, Hillary thought, the cane cutting him once again.

It was time to stop for tonight. He had been satiated long ago, and it was rare that he allowed himself to overindulge this way. It was going on one A.M. and he still had a long carriage ride back to town in front of him. Long and careful.

He needed the release, though. He decided to go to work at seven this morning instead of six. That would give him a couple of hours sleep, anyway. Besides, there were still some more things to do tonight.

"Five more," said Hillary, turning to look at the young girl. "Make them good ones. And then it is your turn." He closed his eyes and stuffed his head down into the pillow to stifle his shrieks of pain and pleasure.

Next morning, in the Confederate war department, the Secretary of War called for Hillary's boss, the undersecretary. A secret and urgent matter had arisen that required deep thought. The secretary had received a most unusual proposition through a most irregular channel and a decision had to be reached quickly.

Little was said about the manner in which the message was received, but the message carried with it the ring of authenticity. A powerful faction in the Union administration wanted to convene a secret meeting to discuss the possibility of negotiations for peace.

First there had to be an initial planning session to work out particulars for a meeting between people who carried weight on each side. The confederacy was to send one man, of middling rank in the hierarchy, to meet with a man of like station in the Union chain of command. Neither side would be willing to risk anyone of true import.

Logistics, here, was the key. What was called for at the meeting, from the Confederate side, was a man low on the totem pole of the power structure but one who knew a little about most of what was going on. Logistics and precision planning were the items to be worked out at the meeting.

The two men discussed the situation for most of the morning. Reluctantly, just before noon, they sent for Hubert Hillary.

Hillary was badly frightened by the summons. His good sense and logical mind told him there was nothing to be feared, but his constant dread pushed his common sense aside.

He walked to the office of the secretary scarcely feeling the pain from the crusting weals on his buttocks, well padded against the possibility of seepage.

A knotted lump constricted his throat as he forced himself to sit down heavily in the chair, gradually diminishing as he listened to the secretary. The lump was soon replaced by a sense of joy which he fought to keep from displaying. He made sure he kept his expression solemn as he considered the invitation.

Yes, Hillary said, he would be honored to serve as liaison for the South.

Earnestly, he thanked the men for their confidence in him and for the opportunity to serve.

Hillary, gloating within, was bowing himself out of the room when such a commotion arose on the street below that he, like the other two men, was drawn to the window overlooking the avenue.

Soldiers and civilians were shouting and clapping their hands as a small group of mounted soldiers made their way up the cobblestoned street. All but one rode black horses. Windows flew up all along the way, and bits of ribbon and torn paper were thrown from them for confetti. Up, too, went the secretary's window and the two men leaned out to join the shouting.

Hillary hurried to the other window, which overlooked the street with even greater advantage. Hillary wished he had a gun and a moment's invisibility to use it, he so hated the figure who led the dozen men. For it was Jackson's creature who rode toward the open window, one who had looked at Hillary, the single time they met, with open mistrust and hostility in his eyes.

Hillary had on that occasion merely simpered some warm sentiment, although his own hostility doubled that of the other man. And so, true to his character, Hillary leaned out the open window, clapped, whistled and shouted.

"Hurrah for Canon," Hillary shouted. "Hurrah for the Stonewall. Hurrah for the Black Horse Cavalry."

Canon was amused and delighted by the spontaneous display from the citizens of Richmond. He reached down his left hand and gave Hammer the special little pinch which put him into an understated but complex prancing gait, making it appear as if the huge yellow horse was almost waltzing down the street.

He had already received three thoroughbred black horses—two mares and a gelding—from partisans who had read of the death of Old Scratch in the newspapers. Only a few sketchy details had been printed about Canon's injury, and that was good. He was well, now, though his head for a week felt like the inside of one of Jackson's lemons. At least, Canon was well physically.

Mentally, Canon had been all at sea since the incident at Antietam.

Many men, including Jackson, had watched Canon brood. All suspected he was grieving over the loss of Scratch, which was greatly true, and that, too, was good in a way. Because none suspected the great turmoil roiling in Canon's mind.

When Jackson had offered, no, insisted on a Christmas furlough for him, Canon had accepted with only token hesitancy. He wanted to see Mountain Eagle, and Buck, of course. But he wanted mostly to talk to his Indian spiritual guide and present this quandary to him. He wrote for the two men to join him in Richmond. In Richmond, because the practical Jackson had not given Canon free rein to go home. During his rest and recuperation, Jackson had said, it would not be much trouble for Canon to make a few recruiting and fundraising trips in the vicinity of Richmond.

Before he could even think to argue, Canon found himself saddled with a great circuit of speaking engagements. He would rather have to face the Yankee artillery at Antietam again, and tried to beg out of the furlough, but Jackson would not hear it.

Besides, Stonewall said, the two months would give Canon time to train the new black horses.

Now, passing the main hotel in Richmond, Canon could see Buck and Mountain Eagle standing among the growing crowd of people on the sidewalk. Both men wore huge smiles. They were not nearly so demonstrative as the crowd of people jostling around them, but he could see pride in their smiles. It meant a lot to him. Those two men were not easy to please. He sent one of his escort to tell them he would join them as soon as he reported in at headquarters, and Hammer danced on down the avenue.

Canon had at first written home often, and had often received letters from Mountain Eagle. Buck could write a smattering, but didn't like to do so. Mountain Eagle's handwriting was flowery as his speech, and his letters were a joy to read.

But Jackson, though he wrote almost daily to Mary Anna, dissuaded others on his staff from writing unless he was allowed to read the letters personally. His penchant for secrecy had been compulsive prior to Antietam. Now it was becoming obsessive.

And the Black Horse Cavalry moved quickly and often, on scouting duty most of the time. Opportunities to write were rare. Correspondence between Canon and home had dwindled to a trickle. But now he, and two of his three main mentors, would have time together.

Canon hoped they would have answers for him, too. The incident at Antietam was not a subject he could, or would, discuss with anyone else. In fact, when he finally made it to the hotel suite, he found he was reluctant to talk about it at all, though he had hinted to the Indian in his letter that something occurred that required deep thought and, if possible, explanation.

The Eagle did not push the matter, however, and two weeks passed before Canon brought it up.

They had been wonderful if vexing weeks. Canon stayed in the army barracks some nights, some nights he spent in the hotel with Buck and the Eagle, some nights he stayed with partisans at their homes in towns where he was recruiting and raising funds.

The two men often accompanied him on these trips, though usually one would stay behind to work with the new horses. Buck had brought two more black Arabian stallions with him to Richmond, giving Canon a stable of five new mounts. But Canon had resolved not to get too close in spirit with these replacement animals.

Their life expectancy could not be great. Already, Jeb Stuart had lost several horses in fights. In the Western Theater, the emerging Confederate hero Nathan Bedford Forrest had had a dozen shot from under him.

Canon had wanted to train the horses at Mulberry. He wanted to go home. The feeling persisted that he would never again see the place he was raised.

If he could prove the feeling wrong, he could stop the worry that had plagued him since Antietam. If he could disprove one of these eerie certainties, the rest could go piss up the road.

Over the past weeks he sought opportunities to test himself. But try as he might, Canon had not been able to foresee anything, could not call up any apparitions or glimpses of the future.

He took it to the level of trying to guess what would happen on recruiting trips, whether he would be successful, whether he would see anyone he knew. He would try to guess what Buck and Mountain Eagle would want to talk about when he saw them, and what would be the war news. He even carried a deck of cards so he could try to predict which card he would turn up.

He was no more successful at these things than he supposed the next man would be, and he was becoming frustrated. Mountain Eagle had caught him, once, with the cards and had watched him closely. Canon had almost gone into it, then, but could not bring himself to speak of it. The Eagle waited for a few moments, then passed on into the next room.

Another thing Canon could not fathom was the Southern attitude toward the war. The Yankees had pretty much gained control of the Southern rivers, establishing lines of communication and supply and bases of operation which Canon knew were strategic necessities. This would ultimately disrupt the South's own lines of supply and communications.

Raids in Mississippi had been accomplished by Federal cavalry brought in by boat, and the confederacy was slowly being pushed out of Kentucky, an important border state.

Food was becoming scarce in the South; inflation was becoming rampant.

Yet the Southern man and woman were willing to put up with nearly anything, any privation, so long as Lee and Jackson continued to win victories in the East. Lee and Jackson, even Canon himself, were looked on with adoration bordering on deification. It was almost frightening.

And now, to match his mood, the weather turned gloomy. Winter arrived. This was the last week of October, and all was bleak. Perhaps it was this bleak mottled sky or the foreboding atmosphere of All Hallow's Eve which finally ended Canon's reticence to speak about Antietam. Maybe it was simply all the mourning.

Buck and Canon attended a plush costume ball at the president's mansion in Richmond. Mountain Eagle, who did not care for such trappings, remained at the hotel.

Canon saw several former girlfriends from Lexington since his return, and found himself invited to many more homes due to his newfound fame as leader of the Black Horse and the Stonewall Brigade. He availed himself of more than one opportunity.

But he took far less pleasure in the game playing which accompanied pursuit and capture. He ruined as many liaisons as he had fostered, but he could not help it.

He had not been celibate while in the Stonewall Army. His many raids and rides into towns had been welcomed by women of the area. He found that he and his men felt far gayer, even foolishly gay, in the face of constant danger and threats of death. But the episode at Antietam had turned his perspective, and he found he was brooding and moody with laughing young ladies who only wanted to amuse him and themselves during his time at home.

More and more, Canon found himself noticing, wherever he went, the great number of people in mourning. Widow's Weeds were in abundance, black armbands surrounded him.

And when his date for the President's Ball came to her door in a witch's black garb, complete to peaked hat and cape, Canon was piqued. Black horses, black dresses, black costumes put Canon in a black mood. It seemed every other woman he saw at the ball was in black, and every mans' arm carried a black band.

With apologies, he returned the fetching young witch to her door all too early to suit her.

Buck, who squired a lovely matron to the ball, told Canon not to wait up on him, and with the advice gave a large wink that let Canon know the old goat was feeling frisky.

A silvery fingernail moon shone through scudding clouds as Canon grumped his way back to the hotel. He found Mountain Eagle in the suite reading a book about the young Sioux mystic, Crazy Horse. Many lurid tales were beginning to come out of the far western territories, most of them promulgated by men like Ned Buntline, whose dime pulp novels were the rage among those with barely enough education to read.

He was surprised to find the Eagle reading such claptrap, and said so, though the book was not of the pulp variety.

Canon knew of Sitting Bull and Crazy Horse. Sitting Bull, the Sioux chief, had been to Washington a decade ago, trying to establish enforceable treaties to stem growing westward expansion.

Throwing himself into a chair, Canon made another uncharitable allusion to the book and the Eagle's wasting time with it. Gravely, Mountain Eagle placed the book on the sidetable which held the reading lamp.

"Is it not the great Shakespeare who warns us that more things exist in heaven and earth than is dreamed of by great philosophers?" asked the Eagle.

Though irritated by his own irrational irritation, Canon testily replied that he doubted the book about Crazy Horse was written by Shakespeare or anyone like him.

"I have met Crazy Horse," the Eagle said. "He is a young man of great power and vision, and he knows much that cannot be explained by any of the reasoning which is possessed by the white man.

"He is not only a healer, a medicine man, but also a war chief. Although he is young, younger than you, he is the only man I know of in the great tribes who holds this dual trust. And if it were not for the leadership of Sitting Bull, Crazy Horse would be the peace chief, too."

Indian tribes selected among themselves a peace chief, a war chief and a medicine man. In time of peace, the peace chief relied on advice from the war chief and the medicine man, but all decisions were made by him and were final. In time of war, the war chief made all decisions, with the peace chief and medicine man as advisors.

Crazy Horse alone held the positions of war chief and medicine man.

"What do you mean by a man of vision?" Canon asked, his interest pricked.

"He can see the future," said Mountain Eagle.

"How does he interpret what he sees?" said Canon. "How can he know what things he envisions are real, and what are just manifestations of mind, maybe meaning nothing?"

"You misunderstand me, my son," said Mountain Eagle. "By seeing the future, I mean he is like your father, who looks about him at the events of society and history, and extrapolates what it will mean to his people two or five or ten years from now."

Canon was disappointed. "I thought you meant he had visions, like glimpses into what is about to happen," he said.

"He does that, too," said Mountain Eagle.

"It has happened to me," said Canon.

"I thought so," said Mountain Eagle. "Shall we talk of it?"

Relief flooded through Canon, and it poured out of him in the form of the story that had welled up inside him so long. He told the Eagle of the events at Antietam, how he had seen the dead man point at Scratch, how he had seen the water filled with bodies, how he had known where the shells would land.

He told him of half-forgotten things that happened when he was growing up, of times when he knew what was about to occur. Throughout the hour long recitation, the Eagle sat without moving.

When finally Canon finished, he looked expectantly at Mountain Eagle, but the Indian only looked back at him. Exasperated, Canon said, "Well, what the hell does it mean?"

"Well," said Mountain Eagle, "I sure the hell don't know."

Canon laughed bitterly. All this time, he thought, I have waited. "If you suspected this thing in me, why have you not said so?" Canon asked. "Why can you not help me?"

"It was not my place to question such a gift as this," said the Eagle, "or to speak of it until you felt the time and need. And I did not say I could not help you. I merely said I cannot understand the power. It is something I have only experienced on its perimeter, as if looking into a shady place. It is too far beyond me for me to comprehend.

"Only on two occasions, when I took the magic cactus bud called peyote as part our religion, did I experience a little of what you have experienced.

"But I have seen others who have seen events of the future with uncanny accuracy, Crazy Horse among them. As I told you, his power as a man of vision lies in being able to read signs in every day life which give him the events of the future. That is what is important to his tribe. The gift you speak of is a personal one, though it can be of equal importance."

Asking the Eagle to wait a moment, Canon stepped into the room he used when he stayed at the hotel, and returned a minute later with his uniform coat and great coat. He pointed out eight holes, nicks and tears in the coats made by bullets, shrapnel or blades that barely missed him.

"At times, in battle, I duck or spin without thought, though I have begun to notice it," Canon said. "It has saved me while others died."

"It is what I meant by gift, and thank God for it" said Mountain Eagle. "Tell me. Have you ever questioned your other gifts? You are strong and swift. Your eyes and ears and hands have capabilities I have seen in no single human before. Have you questioned this?"

"Yes, I have wondered before why I am blessed."

"But not to the point of distraction. You have decided that you are lucky, and have left it at that."

"This is true, Eagle."

"This second sight, then, is another blessing, and perhaps the greatest. Listen to me. It is all right, I think it is imperative, for you to wonder on this thing and ponder it. Only along this path does wisdom lie. But you must understand this. Though you are strong, there are things you cannot lift. Though you are swift, there are things you cannot outrun.

"What I say is that you have through the years learned the limits of your other gifts. With this one, you have not. Yet there are limits, as with everything. Take the gift as it is given. Use it, try to improve it, as you have spent time and effort to improve your strength and your aim.

"But do not punish it for being there, any more than you punish your strength for being there.

"Now, Rabe Canon, I will ask you a question."

"Yes, my father."

"You will answer it, and, knowing you, I know the answer you will make. And then I will give you the best advice I will ever have given you. Are you ready?"

"Yes, my father."

"Rabe Canon, are you afraid to die?"

"No, my father."

"Then do not be afraid to live."

HUBERT HILLARY SHOOK TWO alfalfa pills into his hand from the small metal container the doctor had given him, washed them down with a draught of elixir prescribed for him, and tried to make himself comfortable on the swaying seat of the afternoon train to Fredericksburg. The elixir was vile. Hillary grimaced as he recorked the bottle.

A lowering sun shone orange red through the window. Mostly orange, too; Halloween revelers paced the aisles in grotesque costumes. Hillary thought them disgusting. He had piled his valise in the seat next to him to prevent unwanted company, but the drunken fools continued to harangue him.

The incessant swinging of the coach made him queasy, and he already felt quite ill from the pressures of his job and his own plans. If only these dolts realized the importance of the mission he was carrying out on behalf of their government, he would be afforded some respect. But they were crude, devoid of sophistication.

If they knew what Hillary was really about, the proposal he would make, they would throw him under the coach's iron wheels. He enjoyed the thought until he envisioned it, his body cloven by the racketing rims. It caused his nervous stomach to lurch alarmingly. What made him torture himself with such imaginings? Everything was fine.

The proposal on Hillary's mind had nothing to do with the careful in-structions given him by the Secretary of War. What did he, Hubert Hillary, care for the pokey old South with all its sneering bluebloods? Nothing.

Washington was the place for him. Civilized, exciting Washington, where they was plenty of money for little Hubert. One of the party goers, dressed as the devil, leaned over to grab Hillary's arm, offered him a flask.

Coldly, Hillary shook his head. Looking into the bumpkin's eye, Hillary thought to himself: You are not the devil, fool. I am. The man stumbled on down the aisle. Hillary shook out another couple of alfalfa pills and uncorked the bottle of elixir.

It was dark when he reached the small inn outside the little town. Rain threatened earlier, but the sky had cleared and a crescent moon shone brightly down.

Hillary was pleased with his choice of a meeting place. He had refused the site originally offered, only because he believed the refusal would give him ascendancy in the meeting.

But he truly liked the little inn, ancient but well kept, run by people he knew from experience would keep their mouths shut. He felt it was a stroke of genius on his part to hold the meeting on Halloween, when the roads would be full. No one would remember him. The carriage from the train station had wound its way through many others, but the inn, as he expected, was comparatively empty. Everyone was out to parties and balls.

The night was planned to perfection. Hillary had seen to the rooms, had rented three adjoining. The Yankee would take the room on one end, Hillary the room on the other. They would meet in the middle one at precisely eight P.M.

For once, Hillary was proud of his war department. Even if they acted like idiots most of the time, they had functioned for him this occasion. They had given Hillary a trump card. He knew the identity of his opponent, and doubted the same was true for the other man.

Hillary wanted to hug himself. He had a handful of trumps. And he knew how to play. Evident of this fact, the downstairs clock began to chime. Hillary's choice of the inn was in part based on the train schedule. It allowed him to arrive just in time to get settled and rest a bit, but without leaving enough time for him to get nervous.

At the stroke of eight, Hillary entered the middle room. He was pleased. Though he wanted to check out the room to make sure all was as planned, he figured the other man would probably enter early and wanted to keep him waiting just a bit. Previous stays at the inn gave him confidence the room would be as he wished it.

It was a minor thing, but Hillary liked things orderly and in accord with his itinerary.

The room was perfect. Oak and maple, polished by time, lent a subtle aroma to the room. It was cleared of all furniture save two stuffed armchairs with a table between them. The carpet was new. Two wall lamps, more dim than bright, lent the ambience he had wanted. A carafe of coffee, which he knew would be freshly ground and scalding hot, sat in the middle of a small silver service on the table.

These things increased Hillary's confidence, and he felt a thrill of satisfaction as the small man who occupied one of the chairs rose to shake hands. Hillary was surprised to see the man was about his own height. He thought the man would be taller. This, too, was good. He did not have to deal with some great lummox who thought size to be indicative of skill, and Hillary also knew the workings of the mind of a diminutive man. Things were going well.

"I am Mister Allan," said the man.

I can play that way, too, thought Hillary. "And I," he said, "am Mr. Hubert."

Pinkerton poured himself coffee, offered to fill Hillary's cup; Hillary refused. When the man had set down the carafe, Hillary changed his mind and poured his own. He would remain in control.

The men exchanged amenities. The weather, the holiday, the accommodations were discussed, coffee was sipped. Then Pinkerton opened with a thrust.

"Excellent coffee," he whispered through a smile. "I must get you a bag to take home against the shortage."

Hillary's smile was even broader. "Shortage? No shortage at home, sir. Our blockade runners keep us well supplied. And in the field, our troops take what is needed from captured stores."

"But your army is not in the field," said the major.

"You are mistaken, Mister Allan. It is your army that is not in the field. The intrepid Jackson sits poised like a buzzard over the Shenandoah."

It was bold, Hillary knew, to make such a statement so early, but he was holding the cards, and he felt reckless with power.

Pinkerton felt a little tingle shoot through him. Had he heard correctly? Comparing the great Stonewall Jackson to a buzzard was more than sufficient grounds in any Southern state for a duel.

He chose to be noncommittal. "Yes, Jackson," he said.

Hillary, certain his comment had scored, moved into more neutral ground. For half an hour, the two men talked of the tragedy of war, of the myriad deaths, and finally of the need for peace.

Hillary decided again to press: "It is said that Mister Lincoln is planning to free the slaves, or at least to declare them free. Surely he is aware of the consequences if he does so. There can be no peace."

"Many of us," said Pinkerton, "many who hold more than a little influence in the North, are not in favor of this, but it is so. That is why we feel it is urgent to work toward peace, and put the Union back as it was."

"With our peculiar institution intact?" said Hillary.

"Again, many wish it so."

"But then we are back where we started," said Hillary.

"I think not. If the war is once stopped, if only through a truce, negotiations can begin on the economic structure of the nation, which I think you will agree is the underlying cause of the conflict."

"Do you speak with full authority?" said Hillary.

"As full, I would think, as your own. I speak for the army and for many people who are politically powerful."

"What of Mister Lincoln?"

"The president," said Pinkerton sibilantly, "wants the Union together again. He will bow to the will of the people, however, if they do not like the way he is prosecuting the war. It may be that General McClellan will be looked to as the man of peace."

So intent was Hillary on his own machinations that he missed the gap which Pinkerton opened for exploration. Instead, he opened his own gate.

"It is tragedy and irony that the success of our Southern army is probably the one thing that prevents our leadership from seeking peaceful negotiations. But the fact is, so long as the heroes Lee and Jackson are successful, the Southern constituency would hang anyone who tried to stop the war," he said.

Unsure of this turn in the conversation, Pinkerton merely nodded and waited.

"If our army continues to be successful in Virginia, I am afraid the Southern body politic would face any hardship before it would consent to a truce," Hillary continued.

"It may sound traitorous, Mister Allan, but I believe one great victory in Virginia by the North would do more to further the cause of peace than anything else." Pinkerton could barely believe what he was hearing. The statement did not merely sound traitorous, it was traitorous. Could he actually recruit this man?

Carefully, he said, "A true Southern patriot, a true American, could shorten the war and save many thousands of lives, Federal and Confederate, if he could bring about what you suggest."

"Oh, I have no doubt that such a man could be found," said Hillary, airily.

Pinkerton, in a haze, mumbled, "If we could get troop movements and battle plans, our army could win the victory that we agree is needed." He took the plunge. "And the man who brought the victory about would find a grateful Union very generous."

"With due respect, Mister Allan, I am afraid that Antietam proved that even foreknowledge of troop movements and war plans are not sufficient for your general to overcome Lee and Jackson."

Stung by the criticism of his beloved McClellan, and fearful that he had missed a great opportunity with Hillary, Pinkerton cried out in a voice loud with anguish, "It is that damned Jackson. General McClellan can whip Lee, if Jackson is out of the fight. God damn Stonewall Jackson!"

"I will give him to you," said Hillary, calmly.

"What?" "Who?"

"Jackson. I will give you Stonewall Jackson."

"What do you mean?"

"What I say, sir. I have no love for General Jackson and he is, as you say, standing between us and peace. There is no way to get to Lee and, beside that, if something happened to Lee it would enrage the South to the point that nothing could end the war.

"On the other hand, if Jackson were removed from the scene, it would demoralize the entire South. And Lee without Jackson, though formidable, is no longer invincible. I believe you would win the victory you need."

"But can this be done? What do you have in mind?" said the Pinkerton, reaching for coffee with a shaking hand.

"It will be easy as pie," said Hillary serenely, enjoying himself more than he ever had without a whip in the room. "If you will send me half a dozen good men, I will see that they are placed close to Jackson. It would only be a matter of time before they could kidnap him, or get word to you where to lay for him."

"Mr. Hubert, you are doing a great thing for your country. I will see that men are gotten to you. Your, uh, assistance will not go unnoticed by the North."

Time to dispense with this charade, decided Hillary.

"Let us get down to business, Major Pinkerton," he said. "What I want to do for my country is for me to be a rich man in it. Tomorrow or no later than the day after, you will deliver to me here one half-million dollars in gold. When I learn that the other half is deposited in a certain foreign bank, I will deliver to you General Stonewall Jackson."

Pinkerton displayed his first genuine smile of the night. He was now on firm and familiar territory.

"You will get your million dollars, Mister Assistant Undersecretary of War Hubert Hillary," he said, "with my congratulations. But gold is a bit of a problem. It is awfully heavy, you know. I believe, however, we can make arrangements which will be mutually beneficial."

Negotiations which, after all, were peaceful, lasted far into the night. When Hillary left two days later, he carried a valise that contained two hundred fifty thousand dollars in Yankee thousand-dollar greenbacks and a like amount in Confederate bills. The remainder, in gold, would be deposited in Hillary's name as soon as Jackson was captured.

For officials in Richmond, Hillary also carried a carefully concocted document, a copy of which Pinkerton retained for McClellan. Comprised mostly of jargon and bombast, the document did not sit well in Richmond. An again nervous Hillary could only say the meeting did not go smoothly, but that tentative scheduling was being considered by the North.

Hillary was pressed by the office to explain his delay of one full day. Surely it hadn't taken that long, they said, to discuss a meeting. Hillary lamely said it was the fault of his Northern counterpart, who claimed that unforeseen circumstances were in danger of arising. If so, the plans were endangered.

Hillary could not believe his luck when, the day after his return, it was announced in the North that McClellan had again been removed as commanding general of the Army of the Potomac and replaced by Ambrose Burnside.

Here was the unforeseen circumstance he had prattled of, and it cut cold any future speculation of a negotiated peace with George McClellan. Not only was the pressure suddenly removed from Hillary, but even the Secretary of War apologized for pressing him so. It made Hillary wish he believed in God, just so he would have something to pray to and thank.

In Washington, though sick about losing Little Mac, Pinkerton congratulated himself for the trip and for his own reticence in rendering the truth of what had occurred in Fredericksburg. He had told no one what really had happened, intending to have the whole thing lined up before he went with it to Little Mac.

But now it would strictly be a Pinkerton operation, the capture of Stonewall Jackson, for he was sure that Hillary would carry through with the sale. The man was greedy for money, and Pinkerton knew how to deal with that.

Hillary had been angry at first because he was given no gold, but when Pinkerton showed him the carpet bag full of bills, Hillary had quieted like a babe at the tit. It did not matter, because Pinkerton was prepared to offer two million in greenbacks and Confederate currency, if he had to, rather than gold.

He had access to all the Yankee greenbacks and Confederate bills he wanted, but he did not have any counterfeit gold.

In fact, he had given Hillary real Confederate money, much good it would do him. And the Yankee greenbacks, well, he doubted Hillary would even try to spend any of it until after Jackson was taken care of and Hillary had escaped.

Anyway, the greenbacks were excellent copies. Pinkerton had seen to that.

*10*

# We Will Kill Them All

It had been a touchy situation for Father Abraham.

Lincoln liked George McClellan, but not so much as the army liked him. Moreover, Lincoln did not like McClellan nearly so much as he liked being president. And it was likely that if Honest Abe was to continue to be president, McClellan could not continue to command the army. Lincoln intended to retain the presidency.

Not only was McClellan a Democrat, which did not sit well with the president's Republican constituency, he was also anti-abolitionist. It was heavily rumored that Little Mac was slow to attack Southern troops because he counted on a negotiated peace, in which slavery would remain intact.

Once peace was regained and the South had rejoined the Union, the Southerners would have just enough votes to elect George B. McClellan president of the again United States.

It was also widely known that more than a few powerful persons wanted McClellan to take total control of the army, march on Washington, and demand peace. Many believed that if McClellan called on the army to join him, it would do so with little hesitation. McClellan now generaled a total of one hundred twenty thousand men. There would be no stopping him then.

Lincoln decided to stop him now.

"Dearest," wrote George McClellan to his wife from the Union camp he had set up near Alexandria, Virginia in November, 1862.

> The damned politicians are at me again. There is no pleasing them, and nothing I do is right by them. It is not enough for The Ape that I have by the grace of God saved Washington and the Union. Nor is it enough that I have brought the Army into Virginia, according to his stated wish.
>
> Our line of march was disputed by him and I have been forced to change direction, and move the entire Army. It is about all I will take. I

am prepared now to remain in camp until such time as I am assured of confidence in my command by those in Washington City.

But I retain the confidence of the Army, as The Ape and his ilk may one day learn.


The Young Napoleon had no sooner affixed signature and stamp before the North's Secretary of War was announced, and stepped inside the tent. With him was a very nervous and chagrinned Ambrose Burnside, who fidgeted and pulled incessantly at his bushy muttonchop sidewhiskers.

McClellan recognized the implication of the situation at once. It was late afternoon. Most of the men and all his staff were at retreat or mess. He was being got rid of, at a most propitious time.

Still, he could tell, the secretary was badly frightened. And Burnside was deeply embarrassed. He and McClellan were long-time friends, though Burnside's delay at lower Antietam bridge had seriously strained the friendship. McClellan could scarce believe Burnside was to be given command. He knew Burnside turned the offer down on two occasions, before Little Mac had resumed command. Burnside had honestly stated that he did not feel himself capable of leading the army.

When the trembling secretary handed McClellan a sealed envelope, the little general thought to himself, "They really think I would have done it. They think I would have turned traitor."

Then he realized that it was only now, confronted with ignominy, that he himself understood that he could not have done it. If the choice was up to him, and perhaps it still was, McClellan knew he would refuse a dictatorial role. After all, Little Mac found he was a patriot.

Next day, he gave a ringing oratory to the army, asking the men to proffer Burnside the same loyalty they had shown him. Then he rode away.

Ambrose Burnside, who doubted his own ability to lead the army, was in command of it, like it or not. The zealous veteran had made one promise to Lincoln, the only one asked of him. He would attack Lee wherever he could find him, and he said as much to Little Mac.

The departing commander shrugged, said nothing. He supposed it would not be very difficult for General Burnside to find Robert E. Lee and

Stonewall Jackson. Not difficult at all.

For a moment, McClellan wished he could see into the future. He feared it would be a bloody one for the troops he had turned over to Burnside, but apparently blood was what The Ape in Washington desired.

Maybe those who criticize me have been right, McClellan thought, pounding along the road with his disgruntled escort. Maybe I have been overly cautious. But if I could see into the future, I believe I would learn that Ambrose Burnside will rue the fact that he has not caution enough.

And I wish, thought McClellan, I knew what Pinkerton is up to. McClellan was sure Pinkerton must have known about the coming change in command. He had not heard from the detective in almost a week, not since Pinkerton's sketchy report of the secret negotiation with the Confederate representative, which apparently had not gone well.

No matter now, thought Little Mac, as he rode out of history. Still, he tried for two weeks, after returning to Washington, to find Pinkerton. He could not.

In point of fact, Allan Pinkerton did not know what to do, except to continue ducking McClellan. In the first place, he was seriously discomfited because he had had no inkling that Little Mac was getting the axe. It was a damned shame, keeping secrets from the Secret Service the way Lincoln did.

Now here he was, working at night in the war department to reduce the chance of bumping into Little Mac.

But Pinkerton had his own secret, a whopper, and things were moving along to his own satisfaction. He had opened a circuitous line of communication to Hillary, the greedy pig turd, and had received assurance that the deal was still very much on.

Pinkerton had no idea what the Southern prima donna had against Stonewall Jackson, but Hillary was just as anxious to sell as Pinkerton was to buy.

Only now, with Little Mac gone, it was all up to himself, Major Allan Pinkerton, and the United States Secret Service.

He wished he could see the future. He hoped for all the world that Lee and Jackson would continue their winning ways on the battlefield until he could get the machinery in motion to take Jackson. It meant slow going. He could not afford a mistake. And he could not afford Little Mac's overcaution.

Burnside was in the field, looking for Lee, and Pinkerton could only hope that a stray bullet did not find Jackson during a battle. The odds were against it, he figured. Little Mac was ten times a better general than Ambrose Burnside, and everybody but Lincoln knew it. And Little Mac could not whip Lee and Jackson, even with copies of their battle plans.

I am damn sure glad I am not an infantryman in the Army of the Potomac, thought Pinkerton. Burnside will find Lee, all right, Pinkerton was sure, and the Stonewall Army. And he will get his ass kicked so high that birds will nest in it.

Still, he wished for a tiny glimpse into the future. Wished he knew where the collective asses of Lee, Jackson and Canon were presently located.

That particular part of Rabe Canon's anatomy was at that particular moment taking a verbal scalding from the man who was looming so large in the thoughts of Pinkerton and Burnside.

". . . and you may rest assured, General Canon, that when you are needed you shall be called upon," finished Jackson, who was secretly happy that Canon had returned to camp a week early, but who was not about to let anyone disobey a Jackson order.

Jackson had told Canon to take a two-month furlough. He therefore expected Canon to be gone two months, not a day less nor more.

Canon took the tongue lashing, as harsh a one as he could remember receiving, in good grace. Since the soul-lightening conversation with Mountain Eagle, Canon became more and more anxious to return to camp, the Stonewall Brigade and the Black Horse Cavalry.

He tried unsuccessfully to think up a subterfuge to return early. Finally, he just went. It was early December, perfect fighting weather for an army, and Northern newspapers were full of stories that Federal forces were spoiling for battle. And after all, he had raised more troops and more money than the war department had targeted for him. If he cut a week off his furlough, it ought to be his business.

Canon knew better than to even suggest such a thing to Jackson, who had read him down the road for "presuming too much." Orders are exactly orders, Jackson had said, and not to be suborned, even on the presumption of dedication.

"It is I who will determine when you are fit to resume your duties as commander, General," Jackson said in his quiet, intense way. "Returning for duty before time is an indication that you are not ready, rather than an indication that you are.

"We will see. It is rumored that General Burnside is in the field and seeking battle. General Lee has sent his scouts under Stuart to seek him. You will take the Black Horse Cavalry out tomorrow in similar pursuit.

"Consider yourself confined to quarters in the meanwhile."

Canon suppressed a smile. It was eight P.M. and Jackson had confined him to quarters until the next morning at daylight. Hardly a punishment. Canon saluted and quit the tent, leaving orders outside for his aides to inform the Black Horse they would ride at dawn.

Canon was on his cot and into a deep, dreamless sleep within minutes of leaving Jackson. One day at a time had become his creed. He would not worry about future problems or past mistakes. Evil was sufficient to the day.

Three hours later he was wide awake and in Lee's tent listening intently to Jeb Stuart, confinement to quarters forgotten. Burnside was on his way to Fredericksburg, said Stuart, the Federal Army of the Potomac ponderously slow but steady. Lee sent for maps.

In the morning, Canon was sure, the Rebel army would be on the move. He knew that when Burnside got to Fredericksburg, the Southern army would be there waiting to say hello. It did not take a wizard to look that far into the future.

By noon the following day, Canon and the Black Horse Cavalry sat motionless on the height called Marye's Hill, overlooking a lush pasture almost a mile in length. Bordering the pasture ran the swollen Rappahannock River, on the other side lay the rustic village of Fredericksburg.

Canon idly wondered how many fights Mr. Marye's effeminate sounding last name had earned him in school. Regardless of how many and how bad, he thought, Mr. Marye will see such a fight as he has never seen if he sticks near here.

It had taken Burnside almost a month to bring the Army of the Potomac to Fredericksburg. Now that it had arrived, it found Lee and the Army of Northern Virginia lined up in battle formation on the far side of the Rappahannock.

The next day, December 11, 1862, the entrenched Rebels watched the Union Army move into position near a ford on the river. Lee decided to allow the Federals across the river on the Rebel left side, preferring to dig in at the edge of the woods and force the Yankees to come across the open pasture. On the right side and in the center, Rebel sharpshooters played hell among the Yankee engineers who were laying pontoon bridges. But by the evening of December 12, the Federals had crossed over.

Canon spent the day inspecting the Black Horse and the Stonewall Brigade, checking his own gear as a matter of course. Although he had blacksmiths and gunsmiths on hand throughout the day, they found little to do.

The men in both units were veteran soldiers, the best, Canon was positive, in either army. The infantry in particular was ragged and dirty, but their guns were always clean and gleaming. The cavalry took better care of their horses than themselves. It was rare even to find a horseshoe nail missing prior to a battle.

The horses' harness was piled in front of each mount, the tiniest tear subject to meticulous stitching. Canon made sure he was just as meticulous. His morning inspection had taken nearly three hours. On its completion, Canon ordered parade maneuvers for the Stonewall Brigade and the Black Horse Cavalry, which took another three hours.

The men grumped good naturedly about it, then complied with a will. They trusted their commanders. For three hours they marched, charged, wheeled, feigned attack. And only a few of them cursed, or at least cursed loud enough for Canon to hear, when maneuvers were over and Canon called for another inspection.

He knew diligence was the price paid for being the most feared unit in the Southern Army. The Stonewall Brigade and The Black Horse Cavalry had certain reputations to live up to.

In his tent that night, Canon mused to himself about the strange and terrible power of something so seemingly innocuous as a nickname. And so life-shaping a thing as reputation. It caused him to reflect on the provocative lecture given so long ago in a VMI classroom by the professor, when he had used the analogy of the Chihuahua.

It was now unthinkable for a soldier in the Stonewall Brigade, if not the entire Stonewall Army, not to stand like a stone wall in the face of whatever was thrown their way, including almost certain death. Their collective nickname forced them to fight when it would be better to run.

The Black Horse Cavalry could expect no quarter in battle, therefore could give little. The Stonewall Brigade and the Black Horse Cavalry were seen by friend and foe alike to be larger than life.

Which more or less marked them for death.

There was no question any longer about what troops would be sent to the hottest part of battle or what unit would be given the most dangerous reconnoitering assignments. Jackson, Canon and their men had earned their reputation. Death alone could release them from it.

Casualties in the Black Horse during eighteen months of war totaled thirty-seven percent, forty-two in the Stonewall Brigade. Throughout the rest of the army, twenty percent was considered high. As Jackson had said, the price of glory is horror.

Word had come to Canon earlier in the evening that the Black Horse would fight dismounted in the coming morning's battle as part of one of the division commanders' infantry. Fine by him. A cavalry charge across a three-quarter mile open pasture was less lethal than sticking your head in the mouth of a Parrott gun when the fuse was lit, but just barely.

That was the good news. The bad news, which really was no news at all, was that the Stonewall division would defend the Confederate left, where the brunt of the Federal attack would come. Wave upon wave of Yankees would fall on the left, the obvious point of attack. And what is a better breakwater than a stone wall?

It would be a brutal day tomorrow. Canon found that part of him could not help but look forward to it. He slept.

A FRIVOLOUS MORNING WIND flirted across the field, kicking dull brown clumps of winter grass into swirls, then disappearing, only to reappear a stallion's jump away, curling another set of dry stalks and tendrils.

It frolicked through tense men hunkered behind hastily heaped dirt. It tugged tentatively, playfully, at Canon's hat and he pulled the gray cavalryman's flat brim, right side pinned to the crown, down more tightly on his head. It shaded his face from the winter sun, now risen above the tree tops.

He wanted to check his pistols again, make sure the loads were secure, the caps in place. But he had done that twice already, just as he had checked saber, rifle and bowie knife. Waiting was the hardest part. He was keyed up rather than nervous, wanting something to do. But another weapons check might make him appear fidgety to some of the men, and he needed to show calm. Rather than check the pistols, he checked the men.

Everything looked fine as he surveyed the narrow, shallow ditch in which the army waited. General A. P. Hill had dug in this morning, though Jackson was not one for entrenchments, believing they hampered mobility and hindered a charge.

Hill, who commanded almost half the Stonewall Army in the field, disagreed. He entrenched whenever possible, daring Jacksonian wrath. It troubled Canon that disagreements between Hill and Jackson were increasing in number and intensity. Both were dedicated soldiers, but carried different viewpoints on many matters, martial and moral. They had clashed on several occasions.

Hill was known to be a womanizer who took his pleasure wherever he could find it. Imperially thin, with long brown hair and drooping mustaches, Hill was a mercurial personality. Hill joked with the men, as often did Canon, but the trait was considered unofficerlike among the ranking brethren. The man also poked fun at himself, another trait Canon admired, but he could also become passionately intense.

Canon liked Hill, but found him a bit flighty. It seemed the man was always a little too jolly or a little too severe and, while Canon had no room to complain about anyone's attraction to the softer gender, it seemed Hill had no sense of self-discipline when it came to women.

Women found the passionate planter's son irresistible and Hill delighted in the company of whatever woman was around. Canon disdained most forms of discipline except for self-discipline, and it appeared to be the thing most lacking in Hill.

The fastidious Jackson deplored excess, especially in the area of female companionship. And, unbeknownst to Hill, information concerning his one great dark secret had made its way to Jackson. Hill had syphilis. Incurable. The disease a few years earlier cost him the love of his life.

While at West Point, word of Hill's affliction reached the father of his fiancé, and the stern and righteous man had forbidden her to marry him. Instead, she married Hill's best friend, George B. McClellan. Now, though Hill and Little Mac professed to remain friends, nothing gave Hill more pleasure than lashing the Army of the Potomac whenever possible.

Hill had always been a fiery figure, a fierce fighter, but one who thought he had been held back by lesser men from the advancement he deserved. Now he felt he had proven himself to be as good a field commander as was in the Confederate army. And although he respected Jackson, he was not sure that the feeling was reciprocal.

One dispute between them still rankled both men. On the march to Manassas in August, Jackson had accused Hill of delay and later ordered him to march behind the columns as punishment.

Hill resented and denied the charge, and called for a court-martial to hear the case. Feelings concerning the dispute ran high throughout the Stonewall Army until, finally, Lee had to intervene. Canon thought one of the unremarked facets of Lee's genius was his ability to control the volatile tempers of a diverse volunteer army. But this time, though he calmed Jackson and Hill, and although they shook hands, there was still deep enmity there.

Captain McLaws and Lieutenant Lawson, two of Hill's subcommanders, were vocal in their denunciation of what they considered an insult to their leader. In several instances, the dispute almost led to blows between groups of soldiers. But most men in the Stonewall Army were merely saddened by the rift. They admired Hill, but they loved Jackson. For the most part, men in the Stonewall simply ignored the clash. Little was said about it.

The important thing was that when battle came, Jackson and Hill worked together like soulmates.

Canon was glad of that. Dissension in an army was deadly, and he had ties to one of Hill's subordinates. He had known Billy Lawson from childhood, and was proud that the towheaded sharecropper's son had made good.

Lawson's family had grown cotton on shares for the plantation next to Mulberry. Though from a different social class than Canon, Lawson had been a boon companion to him. They hunted and fished together, and, when Canon could talk him into it, Lawson would accompany Canon to some of the nightspots in Montgomery.

This was frowned on by some of the supercilious newly rich, who made no effort to disguise their contempt for white trash like Lawson. But Billy was more than their equal, bright, witty and mannered, though ill educated and poorly spoken. Lightly freckled, fair skinned and well made, the young man had a contagious smile, a toothy grin that took some of the sting out of his more cutting remarks.

Canon thought Lawson really represented gentry, coming from a good family that had been ruined by ill advised speculation. He was superior to most of the snobbish set in every way but material possessions, and therefore anathema to them. It gave Canon great glee to see Billy cut through the pseudo-socialites like a wolf through sheep.

Lawson had seen the war as an opportunity to regain standing, grace and wealth. And he meant to do it on his own. He was an excellent horseman, Canon had wanted him to join the Black Horse, and had offered him his pick from Bill Kelley's shipment from Texas.

Lawson had smiled, genuinely, and thanked him. He would like to serve with Canon, he said, but he would do this thing on his own. Pride, said Lawson. He had to have his pride.

Like many another soldier, Lawson's pride and willingness were tested early in the war. As a in one of the Alabama troops under Bernard Bee that fateful day at First Manassas, he had seen Jackson's stand, and had rushed to take part in it. But the Alabamians had been hit so heavily the troop was disbanded and its members moved to other units.

Lawson asked for and received permission to join the Stonewall. Ultimately, he had been assigned to Hill. Since then, personal bravery and leadership had gained Lawson a lieutenant's rank, and Canon thought him capable of even higher reach.

Now here was Lawson on Canon's left, at the lead unit of Hill's division. There was no time to talk, but Canon looked forward to seeing the man again when the fight was over, if they both lived. Although Hill and Jackson were often on separate assignments, the Stonewall Army usually camped together. Canon knew Lawson had avoided him. Not because he did not like Canon, but because he wanted no word noised around that his success was coming from a friendship with the leader of the Stonewall Brigade.

Today, after fighting together, Canon felt that Lawson would not refuse a beaker of good Mulberry whiskey and some reminisces. Hoped not, anyway, but even if he did Canon would understand. You pays your money, you takes your chance.

Even as Canon looked at Lawson, he detected a shift in the attitude of the Southern troops. What little muttering had been on going ceased, shoulders stiffened, lips were licked. Canon looked toward the blue masses across the pasture, noted the increased activity as the attack began to form. Without thinking, Canon checked the loads in his pistols again. It began.

Black smoke clouded from the Union heavy guns, but before the roar reached him, Canon felt the earth shake as Southern batteries behind him roared their replies. It was the ritual preclusion to battle, gigantic dances of death between large bore guns that set lines of strain around the hard eyes of men waiting to kill each other.

The shelling lasted a half hour, then, with a huge hurrah, the Federals charged. Musketry opened up all along the Southern line, and the cacophony of twenty-five thousand cracking small arms drowned the artillery noise.

Onward came the blue, though men dropped by rows and exploding shells opened great gaps in the line. Still onward they came. It was a brave charge. The gaps were filled instantly, fallen comrades were overleaped. On came the Yanks. Canon admired it.

Canon knew the Yankees could not be allowed too close to the Confederate artillery and sure enough, after blue troops had covered two-thirds of the field, Lawson led the Southern charge out of the trenches.

The two armies closed like clapping hands. They were within a hundred yards of each other on the open field before the fire became so hot that neither side could advance further. The dark guitar played wherever men stepped, or stooped to shoot. Some men shouted and fell backwards when hit, some grunted and dropped, some fell forward and died without a sound. Slowly, then more quickly, the some turned into many.

Bent to one knee, Canon rammed a load into the breech of his rifle, fired, ejected the casing; rammed in the load, fired, ejected the casing. Rammed, fired, ejected. When the gun finally jammed from powder build up, Canon tossed it behind him and grabbed one of the many lying near him which had been fired only once but which the former owner no longer had use.

Canon looked up to search for Lawson. Finding him, Canon did not like what he saw. The gallant fool had his men too far out, too close to the Yankee line. They had formed a salient, a projection jutting from the rest of the line like a small peninsula. Damn, thought Canon. A salient is fine if fortified, but such a thing on open ground is suicidal.

Canon watched the point grow thinner and thinner, as if whittled away by invisible strokes from a giant knife. No men could stand it. Calling for troops of the Black Horse to form around him, Canon prepared to go to Lawson's aid. It was difficult to be heard amidst the clamor, and it took Canon ten precious minutes to rally his squad. Just when the men were finally formed, Canon saw Lawson's unit waver, then break. Canon gave the call to charge and rushed toward Lawson even as Lawson led his men away from the line.

A great shout rose from the Union troops at sight of the gap left by Lawson's departure in the center of the Southern left flank. The blue men rushed to fill it, hoping to break through the Southern line and push toward the artillery.

As Canon neared the retreating soldiers, he called for them to turn and stand, that help was on its way. Lawson evidently did not hear. He and his men were retreating in good order, but determinedly.

Canon finally got close enough to see Lawson's face, but could not understand what he read there. Certainly it was not fear or panic, but disgust, even hatred, and grim, grim determination.

"Lawson, what in the hell are you doing?" yelled Canon over the roar of battle. "Get back in line, man. You have to rally the troops."

Lawson turned to him, but barely slowed his stride.

"My troops are shot to shit, General Canon, and I am taking them to the rear. I myself will return at once, I assure you, and will fight beside you until hell freezes over or I am in it. But these men can take no more."

Canon had no time to argue. The integrity of the gray line was breached and blue uniforms were streaming into the gap. He threw his rifle to the ground, heard his saber give its raspy steel cough as it cleared the scabbard, drew his left pistol. He rushed toward the gap. With a roar and a shout, the Black Horse hit the Yankees.

Twice, Canon remembered, he had looked up at the sun and could not believe it had not moved. He feared that some Yankee, like biblical Joshua, had been given the power to hold the sun still so long as the battle raged. But conscious thought had left him, then, and he went about the business of killing. Slowly, they pressed the Yankees back.

The North and South broke even that day, so far as death was concerned, on the left side of the field. The Stonewall Army lost three thousand men, as did the attacking Yankee division as it was pressed back.

But on Confederate right, and in the middle of the field, the Union Army suffered slaughter.

As feared by McClellan, as predicted by Pinkerton, as admitted by Burnside, the Yankee general was no match for Robert E. Lee and a stone wall.

This stone wall ran along the edge of the road down the hill from Marye's heights. The wall stood about five feet high, just about to a soldier's shoulders, a perfect shield and gunrest for sharpshooting Southern riflemen. It bordered the same three-quarter mile pasture bordered on the other side by the river.

Time and again, Burnside sent Union troops charging over the open ground toward the wall. Behind it, Confederate riflemen sprayed the most lethal rain of death that one side was to inflict on the other during the war.

Five thousand Union soldiers were killed or wounded in brave charges against the wall. Confederate General James Longstreet, commanding the troops defending the wall, told Lee, "If they keep charging like that, we will kill every Yankee in the North. We will kill them all."

At day's end, the North had lost five thousand men trying to take the wall. The South lost less than five hundred in defending it.

Time and time again, the wild disordered assault was recklessly renewed. Part of Joe Hooker's corps charged with unloaded guns, and in fifteen minutes more than half the four thousand men were down.

Burnside was almost insane, near a state of shock because of the losses his men were sustaining. His one thought was the promise to his Commander-in-Chief that he would attack. The assault continued, and none of his officers could dissuade him. Only darkness finally stopped it.

Next morning, the Federal commander almost had to be physically restrained from recommencing the suicidal charge. But the waiting Confederate guns did not open fire that day. Burnside's staff finally convinced him the situation was hopeless. That night, the stricken Federal Army pulled back across the Rappahannock.

Lee's invasion of the North had been repulsed at Antietam, and now Burnside's invasion of the South was repulsed even more bloodly. The Union Army of the Potomac left the field to the Rebels.

It was a horrible trophy.


IN BLEAK MOONLIGHT, CANON surveyed the corpse-strewn battlefield from the back of black horse number one. He swore he would not allow himself the depth of feeling for another horse, other than Hammer, that he had felt for Old Scratch. Rather than using the names the horses had been given, Canon simply called them by number.

All five horses, under the tutelage of Buck and Mountain Eagle, were well trained. Probably better trained than ninety-nine percent of the animals in the war. But the training was far short of that given Hammer and Scratch.

Canon would have never been able to call Scratch by a number. "One," said to Scratch, would have caused him to rear on his hind legs and dance forward until commanded to stop. But this horse was not Scratch, and this field was no place for tricks.

The stench of death two days old covered the field like a pall. Canon rode through them, around them, and in some places had to detour for hundreds or yards because One could not pass through without stepping on the body of a soldier.

Canon was dreadfully tired, but even more he dreaded what he had to do. He wasted as much time as possible helping direct the burial detail. It was time to go ask a favor of Stonewall Jackson. Reluctantly, Canon turned Number One toward the command tent.

Jackson was inside, alone, and Canon had never seen him so angry. The general sat rocklike still behind his portable desk, formal as always in his fully buttoned, stained uniform. Jackson stared straight ahead, the pale eyes cold as blue ice. Occasionally, a tremor passed through his body as if he were shaken by a chill. Canon knew it was not cold, but anger that vibrated through the man.

Jackson returned Canon's salute, but did not rise. And the look he gave Canon was iced resolution.

"You are here to plead for Lawson," he said. It was not a question. "Hill has been here already. I will tell you what I told him.

"You are out of line, General. It is for me to decide, God help me. It is I who will decide the fate of my men. It is my job, sir, to send men out to kill and to die, and I do not lightly do it.

"Lieutenant Lawson committed an act of cowardice that could have lost the battle. I saw it, sir, with my two eyes. He turned and ran. In fairness to you, General, I also saw you save the day. You are to be commended. I wish all our commanders would do their duty as you do."

"What is to be done with Lawson?" said Canon.

"What must be done."

The answer was the one most feared by Canon. "You won't have him shot, will you, General?"

"He should be shot. An example must be set for the rest of the army. If a man runs from the possibility of being shot by the enemy, he must know that he runs into the certainty of being shot by my firing squad."

"Lawson is no coward. I have known him all my life."

"Then why did he run?" asked Jackson intensely. "I will not have a man disobey orders, and it was I who told Hill to put Lawson out front."

This was news to Canon, but he tried to take it in stride.

"Lawson spoke to me as he took his men to the rear, General," said Canon. "He did not run. They retreated in good order and he was going to personally return to the fight. I know him, General. He is no coward."

Jackson sat silently for spell of time, staring past Canon into space.

"Our army is undermanned and ill equipped," he said. "We have but one chance against those people"—Jackson had taken to using Lee's euphemism for Yankees—"and that is speed. Instantaneous action. The very existence of our army depends on quick and total response, and that means my every order must be obeyed without question or pause." Jackson turned the pale blue light on Canon. "Even when I am wrong. Do you sometimes feel that burden, my friend?"

Canon nodded.

"Increase it by a square root for me, cube it for General Lee, and you will know why I no longer enjoy ten hours of sleep at night.

"Lawson will not be shot, General, but he will be humiliated. He is not saved because you spoke for him, or because Hill spoke for him. He will not be shot precisely for the reason you gave. He did not run. He retreated in good order. If he had run, he would die at dawn.

"But his punishment is to be severe. I am not sure but that he would prefer death." Jackson looked away, waved his hand in Canon's direction. "Go on back to your tent, General. You fought well. But you must leave these bad things to me."

Canon saluted and headed straight for Hill's camp and Lawson's tent. He found Lawson outside it, next to an elm tree. Lawson was on his tiptoes, his arms stretched up, up, up. A rope, swung over a low tree limb and lashed to his wrists, held him at tiptoe. From a rope around his neck depended a wooden sign that simply read:

COWARD

Canon had seen the punishment before, but never for an officer. It was gruesome. Lawson would hang there all night. A fire burned near him, tended by two guards that had been assigned the duty. The fire was not to keep Lawson warm, Canon knew, but to keep him visible.

His old friend looked around up at Canon's approach, and Canon could see the bitter smile in the thin moonlight.

"Evening, General," said Lawson, his voice strained with the pain. "Come to hang around with me a while?" The pain would worsen as the man's weight and the earth's gravity increased the pull on tired muscles. By daylight, Lawson would be a strong man indeed if he were not screaming.

Lawson knew what Canon was thinking, and his lips pulled back in a grimace that tried to be a grin.

"No, Rabe, I ain't looking forward to the daylight, no matter how bad this rope pulls. Stonewall will be calling everybody in at daylight for them to watch him strip me of my rank. I'll be a soldier again in the morning."

"Why in hell did you not just pull back off that salient?" Canon said. "You could have just dropped back to the line."

"Was too late," breathed Lawson heavily. "I know my men and they had took all that was to be took. I led them too far out, in my pride; figured that the other troops would follow us out, but nobody come. Nobody but you nohow, and you come too late, though it wouldn't your fault. I figure you come quick as you seen what was a'happening."

"There was too much noise," Canon said. "It took me a while to gather my men."

"I knowed it. But if I had tried to turn my boys when I seen you, they woulda bolted sure. Then we'd all be getting lined up to face the firing squad in the morning."

The two guards, embarrassed by the conversation, sought and received permission from Canon to go in search of more wood, leaving him alone with Lawson.

"Rabe, I always been proud above my station," he said. "You know that better'n anybody. I joined to improve my lot in life, because I've been looked down on most all of it. Not by you. You've been a friend. But the Jacksons of this world put themselves in front of everything else.

"You know I ain't a coward. I would have died out there before I woulda retreated, but I had the men to think of. We could not a' held no longer, and if I had tried to stop them they would a bolted.

"I took 'em to the rear, and was on my way back to join you when I got grabbed at Jackson's order and put under arrest. All I wanted was to get back out there and find me an honorable death, but I wasn't even allowed that."

Canon tried to tell Lawson that Jackson, too, had come from humble beginnings, and to explain what Jackson had told him, but Lawson would not hear it.

"Just leave me be, General. I'll make it right before the war's over."

From under his coat, Canon produced a square rock, small but with height, he had kept in place next to his body with his right elbow. He dropped the rock and kicked it over near Lawson's feet. Near enough for Lawson to stand on it.

Lawson looked at it a moment, then kicked it away.

"Thanks, Rabe," he said, "but I don't need no 'nother hanging here next to me. "'Sides, like I said, I always been proud above my station."

Canon nodded and walked back to his tent.


# 11

# *Kill Him*


Canon sat on a large stone outside his tent and idly scratched at his thickening red beard. There were things he needed to be doing, he knew, but the warm spring morning felt too good. Although the sun was past the treetops, Canon felt like he had just arisen. He felt like that all too often of late.

The three months spent in winter camp since the Battle of Fredericksburg lay heavily on him. He allowed the beard to grow more from an enervating feeling of malaise than as protection from the quirky Virginia winter. Having nothing exciting to do, Canon grew the beard. Having nothing exciting to do this day, he languidly reached into his tent, got his gear and shaved it off.

Rising slowly to his feet, he stretched and yawned, then cursed as he felt and heard small popping sounds as a seam in the shoulder of his uniform let go.

Hell and damn, thought Canon, removing the deteriorating garment and glaring disconsolately at it. My last one, too. He was also dubious about his boots. Their soles were at least as thin as those of the calf-high moccasins Mountain Eagle had sent him.

Canon wore the moccasins whenever possible, which was mostly at night. He preferred them to his boots but they looked ridiculous when he was in uniform. Stonewall Jackson did not like to see his officers out of uniform. Nor did Jackson approve of unmended tears in officers' garments. Holes were all right, but not unmended ones.

The morning sunshine of mid-April was the warmest of the year and Canon did not want to leave it even to step inside his tent to get needle and thread. Remembering that he was out of thread, Canon again cursed casually but expertly and turned toward the field hospital. He was sure to find thread there. There was no morphine or medicines for the Confederate Army, but there would be plenty of bandages to bind wounds, plenty of sharp knives and saws to cut away limbs, and plenty of thread to sew up bullet holes and bayonet wounds.

Canon knew he should not complain. Would do no good, anyway. The army was at least eating pretty well. People in this area of Virginia were freely sending all the food and clothing they could, and even supplies from Richmond had picked up, though food was again getting a bit spare.

May be about time for another raid North, if Jackson and Lee will allow it, thought Canon. But Lee opposed raids into areas which he thought still might come around to sympathize with the South. So far, such hopes had resulted in nothing but disappointment for Lee.

He had expected people in Maryland to greet the Southern Army as liberators. While few had been openly hostile, most had been apathetic, mainly wanting the war to move away from their homes and families and larders. Lee, the eternal optimist, continued to hope.

It was on one of the infrequent raids Lee authorized that Canon again sensed the presentiment he felt at Antietam.

He took a dozen members of the Black Horse for a quick foray into Maryland, seeking food, horses, shoes, clothing against the winter. A few Yankee patrols occasionally invested the area, but they had been too noisy for one thing, and some local sympathizer was always quick to let the famed leader of the Black Horse know when Yanks were close.

On this day—at the end of it, rather—Canon and his men were return-ing to camp. They always chose different paths for coming and going. Near dusk, they approached a tiny valley, no more than a cut, really, through banked earth.

Without thinking, Canon, in the lead on horse Number Two, raised a hand to call for halt and quiet. There was a buzzing inside his head, to-ward the back, and his scalp seemed to tingle. He pulled the twin Krupp fifty-caliber pistols from their holsters and motioned for two men on his right and his left to flank the hill.

About twenty Yankees, he estimated, jumped up from the cover of the low scrub brush on top of the bank, fired an ineffectual volley and scattered into the dark and the woods. Pursuit would have been more dangerous than useful, so Canon let them go.

It was clear that the Southern Army was not totally among friends in Maryland. Canon thought he could make a pretty good guess which of the men he talked with that day had set them up. He expected to pay the man a visit soon as General Lee removed the sanctions against badgering citizens.

Anyone who helped arrange an ambush was more than a citizen. Southern soldiers did not mind the harassment given out by some of the citizenry. It was their right to speak. Ambushes were a different matter.

A few months ago, the incident would have kept Canon awake nights. Now, after the catharsis induced by the talk with Mountain Eagle, Canon found that any thought he gave it was merely moments of contemplation, as the Eagle had advised.

Canon stopped along the way to the hospital tent, spoke to several sol-diers. They seemed happy enough. Desertion was increasing, though not because of cowardice or lack of faith. Nearly every soldier in the army had lost a friend or relative in the war by now, and the war had become a per-sonal grudge, a feud, for most Southern men. They wanted to kill Yankees, though many believed it was a rich man's war and a poor man's fight.

Still, most who deserted merely wanted to get home long enough to plant a crop to feed their families, and come back. Most would come back, too. Canon shared their pain. He would like to see Mulberry once more.

Canon reached the hospital tent and was grudgingly given a spool of thread. He knew he got it only because of the star on his collar. Canon did not like to pull rank, but, given the mood the Old Man had been in lately, he might not have any rank if Jackson took exception to his dress.

Back on the stone outside his tent, Canon quickly mended the seam and stashed the thread and needle in his bag. Almost as quickly, on giving the other matter second thought, he dismissed from his mind the idea of seeing Jackson to seek permission for a raid.

Word was going around that more than a raid might be in the offing. With the weather warming, and the number of desertions starting to pile up, Canon figured the South would have to get on the move pretty soon, if the Yankees did not come looking for a fight.

Since Lincoln signed that document back in January that declared only those slaves in rebellious Southern states to be free, there was no chance any longer for any kind of settlement except for one army to whip the other.

Problem with that was that while the Army of Northern Virginia was down to about fifty thousand, without prospects of ever again getting much bigger, the Army of the Potomac was around one hundred-fifty thousand.

But Canon learned from Northern newspapers that Mr. Lincoln had also saddled his army with a new commander, Fighting Joe Hooker. Southerner commanders figured that while he probably was not so bad as Burnside, he was still no match for Lee or Jackson.

Fighting Joe Hooker was a braggart, though brave. Canon could hardly think of a way for a commander to court disaster for himself easier than to be a brave braggart. Unless it was to be a brave braggart looking for a fight with Robert E. Lee and Stonewall Jackson.

Still it would be good to have just a few more men, Canon thought.

Canon considered it a good omen when a few new troops arrived the next day. There were not many of them, maybe fifty. What appeared to be the best of the lot were eight men assigned to Hill's division.

It was getting close to the bottom of the barrel when an army commander noticed where each few men were assigned, Canon thought. Still, they had looked like good men, even if they were raw recruits. They were remarkably hard eyed, he noticed.

It was those same hard eyes which had caused the eight to be chosen by Allan Pinkerton to infiltrate the Stonewall Army. The United States Secret Service had grown in the past few months, and Pinkerton was proud he had so many men to choose from for the job of snatching Stonewall Jackson.

Pinkerton knew that Lincoln did not have total faith in him or his abilities. That was all right with him. He had been underestimated before. What he lacked in ability he made up for with hard work and tenacity. When he encountered a problem, he worked at it and worried at it like a dog works and worries at a soup bone until the problem, like the bone, was finally chewed to nothingness.

Whether it was due to inspiration he felt because of his great impending coup, or the confidence he gained in holding such a secret, Pinkerton had managed to cause his department to grow in size and importance. Or perhaps it was merely the magic of bureaucratic inertia, and Pinkerton's artesian energy, that had kept the Secret Service momentum going.

Whatever it was, Pinkerton managed to gather enough manpower to pick eight very hard men and with confidence send them South. It was up to Hillary now. But Pinkerton was confident of Hillary, too. In fact, if Pinkerton had to choose between confidence inspired by loyalty and confidence inspired by greed, well, he could choose pretty quickly. Loyalty sometimes wavers. Not greed.

Before he sent the eight men South, he sent word to Hubert Hillary to get ready for them.

HILLARY'S BODY ACHED WITH terror and excitement as in dark of night he reached under the large rock and withdrew the small roll of paper. He had half-hoped, half-feared the note would not be there. A letter that had to have come from Pinkerton, he guessed, had reached his house, and had scared him badly. He never got mail. Not at home, not at the office. The letter's contents scared him even more:

Brio. Corner Second and Main. Monday noon.

If ever there was an obvious coded note, this was one. Pinkerton was worse than a fool. He was mad. Did not he know that, like Lincoln, Davis had suspended all rights of citizens under the law?

There was no such thing any longer as the Writ of Habeus Corpus in either the United States of America or the Confederate States of America. And the Habeas Corpus was the foundation and cornerstone of any democracy.

Literally, it translated to "bring the body." Intrinsically, it guaranteed anyone arrested the right to a fair and speedy trial. First Lincoln, then Davis, stripped away the right to trial. Anyone, including himself, Hubert Hillary, could be thrown in jail by any ranking officer and left there to rot, with no chance to be heard by judge or jury.

And the mails. The mails were a joke. Anyone even merely suspected of harboring sentiments for the Yanks was subject to a thorough and secret mail search. So Hillary agonized over the letter for three days until Monday finally arrived. He had no idea who or what Brio was, but Hillary followed his orders to the appointed corner.

The block ended there, next to a warehouse raised from the ground by huge, flat rocks stacked beneath it as underpinnings. Hillary waited, hatless in the hot sun, a nervous fifteen minutes before a rough voice came from under the warehouse.

"I'm Brio," the voice said. "You pass here twice a day. From hereout you will walk on Mondays, rain or shine, so keep your ears open for messages." It was true that Hillary passed the spot in his carriage on his way to work and again on his way home. "It will be rare that we communicate with you here, but if we do it will be important. So listen sharp."

The voice went on explaining how Hillary was to place certain men in the Stonewall Army, their names were to be found under a certain rock on a certain road South of town. Hillary could also pass information at the rock, if need be, but only messages of dire importance were to be passed at the corner.

When the voice dismissed Hillary, he almost ran. He tried not to dwell on logistics of the infiltrators; the less he knew the better, but his mind would not let it alone. He figured that Brio, or whatever his name was, probably crawled under the warehouse before light, and crawled out after dark. Perhaps he slept there sometimes. Perhaps he crawled under there Sunday night and did not leave until Tuesday morning.

The volunteer army's discipline, particularly in Richmond, was lax. One man would hardly be missed. Hillary figured the first meeting was scheduled for noon merely to make sure he would obey orders.

Putting the note, still rolled, in his coat pocket, Hillary hurried back to his carriage. It was not yet midnight, and fortunately for Hillary, this road ran right past Hillary's secret house of pleasure.

His heart constricted momentarily. Could they know? He suffered another thrilling bout of agonized wonderment before he decided. No. They cannot know. Hillary reined his horse to the roadside and withdrew the note, unrolled it.

Eight names, none of them Brio. That's all. Eight names. Hillary knew they were to be assigned to the Stonewall Army, but that is as far as Pinkerton went.

But Little Hillary had plans, and damn the Pinkertons of the world, and damn the Jacksons. Hillary knew just where to place the men, and he knew just what to do.

He committed the names to memory, used a match to burn the paper, and went on down the road.

Next morning, Hillary, wincing only a bit whenever he sat, sent secret word to Sergeant Billy Lawson.

Hillary had made it his business to keep up with goings-on in the Stonewall Army. It was a well-kept secret that Jackson was often at odds with his commanders, but Hillary had garnered it and kept it close to him as his pocketbook.

The humiliation Jackson draped on Lawson was widely known amongst the army. As was the fact that Hill stood up for Lawson to little avail and had finally, in opposition to Jackson, re-raised Lawson's busted rank to sergeant. Months had passed since the incident, but Lawson had not recovered. His honor besmirched, Lawson was drinking hard and, in town on furlough last month and in his cups, made threats against unnamed men he considered enemies. No one doubted that Jackson was among them.

Lawson spent an hour in late March in the office of the chubby little undersecretary. Lawson despised the man, and despised himself, too, when he left. But five thousand dollars in new Yankee greenbacks was worth a little despicability.

Lawson stopped on his way back to camp and got very drunk.

Hillary had one more thing to do, and it alternately filled him with dread and wild surges of pure power. He let three weeks pass, until the Monday when new troops were to march out to join Lee and Jackson at the Fredericksburg camp.

On his way to work—he had taken to walking to work on Mondays—his legs trembling so they barely held him, Hillary passed the corner of Second and Main.

"Brio," he said without slowing his steps, and he was pleased by the firmness in his voice. "The plans have changed. Kill him."

12

## Shade for Stonewall

"May God have mercy on General Lee," Fighting Joe Hooker said to the press corps surrounding him, "for I shall have none.

"It is not a matter of whether I shall take Richmond," he continued from atop his big buckskin horse, "but merely a matter of when I shall take it."

With that, he rode to the head of his army, one hundred twenty thousand strong. Hooker had enjoyed great success in the Western Theater of the war, and he screamed out his intentions to his troops.

"You have grown used to running away, to being led away from the fight," Hooker yelled. "From now on, it is the enemy who will run away, and you who will be led to the fight."

He took his army out of Washington on a day in late April when redbirds perched like cherry blossoms among the budding branches of trees.

Watching him go, a reporter from *The Baltimore Sun* said, "Well, he damn sure ain't lacking in confidence." His companion, from *Harper's Magazine*, gave his friend a wry look.

"Lee has caused Lincoln to cashier so many Union generals that the White House is beginning to look like an old soldier's bank," he said. "Fighting

Joe better make sure his western clothes are packed and waiting. Robert Lee and Stonewall Jackson are not inept like Braxton Bragg."

Bands played martial airs as Hooker marched his men smartly out of Washington. Leaving, he thought about returning. He could hear in his mind the tunes that would be played for him as he brought the victorious Army of the Potomac back home.

He had no doubt he would win. Hooker had a surprise for Lee, one he had planned since taking command of the army. He would profit from the mistakes of his predecessors. McClellan tried to take Richmond from the east, had failed. Burnside tried from the north and saw his army slaughtered. Neither thought to tangle their way through the wilderness to the west of Richmond. Hooker would.

Hooker would leave a wing at Fredericksburg to "amuse" the Southern Army and keep it occupied while the bulk of his own army would swing wide, through the wilderness, and come up behind Lee from the west unsuspected.

He would flank Lee, then bring his army up behind Lee's lines, cutting him off from retreat to Richmond. Then General Hooker—dare he dream it—yes. Then future President Hooker would destroy the Army of Northern Virginia and capture Richmond.

Hooker sent word to his regimental band to play something a little more "presidential," in honor of Abraham Lincoln, he said.

Three days later he dropped a wing of the army in front of Fredericksburg and entered the wilderness with the rest. He emerged three long days later on April 29, his army straggled and torn, near the town of Chancellorsville.

Hooker was twelve miles from Lee's Fredericksburg line but well behind it. Night was falling. Hooker gave orders for cold camps, no fires of any kind, as he put the army to bed. In the morning, Hooker and his men would fall on Lee's army from the rear and the war would, in effect, be over.

This has all been confoundedly difficult in the planning and in the getting us here, thought Hooker, but it is going to be simple here out. He slept with confident dreams dancing in his brain; he awoke with that same confidence intact.

He started his army for Fredericksburg and his surprise attack on Lee.

The army was struck immediately by Rebel fire. From behind. Riding furiously to the rear, Hooker to his dismay saw Robert E. Lee and the Army of Northern Virginia arrayed before him, battle flags flying, obviously spoiling for a fight.

Hooker had come to fight. Damn it, he wanted to fight. He had meant to attack and drive the damned Rebels into the ground. But he wanted it on his terms, not Lee's or Jackson's. This development was definitely unforeseen. But all was not lost. Lee was sure now to retreat from Hooker's superior numbers, then Hooker would flank him and flank him and flank him until Lee's lines were spread so thin that sand could be thrown through them.

But even as he watched Lee's veteran army, admittedly the best on either side, the keening Rebel yell began to sweep through it like a sudden sirocco. The fools were going to attack!

Hooker panicked, and later admitted that his nerve had failed. "I just lost confidence in Joe Hooker," he said after the battle.

Rather than attack as planned, Hooker found himself following in the footsteps of every Union general that held command before him. He retreated. The army fell back to Chancellorsville and dug in.

Certain that Lee would not be foolish enough to attack an entrenched superior force, Hooker decided to sit back, bide his time and deal as developments dictated.

Lee and Jackson left fifteen thousand men at Fredericksburg, then quick-marched forty-five thousand men back toward Richmond to confront Hooker. As usual, Lee chose the ground on which the battle would be fought.

As the day of May 1, 1863 waned, Lee and Jackson were where they preferred to be. They were in front of an invading Union force that had abandoned its plan of attack and was waiting on the Southern Army to make the first move. Encamped across from each other, the two armies slept.

The Southern troops were up early next morning. Lee and Jackson at daylight were ready and watching when Hooker began to move his troops into defensive alignment. Master strategist and master tactician scrutinized Hooker's troop deployment for any tiny misstep that would give the Southerners an edge. Through their field glasses, to their disbelief and joy, they watched Hooker make a dreadful blunder.

The Union XI Corps had been placed in the middle of the Federal line. Everyone in both armies knew the raw green troops had taken a fearful pounding at Second Manassas. The cautious Hooker decided to pull the XI Corps from the middle and place it far on his right flank, out of harm's way. The move was accomplished, but Hooker neglected to refill the gap the corp's departure left in the very center of the Federal line.

From the heights, at seven A.M., Lee watched the XI Corps move out. Lee, on Traveller, was next to Jackson, on his little sorrel.

"General," said Lee, "If Joe Hooker has no confidence in those men moving to the rear, perhaps it would be good if we learned exactly where they are to be placed."

Jackson, sucking serenely on a lemon, sent for the Black Horse Cavalry. "It would also be most kind of General Hooker if he were to leave that gap open," Jackson said.

The morning was bright and fair. Canon could see the sunshine outside through his open tent flap, but he would have sworn there was a cold cloud inside his tent. He had come awake slowly, amidst the sound of an army camp preparing for battle. Drowsing, he entered that soft realm that is half-reality, half-dream. He had dreamed through the night, though he could remember none of it, but he had awakened several times filled with unease.

He felt mortally tired. Weariness covered him like damp cotton. His limbs seemed sodden, weak. Groggily, he was aware a battle was looming and that a thousand things must be seen to, but he was so tired.

It took all his strength to raise himself in bed and stretch to his uniform for his pocket watch. Hell and damn, eight o'clock! What a sorry-assed time to pick to get sick. He tried to clear his head, but shaking it only seemed to make it slosh, intensifying the feeling that it was full of warm muddy water.

Then he heard the bugle call for boots and saddles. Anger engulfed him, washing away the unease, drowning the weariness. Canon set bolt upright on his cot. Dammit, he was needed, depended on. This would never do.

Canon stood. Dizziness rushed at his head, dove in his brain, swam in it. Nausea swirled up from his stomach to join in. He took deep shuddering breaths until the queasiness ebbed, but his head refused to clear. Awkwardly, he dressed, then walked outside. Damnation, but he was late.

If he did not hurry, he would not be riding today in the year's first major battle. He would most likely be a walking behind the marching columns, compliments of Stonewall. The thought helped unclog his mind considerably. Calling for orderlies, Canon gave instructions for things to be done that he would normally oversee himself and hurried to his horse.

It was noon by the time Canon gathered the Black Horse and reached Jackson, but Jackson seemed not to notice the lateness of the hour. The professor was in high spirits; Canon still sometimes thought of him as the professor when the man was feeling feisty.

Jackson sat on Fancy, his left hand raised above his shoulder, the right hand holding the reins and a well wadded lemon. Canon had watched many a lemon demolished by the professor during a battle. He likened the lemons to whatever Federal troops the Stonewall faced that day. They both started out fresh and plump and full, then Jackson squeezed them and squeezed them and took the juice out of them until, at day's end, all that remained were pulpy masses that Jackson discarded.

"My friend," Jackson said, entirely apart from normal protocol; Canon thought that getting back to battle must have him feeling fine indeed, "the good Hooker has sent a corps to his far right flank that General Lee would like to know more about. He has also been good enough not to fill the gap in his front line left by the corps' departure.

"You and the Black Horse will scout the Federal right flank and return word to me with all haste. We may have an opportunity here, General.

"It will take them some time yet to locate and set up, but once that occurs, fly here with word soon as you can. And my compliments."

Canon was back in two hours, horse Number One lathered and heaving for air. Lee and Jackson could read the excitement on his face. They returned his salute and the ever polite Lee said, "My compliments, General. What have you learned?"

"Their right is totally in the air, sir, fourteen miles up the road," said Canon, calmly as he could. "It is not only unanchored by back-up troops, it is unprotected by woods, bank or stream. And the men are setting up camp. They are stacking their rifles and building fires to cook supper. They have no idea we are watching them."

"A road, you say?" Jackson asked.

"Yes, sir. An old logging road, right through the wilderness. We struck it immediately. We can come up on them without their knowledge."

Lee turned to Jackson. "Thomas," he said, "it appears our instincts were correct. If you agree, I think you should take your army and attack those people on the flank."

"We will move immediately," Jackson said.

"General Canon," Lee said, "I would prefer that you remain with me. We will allow General Jackson four hours to move his army. If, at the end of that time, the situation is static, we will attack."

Jackson saluted and wheeled away. Canon settled in next to Lee to wait.

Hooker's observers saw Stonewall's Army pull out, and the blue force committed its second great blunder of the day. The company commander watching Jackson believed the pull out to be the retreat which Hooker was sure was going to occur. Rejoicing at Hooker's astute analysis, he pulled his company from the already weakened middle of the Federal line and charged off in pursuit. But first he sent word to Hooker that the Rebels were retreating and he was in pursuit.

Jubilation reigned at Federal command headquarters in the Chancellor home, but Hooker declined to send a full assault after them. "Let the Rebels split much as possible," he said. "We will pursue them in the morning with our full army. Now let us retire to the porch and prepare for a restful evening."

Two hours later, sitting on the front porch of the house and drinking from a tin cup, Hooker heard a sharp but limited fire open. "Ah," he said to his staff, "they have caught up to Jackson." The pronouncement was met with cheers and clapping.

There were no cheers, no hands clapping among the Federal troops who had pursued what they believed to be a fleeing Jackson. Lee's regulars, while only fifteen thousand strong, had caught the Federals and pinned them to the ground. And the gap in the Federal center doubled in size.

Another hour passed with no change in the disposition of the armies. It was growing late, past five P.M., and some of Lee's officers felt it was too late to begin a battle.

"We cannot lose this opportunity," Lee said. He called to Canon. "Take word to General Jackson. We attack all along the line."

Canon was away even in the act of saluting.

When he reached the wooded ridge where Jackson had secreted his army, Canon could hardly believe what he saw. The Yankee flank was totally unprotected and the soldiers apparently unconcerned. Men were at mess, filling plates from large pots smoking over cookfires. He could hear fiddle and harmonica music. Rifles were stacked around the camp like large tripods. There were no sentries.

Even as Canon reached Jackson, a note from Jackson was being handed to Lee. The two flying messengers had missed each other in the woods.

The note read:

> Am in place. Enemy totally unaware of my presence. We are ready.
>
> T. J. JACKSON.

It was Jackson's last note to Lee.

Lee sent his outnumbered troops straight into the gap in the Federal line. They drove through it with a ringing Rebel yell, splitting the Union forces, spearing straight toward the heart of the Federal army.

Twelve miles away, the XI Corps was enjoying supper. Some soldiers were lazing, some were playing cards, some swapped advice. The night would likely be balmy, though not much moon was expected. A good night for sleeping.

Katydids and crickets sang tenor, tree frogs offered guttural bass accompaniment. Facing South, Union soldiers occasionally looked to their right at the orange-gold sphere of the setting sun. Here and there an accordion moaned, squeezing out songs of home and hearth. The sweet aroma of woodsmoke filled the air. Kettles burbled, pans and pots clanked and rattled. Evening songbirds began their nesting trills.

The birds were the first to quiet. Among the trees, tiny frogs quit their croaking. Crickets used their strong hind legs for leaping instead of fiddling. The hush moved slowly through the thin woods atop the ridge.

Members of the Union corps watched in amazed amusement as rabbits, raccoons, deer, and foxes began to run through the camp. No one knew what to make of it.

From the woods, the Stonewall Army suddenly burst free in a line one mile wide, twenty-five thousand strong screaming and shooting.

The shocked XI Corps had one chance, and took it. They had heard the most dread word "STONEWALL" screamed by the charging gray line as if in one huge voice. As it echoed and re-echoed over the plain, the XI Corps fled down the road toward Chancellorsville. A few tarried long enough to grab rifles, but they were dropped soon enough in exchange for speed. The Union right didn't so much collapse as vanish.

Joe Hooker still sat on the front porch of the Chancellor home, leaning back in a rocking chair. Around him, his staff laughed and joked. Each believed Jackson was in retreat, with Lee soon to follow. The Union Army would mop up in the morning.

When they heard firing break out behind them to the right, they whooped and applauded. Doubtless, Jackson had been caught and was being dealt with summarily. A ring of men formed around Hooker, each eager to shake his hand.

Only when the sound of battle intensified did the first niggling worms of doubt creep into their minds. Then the roar of fighting swelled around them and they looked up in shocked surprise as men in blue began to run past.

Hooker's face was a slow study of changing expressions. At first it showed puzzlement, then doubt, then apprehension. His officers called questions to fleeing soldiers but none stopped to answer. One of the staff stepped into the road and all but tackled a beardless young private, returning him to the porch.

"What in the bloody blue hell is going on here?" Hooker thundered, grabbing the soldier by the arms. The young man did not look at Hooker, but twisted his head to gaze up the road.

"The right has caved in totally," moaned the wide-eyed soldier, and then

came the words Hooker feared more than any other. "God help us," said
the terrified man, "Stonewall Jackson is right behind me." Even as he spoke,
the sound of firing rolled nearer.

Hooker dropped his hold on the young man, who immediately rejoined
the throng fleeing down the road. Fighting Joe Hooker turned and gaped
at his staff. Then led them as they, too, fled into the night.

Canon had never seen such chaos. He had led the Black Horse charge
down the hill and was among the Yankees before the Union soldiers could
react. The Black Horse trampled and shot soldiers too slow to get out of the
way, but for the most part they disdained the fleeing troops. The Stonewall
Army was fighting toward the center of the Federal troops in order to hook
up with Lee.

It was difficult to locate the middle of such a rolling tumult. They captured
when they could, killed when they could not capture, but it was impossible
to find the center of resistance where no organized resistance existed.

The Yankees were totally unorganized. The only thing that saved the
Army of the Potomac that evening, other than darkness itself, was the fact
that it fell completely apart. Fifty thousand Rebels were trying to corral one
hundred twenty thousand Yankees, and Canon, for once, did not know
which way to turn.

Darkness descended on the field, adding to the safety of scurrying Yankees. Jackson finally reached the commander of the Southern Army, but
Lee refused to call off the fight. He would not abandon a rout.

A couple of Union batteries managed to form in the confusion and fired
several volleys before they were cut down by sharpshooters and answering
artillery fire.

The scene turned eerily surreal as darkness deepened and battlesmoke
covered the field. It was one of the rare night battles of the war. A pallid
moon rose, but was only a metallic disk seen through dark and cloud and
battlesmoke. Here was a scene weird as any from *Macbeth*.

Entire regiments would charge, only to find no enemy there, and they
could not find their way back. Scouts were lost in the woods. Two messengers, told to meet at a certain time on a certain road, stood within fifty
yards of each other for a half-hour before each discovered the other.

Men from both sides stumbled upon each other in the dark, and in one instance, two platoons ran together in the woods and fought savagely for a half-hour before realizing they were both Union.

At eight P.M., Lee gave the order to call off the attack and regroup. If visibility was sufficient, he said, they would resume the attack and fight all night. If not, he wanted reconnaissance to locate the largest forces of Yankees so they could resume at earliest light.

A strange quiet fell on the field as the battle waned, interspersed by sporadic gunfire. Pockets of soldiers had formed within other pockets. A sharp wind sprang up from the west, twisting sputtered sounds of firing into fluted moans and shrieks that mingled with moans and shrieks of the dying. Garbled, warbled soughs of wind through trees filled the field with uncanny ambience.

Canon, who had thrown off his illness during battle and had fought like a man possessed, felt the weakness return that he had suffered earlier in the day. His head, his entire body was filled with a strange dull throbbing.

He was sitting on his horse, he couldn't remember which one, too feeble to dismount, when an orderly found him, told him that Jackson was forming a scouting party and wanted Canon with him.

Canon did not want to go, did not want Jackson to go, but was ashamed to admit weakness. Why could they not just for once let a man rest? But he only nodded and let the orderly take the reins and lead him to Jackson's tent.

"Hammer is saddled, fresh and ready, General. Shall I bring him, suh?" asked the orderly. Canon nodded absently. He dismounted, half falling, from the horse. He had never been so tired. Canon shuffled, stumbled to Jackson's tent. Gathering himself, he stepped inside.

Having stepped inside, Canon failed to see a tow-headed sergeant slip quietly to the rear of a command tent not far from Jackson's own. Inside the tent, silhouetted by lantern light, a thin tall man sat on a cot as he pulled on his boots.

"Sir," whispered the voice through the thin canvas wall, "be shore to stay back from the scouting party. Be shore, sir." The seated figure inside the tent stopped what he was doing, but otherwise gave no sign the whisper had been heard. The messenger moved softly back into the night.

Inside Jackson's tent, fifteen men selected for the reconnaissance looked around at Canon's entrance. Canon tried to disguise his weariness. If Jackson noticed, he gave no indication.

Stonewall was clearly elated over the day's victory; he was animated, vibrant. "My compliments, to you and the Black Horse, General Canon, are added to those sent from General Lee. Your men did your duty today." It was Jackson's highest form of praise.

"Now we must discover their positions, sir. We will learn where they are weakest and then we shall hit them again tonight or at first light. We will give them the bayonet." The pale blue eyes fairly danced. "We must kill them all, sir. We must kill them all."

The pain in Canon's body had been replaced with a gradually growing numbness. He could hardly breathe. And now this. He had ridden reconnaissance with Jackson before; Jackson preferred to do his own scouting during battle, but Canon had never dreaded a mission as he did this night. But it was his duty to scout, not Jackson's.

"General, let me take the scouts out. You stay here in case of further developments."

But Jackson was adamant. He suspected Canon was concerned about the safety of his commander.

"No, my friend. It is all right," he said. "The fighting appears to be finished for the day. I will learn a little about the lay of the land. Perhaps we will locate campfires."

Canon knew it was useless to argue with a stone wall. Suppressing a groan, he walked out and pulled himself up onto Hammer's saddle. Jackson mounted and they rode out side by side. Canon trotted Hammer alongside Jackson and his little sorrel, thankful that Stonewall had ordered total silence. Canon was afraid if he tried to talk he would vomit. He was racked now with long shuddering body chills so violent they shook the saddle.

Hammer, sensing his master's trouble, became uneasy, skittered and jigged.

Just before the group left camp, General A. P. Hill rode up to join. He apologized for his tardiness and joked, in good humor, that he would punish himself by riding at the rear of the column. It was just past eight P.M.

The strange night and the weird fight seemed to have devolved into Canon's personal nightmare. Body chills shook him head to toe. He began to envision strange forms, wiggles and spots in the dark. The pallid moon cast grotesque shadows. He felt that the earth was undulating, could see the undulations ripple along the ground. Cannot the others see this? he wondered. What is wrong with them? What is wrong with me?

Malaria, he determined. That's what it is. He had heard malarial victims crying out in their fevered sleep about macabre things encountered in their ill dreams. Hallucinations. Hobgoblins. Tricks of the oppressed mind.

And voices. Just beneath the range of understanding, he could hear unearthly voices whispering, whimpering, sighing out bizarre giggles and muted shouts.

Even the trees, even the goddamned trees were talking to him in dry rustling tone, mocking him. He could make out their message. S-h-h-a-a-d-e, they were saying. S-h-a-d-e. We'll give you sh-h-h-a-a-d-d-e.

A part of Canon's mind told him he was delirious, but the knowledge didn't make the delirium cease. Shade, said the trees, more abruptly, as in a muted chant. Shade? Canon wondered. What the hell do I want with shade? It is night. The trees giggled as if they had heard his thought. Canon reeled in the saddle.

Jackson halted the group in the light of a tree set ablaze by an exploding shell. Canon's legendary sense of direction had long since departed. He had no idea where they were. He knew only that he wanted to go home. Home. Not just back to camp, but home, home to Mulberry and Buck and Mountain Eagle.

He could take no more of the death, the pitilessness, the reckless taking of life. He had to get Jackson out of here. A cold chill cramped his innards, followed by an aching emptiness that set his heart pounding. Pounding. He could hear his heart pounding in his head, could feel it pounding throughout his body. The world swam before him. He crimped his insides, afraid he was about to void himself there in the saddle.

Wondrously, Canon identified this new feeling.

Why, I'm afraid, he realized. No, not afraid. I am horrified, terrified,

stricken, unmanned. It was as if one side of his brain were calmly analyz-
ing the other.

From far away, he heard a voice, somehow he recognized it as a real
voice, though it was so low and slow it sounded as if someone were speaking through syrup.

"It is nine o'clock," said the deep, drawn voice. Something in the voice
set Canon on edge. He gritted his teeth to keep from screaming. Slowly it
dawned on him that Jackson was beside him, peering up at him intently
from the short sorrel's saddle.

"General, are you all right?" said Jackson, leaning closer. Canon tried to
form a reply, failed. He could not tell this man he so revered that his nerve
had broken, that his trouble was nothing but sheer terror.

The calm side of his brain tried to work for him. Canon had felt fear
before. It was certainly nothing new in war. He knew that fear in war was
normal and healthy, the father of caution. But this was not just fear, and
he could not hope to control it. This was terror, overwhelming terror.
Stark and naked and consuming. This terror was driving him to the point
of madness.

"Rabe?" Jackson was leaning over to him now. "My friend, you have not
been wounded?" he asked anxiously.

"No, sir," Canon finally managed. "I . . . I guess I'm sick." Sick, indeed,
agonized Canon; sick with fear. My God, I am trembling.

Jackson saw the chills shake Canon. "You are cold to the bone, General.
You should not have come. You should have told me. It is all right. We are
going to camp now and it is but a little way. No, turn loose of the reins.
I will lead you. You hold to the pommel. We will get you to the hospital
tent in no time."

Jackson slipped the reins from Canon's numb fingers and drew them
over Hammer's head. Shamed, Canon held the pommel as Jackson led the
way.

Why am I afraid? wondered Canon. Why am I terrified? I don't think
I'm afraid to die. Hell, Canon knew he would prefer death to the awful
feeling he was experiencing. So the detached part of his mind asked again:
What am I afraid of?

The answer whipped into his brain like an arrow of ice. Rivers and trees! Rivers. Trees. What monstrous things are rivers and trees. Those are the danger. Those are the fear. He saw them in his mind's eye, rivers and trees of pallored hue, surrounded by a white picket fence like those around cemeteries and graves.

Oh, but there is deadly, fearsome danger in rivers and trees. Canon felt his eyes bulge from fright. Why, this is wilderness, he said to himself with despair. There's a river near here and it's surrounded by cold lonely shades of trees, shades like death in the night. He knew he was babbling but he could not stop himself from telling Jackson, "Rivers and trees, General, and picket fences. Danger there. Stay away from them. Keep away."

"He's delirious," said Jackson worriedly to the men who rode around himself and Canon. "We must hurry. Our lines should be near."

A burst of clarity descended on Canon like a white glow. The paralyzing terror lifted. All was not clear to him, but he knew one thing. He knew what was about to happen. The terror he had been experiencing was not for himself.

It was for Stonewall Jackson.

"General, stop! Please, stop," called Canon. "Don't go near the picket line. Fall back! Fall back!" But even as he spoke, a Union mortar crew, lost in the stygian night, stepped out of nearby woods and, seeing the horsemen headed for the Confederate part of the field, opened fire with their rifles.

The bullets whistled harmlessly past, but Jackson kicked his little sorrel into a gallop toward the Confederate camp, pulling Hammer. Jackson galloped toward death.

Canon had heard Mountain Eagle say that sometimes, in extraordinary circumstances, time is fractured. This night, he learned what the Eagle meant. Time did not stop, but everything slid into slow motion. Moved into half-time. Though he could see Jackson pounding at full gallop, it seemed they were barely moving; riding through molasses.

Now aware of what was to happen, he nudged his knees into Hammer, signaling top speed. Slowly, so slowly, as they neared their own lines, Hammer began to draw even with Fancy.

Canon's senses heightened as time slowed. In the dark, he saw six Southern pickets rise from cover. From yards away, through thundering hoofbeats, he heard hammers being drawn and locked.

"Hold fire," he yelled at the top of his voice, "we're friends." And he heard an answering voice thunder, "It's a damned lie, boys. They're Yankees."

Hammer had gained on Fancy, was beside Stonewall Jackson. As Canon left Hammer's back to hurtle five feet through the air, he knew he was too late. Too late.

Maybe you don't hear the shot that kills you. Such had been said to Canon by mortally wounded men. Maybe not.

But he heard the shots that killed Stonewall Jackson, heard the zipping whir of the bullets speeding on their way.

The first bullet hit Canon's left arm, outstretched in his dive, slammed the arm into Jackson's chest. Good! It didn't pass through. Canon had grabbed Fancy's rein with his right hand and he pulled it hard, turning the horse so that Jackson would be minimized as a target. But just as the sorrel turned, the swarm of bullets arrived. At Jackson's left shoulder, just at the proud Stonewall sleeve patch, Canon saw a red flower blossom. The awful wet slap of the bullet was loud in his ear as an artillery blast.

His body was in front of Jackson now, shielding him. He grasped Jackson with his right arm to pull him from the saddle. Then six bullets hit, four for him, two for Jackson. Canon felt the four little pieces of lead make a neat row down his back. They felt like blows from a sledgehammer and blasted the breath out of him.

He tried to hang on to Jackson, tried to keep his body in front of him, but he had no strength. As he slid down, down, down he felt Jackson jerk twice as more bullets struck.

All feeling left Canon's body, his sight dimmed and a low roaring filled his head. But part of his fleeting consciousness remained, and his heightened hearing picked up through the roar a strange sound floating through the air.

His last thought was that somehow the ghostly whisper fit perfectly the macabre day.

"Right in the notch," was the last thing Canon heard. "Right in the notch."

# 13

# *Rivers and Trees*

Jackson sat stunned and still as Canon slid away from him. His left arm, hit in two places, hung useless by his side. A third bullet had cut the fleshy base of his right hand, with which he now gripped the reins.

He was in shock as much from the realization that he had been fired on by his own troops as from the bullet wounds.

Around him he heard the cries and moans of his escort, cut down by the volley. He saw Canon lying on the ground at Fancy's feet. Shifting in the saddle, Jackson made ready to attempt a dismount so he could go to Canon.

But as he shifted, a fresh volley opened up from Union troops on the other side of the flint road. None of the bullets struck home, but one struck the rocks near Fancy's feet and the animal bolted toward the Union line.

Grimly holding on, Jackson managed to turn the horse, but she dashed into the woods out of control. Jackson's forehead slammed into a thick tree limb, gashing him badly and almost unseating him. Although reeling from the blow and his wounds, Jackson finally stopped the little horse and was sitting still in the saddle when, a few moments later, two members of his escort reached him.

Though each was wounded, they had regained their horses and had rushed after their leader. Dismounting, they ran up to Jackson, helped him from the saddle and placed him gently on the ground.

"Are you badly hit, sir?" asked one.

"Do not worry about me," said Jackson in a weak voice, "I will be all right. Attend to the others. See to General Canon. I fear it was he who took the worst."

"He is being cared for, General. I saw him being carried from the road. Sir, we must get you to the doctors. Here is General Hill. He will look after you while we go for a stretcher."

Hill had thrown himself from his horse when the escort was fired on and the animal had run away. Like the other men, Hill hurried after Jackson on foot. He arrived panting from exertion, knelt by Jackson and pulled him up on his lap.

"General, I am sorry to see you are wounded," said Hill. "I trust you will be all right." He looked to the two aides and told them to go for a stretcher.

"No, I think I can walk," said Jackson. "I am afraid my arm is broken, but I think that I am not too badly wounded. Return to your men, Hill, and please find Stuart. Tell him he is in charge."

"I do not wish to leave you, General," said Hill in a choked voice. "I think we are calling off the attack."

"No," said Jackson strongly, struggling to sit up. "We must press them all night. They must not be given the opportunity to reform. Go on, Hill. You fought well today. But make no mention of my being wounded."

The three men helped Jackson to his feet. Though in obvious pain, Jackson made no sound as he rose, swayed, steadied. With a last lingering look at Jackson, Hill walked back toward the Confederate command. Moments later, Hill was struck in the leg by shrapnel and had to retire from the field.

The two members of the escort were helping Jackson down the road when a small body of the Black Horse rode up. They had heard already that Jackson's party had been fired on and that Canon had been hit, but they were plainly aghast at seeing Jackson bleeding and weak.

"Here, General, take my horse," said the foremost rider. "Let me help you."

"No," said Jackson. "I believe I am able to walk but I cannot ride. Go along with us, but if anyone asks who is wounded, simply say it is a Confederate officer."

The group began to walk slowly down the road when a masked Federal battery, hearing the sound of horses on the road, raked it with canister fire. Thousands of wicked iron balls tore sparks from the flint road. Most of the men from the Black Horse were cut down.

The two men holding Jackson were forced to dive for cover and Jackson fell heavily on the hard road. This time, weak from pain and loss of blood, he could not rise. Those not killed or wounded by the cannon fire tended to the others and dragged Jackson into woods. He lay there without complaint while a stretcher was brought for him.

The two wounded men from Jackson's escort finally gave over to repeated demands from the others and relinquished the stretcher. The night had cleared a little. The moon, though pale, was no longer obscured by clouds. In its feeble light, the worried Confederates could see that Jackson was beginning to fail.

The worst wound, high on the left shoulder, had been stanched as best as possible but blood still dripped from the bandage. Jackson's lips were drawn in a thin tight line but he still made no complaint.

"General, it is too dangerous on the road," said one of the bearers. "We must proceed through the woods to safety." Jackson, eyes closed, nodded and the group set off through the tangled underbrush. They moved carefully, men in front trying to clear the way of the worst tangles and deadfalls.

But a hidden root snared the feet of the latter stretcher bearer. He fell full face forward and again Jackson hit the ground heavily. A low moan came from him, the first anyone had heard since the general was hit. Weakly, Jackson asked to be allowed to die. But he was hoisted again and, as they continued toward their lines, he slipped mercifully into a faint.

Canon was running. He knew not where, but he was running fast as he could run. A Yankee cavalryman sat on his shoulders, his legs tucked under Canon's arms, riding him. Canon tried to get his hands up to throw the damn Yankee off his back, but he could not lift his arms.

He was exhausted, but the Yankee wouldn't let him rest. Each time he tried to stop, tried to draw a deep breath, the Yankee lashed him with a riding crop and dug daggerlike spurs into his ribs.

"There is nothing to be done," the Yankee told him sadly. "Nothing."

Canon opened his eyes, then shut them against the light. Opened them again. When finally they focused, he found himself in a bright, airy bedroom. He was lying on his stomach in a big bed in a house, but what house he knew not.

Jesus! He must have overslept badly. The light from the window next to his bed told him the morning was mostly gone. Hell and damn, he had missed the general's staff meeting, and his ass would be to forfeit for it. Jackson would make him walk the column for . . .

Memory flooded in like the light from the window. Jackson! Canon was in agonizing pain but he tried to roll over, couldn't. He realized he was under restraint. Then he looked left and saw Stonewall Jackson, ten feet away, lying on his back in bed and much, much too pale.

Jackson bare chest heaved irregularly. His breathing was a coarse whistle. His shoulders were swathed with bandages and wait, something terribly wrong here, what is it? Oh, Christ. They've taken off his arm. Covered to his armpits with a comforter, Jackson's right arm lay across it. But where his left arm had been there was only an abrupt mass of bandages.

Looking at Jackson, facing Canon, stood two men. One of them Canon recognized as Fulton, General Lee's personal field doctor. Canon knew Fulton's voice. So it was the other man who must have spoken, and invaded Canon's consciousness, he thought. And the man, as if to prove it, said it again.

"There is nothing, nothing to be done."

Dr. Fulton left the room, while the other man, short and round and wrinkled with age, clasped his hands behind his back and rocked back and forth on the balls of his feet. He wore the frocked coat of a doctor. His hair was white and wispy. And he slowly, sadly shook his head as he continued to rock to and fro.

Canon had never wanted anything like he wanted a drink of water. The thought was torture. But the thought fled when he realized the little man had been talking about Jackson. What! Nothing to be done! Could not be true. Stonewall Jackson could not die. Canon tried to shout it, but the sound emerged as a low groan.

The little man heard it, though, and jerked up his head to look Canon's way. He yelled for an orderly as he approached Canon. A head poked through the open doorway. "Bring fresh drinking water," the little man said to the soldier, "the cold spring water we keep packed in sawdust." The head nodded, disappeared.

"Well, well," said the man in a pleased tone. "I am Dr. Roddey, and I am happy to say that in my opinion your crisis has passed. It seemed to me earlier that your breathing had regulated. If there is no infection, you will recover.

"I will loosen these cloths now. We had to restrain you for your own protection, General. I am afraid, sir, that you were entirely in delirium for a goodly while. Frankly, I despaired for your life."

Canon wanted to tell the man to stop his prattle and tell him about Jackson, but his throat was too dry. The little doctor continued to speak as he worked the knotted strips of cloth at Canon's feet.

"You have been unconscious almost a week. It is miraculous, really, that you have regained consciousness. Of course, one of three things had to happen: either you regained consciousness, or died outright, or you slipped into the deeper coma which means death is imminent."

He freed Canon's feet. Canon tried to work up enough moisture in his mouth to swallow.

"You were horribly wounded," the doctor said, moving to the knots at Canon's wrists. "Horribly. Much worse than General Jackson."

Here is hope, Canon told himself, finally managing to swallow. If I am recovering, surely Jackson will. He swallowed again. The constriction of his throat eased a little.

"Yes," said Roddey, "General Jackson insisted we see to you first. Didn't want me to touch him until both Fulton and I had looked at you. He was only semi-conscious himself, you see. Couldn't make him understand that amputation is my specialty.

"I tell you quite frankly that I have never seen anyone take as many bullets as you in such a vital area and not die instantly from trauma, much less recover. The bullet at your left arm was deflected by one of your sleeve buttons."

The knots at Canon's right wrist came free.

"Yes, it is remarkable," said Roddey. "I must write it up for the medical society. It will simply flabbergast . . . awk!"

Canon had grabbed the man by the throat, and he pulled him down close to his face.

"You had better save that man over there. If you don't, you're a dead man, too," said Canon in a guttural whisper.

"You know," said Roddey, in a voice that would have been normal except for the pressure Canon was exerting on his vocal chords, "it really is amazing. General Jackson said almost the same exact thing to me about you. Said he'd have me shot if I didn't save you.

"Of course, like I said, he didn't understand that I was here to work on him." Although Roddey's face was beginning to turn quite red, he did not struggle against or even protest Canon's grip on his neck. "You'd be surprised," Roddey continued, "how often I hear such threats. 'Save my friend over there or I'll kill you.' It is like you and Jackson."

The little doctor lifted his hand to his throat and with one finger gently tapped, tapped, tapped the back of Canon's hand. Canon released him. Roddey coughed and gasped for a few seconds, then resumed his narrative as if nothing untoward had occurred.

Most of the men who threatened his life, he said, did so on behalf of kin or friend. Rarely did a wounded man threaten that his friends or kin would exact revenge if the doctor allowed him to die.

"No," continued Roddey. "It is usually as with you and General Jackson. It is always to save a friend." Canon, who exactly intended to kill the doctor if Jackson died, even knowing the intent was irrational, still glared at the doctor.

"Don't look at me like that, General. I know you mean what you say. I know that you fully intend at this moment to kill me if Stonewall Jackson dies." He pulled up a chair, sat.

"All of them mean it. But no one has ever tried. And I wish you would kill me, actually. Not that I want General Jackson to die. I want me to die. Bother that orderly, where is the water? No. I wish someone who has threatened what you and Jackson have threatened would go ahead and kill me.

"God knows I've lost enough of the ones I have been threatened over. And Jackson is dying, so you will have your chance to kill me, although I can say that in this case I made no mistake.

"But I have killed scores through my own fault and ineptitude . . . well, that and lack of proper medicines like morphiae, but I have killed men I should have saved.

"I told you I am a specialist at amputation? I was not, before the war. Nobody was. But I have probably removed ten thousand arms and five thousand legs in the past couple of years.

"It is a delicate thing, though with proper tools, medication and time it is not in itself all that dangerous.

"But amputation on the battlefield is horrible. There is no morphia to speak of, and the wounded are brought in sometimes hours after they suffered the crippling wound. And we run them through the process as cows are processed into the slaughterhouse.

"Since I have no medicine, and only a few scalpels, timing becomes crucial. The wounded soldier is flopped up on the table and I must quickly remove the limb or limbs. If I cut too fast, the body cannot stand the shock and succumbs. If I cut too slowly, the body cannot stand the pain, and succumbs.

"Even though I have someone behind me constantly whetting instruments as they dull, sometimes he simply cannot keep up, and then I have to gauge the relative dullness of the blade as another factor in the timing.

"Do you know that to save time during the peak hours of emergency I frequently clamp the bloody blade between my teeth so that I can't lose time setting it down and picking it up. Plah! I abhor the taste of blood.

"And another thing. I have told the orderlies and told them to keep legs in one pile and arms in another. Some sense of symmetry must be preserved. At first I demanded the lefts and rights of each limb be placed in separate piles, but that was hopeless. But the idiot orderlies have gotten so remiss as to mix arms and legs in the same . . . ah, here is the water.

"Wait, now, don't gulp it so. An embolism brought on by a fit of coughing would likely kill you after all, and would certainly reopen your wounds. And then you couldn't kill me, and I need you to kill me."

The water restored for the most part Canon's voice. "He can't be dying," Canon gasped out.

"My dear sir, he is so close to dead that I am scarce sure he is here now. Mrs. Jackson has been here. They talked before he went into delirium and finally coma. He has been in the coma for almost a day. And he won't come out of it. He won't last the night."

The words sent corkscrews through Canon.

"I thought he could be saved," said the doctor, staring into space. "The arm, of course, had to be removed. The wounds to his lower left arm and to the right hand were minor, but the bullet to the shoulder had already dangled his left arm.

"General Lee sent a most noble message to him: 'You have lost your left arm, but I have lost my right.' Jackson came through the operation very well. His stump is mending. It is pneumonia, probably developed as he lay on the ground, that is killing Stonewall Jackson.

"I think, strong as is a stone wall, this one had to bear too great a weight for too long a time." He paused. "Everything medically possible was done for him." Again a pause. "I revere him, you know. As does General Lee. As does everyone.

"Nothing was left undone that could be done. So I don't really deserve to die for General Jackson. But I deserve it for plenty of others.

"I want to die, General Canon, but I cannot allow myself the luxury of suicide. I am too needed. It would be desertion. But as soon as this horrible war is over, I will kill myself, I promise you, if someone doesn't do it for me first. The thought of death is all that holds me together."

The little man rose to leave the room. At the doorway, he stopped and looked back at Canon. "I have really gone quite mad, you know," he said with a sad little smile, and he left.

The orderly returned with a stone jug full of cold water and poured cup after cup full for Canon. It was the most delightful thing Canon had tasted in his life.

"General?" said the boy, who could not have been more than fourteen. Canon continued to drain the cup but cut his eyes questioningly toward the youth.

"Sir, I know you lead the Black Horse and that you and General Jackson ain't a'feared of nothing. But why was you yelling during your sleep for some professor to keep away from rivers and trees? We had to tie ye down, General."

Why, indeed? Canon searched his mind for memories of the night. The details were clearer now. The hallucinations had been horrible. And what in hell could his wild babble about rivers and trees have meant? The thought still set a sense of foreboding in his mind.

Now, of course, he realized the significance of the picket fence delusion that had so filled him with terror. Canon almost wept from frustration. What good, he thought, is second sight if it gives no more warning than an obscure hint?

Mountain Eagle's wisdom be damned. And double God damn those raw recruit pickets. He looked over at the ruined Jackson and tears welled in his eyes.

Now, floating unbidden through the thin filaments of memory, came one more remembrance. The hellish, guttural voice that chuckled, "Right in the notch." Canon could not be sure it was a real voice; he had no idea what it meant.

He slept, but the Yankee cavalryman was on his back again, riding him, whipping him, making him chase a running Jackson down a tree lined road toward a river. Each time Canon faltered, he was whipped and spurred. "Right in the notch," said the Yankee in a gleeful whisper. "Right in the notch." And Jackson would spin, blood spurting from his coat sleeve.

When next Canon awoke, a late afternoon light was filtering into the room. Dr. Fulton was standing by his bed. The doctor had been watching Canon stir and begin to waken. "It is almost over, General," he said, going back to Jackson.

None saw Canon tense his blasted body, testing it against pain, then swing his feet to the floor. He bore the agony of rising without a sound. Nor did they see him sway and grimace as his wounds reopened. Canon had decided he would see Jackson alive one more time—at all costs, as Jackson was wont to say.

He walked unsteadily toward Jackson with as much decorum as he could muster. Fulton gasped when he turned to the sound of shuffling feet and saw Canon walking toward him. The doctor moved quickly toward him to return him to bed when a sudden sound riveted them all.

Jackson had taken a deep ragged breath, much deeper than his breathing had been during the coma. His eyes opened, and the pale blue light gleamed in a shaft of afternoon sunbeam.

In a clear, nearly normal voice, Jackson said, "Let us cross over the river and rest in the shade of those trees."

And then, shortly after three P.M., May 10, 1863, Stonewall Jackson crossed the river.

Doctors Fulton and Roddey led Canon back to his bed.

Less than six weeks after the death of Stonewall Jackson, the South lost the war at the Battle of Gettysburg.

# PART II

## 14

# *Pale Blue Light*

Bad news flew through the South like doomed ravens. The appalling defeat at Gettysburg on July 3, 1863 decimated Lee's army. Though almost half of Gettysburg's fifty-one thousand casualties were Union, the Union could afford to lose men. Not the Confederacy. Lee lost a third of his army, men he could not replace.

He sent his troops out to offer battle on the morning of July 4, giving the Union troops a chance to attack. But Union General George Meade had crushed the Confederate invasion and knew it. Southern hopes lay blasted with the thousands of dead at Devil's Den, Little Round Top, the Peach Orchard and Cemetery Ridge.

Gettysburg had been a battle of bad ground and bad tactics for Lee. The Southerners had repeatedly attacked entrenched Union forces, crossing long stretches of open ground only to face huge concentrations of cannon and rifle fire.

Lee said afterward he would have not have made such mistakes had his tactical genius, Stonewall Jackson, been with him at Gettysburg. But Stonewall was dead. Lee turned his troops South, never to threaten the North seriously again.

July is rarely a happy month in the South. Too hot. Too dusty and dry. But the South never suffered a July like that of 1863. On July 4, Union General U. S. Grant accepted the surrender of the huge Rebel fort at Vicksburg, Mississippi and took thirty thousand Rebels prisoner. The chill North wind which sprang up that hot summer was one which nothing could stop. When the spring offensives began in 1864, all the fighting was done on Southern soil.

IN RICHMOND, AT CHIMBARANZO HOSPITAL, Rabe Canon's body healed slowly. His mind healed not at all. He became the scourge of the nurses, charming them out of their fleecy pantaloons one night, scaring them out of their wits the next.

"How can a man be so soft one minute and so hard the next?" one old matron remarked to a young nurse. Canon grinned wickedly and the nurse blushed, putting her hand to her mouth to stifle a giggle. "I meant soft and hard-hearted, you little fool," scolded the matron. She trod heavily from the room.

Difficult as Canon was for the nurses, sleep was even more difficult for Canon. It would soon be a year since Jackson died at Chancellorsville, but he died for Canon every night at Richmond. Even the briefest nap brought on the dream, the nightmare of that fight. Canon fought the dreams, fought sleep until doctors drugged him into unconsciousness. Still, as the long days and interminable nights passed, he began to heal almost against his will.

Buck and Mountain Eagle came to visit at first. They were all right at Mulberry. Food was short, there was little money and it was worth little. But Alabama had escaped serious Yankee raids so far.

The two men had spent nearly every dollar they owned to see that Canon had decent food. They stopped trying to raise his spirits and could hardly bear to see how hollow of eye and cheek he was, how gaunt and wasted. Finally, they told him they were returning to Mulberry.

Canon wished they could be as comfortable as he was. He had the best room in the hospital, one of the few ones. When he finally regained his feet, six months after being wounded, he saw as he tottered around how crowded the hospital was, how critical the food shortage. Only then did he realize what lavish care he had been receiving. He ordered that more patients be put in his room and that they were to share his food.

He learned that doctors would allow no patients in danger of dying in the room for fear of what the trauma would do to Canon. And the other patients refused to stay in a room haunted by such awful screams in the night.

Over and over, more clearly than he could remember the actual night, the dream replayed the scene. How he rode Hammer up next to Jackson and threw himself in front of his general. Again and again he heard the brutal wet smack of the bullets pounding into them. He saw the red flower bloom on Jackson's sleeve. He heard the voice say, "Right in the notch, right in the notch." Sometimes the voice had a sibilant and sinister sound, a snake's hiss. Sometimes it was a maniacal chuckling laugh. Always he awoke howling like a wounded wolf. Canon dreaded the month of May and the anniversary of Jackson's death worse than anything he had known.

Carolina saved Canon's sanity. She breezed into his room on May 2, a year to the day Stonewall Jackson was shot. She stepped into Canon's hell.

Incredibly, the dreams had worsened. They had become so real that Canon awoke in surprise, amidst his screams, to find that he was not covered with blood. For the past week he had vowed each night that he would not sleep. He refused to get in bed. Instead he sat in a straight backed cane chair, preferring the pain that helped him stay awake. When he felt himself nodding, he would rise and feebly rage around the room, fighting sleep. Fighting the dream.

But sleep would gradually take him, and the nightmare would claim him. And sweep him swiftly back to Chancellorsville.

He practically pleaded with the doctors to drug him into dreamless sleep, and was thoroughly ashamed when a couple of times they agreed. Morphia was precious in Richmond.

The day of May 2 was a perfect accompaniment to Canon's worst dreams. Morning rain from a low darkling sky pelted in silver sheets against the window, beat like a demented drummer on the roof. A wild wind rang ragged songs in eaves and gutters. The storm peaked in late afternoon, sizzling its chain lightning down through the blueblack clouds. Then it melted at sundown into a stillness more ominous than the jagged bolts.

Sitting in his nightshirt and robe at the window, watching the last of what had looked like Satan's artillery show, Canon went to sleep. He awoke in a dream, or a dreamworld. Because Canon knew he was dreaming, and he could not awaken.

It was dreamlike, but it was more as if he had been transported into some weird different world, so real did it seem. He felt the chill of the chamber, for in a chamber he was, and one he knew well. He stood in the huge chamber of the capitol in Richmond, not a half-mile from the hospital.

In front of him, a hundred feet away in the middle of the room, lay Stonewall Jackson in his funeral bier.

The dim chamber was empty except for it, and ice cold. Canon was cold. And scared. He could feel himself drawing in the deep ragged breaths of fear. At this temperature, his breathing should have produced plumes, but it was not so.

He tried to turn his head, could not. He tried to look away from the coffin but was unable. Tried to turn, could not move. Nor could he lift his arms. He tried to step back, and stepped forward. Tried to stop, and took another step. Slowly, with the measured tread of a military pall bearer, Canon walked against his will toward the corpse. He felt his own silent gait.

It was as if his consciousness was trapped inside his body, and his body had become a machine controlled by some outside agency. He tried to slow his steps, then tried to speed them. Canon tried to shout but his lips were locked. He could not make a sound. If he could only make some little change of his own accord, perhaps he could gain enough control to waken, or at least flee. But he was half-way to Jackson, now, and it was real.

Jackson was in a full dress uniform and lay in a framework of—what? There was nothing. Nothing but darkness around him, under him. Worse than darkness. An absence of light that was somehow solid and slightly shifting supported the body.

Canon shut his eyes. They popped open. Great God in heaven, he thought, as he realized with miserable fear that he could not even close his eyes. Resisting with all his will, Canon drew closer to the body of Stonewall Jackson.

His tread was stately and slow. The dead march. Twenty feet away, fifteen, twelve—Oh God. Something terrible, something beyond all beyond was going to happen. No! Goddammit, no!

Canon was enveloped, trapped, caressed by the softest sweetest cloud of lilacs. It was bliss. He opened his eyes.

"General, do you always give your nurses such a fright their first night on duty?" said a lilting voice out of the cloud of lilacs. Canon slowly realized he was in his room at the hospital, on the bed, and that a remarkably golden woman was bathing his brow.

Canon smiled at her, and slept a gentle sleep.

He asked for her when he awoke, but she was gone. He sent for her. She came in at four P.M., all briskness and beauty, carrying a nosegay of posies she placed on the bedside table.

"What happened to the lilacs, lovey?" Canon asked her.

"Oh, that's my scent," she said, and colored prettily when Canon grinned at the remark. She was big for a Southern girl, and the loose hospital gown could not conceal what Canon decided must be a truly astounding figure. She was small of waist, though it appeared she did not wear the cursed corset most belles used to pinch their middles. Well shaped ankles. Her hair was pulled back in a severe bun and capped, but Canon could see it was long and the color of dark honey.

Her skin was the milk shade most women would kill for. A little mole, a little dimple, maybe a little too luscious, but exactly what Canon needed at the moment. Milk and honey, and lily skin that smelled of lilacs.

Carolina Lee. No, no relation to Marse Robert, more's the pity. We are the poor Lees, Nashville, she said as she bustled about the room, obviously nervous, straightening this and pulling that and then doing it all over again. She prattled as she dusted and cleaned, but Canon sensed she was not the vacuous pretty young thing that so many Southern belles turned out to be.

She wore no ring, but she was several years past her coming out ball, he thought, if she'd had one. She stirred Canon like he had not been stirred for a while, and he looked forward to knowing her much, much better.

For some reason, as they began to talk, Canon found himself wanting to tell her about the nightmares. That he was having nightmares was no secret, all on the floor dreaded Canon's screams in the night, but he refused to share details with the doctors. He told Buck and Mountain Eagle a little about the first recurring dream, that it concerned the death of Jackson, and they had evidently told the doctors, but only he knew the details.

Buck and Mountain Eagle had taken turns sitting up with Canon, ready to rouse him awake when he started to dream. But it had not worked. In dreamtime, the nightmare lasted long minutes. In hospital reality, they were only a few seconds in duration.

Now he wished the Eagle were here. Canon knew he could not live with this new horror. If it began to be a nightly ordeal . . . the thought struck Canon that he was contemplating suicide. He fell silent, and after a while, so did Carolina Lee.

She sat with him that night through the horror of the new nightmare. The intensity of the dream boggled Canon. It was like the first night, but so real that Canon, knowing it was a nightmare even as he lived it, feared he would not awaken from it. The second night and the third Canon drew one step closer to the body of Stonewall Jackson.

Carolina begged him to tell her about it, as did the doctors. They all thought it was the same dream that had been troubling him but he refused to speak of it.

He wished to God it could be the first dream. He would gladly take it in exchange. He would take anything. His nightmare of Chancellorsville had so little in common with the intensity of this madness as to be almost laughable.

On May 7, three days before the anniversary of Jackson's death, Canon sat outside on the hospital grounds with Carolina. As a diversion from his own tormented thoughts, Canon tried to draw her out about her life in Nashville. They talked for three hours.

The city had fallen early in the war, had been in Federal hands for more than two years, though noncombatants there were fairly free to come and go. Something pretty bad must have happened to her in Nashville, Canon decided, that she was either ashamed or afraid to tell him.

Delicately as he could, he tried to probe the subject, but she kept changing ground. Finally, irritated, she flounced away. For the first time in months, Canon found himself interested in problems other than his own. It felt good.

But that night, someone else waited with Stonewall Jackson for Canon to appear in the ghostly capitol chamber of his nightmare.

It began as usual, with Canon fighting sleep until his weak body had to have it. Shortly past two A.M., holding Carrie's hand, Canon slept. And he was transported to the chamber at Richmond.

Canon barely had been conscious when Jackson's real funeral took place. The Confederacy allowed Stonewall to lie in state in the capitol chamber for two days while the Rebel nation mourned, then moved him to Lexington for burial.

Canon read of the details, had talked with some who attended the wake and funeral. Being in attendance could have been no more real for the mourners than the reality Canon felt in his nightmare. He could feel his neck muscles strain when he tried to turn his head as he walked toward Jackson. He could move his eyes but could not close them.

This night, as he neared within ten feet of the body, Canon shifted his sight when he thought he detected movement at the corner of his vision.

Shock and horror slammed through Canon with such ferocity that he reeled, even in the dream. Jeb Stuart walked into Canon's field of vision, marching with the same stately tread which Canon paced. Stuart, with a huge bloody bullet hole in his stomach, his uniform torn away there by the ripping lead.

Canon tried to call out his friend's name. He strained to speak but he could no more say a word than he could turn from the sight. Stuart finally stopped opposite Canon, with Jackson between them. Stuart's face held no more expression than a photograph. Canon fleetingly wondered whether at this moment Stuart might be having the same dream he was having. He wondered whether the real Stuart was aware of the dream, and whether he felt the maddening frustration, bewilderment and fear Canon was feeling.

For long moments, Canon and Stuart seemed to stare at each other. Then Stuart spoke in a sepulchral tone. "We are dead, Rabe. We are all of us dead." Then Stuart began to step backward at the same measured pace with which he had entered until, like an evening shadow becomes darkness as night continues to fall, he was gone.

Canon looked down at Jackson, from ten feet away, and once again Chirambaranzo Hospital awoke to screams in the night.

When Canon opened his eyes, Carrie gasped and impulsively threw her arms around his neck.

"Rabe, honey," she said, "I've been shaking you and bathing your face with water and calling you. I was afraid I wasn't going to be able to wake you up." With a sigh of relief, she buried her head in the crook of his throat.

But this time Canon paid no mind to the soft skin and the smell of lilacs. He was still so frightened that his body was paralyzed with fear. And Carolina Lee, in her relief that Canon was awake, had said the worst possible thing she could have said. She was afraid she could not wake Canon up.

The only thing that kept Canon from screaming now was that he was absolutely petrified. He was literally too scared to scream. Oh, Jesus and Mary and Joseph. He couldn't take this. No human could take it. What if he got trapped in that dream and had to stay there for the rest of his life? Forever. For ever. He could not tolerate the thought.

If he did nothing else this day, he would send word to Stuart to be careful.

Stuart coming in was bad beyond telling. It had been awful. But it was not the worst. That was the real horror of it. Each time Canon thought it could get no worse, something happened in the dream to make him realize it could get infinitely worse. Like tonight.

Stuart's bullet-shattered appearance was bad, but it was not the worst.

It had not been much, but Canon was sure of it. Positive. Certain. Beyond doubt. Beyond reason. Beyond sanity. It had not been much, but right before Canon awoke, Jackson's head had turned toward him. Just a little bit.

HE LAY IN THE CLOUDLESS AFTERNOON SUN, on a quilt thrown on a freshly cut lawn. The temperature was perfect. Dogwood trees had gone to full bloom almost overnight. Daffodils and lilies had leaped from the earth. Honeybees droned, drew nectar from wild honeysuckle.

And the magnolias. God, the magnolias were blossoming, their rich floral smell permeated the breeze. When the playful wind shifted, Canon caught the fruity fragrance of Grancy's Greybeard, the most wonderful tree in Southern woods.

It is a delicate tree, never growing taller than a pine sapling. Its bloom resembles a gray beard, hundreds of tiny blossoms depending like a cluster of grapes from its thin branches. Canon could almost taste the aroma.

This was the kind of day Southerners lived for. And died for.

Canon reached for the last of the cheese sandwiches Carrie had prepared, then changed his mind. Rather, he had finally made up his mind.
They were in the most remote section of the hospital grounds, on a little
hill overlooking Richmond.

"Carolina, I think you are a brave and wonderful girl. You know that,
don't you?" Canon said.

"I hope you do, Rabe."

"If you weren't, I couldn't ask you what I'm about to ask you. So you'll
have to promise that you will never say one word to anyone about this."

He could tell Carolina did not like the tone of this. She was sitting next
to the picnic basket, but close enough to Canon to fan him every now and
then with her flimsy little fan.

"Why are you so serious, Rabe? What is it?" she said.

"The nightmares."

"Yes?"

"They're so bad that I can't speak of them. Not even to you. But the
dreams themselves don't scare me nearly so badly as something else I have
been thinking."

"Rabe, you're frightening me. Just say what it is you want."

"I'm afraid I'll go mad, lovey, if it gets any worse. I'm afraid the dream
will take me, and lock me in, and for the rest of my days I'll be locked in
a place that is worse to me than anything I can imagine. No way out. The
thought is beginning to be more than I can stand."

"What do you want me to do?" Carrie said, in a small voice.

"If I reach the point where I can't wake up, Carrie, I want you to promise
me that you'll kill me."

"Rabe. Don't say that, please."

"Believe me, lovey. Death would be candy compared to what I fear."

"Tell me the dream."

"Telling the dream is nothing. Living the dream is impossible."

"Tell me or I won't promise."

Canon looked at her for a moment. She was truly lovely. The set of her
jaw convinced Canon she meant what she said. With a sigh, part resignation
and part relief, he told her about the nightmare.

He did not tell her of the first dream of Chancellorsville, he did not tell her about Jeb Stuart, from whom he was awaiting a reply to the telegram he had sent this morning. He told her of approaching Jackson's coffin. He did not tell her that Jackson, in death, had moved.

When he finished, Carrie stared at the ground for a while, occasionally reaching over to run her fingers through Canon's hair. She wouldn't look at him, didn't speak. When finally she did look toward him, he saw tears streaming down her cheeks.

"Oh, Rabe, that is truly terrible."

"So you will do it?"

"But how?"

"You won't get in trouble. The doctors are afraid I've gotten too weak for my heart to stand the strain I've been under. Here." From the pocket of his robe, Canon took a small vial filled with white powder. "I took it from the dispensary. Just pour it in some coffee or some water and get it down me. You won't be suspected."

She stood, paced a bit, came back and sat.

"Very well, Rabe. I'll do it," she said.

"Good girl."

"On one condition."

"What condition?"

"Rabe, you've been fighting this dream for a month."

"Yes."

"Stop fighting it. Go with it. See what happens."

It was something Canon had not considered, and it was his turn to pace. He did so a long time. When he returned, he sat and took her hand.

"And if I go mad, lovey?"

"I'll kill you."

Canon hesitated but a moment.

"All right," he said.

When they returned to his room, a doctor was waiting for him. If ever bad news was written on a face, Canon thought, I am looking at it now. Canon sat on the bed, stared at the doctor until the man cleared his throat a couple of times and spoke.

"General," he said, "before I pass along this request I must tell you that all the doctors feel you should refuse it. We fear a shock right now might totally undo you."

And Canon knew.

"It is Stuart."

The doctor looked at Canon strangely, then slowly nodded. "I don't know how you knew, but General Stuart intercepted a Yankee raid a few miles outside of Richmond this morning. The raid was repulsed, but General Stuart sustained a terrible wound. He's dying, but he wants to see you."

"Where is he?"

"Just down the hall. General, you really should not see him."

Canon was already going out the door.

The doctor caught him, insisting that if Canon had to see Stuart, then he was going to stay right by Canon in case he collapsed. Canon was in too much a hurry to argue. He pushed the doctor in front and followed him to see Jeb Stuart.

Canon's friend and comrade-in-arms was lying on bloodstained linen on a narrow surgical bed. His stomach was swathed in bandages. Stuart's face had already taken on the sickly gray pallor of encroaching death, but he looked over at Canon with eyes bright as ever. He smiled and with a great effort held out his hand, which Canon clasped.

"Thank you for trying, Rabe," he said in a slurred whisper. Thank God they've given him morphia, Canon thought. He knew exactly how terrible was the nature of Stuart's wound. "I considered it," continued Stuart. "I paid it heed, as you asked. 'Stuart, I dreamed of your death last night. Please take heed.'"

"I have seen too many strange things in this godforsaken war to discount premonitions, Rabe." Stuart began to cough blood. The doctor hurried over to wipe it from his mouth.

"Stuart, I am dreadfully sorry," Canon said.

Gradually, Stuart recovered himself. "No, do not grieve," he said. "It is all right for me to die now. The South is dying, Rabe, and I would not want to be alive at the end of this war. It is that thought that made me ride on out this morning. I decided that if it was time, I would not shirk it or shrink from it. I put your warning out of my mind. It was not until the bullet struck me that I remembered your telegram.

"I think I will sleep now. If it happens that I do not see you again, I want you to know that I thank you for the warning and for your friendship to me. Remember me, Rabe, and remember that we must fight on."

Canon started to reply, but the little cavalier was unconscious. Canon hurried back to his room.

"Carrie, give me the powder," he said, reaching for a glass of water.

But she backed away, shaking her head. He followed her, desperate now to die. "Give it to me, Carrie, or so help me I'll take it from you."

"Rabe, please listen to me. You did your best for Stuart."

"He said in the dream that I am to die, too. He said, 'We are all dead.' Why live through torture just to get killed in battle? Give me the powder, Carrie."

Desperate now herself, Carrie kept backing away. "Listen, Rabe. He just now said the South is dying. Maybe that's what he meant in the dream. Rabe, I've got a feeling about your dream. Maybe it's a good dream and fighting it is what is so bad. The dream let you warn Stuart. It was his choice.

"It might be a dream that will do some good if you let it, Rabe. For God's sake, at least try it."

"For pity's sake, give me the powder, Carrie."

"I will not pity you and I think you are forty times a fool and a coward for pitying yourself. For your sake and mine, I'll not give you the powder. You'll have to rip it out of my dress to get it."

A dark flush of anger and embarrassment reddened Canon's face at the word "pity." Carrie continued to stare at him. He moved back to the bed, stretched out on it.

"Remember your promise to me, Carrie," he said.

"With all my heart."

Canon closed his eyes and thought of Stuart down the hall, dying a hero's death. In minutes, perhaps seconds, he was asleep.

Watching him, Carrie saw to her surprise Canon beginning to smile. As she watched Canon's lips pull back into a grin, she sighed with relief.

What Carrie took for a grin was a grimace. It was not a smile she saw, but the rictus of pure terror.

Canon was inside Stonewall Jackson's tomb, and no longer cold. The air was fetid, and it shimmered with heat, casting its own eerie light. God, this was beyond bearing! Panic coursed through Canon as he struggled to wake up, strained not to look at the closed coffin resting on its stone pedestal ten feet away.

Then he remembered his promise to Carrie. Tentatively, Canon tried on his own accord to take a small step forward. He took the step, and as he did so the coffin creaked open a few inches. Involuntarily, he tried to step back, could not.

He stepped forward, again on his own, and the coffin rose a few more inches. Enough, thought Canon. More than enough. Too much. He had to get this over with. If it be madness, he said to himself, then let madness come. He walked toward the coffin, which opened wider at each step.

Eight feet away, five . . . now he could see the chiseled profile of Jackson in the faint light . . . and he stepped up to the coffin as the lid raised wide open. I'll fight it no longer, thought Canon, and then he yelled it. "I will fight it no longer." He looked down on the dead face of Stonewall Jackson.

A hot wind sprang up, swirling inside the tomb, dust flew and cobwebs were ripped from the corners. Howls and shrieks echoed, running through Canon like the bayonets of which Jackson was so proud. Canon screamed but made no sound.

God in heaven! Jackson's face. Moving. Features writhing as if in great pain. Jesus! Now Canon could see the empty left sleeve. The wind quit suddenly as it had sprung. Howls and shrieks were replaced by the total absence of sound. Canon looked at Jackson's face, and now the thin blood-less lips were moving.

"Murder," Jackson whispered, in a low moan, and suddenly a bright gout of blood geysered up from the empty left cuff where the first bullet had hit him.

"Murder," groaned Jackson, louder, and the red flower bloomed at his elbow.

The lidded eyes suddenly snapped open, and Canon would have gladly died if he could have. There were no eyes. Only a flooding of pale blue light emanated from the empty sockets. And bright arterial blood splashed, gushed from high on the empty sleeve at the shoulder patch where the bullet struck that took Jackson's arm and life.

"I WAS MURDERED!" Stonewall Jackson screamed.

CANON AWOKE TO THIN DAYLIGHT. The room was gray as Jackson's greatcoat. Doctors surrounded Canon, staring down at him, smiling nervously. Carolina sat beside him, wringing a damp cloth in her hands.

Canon felt weak, yet almost unbearably light, as if he could float. What a terrible, wonderful, joyful feeling he was experiencing. All in the room seemed to be waiting for someone to break the silence.

"All of you, just to bring one little bedpan?" Canon said.

"General, you just loosed a scream that would make a Rebel yell sound like a whisper. Probably half the Yankees in America need a bedpan right now. Have another nightmare?"

"No thanks," said Canon. "Just had one."

The doctor shrugged off the pun. "Did you have a nightmare, General?" he insisted.

"Yes. It was horrible."

"Will you tell us about it?"

"Well," said Canon, "I dreamed I ate my feather pillow."

"Really! How extraordinary. Tell me about it, please."

"Not much to tell. Made me feel a little down in the mouth."

When the doctors had gone, Carolina leaned over to him. "What happened, Rabe, honey?" she said.

He looked at her, gratitude mingled with the Jacksonian penchant for secrecy. "I expect I will tell you all about soon," he said, "but first I must think it through. But I can tell you this: I'm well now, lovey, and it is much, if not all, thanks to you.

"I have work to do. Carolina, find me a house in town, close to where you live. It is time I moved out of here, but I don't think I can get along yet without my nurse." Canon pulled her to him and kissed her slowly and deeply. When he released her, she stepped back and saluted.

"Yes, sir, General. One house near mine. My pleasure, sir," she said.

"Our pleasure, darling, soon as possible. And have them bring me breakfast, as much as they can get on the plate, no, on two plates. I'm famished."

He saw a cup of coffee on the bedtable and reached for it.

"I don't think I would drink that particular cup of coffee if I were you, General," Carolina said.

Canon looked at the cup, then at Carolina, and sat the coffee back down quickly.

Next day, as Canon was packing his few items preparatory to leaving the hospital, he learned Jeb Stuart had died.

I will remember you, my friend, Canon said to himself, and your last words to me. I will fight on. You may rest assured of that, and may you rest well.


# 15

# *Nothing Could Be Finah*


Rabe Canon looked to his left at Carolina Lee, asleep on the pillow next to his own. Her long butterscotch hair was tousled after the night's lovemaking. The first wisps of Monday morning light licked at it through the windows of the comfortable little two-bedroom house she found for him near her own next to the Confederate garrison.

The oversized bed, on which even Canon could stretch, was the most comfortable he could remember. But he was not comfortable. He realized he could care a lot for this woman, but he wondered about her and worried.

Canon had enjoyed many women. Here was one he could not fathom. She came willingly enough to his bed left the hospital three weeks ago, and seemed to enjoy their lovemaking. He had never seen a body so lush as hers. But she was shy about her nakedness, would only make love in the dark.

She was passionate. Her climaxes weren't pretend. But she never really let go the way she seemed capable of doing. At a point when he thought she could have become truly abandoned, as Canon thought lovemaking should be, she would smother her passion. Canon tried everything to draw her out, but affair was cooling. It was more and more difficult to get her to bed.

Canon wondered what made her as she was. She still would not speak of it, and Canon stopped pressing. He was happy to have her with him, but if he knew more about her past, he felt sure he would know why she held herself back.

He watched her now, as the sun rose. She lay on her back, her full breasts pushing up the thin sheet. Carefully, Canon eased the sheet down her body. How magnificent were those breasts! Gently scratching and tickling her nipples, he watched the pink-red points jut out like twin telescopes from pouty crowns until they became bullet shaped spikes.

Her breathing, regular in sleep, deepened until it became ragged and she moaned softly. Her eyelids fluttered and she was awake. She closed her eyes again as Canon leaned over and captured with his mouth the nipple nearest him, still gently fondling the other.

"Rabe, honey, don't do that, please," she said softly. "I can't stand it when you do both of them, and I've got to get ready to go to the hospital." The damned hospital again. In their time together, the only disagreement they had was her insistence on continuing to put in such long hours at the hospital. The place depressed her, and there were plenty of volunteers, but she would not listen. Finally, feeling rotten for trying to take her away from what she obviously considered her duty, Canon desisted.

He understood duty. He was ready to return to it. He owed duty to Stonewall Jackson. The dreams had not returned. No need to. The message, so obvious, had come through immediately when he had let it. It was another thing he could thank Carolina Lee for giving him.

Carrie gently pulled Canon's hair, raising his lips from her glistening nipple, and kissed him deeply but gently. Canon probed her mouth with his tongue and for a moment she clung desperately to him, molding her moving body against his own. But she pushed him away, and with deliberation removed his hand from her breast.

Canon laughed at her. "All right, lovey," he said, "go ahead. I have an appointment this morning, too."

"Really, General? And who is the lucky girl that is to take my place."

Canon became grim. "No girl, lovey. General Lee," he said.

"Lee? He is back?"

"He will be in Richmond today, and I have been waiting to see him for three weeks. I am to have lunch with him and President Davis."

"Rabe, you've not said one word to me about this. Honey, you're not planning to go back in the field, are you? You aren't strong enough yet."

Canon knew he was strong enough. In three weeks, his body had improved more than in the previous year. Once his mind had cleared, his body responded. He was still thin, but he had been riding and running while Carrie was at work. Ropes of muscles returned. Canon felt he had regained at least ninety percent of his former strength.

He wanted his strength, now, needed it. He had a job to do. Since he got out of the hospital, Canon had been checking into the details of Jackson's death. It had not taken him long to get information enough to be sure that Jackson been assassinated. He hounded headquarters for an appointment with Lee. He probably could have taken the information to President Davis at any time, but he wanted Lee there, too.

Lee, however, was trying to hold off the bulldog of the Union Army, Ulysses Grant. Earlier in the month, on the fifth and sixth of May, and again last week, Lee had fought furious battles against Grant in the wilderness and at the Spotsylvania courthouse. The battles had been bloody draws. Lee could not force Grant from Virginia, but neither could the Union advance.

Finally, last Friday, he learned Lee would be in Richmond today and secured a luncheon appointment with Lee and Davis.

"Rabe, honey, please tell me you won't go back into the field just yet," said Carolina. When Canon did not answer she became miffed and, gathering the sheet about her, padded softly into the bathroom to wash and dress.

Canon dreaded telling his suspicions to Lee and Davis, but he was in a hurry to lift the burden from his mind, and he had a special request to make of the men. Canon rolled out of bed and took the big package from Mulberry from under it. He knew what was in it the day it arrived. The note with it said, "Glad you are better. Wear this when the time comes."

Out of the huge box Canon took a pair of new cavalry boots and a tailored

Confederate general's uniform, noting the dual Stonewall and Black Horse shoulder patches with pangs of grief and yearning for revenge.

When Carrie walked back into the room, all lilacs and white lace, she saw the uniform. Her face went white and she sat down heavily on the edge of the bed.

"So you're going back out."

"I have to, lovey. I'm going after the men who murdered Jackson." Carrie gasped at the word, putting her hand to her throat.

"Murdered?" she said. "But, Rabe, it was his own men who shot him accidentally. Everybody knows that."

Canon inwardly cursed himself for the slip. The knowledge of the assassination had been on his mind so much, and the fact that he was finally going to speak of it today, brought it out of him. Well, it was out, and perhaps if he demonstrated his trust to Carrie, it might cause her to trust him more, too.

He sat down on the bed next to her, took the hand she still held to her throat.

"Carrie, you must promise that you will tell no one else what I am about to tell you."

"Promise."

"All right. I had another dream, another recurring dream before the one about Jackson in his coffin. I dreamed over and over about how I was wounded that night with Jackson."

"Yes."

"No one knows it, but I realized what was about to happen that night, and I jumped in front of Jackson as the pickets opened fire."

"Rabe, what a brave and noble thing."

"It was instinct, Carrie, but that is not the point. The point is that I was in front of Jackson when the bullets were fired. All the bullets that hit me were aimed for him. That entire first volley was for Jackson. He was assassinated."

She pondered the information for a moment, then, "Rabe, you can't be sure. It was dark. He was in front of you."

"No. I was even with him when they fired. I was moving faster, I was a bigger target. And it was light enough for the pickets to place their bullets where they wanted them to go."

"But, Rabe, there was an inquest. All the pickets were, uh, were . . . what's the word?"

"Exonerated. Yes, damn it, they were. Because I was too stupid to realize what had happened. And it is true that men on both sides have been accidentally shot by their pickets.

"But that's what made it so perfect for them. It appeared to be a horrible accident, unusual but not rare. The Confederacy and the board of inquiry were still in shock over Jackson's death. They just wanted the thing over and done with. I looked up the newspapers. The inquest was light as feathers.

"I also checked the rolls for information on what happened to the eight men who fired the first shots. After they fired that night, of course, many others fired. But those eight who stood at the inquest are the ones I want."

"What of them?"

"All eight have been reported killed in battle or missing in action."

"Thank God for that."

"No. It will not wash. I have seen too many shirkers and deserters use the trick. Three or four of them will simply fall down on the battlefield as if shot and later slip away in the night. Their friends volunteer for burial detail and simply report them dead.

"And the other bastards probably just allowed themselves to be captured. But if Lee and Davis will allow me, I will put together a special detail to go after the murdering scum, and I'll track them to the ends of the earth if I have to."

With the last statement, Canon's voice had changed into something Carolina had never heard. It became a soft deadly whisper with an edge of intensity, a lethal oath that caused tingles of fear to shoot through Carrie's body.

She looked at Canon and scarcely knew him now. His face flushed; his grey eyes, staring at and through her, became bloodshot. Veins stood out in his neck like thin cables and his whole body seemed to swell. He squeezed her hand until she thought she must cry out. She was terrified of him.

"Rabe, you're hurting me," she said breathlessly. "Rabe. RABE!"

Canon released her hand, and took a few seconds to calm. When he did so, he looked away from her. "I have their names. I doubt they are really their names," he said, "but it's enough to start. I will get their descriptions, and I'll find them."

She looked at him, kissed him lightly, and rose. "I have to go now, Rabe. But promise me you'll be careful."

Canon had retracted the wolf, put him back inside himself. He rose, too, and kissed her gently. "Yes, lovey, I will be careful. Don't worry."

Still pale, Carolina turned to leave the room, stopped, looked back at him. "I might take a little time off this afternoon, Rabe. If so, I will need your advice on how best to spend it." She turned and swiftly left the room. Canon watched her go with a smile on his face, then turned to his own toilet.

Half an hour before noon, Canon began the five-minute walk to the stable where Hammer was kept. It was the last day of May, and the May of 1864 had been one of the most beautiful he recalled. For this, too, he could at least in part thank Carolina Lee. For the first time in his life, Canon began to think seriously about a woman in his future.

As Canon set Hammer into a trot down the street toward the capitol building, he smiled. The smile vanished as a long dormant prickle began to tingle and burn at the nape of his neck.

"One," he called to Hammer, tugging and lifting both reins. Hammer reared high, sitting on his back legs, as a rifle's boom cut the air. The heavy bullet struck Hammer high on his right withers, right in front of Canon's chest. Hammer dropped at once, taking his rider down with him.

Canon's left leg was trapped under the palomino's limp form, but he was unhurt. It took a couple of minutes to free it. Then he bent to examine his horse. Hammer was coming back around, having been knocked unconscious by the impact of the bullet. The bullet had torn through the muscled upper leg and exited right under the saddle horn. Canon believed the damage not serious. Already, the big horse was struggling to rise.

"Six, Hammer, six," he whispered urgently to the horse, and Hammer lay still. A crowd had begun to gather. Gunshots near a Confederate garrison were common, but some had seen the horse and rider go down.

Canon had automatically reached for his right pistol when he felt the warning, but his Krupp revolvers were still packed away. In the crowd, however, were several off-duty soldiers, some armed. He pointed to three of those. "I am General Canon," he said, "and someone just shot at me from the roof up there." Canon pointed to the top of a hardware store. "You three come with me." Two others, unarmed, he sent for a veterinarian. Before they left, he said to them, "The horse will stay as he is until otherwise instructed. If the vet needs him to stand, you say, 'Eagle one,' and he will allow you to lead him. Understand?"

"I know of you and this here horse, General," said one. "I understand and will do as you say."

Canon nodded, and with the armed men ran toward the store. For fifteen minutes they searched the roof and surrounding grounds, but found no clue or anyone who had seen anything amiss. Canon ordered the three to return to the spot the next day to question anyone who passed by regularly at this time of day, but he knew the odds were against learning anything useful.

When he returned to Hammer, the horse was standing. Hammer nickered softly when Canon stroked his nose.

"He will be fine, General," said the vet who was putting the final touches on the dressing of Hammer's wound. "Can't be ridden for a few weeks, but the bullet just went through some muscle. He'll heal, all right. You take my mare, and I'll lead Hammer back to my place on Confederate Drive, one block down and one to the left. And don't fret. This horse will be just fine."

Gratefully, Canon mounted the vet's horse and rode full speed to the fateful meeting he almost missed. He arrived ten minutes late. The two leaders of the Confederacy sat in stuffed armchairs, a coffee table between them practically covered with a silver coffee service. They rose, motioned Canon to the third arm chair and handed him a cup of coffee.

Canon was tempted to fill the coffee with the fresh cream and pure sugar sitting on the service, it had been long since he had seen such, but it had been long, too, since he had real coffee. He savored its rich texture and aroma, and drank it black.

Lee and Davis already knew about the shooting, and they knew Canon had not been hit. As they questioned him about the incident, and expressed relief that Hammer would be all right, Canon took stock of the two men.

Lee's right hand, broken a week ago when Traveller threw him inadvertently, was tightly wrapped and in a sling. Lee had stopped by to visit his hospital room a couple of times earlier in the past year, and Canon could see how the constant strain of war was ravaging Lee.

The weatherbeaten face had lines cut in it far more deeply than they had been when Canon had seen him last. The graying hair of a year ago was now solid white, though neat and trimmed as always. Every line in that composed countenance represented strain that would have broken a lesser man. Canon thought God probably looked a little like Robert E. Lee.

Jefferson Davis was thinner than when Canon saw him last, and Davis had been thin then. He was dressed in his usual tailcoat, a fashion that was practically out of style. But Davis knew politics. He dressed as he was expected to dress. Both men seemed preoccupied as they made small talk, and Davis had a high tea sent up from the kitchen.

As they finished eating, the subject returned to the attempt on Canon's life.

"It is ten times a shame and sin that Southern ranks have been infiltrated to the point where a Confederate officer cannot safely ride down the streets of Richmond," said Davis.

Canon knew he would have no greater opportunity than that to broach his reason for the meeting.

"President Davis, I am afraid it is far worse than that," he said. Both men looked at him, and Canon told his story. He told it all. About the dreams. About the night. About the bullets all meant for Jackson.

When he finished, Davis rose and began to pace the room. Lee buried his face in his hands. Then Canon stressed the point that he had not made to anyone, including Carolina Lee.

"General Lee, you know that General Hill hated General Jackson," said Canon. "It has been the one interarmy feud you could not quash. McLaws has been Hill's main supporter, and it was his North Carolina brigade that opened fire on us. General Hill was the only man in the company not hit. I must not say more."

Silence grew, lengthened, thickened in the room. Finally, Lee said, "I refuse to accept it." Canon hung his head.

But Davis said, "General Lee, I realize this is all quite circumstantial, but good, great God, General, how many coincidences does it take? Don't you know what General Canon has just said?"

"Very well," said Lee in an angry tone that shocked both Canon and Davis. "I will tell you what I know. I know we are losing the war because we lost Gettysburg, and we lost Gettysburg because we lost at Chancellorsville the best general on either side.

"I also know I cannot afford at this time to lose the best remaining field general I have, and that is Powell Hill. There is yet one other thing I know. I do not believe A. P Hill would have ordered a deed done such as the one you have described." Lee's voice softened. "But I fear his complicity."

"This is how we must handle it. We cannot afford to have this become public. We would have the two halves of our best army fighting each other to the death. The Confederacy cannot afford such a scandal within in its ranks, either.

"At the proper time, I assure you I will confront Powell Hill with these things you have laid before me, General Canon, and he will answer me. And I will know the truth. If it is so, then I promise you the situation will be rectified. At the proper time.

"I will leave you now. General Canon, you are the only soldier in the Confederacy that I would admit had a greater admiration for General Jackson than I.

"But nothing can be accomplished right now by seeking revenge. President Davis has a far greater task for you, if you will accept it. I ask you to do so to further the ends of the Confederacy. It may be our last chance.

"We had planned to call you here today had you not already asked for a meeting. With your leaves, gentlemen, I will withdraw to let the president give the particulars. I am much distressed, now, and must be on my own a while."

Bowing, Lee left the room.

Davis continued to pace the room in silence for a while, then abruptly resumed his seat.

"I have thought it through, and it as General Lee says," Davis said in a low voice. "We cannot afford to pursue this grave matter openly right now. It would tear us apart internally. We must investigate for a traitor in our midst, but it must be done quietly. And while I would personally like nothing better than to send you after the men you have named, I have a much more important mission for you."

Absorbed, Canon leaned forward in his chair and gave his full attention to the little president.

"Matters are grave within the Confederacy at this time, as everyone knows," said Davis. "But far from hopeless. We have been in dire straits before. Everyone is tired of the war, but the population of the North is even more tired than we. Our cotton embargo is finally taking effect. The voters and the influential businessmen of the North are calling for relief.

"So long as Petersburg and Atlanta are safe, the Confederacy is safe.

"Our main problems now are money and manpower. We cannot get more men, so there is no use to worry about that. We still have sufficient, I believe, to the task. We have to supply them, though. If we have enough weapons and enough food for another year, we will hold and we will win. We will win." Davis emphasized the last three words by slapping the back of his right hand into his left palm.

"Unfortunately," Davis continued, "we do not have enough money to last another year. Our credit is overextended, our money is down to a tenth of what its buying power was a year ago. We must have financial help. We must have gold.

"General Canon, what do you know of California?"

Canon was surprised by the question, but answered promptly.

"Only what I have read, sir, and that has been quite enough to make me wish to visit there some day. It will certainly be a state soon. They clamor for it. And this war will determine whether it will be a state of Southern influence.

"You spoke of gold, and that of course is what everyone knows about California. It is said that a man can get rich in a day there just by finding the right spot on a river to pan for gold.

"As to the feelings in the territory about the war, I understand that it is about half in favor of the North and half in favor of the South. I suspect the Southern half is stronger in wealth and influence.

"Much of the exodus in the gold rush was from the South, our being nearer and more pioneer in spirit. I would like to go there before it becomes too crowded."

"Excellent, General. I commend you on your cosmopolitan knowledge. And I hereby grant your wish."

"Excuse me, sir?"

"You are going to California, if you will do what your country asks of you."

Puzzled, Canon only nodded.

"As I told you," continued Davis, "we need gold. It is critical. The Yankees have flooded us with counterfeit Confederate bills. Frankly, the only way to recognize them is that their quality is better than that of the ones we print ourselves. Inflation is driving us down far worse than bullets. Our credit is all we are living on, and it is almost exhausted.

"But a gold-rich Californian, a real billionaire, has contacted us. He is a true Southern sympathizer and is prepared to lend us five million dollars in Yankee greenbacks, which suits our purpose even better than gold. The Yankee greenback is backed by gold, and is redeemable with no questions asked. If you or I or General Lee walked up to the main bank in New York and presented a million authentic greenbacks, the bank in theory would have to hand over a million in gold.

"It wouldn't work that way in reality for us, of course. In reality, we could put five million Yankee greenbacks to far better use than simply cashing it in for gold. It would pay off some of our debt and reestablish our credit. Five million dollars in Yankee greenbacks would be worth fifty million to the South."

"I am overjoyed to hear it, sir, but what has this to do with me going to California?"

"General, if you wish to save the Confederacy, you must go to California and bring back the five million."

For a moment, Canon could say nothing, then, "But, Mr. President, to California and back is a six-month trip, at the least."

"At least."

"Surely there is a quicker and better way," said Canon.

"If there is, we cannot think of it."

"What about letters of credit? I know very little about financial dealings on that scale, sir, but it seems that banks move sums like that all the time."

Davis sighed. "A year ago, it would have been no problem. We could have merely had our ambassadors in France and England make the proper connection and representatives from either of those countries would have gone to the Bank of San Francisco and arranged everything in an hour's time.

"But England and France are now reluctant to involve themselves in any dealings on our continent. The Federal government, and more importantly, the mighty Federal treasury, is on the lookout for any effort to aid our cause.

"Every bank outside the South is threatened with economic reprisal if it lifts a finger to help us. Every government is threatened with economic reprisals if it helps us. Real money can be withdrawn in relative secrecy, if the banker is willing to help. We have that banker, and we have the funds, in California. And once the money is safe in Confederate banks, the Federal government can have no control over what is done with it."

"Sir, if you want me to go to California, I will certainly go. Tell me what I am to do."

"Very good, General. I knew we could count on you. In the first place, Mr. George McClavel, our benefactor, asked specifically for you. In his message, he said he had read of your exploits and wanted very much for you to be the man for the job. He is fully aware, of course, of the strictures threatened by the Union. He insisted that you are the man for the job, and I quite agree.

"Our war department has checked out Mr. McClavel. We were at first inclined to treat his telegram as a joke. But McClavel apparently has a long history as a businessman in San Francisco, though he is not actually from the town. He is, as I have said, a gold miner on a large scale. However, Mr. Adam Trask, who owns the Bank of San Francisco, has backed McClavel in every particular. McClavel is not that well known in San Francisco, but everyone knows Trask. Million-dollar deals have been made on the strength of Trask's word. We do not have to fear duplicity.

"Our problem is ways and means. How do we get you there, you are famous, General, and how do we get you back safely with five million dollars?"

"Yes, sir."

"Our shipyard, as we speak, is making a Confederate raiding vessel seaworthy for you. It was damaged last month while running a blockade, but it will be shipshape in two weeks. It will get you to California within three months, easily. Getting back is another problem.

"McClavel and Trask have promised a thousand men to escort you back and who will then join the Confederate Army. You will induct them into the army while you are in California. But there are thousands of Yankee soldiers in the west, fighting Indians. If the Union learns of this, they will send every one of them after you. So strict secrecy must be maintained.

"However, once you reach Texas on your return, you may deposit the funds in any major bank and the money will be safe. The raiding ship will also stay in San Francisco to be at your disposal in case you need her. But, again, if word gets out, the Union will send its entire fleet against the ship. You must guard against any slip."

"Yes, sir."

"Good luck, General."

"Thank you, sir, but may I ask for something before I leave?"

"If it is my power to grant it, I will probably give you anything you wish."

"Merely this, sir. I realize the importance of this mission and if it is possible to succeed, I will do my utmost to succeed. When I get back, sir, will I have your permission to go after those men who killed General Jackson?"

"Granted, with all my heart, General Canon. Though I fear the trail will be so very cold by then."

"Yes, sir. But I have picked up a new lead today which I hope will throw some light on the particulars of it."

"Really. You astound me. Please tell me about it."

"With your permission, sir, I would first like to check it out. I promise to keep you informed of any result."

"I must remind you of the secrecy involved concerning this matter, too, General. If there is anything that can be done here while you are gone, I will put our very best people on it."

"Thank you, sir, but that is one reason why I want to use the next couple of weeks working on this myself. There will be no slips from me."

"Very good, General. The best of luck to both your endeavors. Come see me again before you leave."

Canon rose and saluted. Davis shook his hand. And both men bowed as Canon took his leave.

As Canon mounted his borrowed mare, he chided himself because he had promised Davis he would make no mistakes. He corrected it in his mind. He had made one already. He promised himself he would now make no more. He rode hard. First, he would pick up Hammer, then it was home to Carolina Lee.

# 16

# *In the Notch*

It was only a few blocks from the Veterinary/Blacksmith shop to Canon's house. He would rent a horse to ride while Hammer mended, but he chose to walk Hammer home. As they rounded the last block before turning toward his house, Hammer began to crowhop and fidget.

Wondering what the hell could be happening now, Canon dropped to a knee with a curse. He still had no weapon and felt a fool. Scanning the rooftops, looking around behind him, he saw nothing but a fairly busy street. The palomino let out a shrill whinny that was answered a block away.

"Hammer, what in hell is going on?" Canon said. He couldn't remember the horse acting this way since he was a colt. Hammer was tugging to run, even breaking into a limping trot, pulling Canon along. The street had been watered at noon, but the afternoon heat had evaporated most of it. Canon's boot heels dug dusty furrows into the unpaved back street.

Rounding the corner, Canon saw a sight that stopped him cold. Hammer broke away into a gimping lope. How many ghosts, wondered Canon, is a man entitled to?

Old Scratch, fully saddled, was hitched to the post outside his door.

Ghost or no, Canon called out, "Scratch!" and almost caught up with Hammer before the wounded palomino reached the whinnying black Arabian.

It was a strange sight that greeted Carrie Lee when she stepped out of Canon's front door to learn what the commotion was all about. Canon had an arm around each horse's neck. All three were literally dancing for joy at the reunion.

"Well, General Canon," she called, "I hope you will not be so enraptured by two horses that you fail to pass the time of day with your visitor."

Canon stopped frolicking with the horses and stepped up on the small front porch of his house. Carrie handed him a note. "I found it tacked to the front door," she said. "It's from Mrs. Jackson."

"Dear Rabe," it read, "Scratch was horribly wounded at Antietam, but to the surprise of my husband, walked unsteadily into camp while you were unconscious.

"Thomas could not bear to have him killed, but he did not want to tell you because he was afraid the horse would die, anyhow. It was a year before I, and half the veterinarians in Lexington, were sure he would be all right. By then, you and my husband had been wounded.

"I apologize for not having come see you sooner, and for not sending word, but you will understand that I have been in mourning and could see no one. Perhaps it was selfish of me, but I did so want to present Scratch to you myself.

"The nearer I came to your home today, however, the more reluctant I became to see you. He was so fond of you, as I am, General. But I am not sure I can deal just yet with the memories seeing you would bring. So I left Scratch for you.

"I am to visit in Richmond for a few days. If you do not mind, let me send word to you later of where I am staying, and perhaps you would be kind enough to visit. But, if you do not hear from me, please understand. I want very much to talk to you one day about Thomas, Rabe, but I am not sure when I will be able to bring myself to do it. Forgive me." It was signed, "Mary Anna."

Canon walked into the house, blinking back hot tears, trying to gulp down the lump in his throat. He also fought down the rage that rose up in him. He willed the rage to ice. He could not afford to kill. Not yet.

He turned to Carrie, who had followed him in and shut the door behind her. He smiled a grim and terrible smile. Her returning smile was puzzled.

Canon grabbed and shook her, lifting her off her feet, his hands wrapped around her arms like steel bands. He was hurting her, he knew. He wanted to hurt her. He threw her from him. She struck the wall and fell limp to the floor. He lifted her, placed her on the couch and went for water and a cloth.

He bathed her face with one hand while he searched her purse with the other. He found nothing of consequence in the purse, but his repeated ministrations with the wet cloth finally caused her to stir. She came to with a series of whimpers, groggily reached her hand up to her swollen cheek.

"Rabe, what in the name of God is wrong with you? Why did you do that?" she moaned weakly. "Have you gone mad?"

"Carrie, it isn't going to work. Now, who did you send to shoot me?"

She opened her eyes wide. "Shoot you? You are mad. What are you talking about?"

"You're going to tell me who you're working for and why they want me dead. Why you want me dead. I don't want to hurt you any more than I have to, lovey. Now tell."

She tried to struggle to a sitting position, but Canon grabbed her arms and held her down. "You cad!" she strained out angrily. "I'll tell, all right. If you don't let me go this instant, I'll tell everyone in Richmond what you . . ."

Holding her down with his right hand, Canon slapped her left cheek hard with his left hand, rocking her back into the couch pillows. She opened her mouth to scream and he stuffed the rag in it. Choking, she raked her nails at his face, and Canon thumped her nose.

Carolina squealed, from rage and pain, almost loud enough to be heard through the gag. She grabbed her face with both hands and kicked her feet up and down. Abruptly, she stopped her struggles and began to cry. Softly, at first, then she wept with great racking silent sobs.

Canon let her cry for a while. When she opened her eyes and looked at him, he shook his head.

"None of it will work, Carrie. Not the enraged lady, not the wounded nurse," he said roughly. "You are hard as nails, lovey, and sharp as briars. I could get to like you all over again if you can prove to me that you had nothing to do with Jackson's murder." She reached for the gag, wanting to protest, but Canon stopped her.

"You don't know me very well, lovey. Not very well at all," Canon said through clenched teeth. "You only saw me as a confused convalescent Confederate soldier." Canon reached under the couch. He saw her wince at the unmistakable sound of a bayonet rasping out of its steel sheath. Canon thought of Stonewall Jackson lying, dying in the house at Chancellorsville. He did not have to playact. He showed her the razor-edged bayonet.

"I am the leader of the Black Horse Cavalry and the Stonewall Brigade. I have killed more men than you have got fingers and toes. I can be a very bad man, lovey, and I am gong to be a very bad man to you unless you tell me some very large truth very quickly.

"I'm going to remove the rag. If you try to scream, or do anything at all except what I tell you to do, you will regret it." Canon flashed the bayonet across her throat, felt her jerk, saw the thin red line open where the tip had grazed her.

"I'll turn you into the ugliest creature anyone ever saw," he said calmly. "Children will scream at the sight of your face, lovey, if you try to make me play the fool again. I will cut out your lying little tongue." Canon drew the blade lightly down her body, cutting her dress and leaving little beads of blood on the exposed skin. He removed the gag.

"You bastard," she hissed, "I wish they had killed you."

"That's a start," Canon grinned wickedly. "Just remember female spies are hanged, too. Now tell me something, or I swear on Stonewall Jackson's grave that I'll cut your lips off right here and now."

"I work for whoever pays me," she spat. "I always have. I guess it has to be the Union but I never tried to find out for sure. My money and orders come to me at the post office. When I have information I leave it under a rock outside town, then I leave a candle burning in my window.

"On Mondays, if there is something urgent, I go by a house down the street and just say out loud whatever it is I want them to know. That's what I did this morning." She softened. "But, Rabe, I swear I didn't know General Jackson was murdered until you told me. I don't know anything about that at all. And I didn't try to get you shot. I was trying to save you.

"When you told me about the general, I was afraid they'd shoot you, too. When I went to that house, I stopped there to fix my shoe and waited until nobody else was around. Then I just said out loud that you had told the war department last week that Jackson had been murdered and that they were looking for the killers. I thought they would run, if they were the ones who shot him."

Canon sat back. "That is strange, if you are telling me the truth, lovey. They should have run. Now come on." Canon grabbed her arm, pulled her up.

"All right, don't jerk me so," she said angrily. "You bastard. Where are we going?"

"Lawsy me, what language, lovey. First, you're going to tell me which house you're talking about. Then you're going to your house, where you will stay until I come back for you. As soon as it's dusk, you'll light a candle for the window, then we'll go to message rock. In the meantime, I am going for a little stroll."

Before they left, Canon went to a trunk in his bedroom and took out a glossy wooden case wrapped in an oiled chamois skin. When he returned, the twin Krupp fifties were in the holstered belt he strapped around his hips.

Canon took Carrie with him behind the house to the stable he had never used. Calling to one of the street urchins who were always about, Canon flipped him a silver dollar and watched his eyes widen.

"You know anything about horses, son?" he asked the youth.

"Yessir, reckon I do."

"Well, from now on, you're my stable hand, if you want to be, and you'll get one of those dollars every week."

"Yessir."

"Set the stable to rights. Clean it up, fill it with hay and fresh water. Go get oats and a curry comb. Be careful of the palomino's shoulder. You do all that?"

"Yessir."

"Then I reckon you're my new hand."

"Yessir."

As Canon and Carrie walked the half-block to her house, she said, "I can't believe that fool shot at you. Pointed the finger right at me."

"Well, he did not intend to miss, lovey. Thing that puzzles me is why he'd do it if he thought I had already talked about Jackson being murdered. You know what I'll do if you're lying about that."

"I'm telling you the truth, you bastard."

"Maybe you are, lovey, but wherever there's a maybe, there's always a maybe not. And your track record in the truth department stinks."

"You bastard."

"Now, lovey. Tell me where the house is, and what this man looks like."

"It's the little gray house on this corner of the garrison that nobody lives in. I've never seen any of them, if there is more than one," she said bitterly, "and that's God's truth. I've never had reason to. I didn't want to see him. There was just a letter one day, with money in it, telling me what to do. I did it."

They reached her door. "All right," said Canon. "We'll talk about this some more later. You go on in, and don't try to run away. I'll be back at sundown."

Canon walked toward the Confederate garrison, checking the loads in his pistols. Anyone watching him as he approached the small abandoned house, its gray paint peeling and its yard gone to knee high weeds, would have thought him just another passerby. But Canon was taking in every inch of the terrain around the tumbledown dwelling. He had slipped the rawhide thongs off the hammers of his pistols.

The house was on Canon's left as he approached it, ambling slowly down the cobblestone street. The lowering summer sun was in his face. Canon closed his left eye, half-lidded the right against the glare. Once inside the darkened house, he wanted his eyes to adjust quickly.

As he paralleled the ramshackle porch, Canon turned toward the house and stepped up on the board sidewalk. Now he opened his eyes wide, taking a mental picture of the grounds and house. It took only a second, then Canon was again walking toward the garrison. He did not look at the house as he passed it, but tuned his hearing toward it. He again hooded his eyes against the sun.

The silver dollar made a clinking, rolling sound when he dropped it. He took a few paces more, then turned back as if to search for the dollar, the sun now at his back.

Richmond had grown toward the Confederate garrison, but the town had played out as it neared the place. The old house predated the garrison, its warped boards and mostly paneless windows looking all the more dilapidated next to the tended grounds and new buildings nearby. Canon scanned the house as he ostensibly searched for the dollar, took in the broken windows, the weather swollen planks and boards.

He saw nothing, heard nothing. No one was around outside, it appeared there was no one inside. Canon bent to retrieve his dollar, accidentally kicked it into the tall grass next to a window in the side of the house.

Bending to his knees to search the grass, Canon looked under the house, which rested on columns of large flatrocks used for the foundation. Standing, he peered in the window. The house was empty. No marks to speak of in the dust of years that covered the floor. No need to look inside.

Moving to the back of the house, Canon took a quick look around him, dropped to the ground and crawled under the back porch. He had so far seen no sign that anyone had been in or around the house for any length of time in years. By God, he thought, if Carolina lied to me, I'll make her sorry. But Canon sensed she had not lied; there was something here for him, he was sure. An anticipatory tingle ran up and down his spine.

He recalled the witches' rhyme from *Macbeth*: "By the pricking of my thumbs, something wicked this way comes." He was after someone, or evidence of someone, very wicked indeed.

And he soon found a small depression in the ground underneath the front porch. It was enough to show that Carrie was telling the truth, at least about this. Canon reached back and slid the bowie knife from his boot, dug into the soft earth. He uncovered a few fairly fresh scraps of food, and some sticks of jerky in a small leather pouch. Whoever had been here planned to come back. It was someone, Canon thought, who meticulously erased all tracks of comings and goings. Someone very careful.

Canon meant to be just as meticulous. He rearranged everything just as it had been. He crawled backwards, covering his marks, until he neared the back of the house. With difficulty, Canon swung his bulk around under the floor. He drew one of his pistols. Then he found a small patch of sunlight streaming down through the punctured back porch and accustomed his eyes to brighter light. When he came out from under the porch, he would be ready.

Sunlight, however, was the only thing awaiting him. He stayed under the porch for a half hour, by his watch. At four P.M., he came out, holstered the pistol, hooked the thongs to the hammers.

He would begin his vigil at this house as soon as he and Carrie returned from message rock. If nothing happened there, he would wait near this house; until the following Monday if necessary. Canon finally found a trail.

Dusting himself off, he started walking to Carrie's house, past the Confederate garrison. It had been long since Canon was there. He turned toward it.

A tall plank fence ran down the sidewalk on each side of the street, screening in the barracks and protecting shy Southern ladies from the possibility of seeing shirtless soldiers.

Canon started down the sidewalk. Behind the fence on the right side of the street, he knew, were barracks and a parade field. To his left, behind the fence, Canon was passing a training field and coming up on the firing range.

With his mind on the unknown man from under the house, Canon had no thought of the firing range. When the heavy caliber rifle went off, only a dozen feet away behind the fence, Canon reacted instantly, instinctively.

He dove to the ground and rolled twice as he drew his right hand pistol.

It quickly dawned on him where he was, and how foolish he had been. The damned firing range! Grinning wryly at himself, Canon holstered the pistol and looked sheepishly around to see if anyone had witnessed his acrobatics. He rose to one knee and began dusting off his uniform when he heard a hoarse whisper from the other side of the fence. The words chilled him, froze him.

"Right in the notch," said the voice. "Right in the notch."

Canon would not remember going over the eight-foot high fence. Rage filled him quickly and completely. One second he was kneeling on one side of the fence and the next he was on the other side with his huge hands around the throat of a grizzled Rebel soldier, shaking him so that long greasy gray locks pendulumed on the soldier's hatless head. He pulled the man's face within an inch of his own.

"What does it mean?" hissed Canon. "Who are you, and what does it mean?" The soldier, eyes wide, looked at Canon and struggled briefly, then went limp. Only Canon's grip on the soldier's throat kept the man from slumping to the ground.

Canon dragged the soldier, a corporal, according to his sleeve marks, over to a water trough. Taking the huge Sharps rifle, still locked in corporal's hands, Canon placed man and rifle on the ground next to the trough. A few splashes of water brought the groggy trooper around. "What's happened? Why you here?

"Tell me who you are," Canon ordered harshly, standing over the man.

In almost comic fashion, the soldier gaped at the rank marks on Canon's sleeve, saw the twin patches of Stonewall and Black Horse. For the first and only time in his life, Canon saw a soldier struggle to salute from a prone position.

"Corporal Ben Roy Rodgers, suh, attached to General John B. Hood's Texans and proud of it." It sounded like he said, "proud uv hit." Here's one from the sharecrops, thought Canon, still on guard.

"What does it mean?" Canon prodded.

"Whut?" said Rodgers. "Gimme jist a second, Genral Canon . . . you is Canon, ain't you? Thought you wuz. Lemme get my air back, suh. I still ain't quite right." The man gave an embarrassed chuckle. "Reckon I never dropped like that in my life, and I've seed aplenty of bad sights.

"But when ye fell on me outta the sky, sort of to speak, like God's vengeance, I thought my time was up. I knowed you right off, and when ye grabbed me by my neck, I purt near figgered I'se a goner." Canon wanted to interrupt, wanted to know what the phrase meant, but the man was obviously still woozy.

"I seed you at Fust Manassas, suh," Rodgers continued, "down to the Stone Bridge when you and the Black Horse sailed over the wagon. Youens wuz the most terriblest, awesomest sight I seen in my time." He chuckled again. "You still is, and it's a fack. I be a perty tough old bird, and I do say so muhself, genral, though I ain't sure my legs'd hold me even now.

"I seen action, and a plenty of it, but I ain't never seen nothing that looked the way ye looked when ye grabbed me. The Yankees claim you to be the devil. I know a'cause I was they guest for a spell up in they establishment for Rebel prisoners at Cairo, Illinois, till I'se exchanged.

"I even had a joke about ye, up there. If I heared 'em mention yore name, I'd ast if any of 'em ever seen you. Then afore they could answer, I'd say that I knowed none of 'em had seen you, acause they wuzn't dead."

Canon was itching to grab the man again, but he waited out the ramble.

"Now, lemme see," said Rodgers. "You asked me sumpin. What was it agin? Oh, yes, thankee. In the notch. Well, that be easy, General. Prison I wuz in at Cairo was a Yankee barrack, and they gambled on a game at the firing range. Let me show ye." Canon helped Rodgers to his feet, then walked with him fifty yards down range to a target pole. On the post was a square of white paper the size of a man's head. A deep vee was cut in it from the top almost to the bottom. At the juncture of the vee, touching each side of the vee, was a bullet hole.

"Thass it," said Rodgers, proudly.

Straining to keep his voice level, Canon said, "What's it?"

"Why, the notch, genral. Thought you knowed by now. Whosoever puts a bullet clostest to the bottom notch of that vee hittin both sides of the paper is the winner. Them Yankees let me play the game with 'em some when they found out what I do for the Rebel army, and I won me some Yankee greenbacks thataway."

"And what do you do, corporal, for the Rebel army?"

"Why, the very same that them Yanks was training to do. 'Tis what most of them Yankees train for there. I be a sharpshooter, suh, and one of the best, ye don't mind me saying so."

Rodgers stuck his finger in the bullet hole and grinned at Canon.

"See," he said. "Right in the notch."

Canon wanted to question him more, but the trooper, still shaky, begged off so he could go to evening mess. And Canon knew preparations had to be made to get to Carrie's rendezvous site. Reluctantly, he let the man off with the promise of an eight A.M. appointment next morning at the firing range.

Canon's head was buzzing as he walked back to Carrie's house. How could eight Yankee sharpshooters infiltrate the Confederate Army to the point of being posted pickets at Stonewall Jackson's headquarters? Canon, like Lee, did not believe A. P. Hill capable of so monstrous a plot. He needed to see Lee, but Lee had gone back to his troops this afternoon.

Just as well, perhaps, thought Canon. He needed time to think matters through. He would begin tomorrow by checking out Corporal Ben Roy Rodgers. Tonight, he thought, might bring even more developments. Canon hurried back to his house and changed into stalking clothes—dark buckskin shirt and pants and calf-high moccasins. He looked, ruefully, at the new uniform, now dusty and sweat stained, as he hung it in the closet. Before buckling his gunbelt back on, Canon slipped the sheath for his bowie knife on it and secured the big blade in it.

Carolina Lee was not a happy person. She turned on Canon like a viper when he let himself into her house.

"Look what you did to me, you son of a bitch," she said in a furious undertone. She was standing in front of the mirror, trying to cover her swollen eyes with facial powder. She walked up and stuck her face two inches from Canon's.

She walked back to the mirror, looked in it and gave a little moan. "If you think I am going out in public looking like this, or anywhere else with you, Rabe Canon, you are just simply crazy as hell," she said, stamping her foot.

Canon reached for the bowie knife, sent it a twinkling fifteen feet where the point imbedded deeply into the wooden wall next to Carrie's head. Canon knew she had felt the blade's breath as it winked past her. The handle quivered, almost touching her ear.

"On the other hand," she said, "it will be dark soon."

"Lovey," said Canon, "I'm glad you see my point."

It was still a half-hour until sundown. Carrie was dressed in calico, off the shoulders, her honeyed hair tumbling thick and loose down her back. Canon had to admit she was a fetching sight. She knew it, too. Coming close to him again, she put her arms around him, drew him down to her, kissed his ear.

"Honey, let's kiss and make up," she said, breathing into his ear. Canon wanted to smile at her naiveté, but led her to the couch. For the next half hour Canon toyed with the delights of Carolina Lee, moving his hands expertly on, in and under her clothes. He caressed every part of her body while she moaned softly.

But when the sun dipped below the horizon, Canon rose from where he knelt beside her. "Time to signal our friends, lovey," he said.

"Oh, Rabe, do we have to?" she said. "Can't we just let it drop? I'm afraid, Rabe."

"You're a little bitch, lovey," Canon said. "Now say hello to your friends. I'm going out the back, and you go out the front. I'll follow you to the blacksmith's shop next to the general store. We're going to rent a nice carriage so I can keep a close eye on you. Light the candle."

With a murderous look at Canon, Carrie took a candelabrum from the table, lit the candle and placed it in the window. Canon watched her go out the front door, then he quickly went out the back.

The streets of Richmond were empty. Suppertime comes early in the South, especially when there is little for anyone to eat. Other than food, only sleep takes the edge off hunger. The one person they met as Canon trailed twenty yards behind Carrie was an abashed Corporal Ben Roy Rodgers, who walked out of the general store and slammed straight into Carolina Lee. Rodgers dropped the Sharps rifle he still carried and grabbed Carrie's hands. It was the only thing that kept her from falling.

Canon was almost on them as the clumsy trooper righted Carrie, tried to pick up the rifle, dropped it, picked it up again. "'Scuse me, ma'am, General, suh," he said, bowing thrice and saluting a like number of times, "beg to be 'scused." The befuddled trooper backpedaled away. Canon solemnly returned each salute.

Canon and Carrie walked the remaining block to the smithy. The sidewalk ended at the smith's, where the huge Scotsman, dwarfing his chair, sat outlining horseshoes on a three-foot square of iron resting on the edge of the walkway.

Brusquely, Canon ordered a buggy. The man nodded and stepped inside his barn. As they stood waiting, Canon felt Carrie sway against him. He was about to tease her, accuse her of being oversexed, when he saw her features slacken, heard her mumble that she felt faint. Canon grabbed her waist with his right hand and looked over to reach for the smith's chair with his left. Then several things happened at once.

Canon's warning sense lit up like a lightning strike. He looked back, saw a knife gleaming in Carolina's upraised right hand, ready to put the blade in his back. Then he heard the lethal clickclack of a rifle hammer being drawn and locked, shifted his vision, and saw Rodgers kneeling and aiming the Sharps. Aiming at Carrie Lee.

Canon reached past the chair, grabbed the square of iron the smithy had been working, and slammed it broadside into Carrie's chest simultaneous with the rifle's bark. The knife flew from her hand. The bullet ricocheted off the iron. Carrie sighed and sat down hard on the ground, toppled over.

Canon picked up the knife and was gazing at it intently when Rodgers ran up. The trooper stopped, spat a stream of tobacco juice onto the side of the shop, wiped his mouth with the back of his hand.

"I seed she was gonna stab ye, genral," he said, "so I throwed down on her. What come over the gal? Why'd she want to stab ye, anyhow? Lord, but you wuz quick."

Canon stood silent, fingering the long knife blade. He took the rifle from Rodgers, who seemed reluctant to let it go. He gave in to Canon, who leaned the Sharps against the wall.

The smith had come out at the sound of the shot. He heard Canon ask the corporal a seemingly strange question.

"You have a pocket knife, Rodgers?" Canon said.

"'Deed I do," said Rodgers, haltingly. He reached in his pocket, brought out a new bonehandled knife similar to the one Canon held. "Spankin new, too. Just bought it."

"Let me ask you one more question, Rodgers."

"Certain, genral."

"Did your bullet hit me or Jackson at Chancellorsville?"

Rodgers, eight feet away, dropped to a knee and pulled a small pistol from his boot. Canon took a step toward him, saw he could not reach him in time, thought "Dammit," and threw the knife. Smoke and noise billowed from the pistol, the bullet cutting through a fold of cloth on Canon's coat.

Rodgers slowly lowered his other knee to the ground as he plucked weakly, uselessly at the knife handle protruding from the side of his throat. Canon knelt beside him.

"That's for Stonewall Jackson, you miserable scum," he said. He grabbed the man's greasy hair, yanking the head back until Rodgers' throat pointed toward the sky. Canon picked up the new knife Rodgers had dropped, opened it with his teeth and put the blade at Rodgers' throat. "Where are the others?" he demanded Rodgers said nothing. Canon savagely shook the man's head, looked into eyes now growing glassy.

"Where?" demanded Canon.

Rodgers opened his mouth, but only blood frothed with tobacco juice issued from it. Canon heard the death rattle as Rodgers' last breath bubbled out. Canon removed his grip from the man's hair, and the corpse huddled down like a load of washed clothes.

"Hell and damn," yelled Canon, "I should have known the bastard would have a hideaway." Placing a boot on the dead man's chest, Canon pulled at the knife handle. The blade made a wet sucking noise as it came free. The empty sack that used to be Rodgers fell back onto the street.

A small crowd, mostly soldiers, gathered at the scene. Though gunshots weren't unusual at the garrison, some of the trained ears of the soldiers had picked up the sound as being out of the normal vicinity. The blacksmith stood between Rodgers and Carrie, gaping first at one, then the other.

Canon waited until the crowd settled. "Anyone know this man?" he called to the dozen spectators. The crowd buzzed but there was no answer. "I am General Canon. The smith here will testify that this soldier tried to shoot a woman," he pointed to Carrie, still on the ground. "Is that right, smith?" The man nodded vigorously, ready to agree with whatever Canon might say.

Carrie groaned and stirred. Two women and one of the soldiers moved to help her. "Put her in the buggy," said Canon, watching them do so, "and I will take her for treatment.

"I will make a full report of this tomorrow," he continued. "Now I am going to search this man for identification. You and you," Canon pointed to two soldiers, "will witness. The rest of you please go about your business." The people slowly drifted away. Canon motioned the two nearer as he bent over Rodgers' body.

He cursed under his breath at the first find. It was a leather tobacco pouch, containing a few plugs of twist tobacco. The pouch was identical to the one Canon found underneath the house. He doubted that anyone would be going back to the house to get it.

The only other item of interest was the man's wallet, which matched the two leather pouches. Pretty fancy stuff, thought Canon, for a Rebel corporal. Inside the wallet was $280 Confederate money, a ten dollar gold piece and a five dollar silver piece.

"Take the body to the hospital morgue," Canon ordered the men. "I will be responsible for the wallet and rifle." The men lugged the body away as Canon stuffed the wallet into the waistband of his pants and put the Sharps in the buggy. He demanded and received a clean cloth from the smith, wet it in a horse trough, and climbed in the carriage.

"I will see to the lady," Canon said to the smith, who nodded dumbly and went inside the barn. Canon set to work on Carolina, bathing her face with the wet cloth. Her eyes opened almost immediately.

"One thing about being with you, General Canon," she whispered weakly, "is that a girl can count on being buried with the cleanest damned face in Richmond. Your company is great for the complexion, but hell on the rest of the body." She tried to sit up, gasped in pain.

"I think you broke my rib, you bastard. I ought to kill you for that," she said.

Canon gave her a wicked grin. "You've tried twice to kill me, lovey," he reminded her, "and it has gotten you a swollen face and a cracked rib. Don't you think you ought to find a new way to amuse yourself?" She looked sullenly at him. "Which way to your little rendezvous rock?" said Canon. She pointed west, and Canon clucked up the horse.

They rode wordlessly for a few minutes, then, "Rabe, he tried to kill me, didn't he?" Canon stopped the horse, looked at Carrie and nodded. "And you saved my life." Canon nodded again. "Why?" she said.

"He tried to kill you because he knew I was on to you. When he failed to kill me this morning, he realized that I would have to be stupid indeed not to know it was you that set me up."

"You already told me that, Rabe. Why did you save my life?"

Canon considered for a moment, then said lightly, "Have you ever seen the size bullet a Sharps rifle carries? Makes a really nasty hole. You were standing right next to me. It would have splattered blood all over my new buckskins."

"Be serious for once, Rabe. This is important."

Canon thought it over, took in a deep breath, blew it out again. "All right, Carolina. I saved you because I think, for some reason I can't explain, that you are worth saving. And I believe I could care quite a lot for you. I don't know why. It doesn't make sense, except that perhaps you and I are quite a lot alike. Anyway, I can't explain it and I don't care."

"Rabe."

"Lovey," said Canon, snapping the reins so that the horse started into a trot, "if I can just get you to stop trying to kill me, I think we'd make a lovely couple."

Canon laughed, but Carolina Lee was very still and solemn.

They rode west at a clip along the rutted red clay road. Message Rock, as Carrie called it, was a half-hour's ride from town. Canon hurried the horse.

Carrie's signal candle had been burning throughout the killing of Rodgers, at least half an hour had been lost. Canon meant to be first at Message Rock.

Carolina gave him a brief but thorough description of the landscape around the rendezvous and Canon, who was slightly familiar with the area from previous rides, put it all in a mental picture, questioning her on a couple of points, until he was sure he could find his way around there in the dark.

Dark would not be a problem this night, though. Dusk had dropped on the day, a pale luminescence permeated the warm, clear evening, precursor of the shining to come.

Halfway to their destination, Carrie leaned over and buried her head in the hollow of Canon's neck. He knew better than to trust her, but he also knew he held her life in his hands. With proper persuasion, even if it meant putting her in fear of the hangman's noose, she could perhaps become a double agent and spy for the South.

"Rabe, honey?"

"Yes, lovey?"

"How did you know it was that man back there? I didn't even know until he . . ." She fell silent.

"Until he slipped you the knife when he bumped into you at the store."

She sat back in surprise. "How did you know that?" she said.

"Because I searched you earlier, lovey. Remember? On the couch when you wanted to make up? It was fun, but I also wanted to make sure you didn't have any little surprises hidden on you. And the blade you used had tobacco stains on it where he had cut his plug. Besides, he had told me he had been in town several days, yet he had just bought a new knife.

"A trooper with money in his pocket, particularly a tobacco chewing trooper, won't go without a knife. If he had a new knife, it's reasonable to think he had just gotten rid of the old one.

"And I didn't realize it at the time, but he told me this afternoon he was a Yankee."

"Told you?"

"I saw him at the firing range. He was a bit woozy and let something slip. He said he had seen the Black Horse crossing Stone Bridge at First Manassas. He was right. We did. But there was no Confederates out that far except the Black Horse. If he saw it, he saw it in a Yankee uniform.

"And then he tried to kill you, lovey. When he didn't have to. At that distance, Rodgers, or at least he called himself Rodgers, could have hit your arm or leg. Could have probably shot the knife out of your hand and never even caused a hangnail. But I saw where he was aiming. At your heart."

Carrie shuddered.

"How did you know he was trying to kill you, lovey?" said Canon. "I thought you were out."

"I could tell he was aiming at my heart, too, darling. That's why I froze." Carrie gave a little sigh and snuggled back into Canon. "Since you kept that big ole bullet out of my little ole heart," she said, mocking her own accent as she caressed Canon's thigh, "I guess my heart belongs to you."

"Carrie, stop that right now. We're here."

Canon had slowed the horse, looking for the small cut in the woods he learned of from Carrie. It was a good quarter-mile from the rock and a perfect place to leave the horse and buggy. Canon picked up the Sharps, leapt from the buggy and tied the horse to a small sapling.

"Rabe, I want to go with you," said Carrie.

"No."

"You should have at least brought more men."

"Until I know who I can trust, lovey, I trust no one. Besides, I've got a personal score to settle with these bastards if they had anything to do with shooting Jackson. And I work well alone. Stay here and hold the horse, Carrie. I'll blindfold her so she won't whinny."

"All right, Rabe. I'll pinch her nostrils if she starts to act up."

"Well, listen to you. Very good. I'll be back soon, I hope." He started to turn away, thought better of it. "Here," he said, handing her the small pistol Rodgers had used. "Just because you've tried to kill me twice, I see no reason not to hand you a loaded pistol."

Carrie made a little moue as she took the weapon, broke it down and checked the loads. She smiled at him, tucking the tiny pistol into the bodice of her dress. "If it gets lost in there, you'll have to help me look for it," she said.

"I'm getting to like you more and more, lovey," said Canon. Carrie looked down to adjust the pistol nestled in her cleavage. When she looked up, Canon was gone.

Years of Indian training rushed back on him. He was in an element now where few white men could match his stealth. He knew it and gloried in it. The rising three-quarter moon turned everything silver and black. Canon moved through pine and scrub like a whisper. There was no wind, but Canon paused on occasion to take deep sniffs, using all his senses to search for anything that might add to his edge.

He had not intended to bring a rifle, trusting instead to the long range of the Krupp pistols and his own shooter's eye if the night required gunplay. He wanted this to be close work, and he intended to capture, not kill. But the Sharps had changed his mind. If a truly long shot were needed, Canon wanted to have the best tools to hand.

As he closed in on the rendezvous point, Canon stopped, closed his eyes for a slow count to two hundred. This would "open his eyes," and enhance the light of the moon, Mountain Eagle had taught him. Canon merged his mind with the surroundings. The gentle roll of the terrain, the curve of the road, the big flat rock at the intersection a few hundred yards away; these things Canon saw without seeing.

When he reached two hundred, Canon opened his eyes and moved. He circled wide, approaching the rock from the south, moving instinctively in an arc to high ground so that all before him was in panorama. Fifteen minutes brought him to the position he sought, knew would be there from reading the terrain. He was on a grassy knoll overlooking the rock a hundred yards away.

Canon settled to his haunches, Indian style, to wait. He had no idea how long it would take. Although this road was lightly traveled, except for troop movements, and particularly at night, Canon figured the Yankee accomplices would prefer late, late night. He would wait an hour, he decided, then slip back and check on Carrie.

He cleared his mind of thought and got set to send his senses winging like invisible birds over the territory. First he determined to scan the panorama, then slowly go over it in detail. Then he would open his hearing to all sounds of the forest, whittling them away one by one, focusing on each for a moment, moving quickly to the next.

Still no wind. When he heard the faint belling of horse harness jingling, he cursed Carolina under his breath for not keeping the mare quiet. Then he realized with a full vented oath that Carolina's horse did not have the only harness that jingled. If the place he chose to hide the horse and buggy was perfect for him, it would also be perfect for others who came in the night.

He directed his trained ear toward the sound. No need. Carolina's scream and the report of the small pistol he had given her were simultaneous. Canon cursed again as he bolted toward the road, leaving the heavy Sharps behind. The tripled damned Rodgers thwarted him, even while dying by his hand. Rodgers' death gave the watchers time to move. The bastards beat him here!

Canon gained the road and pounded down it at top speed, all attempts at stealth forgotten. He ran the quarter-mile in a minute flat. But sixty seconds seems like forever when you know it's just not enough time.

They were dots in the darkness when Canon came on the scene. But he thought he made out five figures on horses. He stopped by the buggy, reading the ground for sign. They had taken the mare, cutting the harness in haste. Canon saw a swatch of cloth, part of the bodice from Carrie's calico dress. The blood on it, fresh though it was, looked black in the frail moonlight.

Cursing yet again, Canon took a deep breath and did the only thing he could do. He began to run, moving into the Eagle's low long-distance power lope.

Three things were in his favor, he felt. First, they would not think he would follow them on foot. Second, Canon guessed they had a shelter of some kind nearby, since they evidently came often to this place. Third, given the right circumstances, he knew a man could outrun a horse.

Canon learned early in life to take Mountain Eagle's teachings as gospel, could not hide the doubt in his eyes when the Eagle told him it was no great feat for a man to outrun a horse.

Seeing the doubt, the Eagle said nothing else.

Three days later, Canon and Buck set off one morning for a hunt forming at a neighbor's house, ten miles away. They were late and left in a flurry of pounding hooves and clouds of dust. The Eagle waved goodbye from the front porch. They rode hard for an hour, but when they arrived at the neighboring farm, the Eagle waved hello from the front porch. The Indian, at least fifty years old at the time, Canon reckoned, was not even breathing hard.

Canon was amazed. The road was the only way to the neighbor's, except through primeval forest that made horseback riding practically impossible. There was simply no other way for the Eagle to have gotten there except by running or flying. At that moment, Canon would have believed the Indian capable of either.

Buck, though unaware of the conversation between the two, knew immediately that another lesson had been taught and learned. His eyes twinkled as he winked at Rabe.

"That derned redskin has got his wings on today, I reckon, boy," said Buck.

The other men in the hunting party had been surprised when the Eagle ran up to the farm out of the woods, but nothing further was said about it that morning. Mountain Eagle joined the hunt. That night, around the campfire, after the jug had gone around a few times and tall tales were being swapped, Buck asked the Eagle to elaborate on the lesson Rabe had learned.

It was elementary. Plains Indians often chased down on foot marauding tribes who raided their horse pens. The victims usually knew which tribe raided their corral, so they knew what direction the raiders would take going home. They also knew the raiders would stop along the way to celebrate the raid and argue over the horses. Usually, too, there were certain trails everyone rode—trails that avoided obstacles such as hills, draws and deep water.

These were easier for a man to cross than for a horse. And the heights allowed the pursuers to observe the raiders. It was a relatively easy matter to overtake the raiders and lay an ambush for them.

Today, for instance, said the Eagle, though the road to the farm might be ten miles long, the distance through the forest was half that. It would be a sick Indian who could not run five miles in fifty minutes. Next day, with Buck leading Rabe's horse home, the Eagle showed Canon the trails he took. They beat Buck home by fifteen minutes.

Canon knew he could catch the men who had Carrie. He just hoped he wouldn't be too late. They would rape her before they killed her, he was sure. He figured he would catch them at it. There were four of them, by their tracks, and Carrie. Canon wondered if he was right about Carrie's fear of letting herself go while making love. Wondered if it was due to being raped or mishandled when she was young. If so, and these pigs brutalized her . . . Canon ground his teeth in anger and frustration. He needed to conserve energy if this was going to be a long trek. But anger burned away his resolve. Digging in with his toes, as the Eagle had taught him, Canon began to sprint.

He made a map in his mind. His enemies would not take the girl back to Richmond. They had to turn off, and Canon began to believe he knew where they were heading. A road branched south from this main thoroughfare, leading to an abandoned sharecropper's hovel. The mile-long road was disused, the sharecropper long gone. But there was a spring there. It was a livable place.

Canon turned and ran into the woods on his left. He slowed somewhat, but the thick canopy of the ancient forest had for years kept direct sunshine from reaching the forest floor. There was practically no undergrowth. It was like running on carpet.

In less than an hour, Canon emerged on the sharecropper's track, stopped and read the sign. A wolf grin stretched his lips wide. They had passed here, only minutes ago, moving at a trot from the look of the hoofprints. One of the horses had stepped on the long stem of wooodsbriar, mashing its tip into the dirt. Even as he watched, Canon saw the springy stem pull its tip free of the dirt. He was close.

Slowing to a trot, he warily topped a small rise in the road and dropped immediately to his knees. He quietly backpedaled down the hill. Five horses were tied to saplings next to the little spring three hundred yards away. Canon left the road and began to creep through the thinning woods.

A tiny stream bubbled down the hill to join the spring at the bottom. They had stopped to water the horses. The clear rivulet beckoned Canon to stop and drink, but he put the thought from his mind. Though the horses had probably muddied the spring, he would take no chance, unlikely though it was that he would muddy the rivulet and one of the outlaws notice it.

Canon waited for his breathing to regulate, then eased forward. One hundred paces nearer, he picked up the sound of voices, muffled by the trees between himself and the men. Canon was part of the forest now. Each step was planned and exact. Automatically, he chose the path that afforded the best combination of cover and least resistance.

When he was within twenty-five yards, he stopped. The voices, vague earlier, became distinct, and began to rise.

"I go first. I'm the one spotted her first," said one, petulantly.

"Yeah, but I'm the one with a arm shot near about off," said another. "If I'm aim to bleed to death, which I might just do and I don't get the blood stanched, I wanta die happy."

Then Canon heard Carolina Lee, and he had to smile.

"Now, gentlemen," she said in her coziest voice, "there's plenty for the three of you, I promise." Her voice was soft and fluttery as a magic flute. "Truth to tell, I'm starting to want it. I've had this fantasy for the longest time about being taken again and again by strong, tough men like you. I know it isn't ladylike, but I guarantee you that whoever has me first won't likely forget it, ever. I think I want it to be Billy over there. He's so cute."

"Hear that?" said a younger voice. "She picked me. Ya'll get the hell outta my way. Go argue about who gets second."

"She got no choice here and you sure don't, squarehead," laughed the first voice. "It's me that found her and it's me that's to unwrap her. Anybody who says me different will find me disputatious."

"Hell you say," cried Billy, and Canon heard the sound of scuffling, the thudding of blows. It lasted only seconds before he heard a whooshing "Oof," then silence. Edging closer, Canon knelt and peered out from under a bushy shrub. He saw the young one, Billy, step back, loosing his hold on a hunting knife he had plunged in the other man's chest.

Stabbed to the heart, the man swayed a moment, took a lunging step, and fell face down in the dirt.

Carolina stepped out of the shadows. Canon saw that the bodice of her dress was in tatters, as he expected. Part of it had been left back up the road, part of it had been used to bind the wounded man's arm. She held the shredded material to her shift, covering her breasts. She was not trying very hard to cover them, Canon noted with another grin.

"Oh, Billy, that was brave of you," she cooed. "You're going to get a little something extra for that," she said, running her tongue over her lips. Even in the moonlight, Canon could see Billy's eyes widen at the thought.

"What in Sir Harry's hell is happening here," roared a new voice. A thin, dapper looking man stepped into the glade, glanced down at the body on the ground.

"Jesus! He dead?" said the man, using his boot toe to roll the corpse onto its back. "What the Harry's hell is this shit? We stop to water horses and look at Tilman's arm, and now Henry's dead. I turn my back one goddamn minute to scout our back trail and look here. You goddamn fools!"

"Ain't no great loss, Captain," said Billy. "Me and Henry been at one another a long time. Had to end sooner or later, one way or t'other. Might as well be over a piece of Miss Purty Pie here as anything. Ain't that right, sugar." This last was spoken more as a confirmation than a question.

"Yes, Billy," Carolina said. "But I do believe now that I've seen him good that I would like the captain to go first. Captain, you have a feeling for me?"

"What?" cried the spurned youth, almost in tears. "You damn bitch. Here I just kilt a man over you. I ought to . . ."

"Stop this shit right now," yelled the captain, breaking Billy's threat. "You see what she's doing? Done shot Riley here and then got you to kill Henry. She's practically halved us already, which is more than the damned Rebels could do in three years.

"This shit is over, as of right now. The shack ain't a mile away. Once we get here there and find out what she knows and how much she's told, we'll all have fun. There's ways where we can all be first. Now hit the saddle."

The sound of hammers locking froze them all. Canon stepped into the clearing, guns pointed.

"Stay real still," he said, hoping they would do so. He needed at least one alive and wanted to take all three back. But the dapper captain immediately dropped to one knee and reached for his flapped holster.

Canon could scarcely believe how desperate these men must be, when one tries to draw from a flapped holster against a dead drop. Canon had time to direct his shots, and he wanted to make sure the man was incapacitated. The Krupps roared, the bullets took the captain high in each arm. He pitched backward and began flopping around on the ground. Riley ran. Canon shot him in each leg. Then Billy pulled a gun from his waistband, too quickly for Canon to worry about precision. Canon shot him once through the body. Billy's convulsive jerk triggered the pistol, the shot harmless to Canon. But Canon heard the captain, who had managed to gain a sitting position, grunt. The captain, both arms broken and dangling, looked wonderingly at the hole that had appeared in his chest. Billy's legs jerked twice and were still.

Carrie ran to Canon as he went to the captain, who in vain was trying to lift his broken arms to the wound. The captain rolled onto his side, his torso already beginning to loosen.

"Who sent you to kill Jackson?" Canon said, grabbing the man by the shirt collar. The captain, as though very tired, shook his head.

"I know you, Canon," he said hoarsely. "We hadn't planned to shoot you—just Jackson—but we was lucky. I admired you and General Jackson, want you to know that. But I don't rat." The man coughed an awful wheezing cough. "Time to go see Harry," he said, and died.

Canon turned to Riley. "Oh, you bastard," said Canon, angrily, "don't you dare die. Help him, Carrie." She ran to Riley, who was sitting in a growing pool of blood.

"Give me your knife, Rabe," she said. Canon was beside them in an instant, cutting away Riley's pants. One of the bullets had cut the man's femoral artery. He was already in shock. Carolina looked at Canon, shook her head. They stood and watched Riley die. It took little more than a minute. "Hell and damn," Canon shouted.

## 17

# *Hurry, General, Hurry*

Canon searched the bodies and boots of the four men. Three were dressed, like most volunteer Rebel soldiers, in homespun butternut uniforms. The captain wore storebought pants and shirt.

The search turned up nothing unusual except that each man carried fifteen thousand dollars in new Confederate issue. The sharecropper's shack yielded only a lamp, sleeping pallets of boughs and ground sheets, and a few changes of cheap clothing. Carolina took a shirt to cover the ripped bodice of her dress.

It took some time to re-rig the carriage, but Canon was pleased to see that Carrie knew her way around a horse and harness. She slept, snuggling into Canon, on the ride back to Richmond. She seemed to pay no mind to the four bodies tied to the saddles of the horses strung in a line behind the carriage.

The young sentry at the Confederate garrison in Richmond paid mind to the bodies, though, and tried to question Canon. He said General Beauregard, who was with Davis in Richmond now that Lee was back in the field, would want information.

"Just report the matter to the general in the morning, Private," said Canon, "and ask him to learn everything about these men he can. I will make a full report to him at earliest tomorrow."

The sentry wanted to protest and mentioned arrest, but thought better of it. He decided it would be unwise to argue with a man who brought in bodies by caravan at two in the morning.

Canon drove the rig to Carrie's house and woke her gently. He knew the cool night air would have her stiff and sore after the battering she had taken this day. Broken ribs and a bareback horseride would have anybody sore.

She groaned as she sat up. Canon came around the carriage and lifted her out, carefully as he could, and carried her into the house. He left the horse and buggy where they stood.

As he started to put Carrie to bed, she begged him instead to fill the bathtub for her from a barrel of tepid but fresh rainwater on the back porch. He obliged, then went in and dropped on the couch, removing only his moccasins and gunbelt. He, too, had expended some energy.

Canon needed sleep, but the extraordinary events of the day had his head in a whirl. So little had happened in his life since Jackson died, and now things were moving so fast he could scarcely find a starting place to sort them. He lay there, deep in thought, listening with part of his mind to Carolina splash around in the tub.

She was certainly a remarkable girl, Canon conceded. He wondered what she would have done if he had not arrived on the scene at the spring. She had seemed serene enough at the prospect of taking on all the outlaws, though he knew she had used her sex appeal to sow discord among them.

Canon did not blame her for that. And certainly could not have blamed her if she had been forced to follow through with her promises. Hell, he couldn't really blame her for trying to get away from him, even though she had tried to kill him in the attempt.

He cared for the girl. He couldn't deny it to himself. But neither could he deny she was a cold, calculating Yankee spy. Well, a calculating Yankee spy, anyway. The splashing ceased, and he heard her soft tread on the wooden floor as she went into her bedroom.

Canon had a strong impulse, a desire, to go to her, but he stifled the urge. Breaking a girl's ribs was not exactly foreplay, even if she deserved it. He would probably have to turn her over to Confederate authorities more skilled at dealing with spies. But he sure as hell dreaded the thought.

She would be asleep soon, thought Canon, though he could see her lamp still burning. From under the door to her room it slipped its soft yellow glow into the living room. The glow intensified, brightened into light as the door to her bedroom opened. What now? wondered Canon. Hell, he had not even searched her house. She could be coming out with one of those new Gatling guns for all he knew. He had tested her back at the rendezvous with the little pistol, but he and she knew that it would have taken a very lucky shot to stop him with that little gun. He reached down to his holster.

Carrie came into the room. She was fit to kill, all right. Dressed fit to kill. Canon thought he had never seen anyone so lovely. She was wearing a green satin evening gown, petticoats flaring out the dress and rustling like wind through autumn leaves, so low-cut it would have scandalized half of Richmond had she worn it in public. A cameo was strategically placed to highlight the swelling breasts rounding out of the bodice. She wore a green ribbon around her neck. Canon had no idea how she had managed to arrange her hair in so short a time, and he didn't dwell on it. It rose to a crown, with long soft curls hanging from it. She walked toward Canon; he noticed she was still not quite steady on her feet. She stopped, just out of reach. Canon was definitely considering reaching for her.

"I know I've been bad, Rabe," she said in a breathy voice, "and I don't blame you for not liking me. But I have always cared for you, truly, even though I did those bad things." She began to unbutton the dress. "And I have been dishonest with you. Very dishonest." The dress fell to her ankles. She stepped away from it, turned her attention to the petticoats. "I've been dishonest with you in bed." The petticoats rustled silkily to the floor. She began untying the strings to her shift. "The times I have been with you in bed were very difficult for me. One of the reasons I wouldn't let you make love to me more often is that, well, I had to control myself too much, and it is very hard for me to control myself with you." One string gone, two strings gone.

"One of the things I've really wanted to do is be with you like this," the shift slid down her body, puddled at her feet, "and really let myself go. Only one other man has ever really seen me like this." She pirouetted, her butterscotch curls flying around her face, the full breasts pointing out, pale pink tips swinging. The thick blondgold patch of pubic hair was damp along the furrow, the globes of her nether cheeks thrust out, firm and tight.

She walked closer. Canon could smell lilacs. She took his hand and began rubbing it over her body. It was soft as young cotton fresh out of the boll.

"I'm a very naughty girl, Rabe Canon. Have been for a long time. Was even, for a time, what people out west call a 'soiled dove,' you know what that means?" Canon nodded, and began to move his hand, tickling here, pinching there. Her breathing deepened, became ragged.

"I like the things men and women do together. Things that would shock most women, maybe even most men. Do I shock you, honey? I didn't think so." She began to move while standing still. Another aroma, pungent and earthy, melded with the scent of lilacs. She was writhing now, and occasionally a small moan escaped her. Canon aided and abetted all he could.

"I've always dreamed of total abandonment with a man I loved," she said, "that I, uh, uh, wait a bit, my darling . . . that I couldn't dominate but who wasn't cruel to me. But I've never had a love like that. Uhhhh. Not until today. So, ahhh, so if I should shock you, my . . . darling! Ohhhh. Forgive me. But this once, I am going to give, uh, and give, ummmm, and . . . ohhhh."

Canon drew her down to him.

He awoke with a start. Sunrise cast gold paint through the window of the bedroom. Carolina Lee was staring at him, a lewd smile on her lips. She twirled her fingers in his hair, said, "You lovely, lovely man. That was even better than my fantasies." She rolled on top of him, brought her face down inches from his own. Her morning breath was sweetsharp, like a loamy cloud rising from black dirt following a spring rain. He kissed her, deeply but not harshly. She pulled away a little.

"Rabe, listen to me, darling, and please try to believe me. I never, ever wanted you dead. I've cared a lot for you ever since those days in the hospital. I think I've fallen in love with you."

Canon's smile was wicked. "Happy to hear it, lovey. Can't think what might have happened if you had developed a dislike for me."

"I mean it, Rabe, damn you."

"Of course you do. You proved you were fond of me by trying to get me shot. Then you proved you were falling in love with me by trying to knife me in the back. I expect that if I ever propose marriage, I'll have to bring along an ax for you so you can chop me to pieces."

"I explained about the shooting, Rabe. I thought they would run. I was trying to save you."

"Yes, lovey, and the knife was for my protection, too, I'm sure."

"All right. I'm sorry about the knife. But I wasn't going to kill you, Rabe. I was afraid you would turn me in, so I wanted to, uh, incapacitate you so I could get away. I just wanted to slow you down. I'm a nurse. I know where to stick you without killing you."

"Well, I'm not a nurse," said Canon, lifting Carolina's supine body into the air and turning her upright to a sitting position, "but I know how to do that, too." He set her down on him. She squealed. A little at first, then a lot.

Later, Canon said, "Lovey, I have something important to ask you."

"What is it, darling? I've told you all I know. I swear it on, on . . . on this." Canon yelped and cuffed her lightly. "Behave yourself," he said, "and tell me the truth when I ask you this."

"Yessir, General," she said with a pout.

"Carrie, did you get a payday recently? From them?" Canon believed she had. The abductors had apparently been freshly paid, since all carried the same amount of new money. It was another little test for Carrie Lee, who now pouted for real.

"Darling, please don't take it," she said. "I truly need the money. I'm almost out."

"I won't keep it," said Canon, pleased she had told the truth. "Promise. I just want to see the envelope."

"I burned the envelope, but all it had was my name on it. They all have been like that."

Canon watched as she rose naked from bed and walked out of the room, twitching her truly glorious derriere for his benefit. She returned with a hammer, which she used to pry loose a section of door facing. She brought him a thick sheaf of Confederate bills.

Canon, naked, too, got out of bed and went in to search his gear. He returned with the things he took from the bodies last night, and those he took from the body of Rodgers.

All the Confederate money was of a series, though not consecutive. Except for that of Rodgers. It was a different series, but it did have a characteristic in common with the rest of the money. All the bills were counterfeit Confederate. The money was incriminating evidence, but did not provide much of a clue.

Canon figured Rodgers and his friends each had a haversack and locker in the barracks, which he would search, but it was unlikely they would leave money or anything incriminating in them.

He picked up the leather wallet that he took from Rodgers and reached down to his gunbelt for the bowie knife. It took only moments for him to locate the hidden flap, sewn tightly to the lining, even less time to cut away the thread. His low, tuneless whistle attracted the attention of Carolina Lee, now lolled back on the bed.

"What is it, Rabe?" she said.

"A coincidence, lovey," he replied. "One that I have to speak to General Beauregard about. No, don't ask me about it. You know too much already." She pouted again.

Canon put the wallet in his clothing, sat down on the edge of the bed. Things were more muddled, more tangled now than ever. Inside the wallet's flap rested a neat sheaf of new Yankee greenbacks amounting to five thousand dollars. And a ticket for ship's passage. To San Francisco.

Hello, thought Canon.


"HELLO, GENERAL BEAUREGARD," CANON said a few hours later, saluting the little man who had answered Canon's knock on his door. Pierre Gustave Toutant Beauregard returned the salute with a flourish, then took Canon's arm and walked him over to the chair opposite Beauregard's oversized desk.

Canon wondered for a moment on small men's penchant for large things. Many great generals and great leaders were men of small stature, making up in accomplishment what they laked in size. Lee was of medium height, and well made. President Davis was almost a gnome.

Beauregard matched Braxton Bragg in size, but was wiry where Bragg was merely thin. Beauregard's thick graying hair was neatly trimmed, as was his tiny moustache and goatee. As they took their seats, Canon noted maps on every wall. They were marked with blue lines that represented the Federal noose cinching ever more tightly around the neck of the Confederacy.

Beauregard ordered coffee and biscuits for them, made polite chitchat until it was served. The orderly placed the food, then stood next to the closed door.

"Shut the door," Beauregard said to the orderly.

The orderly looked confused. "General, the door is shut," he said.

"From the outside," said Beauregard. The orderly saluted and was gone.

Beauregard was Cajun, looked French, and cultivated the look, but he spoke soft Southern with no trace of French accent.

"General Canon," he said, gently, when they finished eating. "Perhaps you would be good enough to tell me just what the hell is going on."

Canon was ready to tell the whole story. He talked, uninterrupted, for an hour. Beauregard nodded from time to time, as if agreeing with what Canon said. Canon supposed that Davis, or Davis and Lee, had already told Beauregard of the suspicion that Stonewall Jackson had been assassinated. Beauregard just wanted a first-hand account.

Beauregard perked up when the recitation reached the events of the previous evening. Canon considered trying to downplay the role Carolina Lee had played. He did not want to see her hanged. Hell, he admitted to himself, he did not want to see her exchanged for a captured Southern spy, either, as was often the case. He felt that the aging Southern aristocrat sitting across from him would agree that Carrie would best serve the South if she could be turned to a double agent. He told Beauregard everything.

"Last night, one of the men admitted to me, before he died, that he was one of the eight pickets who shot me and General Jackson, and I believe the other men with him were on the assassination team, too," said Canon. "The man I killed earlier yesterday tried to kill me when I accused him of being one of the assassins."

"A pity none of them could have been taken alive," said Beauregard, accusingly.

Canon explained what had occurred. "At any rate, five of the ten men responsible for the death of General Jackson are dead."

"Then you, too, accuse General Powell Hill of complicity."

"No, sir. Not at this point. Eight Yankee infiltrators fired on Jackson and me. Someone in the Confederacy sent them there, and someone at Chancellorsville placed them on the picket line that night."

Beauregard was silent for a moment.

"Then you do not know?" he said.

"Know what, sir?"

"Captain Frank Lawson has deserted," said Beauregard stiffly. "He has joined Quantrell's band of outlaw raiders and is now condemned by North and South."

The news shook Canon. "Frank Lawson?" he said in disbelief.

"Yes, Captain Lawson. It was Lawson who placed the pickets that night, and who later reported them missing in action. Lawson."

Lawson, who bore a grudge against Jackson for his punishment at Fredericksburg, had served in McLaws' brigade under A. P. Hill. Hill's hatred for Jackson was well known within the army.

Canon drew from his uniform the greenbacks and the ticket for ship's passage to San Francisco, handed them to Beauregard. "Then that makes it eleven, sir," he said, "and one of them has to be a member of the Confederate cabinet. I take it that only cabinet members like yourself know of my mission to San Francisco, and this ticket was purchased, according to the date, yesterday afternoon. Someone worked very quickly."

Beauregard's features contorted, a look of intense pain flashing across his face. He smashed his fist on the desk.

"We are surrounded by treachery," he said in a strangled voice. "By God, I will look into this personally."

"Who knew about my mission, sir?" asked Canon.

Beauregard's eyebrows beetled. The anger was still there, but his voice sounded very old, tired and sad when he replied. "Too many, Rabe, evidently. Too damned many. It was a full cabinet decision. That's a dozen men, plus their assistants and undersecretaries, but President Davis felt he had to put all resources into this to learn whether the offer from California was legitimate.

"With the information you've given me, we can start a weeding process, but it will go damnably slow. It is a delicate business. It is bad enough to suspect that General Hill was at least aware of the plans for Jackson's assassination. To think that a member of the Confederate cabinet took part in it is no less horrible.

"It stands to reason. The same people who assassinated General Jackson are out to destroy the San Francisco mission. We now have to assume the

Yankees know every detail of your mission, and will stop at nothing to thwart you."

"Yes, sir."

"The Confederacy's fastest ship, the blockade runner *Southern Star* will be at your disposal. The voyage to San Francisco normally takes six months. *Southern Star* will make it in three. It will get you there. Nothing the Yankees have can touch her, and they won't be expecting you to sail. They will be expecting you to railroad out to Texas and then stagecoach the rest of the way. At least," Beauregard said with a deprecatory smile, "that was the decision of the cabinet.

"Since the cabinet is evidently compromised, it has been decided that you and your companion will ship out day after tomorrow. The Yankees will likely learn quickly enough that you are at sea, but they won't be able to shift a fleet soon enough to stop you from reaching California. You'll be put ashore somewhere on the coast near San Francisco.

"Getting you back, I'm afraid, will be a different story. Every Yankee clipper will be looking for the *Star* by that time, and the chances are too slim of her getting back home quickly enough with you aboard. You will have to ride back, so take along one of your much heralded horses.

"Our benefactor in California promised to provide an armed escort to get you back here safely, but the Yankees will be expecting that, too. Once you have the five million dollars, send the escort Southward without you. The escort and the *Star* will each act as a ruse to draw the Yankees, while you return as swiftly as possible by another route. Your companion will remain in San Francisco. Is all understood?"

"Yes, General," said Canon hesitantly, "but I have no plans or need for a companion. It is the first I have heard of it."

"Miss Lee."

"But, General . . ."

"No buts, General Canon. It is decided. Your mission is already largely compromised, but if the Yankees are as inefficient as we seem to be, there may yet be one or two of them who are unaware of what you are doing. If a story is needed to cover your absence, it will be that you have been sent west to recover your health. You will need a nurse. That will be Miss Lee."

Canon thought the story damned silly and a damned nuisance, but since he could not argue, he did not try to do so.

Beauregard waited for a moment to see whether Canon would speak. When Canon did not, Beauregard continued.

"We aren't sure just how Miss Lee fits in. She was passing information, but nothing of great import. We have watched her for some time. She seems to be of little consideration in the overall scheme of Yankee intrigue.

"There is one thing that makes her suspect. We have traced her back to Nashville. She arrived there about the time it was occupied by the Federal Army. Then we traced her further.

"She grew up in San Francisco, and her guardian was Adam Trask."

Canon almost said "Goddamn" in front of the straitlaced Beauregard.

"Our benefactor's banker," Canon said, instead.

"Precisely," said Beauregard. "But we can find no connection between Miss Lee and the five million dollars, other than the fact that she was under the care and protection of Mr. Trask for several years.

"She left his care rather abruptly several years ago. Much too long a time ago for her to have anything to do with any of this. I would prefer to think of it as just an oddity, but it is too damned odd for that, and this mission is too damned important. Do you realize how important, General?"

"I think so, sir."

"If we are continue to prosecute this war for two more years, which is our estimate of how long it will take to win it, we must have the five million. We must have it by next spring, at the latest."

"Yes, sir."

"Everything appears to be on the up and up with the money. Several important people, Southerners whose reputations are beyond refute, have seen the money and met our benefactor. The money is genuine. There is no question about that. It is five millions Yankee greenbacks. That is reason enough for the mission. But there are two things I want you to do for me, General Canon."

"Yes, sir."

"Watch your back . . .

"Yes, sir."

"And hurry, General. Hurry."

CAROLINA SQUEALED WITH DELIGHT when Canon told her she would be accompanying him to San Francisco. She had waited for him at his house, wondering whether he would expose her.

Canon had wondered about her, too, as he shopped away the afternoon in preparation for the trip. Beauregard was right, of course, Canon thought. Carrie had been too long gone from California to have anything to do with the five million, but her connection to Adam Trask surely must have some tie-in. What that could be or mean, he could not fathom now.

Looking at her, now, listening to her little-girl laughter, Canon wished he could trust her enough to simply ask about it. He guessed her ribs were sore as hell, but she made no complaint. Well, he thought, there was a three-month voyage ahead of them. She would heal on the trip, and much could be accomplished and learned in three months.

Carrie quieted. When Canon looked over at her, he was surprised to see tears coursing down her cheeks. Now what the hell, he thought. Noticing his baffled look, Carolina said, "I'm sorry, darling, it's just that I promised myself if I ever went back to . . . uh, ever went to someplace as glamorous as San Francisco, I'd go in the finest style and set people on their ears."

Jesus, thought Canon, what kind of spy is this? She almost admitted having been to San Francisco to me right then. He decided that Carolina Lee must be either the best or worst spy in the world. He had no idea which.

"All I have in the world are three ratty old dresses and two half-ratty ones, and some Confederate money that barely keeps me eating," she said. "But don't pay any attention to me, sugar. I'll be all right in a little while. I don't need new clothes to knock a stupid town on its ear."

Canon smiled. "You sure, lovey?"

She straightened up, lifted her chin. "Damn right," she said.

Canon sighed theatrically. "Then I guess I better send him back. Seems a shame, though."

She was instantly alert. "What's a shame; send who back?"

"Him," said Canon, drawing back the window curtain and pointing to a man on the wagon Canon had heard as it pulled up in front of the house.

The wagon bed was piled high with beribboned boxes of varying sizes and shapes. Carrie let out a squeal that put her earlier one to the utmost shame, and ran from the room.

Minutes later, an utterly bemused Canon watched a naked Carolina run from room to room where she had laid out the half-dozen gowns, frocks and dresses he had chosen for her.

"Honey," she said, twirling around in one of the gowns, "how did you ever size them so perfectly in all the right places?"

"It was easy, lovey," said Canon. "I just had them measure different portions of my mouth."

Her answering laugh was full-throated.

"Rabe, I have a marvelous idea," she said.

"Oh?"

"I'll put on the dresses, and you take them off me."

"You are a lazy bit of baggage, lovey."

"I know, dear," she said with a sigh. "It will probably take the entire afternoon."

Smiling, Canon reached for her.

That evening, as an exhausted Carrie Lee slept a happy sleep and an equally exhausted Canon wrote a couple of long letters to be posted next day. Then he, too, eased into the arms of Morpheus, the god of dreams.

He didn't tell Carolina that the dresses represented more than half the money he had taken from Jackson's killers. Beauregard's search of the men's haversacks and lockers turned up nothing unusual, and he had given Canon all the Confederate money taken from the men, plus the five thousand dollars in greenbacks plus another five thousand dollars in gold. Canon protested that it was too much.

"Everything must be first class, Rabe," Beauregard had insisted. "Even our benefactor must not know what desperate straits we are in."

"But, General, the Confederate bills are counterfeit."

"We will exchange them for real ones," said Beauregard. "They are worth just about as much as ours."

# 18

# *Bait; and Too Many Tangles*

The big clock on the capitol facade in Richmond belled noon. Canon looked over at Carrie, beside him in her bed. She was still in deep sleep. He counted the booming gongs, distractedly, just as he had counted them that morning at nine, ten and eleven.

His legs were bitingly sore from his long run Monday night. They had been merely stiff Tuesday. He thought he would be fine by Thursday evening, when he and Carrie sailed with the tide. He made a mental note to exercise every day on the ship.

He had reached another decision earlier. Old Scratch would go with him to California. He had not been able to spend much time with the black Arabian since Mary Anna had brought him, but it was evident that Scratch was in fine form. He would not risk Hammer's wound getting infected.

Nor would there be time to visit Mary Anna in Lexington. Canon wondered for the thousandth time if she had any suspicion her husband was murdered. He doubted it, knew he could never bring himself to tell her. At least not until the men who did it were in hell.

The thought of Jackson's death returned Canon to the problem. Too many tangles, he thought. It was Rodgers who tried to kill Canon from the rooftop. He was sure, remembering the sound of the Sharps. Then Rodgers had set Carolina up so he could kill her instead of Canon. The question was why? And Carolina could not have told Rodgers that Canon was going to California. She didn't know. Yet Rodgers had the damned ship's passage to San Francisco almost as soon as Canon himself knew about the trip. Tangles.

And Carrie. Canon cared for her but he knew he would be foolish to fall for someone he could not trust. Then there was Adam Trask. An honest banker, according to Confederate information. Canon snorted. He had always considered "honest banker" a contradiction in terms, just as he considered "shyster lawyer" a redundancy.

Trask, Carolina Lee and a mysterious benefactor willing to put the bankrupt Confederacy back on its feet: These people were destined to play large roles in Canon's life in the not too distant future. Whatever the roles, Canon was certain of one thing. He would bring the money back to Richmond or die trying.

At least three men who pulled triggers to kill Stonewall Jackson were still at large. One of the dead men had planned on going to San Francisco, probably figuring it would be a lot easier to kill Canon there than here. Maybe the other three felt the same way and were even now heading for California. Canon hoped so.

Carolina stirred beside him, opened puffy eyes, groaned in pain.

"Oh, Rabe, why didn't you just go ahead and kill me," she moaned. "I think I'm dying anyway. My body is one big bruise."

Canon flipped back the sheet tucked under her chin, looked her up and down. "If that is what a bruise looks like, lovey, women would be cracking their own ribs every day. All you need is a hot bath. I'll light the stove and put water on to heat, then go out to get us something for lunch."

"Please do, Rabe. Something good, and a lot of it. I'm starved."

"On second thought, you should do the shopping. After all, you're my nurse, you know, and I'm the invalid. We have to play the game, for anyone interested. I'll do the stove and water, then ride Scratch down to the dock. I need to check in with the captain of the ship.

"And if anyone tries to shoot me on the way back, lovey, I'll wring your lovely little neck when I return."

Canon meant the remark lightly, but some of the doubt in his mind crept into his voice. He saw tears start to well in her eyes and he turned away. Angry now at himself and her, he rose and hurriedly dressed in civilian clothes. He lit the stove and laid on a bucket of water. Before he stormed out the door, he buckled on the Krupp fifties.

Scratch crowhopped for sheer joy as Canon petted him, talked to him and fed him apples, one item which was now abundant in the South. The Southern harvest was going to be a good one, enough to feed the army and civilians through the winter. But unless Canon could bring home the greenbacks, the Southern spring would herald a hard summer.

Canon saddled Scratch, swung onto his back and rode up the street.

He stopped on the way to mail letters and send a telegram to Mary Anna.

At the dock, Captain Henry Jenson appeared as delighted as Scratch had been to see Canon. He looked to be middle-aged, though spry in his movements. His hair was thick, blond and curly, going to grayish white on the sides. The most famous blockade runner in the South, Jenson was the darling of Richmond. Earlier in the war, he made a fortune carrying out cotton and bringing back guns, a few staples and some hard-to-get luxury items for the wealthy.

As the war lengthened, Yankee blockades tightened and times grew lean. Jenson stopped bringing anything back for the wealthy few who could still afford luxuries, although the captain could have tripled his already large fortune. He still carried out cotton, but he returned with staples only.

The four-member crew swarmed down from the ship's rigging to meet Canon when he stepped aboard. They looked so much like Jenson that Canon was amused. Two were Jenson's sons, the other two were his nephews.

"And is the fine horse yonder the one we'll be boarding, too?" said Jenson, pointing at Scratch on the dock. Canon merely nodded, unwilling to let out more information than necessary.

Jenson took it in stride. He nodded, too, and changed the subject.

Richmond was practically the last deepwater port left to the Confederacy, and the *Southern Star* rocked gently at her ropes, lifted by swells of deep clear water. Canon stayed around for a couple of hours, getting to know the ship and crew. It should also be ample time, he figured, to receive an answering telegram from Mary Anna Jackson.

Canon had spent considerable time at sea, sailing to and from university. But he had never been aboard anything like the *Southern Star*. Even at her moorings, the ship looked as if she were cutting the waves. She was long and sleek and dark, carrying four masts. The *Southern Star* was built for speed, but also comfort. After talking with the crew, who knew only that Canon's mission was top secret and of great importance, he was sure the *Star* would get him to California. He hoped she would bring him back.

They would leave at midnight the next day, Jenson told him. "I don't know why you make this trip," said the captain, and for the first time Canon thought he heard a trace of Danish in the voice, "and I need not know.

But you have much on your mind, 'tis easy to see. Remove this one thing from your mind, sir, and worry on it no further. We will see you safely to your destination."

Canon believed him. On his way back to Carrie, another worry replaced the one of which Jenson relieved him. There was no answer at the telegraph office from Mary Anna. It was a small thing. There could be a hundred reasons for it. But it nagged at him. He sent another to her.

It was past three when he returned. Carrie had bathed, powdered, perfumed. If she was still angry or hurt, she gave no sign and Canon was grateful to her for it. She was humming, happy as a mouse, and lightly scolded him for making her wait to eat. She wore a light gray frock Canon had seen her wear many times before, but with a difference. He was pretty sure she was naked underneath.

She smilingly slapped his hands away when he reached for her, and set to work with the three huge skillets which had been heating on the stove. Minutes later, she dumped out mounds of eggs with peppers, and fried green tomatoes, cornbread and hominy grits. Canon did not ask where she got the coffee. It was dark and rich and real. He set in with a will.

He had left word at the telegraph office that reply to his telegram should be brought to him immediately, and had given his own address. When he was full to bursting, Canon groaned theatrically and pushed back from the table, ready now to face the rigors of packing. Carrie, having packed most of her things in his absence, walked with him down the street to his house to help him. Canon also wanted to bathe, and he wanted his own king size tub.

Joyfully, Canon filled the oversized tub. It was almost as much a comfort to him as his huge bed. He was soon soaking in cool water. He reached for a cigar just as Carolina stepped into the bathroom and began to unbutton her dress. Canon forgot about the cigar.

She removed the frock slowly, teasingly, delightfully. Canon smiled. He had been right about the underneath.

Without a word, Carrie walked over to the tub, knelt and took the soap from Canon's hand, placed it next to her on the floor. What she did next brought a gasp from Canon. And he wondered for the first time whether huge breasts also meant expanded lung capacity. Whatever the reason, Carrie could certainly stay under water a long time, he thought.

They spent a playful hour in the bath, after Canon pulled her in on top of him, and sloshed considerable water before he shooed her out with an admonition to get his bags out while he toweled himself dry.

"Have you ever been at sea, lovey?" he called after her.

"No, darling," she called back, as she buttoned the frock.

"I think you will be a natural sailor," said Canon. "If you didn't get seasick from all that sloshing around, I doubt you ever will."

Canon, still naked, had just joined Carrie in his bedroom when the knock sounded at his door. He pulled on bathrobe and slippers and stepped out to answer.

Expecting a messenger with a telegram, Canon was thrown into momentary confusion when he opened the door to find the prudish Beauregard standing on the porch. He quickly brought the general in, led him to the settee, and began to withdraw to put on clothes. Beauregard stopped him.

"I won't stay long, Rabe," he said, and Canon felt a twitch of uneasiness. He could not remember Beauregard ever beginning a conversation with another soldier by using the first name. Beauregard considered such to be beneath him.

Canon pulled the robe around his body and sat down in a chair. He looked expectantly at Beauregard, who appeared to be taking time to marshal his thoughts.

"Let me put this in perspective, Rabe," he said. "For some months now we have been monitoring all outgoing mail, including telegrams, from Richmond and the other cities of the Confederacy which are of utmost strategic importance.

"Following the recent revelations concerning the probability of, uh, treachery within this city, we have increased the amount of surveillance of the mails. I tell you this to make you understand that there has been no effort to single out your, uh, activities in any way.

"Each telegraph office has orders to report anything suspicious, and to report anything at all which is sent to certain individuals. The list of individuals is long. Some are on the list because they are suspects, others are on the list as a matter of protection for the person. Threatening letters and the like, you know."

Canon, wondering where all this was headed, merely nodded.

"Mary Anna Jackson has been on the list as a member of the latter category," said Beauregard. Canon inched up on the chair. "So we are aware that you have sent telegrams to her today." Again, Canon nodded.

"I have debated since yesterday whether to tell you this, Rabe. I will tell you frankly that I decided against it, in the interest of your mission. Now, since you have sent telegrams and will wonder about not receiving a reply, I feel it is best to tell you that Mrs. Jackson has been missing for two days. She went shopping for groceries in Lexington and did not return home.

"In all likelihood, she has been kidnapped, whether for ransom we do not know. Whether it concerns your mission, we do not know. Nothing has been heard from her since noon on Monday last."

Beauregard awaited Canon's reaction. There was none, or at least no outward appearance of reaction, except that Canon's fists clenched until the fingers whitened. It was the single manifestation of the cold resolve which filled Canon to the exclusion of anger. Making war on innocent women was too damned much. Spies like Carrie took their chances, but to victimize a lady like Mary Anna Jackson was unconscionable. When he spoke, the calmness of his voice surprised Beauregard.

"Sir, I respectfully request to be relieved of the California mission," said Canon, "and placed in charge of this investigation."

"Request denied, General," said Beauregard gently. "It is what I expected you would want and it is the reason I was reluctant to inform you of what has happened. The California mission must take precedence over everything. Any life—yours, mine or Mary Anna Jackson's—must be subservient to the cause.

"I give you my word as a gentleman that nothing will be spared in our search, and search we will. There is no reason for any sane person, especially anyone connected with the union, to want to see Mrs. Jackson come to harm. The operation was done too smoothly to have been the work of a madman.

"Still, it is baffling. You will be gone for six months at the very least. If

Mrs. Jackson is to be used against the mission, it would seem that it would have been better to wait until completion of your mission was imminent and assured before this action was taken.

"If Mary Anna Jackson is still within the bounds of the Confederacy, and it is difficult to imagine she is not, then we will find her. However, here is the thing you must understand, General. Mary Anna Jackson would willingly give up her life, as her husband did and as you or I would do, for the Confederacy. We must do our duty, General, and trust in providence."

Beauregard rose to leave. Canon saw him to the door, opened it. Before stepping into the waning afternoon, Beauregard said, "You have very few trumps in your hand, General Canon. Hold them as long as you can, but play them when you must." And he was gone.

Woodenly, Canon turned to the hatrack next to the door. Hanging from it was the gunbelt that held the heavy Krupp revolvers and the bowie knife. He reached first for the knife, had it halfway out of the sheath, then pushed it back down and slid one of the big pistols from its holster. It had never felt so heavy.

He approached the bedroom door. Even before he opened it, he could hear from within the room Carolina Lee. She was sobbing. He pushed open the door. Carrie sat on the bed, her frock on but only half-buttoned. Her face was down in her hands as she cried. Canon placed the cold steel muzzle under her chin and lifted up her head with it. She did not resist. Tears cascaded down her face. He put the muzzle between her closed eyes. The sound of the hammer cocking seemed somehow the loudest sound he had heard in his life.

She was trying to control the sobs now, hiccoughing from the effort. Her breath was in gasps between the sobs. She had heard it all, as Canon knew she would. As Beauregard, who doubtless was aware of her presence, also knew.

"I threatened once before with a knife if you lied to me" said Canon, softly. "or I could turn you over to Beauregard to hang, but I can't stand the thought of your delicate neck twisted and bent.

"It has to be quick and complete devastation for you, lovey, of your beauty. That's the only way I could bear it. This bullet is extremely large caliber. It won't leave much of your head, much less your face. But it's the best way. It'll haunt me, but not as badly as the other ways. I'll get over it in time. But even if I don't, it has to be this way. Because if you tell me you know nothing about Mary Anna Jackson, I'll pull this trigger. And even if you tell me where she is, I'll pull the trigger. So there is no way out for either of us. You'll be dead, and I'll be haunted."

The weeping woman fought to control her sobs. When she had done so, she looked at Canon, eyes flashing through the tears. "Then pull the fucking trigger," she said, anger stifling her sobs. "I don't know where the bitch is."

The words shocked Canon, but he knew she was telling the truth. Canon lifted the muzzle away from her face and disengaged the hammer. "I didn't think you did," he said. "But, my, lovey. Such language."

ONLY ONE MAN IN RICHMOND knew the whereabouts of Mary Anna Jackson. And Beauregard was wrong about him and about her. She was no longer in the Confederate states and the man was not sane. At least, he was no longer sane. Sanity had been gradually departing Hubert Hillary for years, like a tiny trickle of sand dropping from the top of an hourglass.

The trickle had grown exponentially the past few nervous months of Hillary's life. But as sanity departed, the innate sense of cunning sharpened. It sharpened to the point that he was able to conceal in all but the most depraved moments of his life the hysterical titter he had developed.

It was oh, so tasty, thought Hillary, the way the drugged widow of Stonewall Jackson had been slipped aboard ship in a steamer trunk. And it had been oh, so expensive to make arrangements with one of the seedier blockade runner captains to rendezvous with the Union vessel off the coast. Dangerous, too. Delectably so. Fear still thrilled through Hillary at the thought. The Rebel blockade runner and the piece of flotsam who was her disreputable captain would be at the bottom of the sea by now. The Pinkerton man, Wilson, was apparently very good at such things.

Hillary grunted, then groaned when the thin riding crop stung his flaccid penis as he lay supine on the couch. Then he tittered.

Carolina Lee languidly twirled ringlets into Canon's long blond hair as they lay in bed like spoons. Reaching around, she pulled at his chin until he turned to kiss her.

The hot August night had finally filtered away into the cooler hours of approaching dawn, but a light sheen of sweat from their lovemaking glistened in the dim glow of a single candle. When the long kiss ended, she looked into Canon's eyes.

He wondered again what strangeness motivated her. When he had put away his pistol, she had come after him, ripping away her dress in desire. They had coupled frantically, ecstatically on the floor, then she had dragged him to the bed for more, mewling and crying out as he took her again and again, aroused as he had never been. A soft gleam in her eyes now replaced the animal glint he saw in them as they made wild love.

"Can you love someone without trusting them?" she asked.

"Daybreak is no time for philosophy," said Canon. "Daybreak is time for breakfast. Now be a good little lovey. You will have a choice. I will cook while you sleep, or you cook while I sleep. If you choose 'B,' I will buy you a pretty when we reach San Francisco."

"Answer me, Rabe, damn you."

"All right. I think there are varying degrees of love, just as there are varying degrees of trust. But, basically, love *is* trust, in its deepest sense. A person can be enamored of another, without trust. And a person can certainly want to possess another, but possession, by definition, excludes trust."

"Do you think either of us could ever trust the other, darling?"

"Of course, lovey. Whichever of us finally kills the other, I promise the remaining party can truly and completely trust the corpse."

"You are a louse."

"Yes, Carrie, darling. I am a grayback. And you are a bluebelly, if not a blueblood."

"Rabe, I don't think you've ever called me darling before. Always 'lovey,' like you call all women. It sounds . . . nice. And I am a blueblood, or once was, if blueblood means being rich."

Canon felt his insides tighten, and hoped he could keep his breathing normal. He waited for her to continue.

"I won't tell you everything about me, not yet, Rabe. I already told you once what I was for a time in San Francisco. I was . . . a whore. I was very expensive, and very exclusive, but I was a whore." Her voice had gone throaty. Canon knew she was near tears.

"It's all right, darling," he said. "Your job was to make love and make people happy. My job has been to make war and make people dead. I suspect that neither of us had much choice, and your job sounds ever so much nicer."

Canon felt her hot tears fall on his shoulder. "Before that," she whispered, "I was kept by a man, an important man, in San Francisco. I ran away from him." She took a deep breath. "One of the reasons I wanted to go to San Francisco with you was so I could find that man and beg him to take me back."

"And is that what you still want, Carolina?"

"No. Maybe. I don't know. I don't think so. I think I want to stay with you, but you frighten me sometimes. And you hurt me, and I don't mean outside, I mean inside. This afternoon I really thought you would kill me, Rabe, and I didn't care. I just hated the thought of you killing me for something I didn't do." She broke down. "Damn you, I didn't care a fig that you were going to kill me, but I couldn't stand the thought of you hating me while you did it."

He held her as she cried herself to sleep.

Canon could not sleep. Carrie had said little that he did not know already, but the fact of her telling him mattered to him a great deal. It was one of the things for which he had cherished hope for many weeks. Now he wanted to wake her, tell her that her past life meant nothing to him except that her telling him about it would prove trust. He hoped she would truly come to trust him and was sure the voyage would decide it. Three months at sea would be perfect for them.

He dreaded the thought of her going back to Adam Trask, for it was no doubt Trask of whom she spoke.

For a few moments, Canon allowed himself the luxury of fantasy. He could take Carrie home to Mulberry, quit the army. They would sell the place, and he, Carrie, Buck and Mountain Eagle would head west. They would buy horses from Bill Kelley in Houston and go on to the plains, where they could live in peace and freedom with the Indians of Mountain Eagle's tribe.

But as dreams break with the dawn, so did Canon's fantasy. He knew he could not break faith with his duty. He could make little sense of all the tangles that now enmeshed his life, but he had to try to follow that tangled thread until it unraveled in his hand. Stonewall Jackson, Mary Anna Jackson, the Confederate nation itself were all his responsibility. So was Carolina Lee.

Another thought had come to him as he listened to Carrie. He now understood P. G. T. Beauregard's enigmatic parting instructions about playing trump cards when they must be played. Beauregard had seen it from the first. For some reason, the Yankee assassins now wanted to kill Carrie. She had somehow become a danger to them, and she would draw them out. She was the trump card of which Beauregard had spoken. She was bait, and Canon had been instructed to use her as such.

It was a hell of way for him to repay her trust, Canon thought. One hell of a way, he thought, drifting into sleep.

They slept until noon. He tried his best to put on a cheerful face for Carrie the rest of the day, but the helplessness he felt over leaving while Mary Anna was missing made him uncharacteristically fidgety. Everything was packed and there was nothing to do but wait for the wagon the Jensons would bring at dark. He paced away the hours.

The captain had chosen tonight for departure because there was no moon. Darkness was necessary now for the departure of any Confederate ship. Union Admiral Farragut had won the Battle of Mobile Bay on August 1, and the Federal fleet roamed the waters off the Confederacy unchallenged.

Slipping the blockade had been a constant worry to Canon. He was afraid his mission might end before it was hardly under way. Jenson, when he arrived that evening at eight to pick them up, recognized Canon's fears and laughed at them.

"The papers say you have never been successfully ambushed, General," Jenson said. "Neither have I. We'll be through the Yankees before they know we are gone."

Jenson was good as his word, and his abilities were apparent to Canon, novice as he was at the workings of a clipper. Scratch was skittish at first, but his master had put him through so many unusual tests, he decided this swaying slippery planking was just another game.

Canon spent an hour with him below decks, calming and soothing. The horse was fine.

At midnight, the *Southern Star*, a dark ship on dark water in a dark night, slipped her moorings and eagerly shot out to sea as if her sails were wings. By morning they were sailing the open sea.

The *Star* was sighted by Federal boats four times in the next three weeks, but only one Union vessel, another clipper, even offered to chase them. Jenson stood on the deck and laughed as the *Star* left it behind.

Canon made good on his promise to exercise at sea, though over the captain's objections. He began climbing the rigging the second day, wanting to learn how to scamper in, through and around it as the Jenson boys did. The captain threatened to pull rank and order Canon to cease and desist.

But he frankly loved to see someone as huge as Canon crawl among the high ropes and sheets like a great spider. By the third week, Canon felt at home amongst the masts and spars.

Scratch, too, got exercise, on board and in the sea. On calm days the horse was brought topside and put through his paces. After an hour's coaxing, Scratch, with Canon riding bareback, leaped over the railing and into the sea.

Thereafter, three times a week, Canon and Scratch swam once a day. Then Scratch was carefully hoisted aboard with the big boom used for lifting bales of cotton.

The long trip also gave Canon ample time to become thoroughly happy with yet another wartime invention that escalated the number of casualties exponentially. The self-contained cartridge had been perfected. It was no longer necessary to load cap and ball in the Krupp fifties. One deadly cylinder slid snug and smooth into each chamber of the Krupp specials and stayed there, still and ready as death, with no chance of spillage or becoming wet.

Jenson brought a crate of the ammunition along. Canon practiced with his pistols every day, and with his rifle, and he practiced his knife throwing. Proud of his marksmanship, and needing the work, Canon delighted in the amazed expression of the crew as he blasted thrown bottles with bullets from either pistol, and placed round after round, snap shot, into a tiny circle drawn on a hunk of driftwood Jenson tied to the mast.

Carrie was amused and touched by the change in Canon at sea as the miles and the leagues and the war fell away behind them. His dark mood lightened as the days passed, and his skin darkened. He wanted to fit in with the Californians, who would be dark from the sun, so he worked the rigging dressed only in cut off canvas pants.

Halfway into their journey, Canon was in top physical condition. Gradually, the cares of war and death and kidnaps waned and finally ceased.

Carrie would have sworn that worry lines disappeared from Canon's face as time passed at sea. Strain slid behind them like the smooth wake that marked their voyage.

On deck one day, near the midpoint of the trip, Carrie slipped her arm through his and told him she loved him. And she silently wished on a star that night that they could be through with war forever.

Canon instructed the crew to begin calling him Robert Johnston, as he was to be known in California. The name was half Robert E. Lee, half Albert Sidney Johnston, the first Confederate commanding general. Johnston had died at Shiloh.

Carrie was to be Mrs. Johnston. That day, he moved her into his cabin. Canon and Carrie had tried to be secretive about their trysts, finding excuses to be alone in his cabin or hers. But there can be no secrets on a small ship with a small crew, and when the Jensons began to wink goodnaturedly, Canon and Carrie winked back. He moved her in with him.

One occurrence marred the marvelous trip, but another close behind it made up for much for the calamity. On a particularly calm and balmy morning, *Southern Star* cruised quietly into a foreign and exotic port to take on supplies and fresh water. They would have to wait a day for the tide to take them back out. The captain announced the crew and passengers would have a day of relaxation ashore.

They took full advantage. Canon and Carrie dressed in their finest, it being their first chance to wear their new clothes.

No one could possibly interfere with them. Jenson had only chosen the port a week earlier, when supplies began to run low. They were completely safe, and for a day the seven of them mingled with the colorful people, making friends who joined them for drinks and exotic fare on which Canon gorged himself.

That evening they all became deliciously, hilariously intoxicated. The night sealed for the seven a friendship that began on board. Canon had feared that close quarters on ship would finally begin to grate on nerves, but the Jenson boys were a rollicking crew, always laughing, and the master of the ship was the type of person who invites and treasures trust.

When the first pearly fingers of dawn crept into the garden bar in which they had chosen to end the night, the Jensons offered a last toast to "Mr. and Mrs. Johnston" and went back to relieve the guards Jenson had hired and to direct the loading of supplies.

Canon and Carrie rented for the day a small cottage away a bit from the town. They had enjoyed each other many times aboard ship, but Carrie confessed she had been looking forward to time alone.

"If I groaned and squealed on ship as much as I wanted to, they would think me the most depraved wanton they'd ever seen," she said.

"You are a depraved wanton, lovey," said Canon. "It is what I find most attractive about you."

When they returned to the ship that evening, Canon thought Captain Jenson seemed troubled, but put it down to the blasting hangovers all developed that day. Jenson kept throwing troubled looks that had Canon on the verge of taking him aside to ask about them. Soon after the *Star* was at sea, though, he asked Canon to his cabin.

Jenson had terrible news. Atlanta had fallen September 1, less than a week after the *Star* had sailed. Canon could hardly believe it. Sherman had made stabs and forays and sieges at Atlanta, but had always been driven away with awful loss. Now the Queen of the South had fallen. Atlanta was the gateway to the inner South, the granary, and Sherman was through the gate and into the pantry. It was catastrophic, and it tripled the importance of Canon's mission.

It weighed heavily on him as the voyage, in mid-October, entered the last leg. Jenson estimated they would reach landfall the first week in November.

With the announcement, Carrie saw Canon begin to revert to his role of warrior, to the rock-hard leader of the Stonewall Brigade. It was difficult for both of them. Canon had forgotten, before the voyage, what it was like to be truly carefree. Now that he had recaptured that feeling, it was time to lose it again.

He was charged with responsibilities grown more awesome than before. Canon still believed within himself that he had cost the Confederacy its main weapon by letting Stonewall Jackson get killed. Now he had to redeem himself for it, and he owed Jackson double duty, for Canon also had to find out what happened to Mary Anna, if she had not been found when, and if, he returned.

After the *Star* resumed its voyage, Carrie saw that Canon joked less, spent more time alone. His jaw began to tighten, bringing back some of the worry lines on his face. She understood that San Francisco and whatever awaited them there was little more than a month away. And she knew that Canon must start mentally preparing himself for it.

Before this side of Canon that was new to her, this carefree Canon she had come to truly adore, disappeared, she decided she would cling to it closely as possible.

That night, after they had made love in his cabin, she said, simply, that it was time he knew about her. Canon, who had been lightly stroking her and was on the verge of sleep, came instantly awake.

"I was born in Carolina, and my mother named me for the state as she was dying from my birth," she said. Canon, thinking of his mother's similar death, felt a pang of empathy. "Daddy couldn't live there any more, he later told me. Soon as I was old enough to travel, we went west to the gold fields. He struck the gold, too, but it took him years.

"I was raised pretty free, around the gold camp, until then. But I was treated better by those rough men than anybody has treated me since. They were always perfect gentlemen. But by the time Pa hit the vein, I had started turning into a real girl. I still would have been safer in that camp than anywhere else, but he wanted to polish me up and have me become a lady. He took me to San Francisco and put me in a fancy school.

"It pleased me to find that though I was raised in a gold camp, I wasn't far behind the school's spoiled brats in my lessons. You'd be surprised at the amount of educated men who get gold fever and they had been happy to tutor me.

"Anyhow, I was in school and doing well, and we lived high, Pa and I. The mine was doing wonderfully. Then Pa went back to check on the mine and got himself claimjumped and killed. I was seventeen, and all of a sudden I was broke and alone. Lots of the miners wanted to take me in, and they would have been a pa to me, with no strings.

"But our banker, his name was Adam Trask, took me. In lots more ways than one. Within a month, virgin that I was, I was in his bed begging for it. He has that effect on women. But he had also staked my Pa and treated us both decent. I grew up with a crush on him.

"I loved him, Rabe, or so I thought, and I thought he loved me. He sure could get me in a lather.

"After I had been with him a couple of years, though, he started taking me for granted. Then one night he arranged a dinner for me with another man. There wasn't much doubt of what was expected of me. Adam said it was a measure of my love for him and that it would excite him, seeing me with another man.

"I didn't mind it much, Rabe. The man was very handsome and powerful and polished, just like Adam.

"All of them were, that he had me 'entertain.'

"It went on for several months, then I came home one night from some errand he sent me on and he was half-drunk by the time I got back. He didn't drink a whole lot very often, because he knew it changed him. Bad. But he said he had a surprise for me. He made me drink with him . . . and he had put something in it. It didn't make me pass out, it just put me in a sort of dreamy, pleasant way. Everything seemed about half-real and sort of warm and fuzzy. I even helped him undress me and tie me to the bed.

"Then he brought in a woman. She was older, about his age, but very attractive. I did everything they wanted. And as long as I'm telling the truth, you might as well know it all. I liked it, too. I thought he wanted me to like it. Even when the drug started to wear off and she left, I wasn't upset about it. But Adam was.

"I guess he wanted to humiliate me, and hadn't really wanted me to enjoy it. He called me horrible names and started slapping me. Then he got out a quirt and really beat me." She paused. "When he started burning me with his cigar, I fainted.

"When I fainted, I guess he decided it wouldn't be fun to burn me while I was unconscious, I don't know, but anyway he didn't burn me much more. When I woke up next morning he was all humble and apologetic and sorry. And I let on like I forgave him. A week later, when I was well enough to walk, I waited one day until he left for work and then I took all the jewelry and money I could find and cleared the hell out.

"And then I . . . whored for a couple of years in another part of town. It's a wonder he didn't find me, because I knew he was looking for me. But the lady who ran the place knew Adam, and had hated him already because of a couple of girls he had ruined. She only got me patrons who were on their last night in town and were going far away, so there would be no chance of Adam hearing about me.

"Then about two years ago, this nice man I had been with took a liking to me and moved me to Nashville. And I became a spy. And now I've fallen in love with you. Rabe, whatever it was I felt for Adam was different. I loved him for his smoothness and power and money and his pretty ways.

"But the difference of what I felt for him then and what I feel for you now is the difference between heaven and hell. I love you, Rabe." Her soft voice became a whisper. "But what about you, Rabe? What are you going to do with me? Do you hate me?"

Canon did not hesitate. "Listen to me, darling," he said. "I'm sorry you had to go through those things, but I'm also glad, if they're what made you into the girl you are. I think you're the most wonderful girl I've ever known."

"Truly, Rabe?"

"Yes, truly. I wish I knew how this mission will end, but I suspect it is going to get very dangerous. But it will be quick, our time in San Francisco, and then we'll be together. I want us to be together for a long time. All right?"

"Yes, darling."

"But you must promise to do as I say, without question, and to trust me. Just like I'm going to trust you. Will you do that, Carolina?"

"Yes."

Their lovemaking that night was urgent but tender. They loved like they were storing up love for whatever disaster lay ahead.

A storm hit as the *Star* neared her destination, and for three days the sleek ship fought for life. Captain Jenson admitted later it was the roughest he had seen. The morning after it cleared, Canon, in the crow's nest, shouted, "Land, ho!" He saw the misty outline of the California coast.

Jenson called the storm a freak. Canon feared it might be an omen.

# 19

# *Not Nearly So Many*

San Francisco seemed more than real. It was gold rich and booming. Canon looked on in amusement at men who the day before had been penniless prospectors, and who now wore top hats along with their ragged overalls and clodhopper shoes, and smoked ten-dollar cigars. Almost any cigar cost ten dollars. Supply and demand in the city had sent prices soaring, and the new rich were willing to pay almost anything to get the luxuries they wanted.

Canon was glad Beauregard had insisted on being generous with funds. Rooms in the middle class hotel in the nearby town, where he left Carolina, cost twenty-five dollars a night.

She begged to go into San Francisco with him, but Canon had been adamant. She would stay here, fifteen miles away, while he scouted the city and met the benefactor. Once matters were squared to his satisfaction, he promised, he would send for her.

They waited until night to go to shore. Captain Jenson rowed Carolina in as Canon and Scratch swam after them. Jenson saw to a covered carriage for her, shook hands with Canon and wished them well. The *Star* would patrol off shore. Canon would light two signal lanterns when he wanted to board, and Jenson agreed to previous plans. If he saw Yankee ships, he was to run the *Star* homeward to try to draw pursuit away from Canon.

Canon hoped everything would go smoothly so he could bring Carolina Lee to San Francisco. He dreaded her meeting Adam Trask again. Perhaps she would find that she still loved Trask. Canon knew better than to try to prevent a meeting, though. That was a coward's way and solved nothing. Still, he dreaded it.

He spent the night and morning with her. At noon, she waved goodbye to him from the window, fluttering a lacy handkerchief as he rode away on Scratch. Canon was almost out of sight before he realized the "handkerchief" had been her underwear.

Canon shopped that morning, and was dressed western. He wore black canvas pants, a dark checkered longsleeved shirt and a black broadcloth vest and coat. He wore his calf-high moccasins, disdaining heavy cowboy boots. He also wore a black western hat with the lowest crown he could find. He wanted to cover his long blond hair, but did not want to add to his height.

A third of the cowboys he saw were wearing gunbelt and pistol. Canon carried the Krupp fifties and his gunbelt in a small canvas bag along with a change of clothes. Before leaving, he slipped the big bowie knife in one moccasin and a small caliber hideaway gun in the other.

Three hours later, he reached the cauldron of 1864 San Francisco. It was a cowtown on the verge of becoming a great city. An opera house and a stockyard were on the same street, two blocks apart. Cowboys, prospectors and swells gambled side by side in saloons. Canon blessed the homogenized population. His six-foot-seven inch frame, while certain to draw a look or two, was no more than a slight oddity in a hodge-podge of strange beings come to California to get rich fast. Canon would employ the techniques Mountain Eagle taught him to diminish the appearance of his size.

He toured the town for two hours, familiarizing himself with streets and landmarks and waiting for darkness to fall. He saw some bluecoated soldiers, but they wore the garb of fort cavalry instead of the Northern army's uniform. Canon sensed no threat from them.

In the middle of town stood the imposing edifice of the Carlton, one of the finest hotels in the world. Its six stories were of shining red brick, and even in Montgomery men who had never seen it and never would spoke of the luxurious Carlton.

Canon circled it a half-dozen times. Inside it, on the second floor, Mr. Orbi was supposed to be waiting for him. He said he would wait for Canon at the Carlton through the first two weeks of November. Canon was a week ahead of the November 14 deadline.

It was nearly eight A.M. when Canon grabbed his light luggage and left Scratch at a stable two blocks from the Carlton. Saloons and music houses were lit up like Christmas trees, sidewalks were crowded, and Canon drew little notice in the bustling throng. He moved in a slight crouching slouch, bending his knees just a bit more deeply than normal, rounding down his shoulders the merest inches to hide his height. Nobody paid him any mind.

Canon passed the enormous revolving door of the Carlton twice and noticed nothing he considered suspicious. On the third pass, he went inside and thought for a moment he would sink to his knees in the rich crimson carpet, so thick and deep it was. His stride never faltered, and he took no time to marvel at the splendor of the room's interior. He moved easily, un-hurriedly to the least occupied corner of the crowded lobby, automatically choosing the lowest chair so he could further disguise his height.

In accordance with Mountain Eagle's Rule Number One, Canon noted ways out of the place soon as he was in. Exits, stairs and places for cover were automatically filed in his mind. Then he scanned the room for people who might be inordinately interested in his presence. Canon spotted them right away.

Three men, perhaps four, were waiting for someone, and trying not to be conspicuous about it. They, too, had chosen corners of the room. One of them, the one nearest Canon, was just a few seconds slow in raising the newspaper back up in front of his face. The fourth man, the one Canon wasn't sure about, suddenly got up off the settee near the front desk and put his arm around a beautifully gowned and coiffed woman who had come through the door. They left.

So it is three, thought Canon, who are waiting for Mr. Johnston. He rose and walked to the desk. A momentary flicker of interest flared on the face of the clerk as Mr. Johnston signed the register. Canon dropped the pen he was holding, bent to retrieve it.

In the polished brass plating of the desk front, Canon saw the man with the newspaper rise, glance toward him, and head for the stairs. Mr. Johnston's arrival would soon be announced, no mistake. Canon was given the key to 211. He asked the clerk if Mr. Orbi had by any chance checked in. Mr. Orbi was next door to him, in 213, said the smiling clerk. Orbi had the corner suite.

Canon gave the liveried bell captain ten cents to see to his luggage, then wandered through the double doors at the back of the room. The doors opened, as he thought they would, on the huge walled courtyard he had glimpsed through a wrought iron gate as he circled the hotel.

Lanterns flickered throughout the groomed yard, making the leaves on manicured eucalyptus trees and tended islands of grass shine like emeralds. The brick courtyard wall encompassed the back and both sides of the hotel, but the sides were given to garden paths through flowers and magnificent ancient oak trees.

Canon guessed the half-dozen oaks covering the courtyard had presided over this spot of ground for the past century. Lantern light was dim here, away from the marble tables and cobblestones of the main courtyard. He wished he had Carrie with him to stroll this secluded area, rich with the mingled aromas of eucalyptus and loamy ground.

The oaks, with trunks the size of size of siege mortars, were still in green foliage, blocking light from street lamps on the sidewalk. Lower limbs, so big that Canon could not have gotten his arms around any of them, stretched out over the courtyard in one direction and over the six-foot high wall toward the street.

The courtyard was deserted. It was likely more popular at lunchtime, Canon decided, with the huge limbs casting shade over the dozen tables set among the islands of grass. It was a likely luncheon spot, and he could envision the place filled with frilly parasols and fruity frappes.

The limbs ran like yardarms over the wall, providing shade, too, for passersby on the street. Toward the hotel, the limbs had been pruned and shaped, but still were of such size and plenty that they must also provide shade for the occupants of rooms.

No harm in checking out everything that can be checked, thought Canon, glancing up into the greenery of the oak nearest the courtyard wall. He ambled back into the lobby and stepped toward one of the bars. The lobby itself was richly done in gold, silver and crimson. The doors of small shops dotted it and Canon perused the window displays with wonderment. He could buy anything from cigars to a frock coat within the hotel.

The bar was full of people and dimly lit. Canon was glad of it. He moved quickly through the crowd, again noting exits and entrances. One door left of the bar would exit into the courtyard on the left side of the hotel, the door at the far right would be a street entrance. A smaller door, near the courtyard exit, had a hat and coat rack next to it. That would be the way to the privy. Canon went to it, hung his coat on a hook, then moved fast as he dared without calling attention to himself.

He was standing in the shadows next to the front entrance when two of the men he had noticed in the lobby entered the bar. They spotted his coat almost immediately. When they headed toward that side of the bar, Canon walked out the front door.

An alley bordered the courtyard at the left and at back. Canon cut back to the deserted alley. He took one quick look around, then pulled himself to the top of the fence, lay flat and looked over the courtyard. He waited five minutes, by count, in which time one of the men who had followed him into the bar walked out into the courtyard, looked around, and walked back inside.

In one fluid motion, Canon stood and jumped for the oak limb, big as his body, just over his head. The rough bark felt good to his hands. In seconds, he was high up in the tree above the yard. After months of climbing the ship's rigging, it was the work of seconds for Canon to scurry like a squirrel through large interlocking high limbs of the trees. He was soon sitting in the fork of a tree less than fifteen feet from the open windows of rooms 211 and 213.

There was no one in view in what he could see of Orbi's suite. In his own room, Number 211, two men were hurriedly going through his luggage.

Canon was not surprised. His main concern was whether the men were Orbi's or Yankees. The answer came quickly. A dapper man in slippers and green silk smoking jacket appeared in 213 and walked through the door connecting it to 211. He watched them finish their search, then took them back through the door to 213. He locked it and placed the key in the pocket of his jacket.

Very accommodating hotel, the Carlton, thought Canon.

When the little man began to talk, Canon inched his way up the limb until he could hear.

". . . knew there would be nothing untoward in his luggage," said Orbi, or so Canon would consider the man to be until he learned differently. "It is the general, no doubt. But he should have been here by now. One of you fools, you, Williams, go out in the corridor, get Casey and get your asses down to the bar and surveil him, and don't let him see you. Flannigan, you take the corridor watch."

Canon noticed that Orbi constantly rubbed and scratched at a thick red rash on his face and neck. That must be hell even in this mild climate, Canon thought. He waited in the tree. Williams returned to the room ten minutes later, hesitantly said to Orbi, "He's just not in the bar, sir. The bartender noticed him. Said he went out the front door. He's probably just looking at the town, sir."

"And you'll be looking for another post, you idiot, if anything happens to him. General Canon is well known, even here. His photograph has been in every newspaper and his size will attract attention wherever he goes.

"All our men have been alerted to watch for and protect him, but what if some hothead union fool recognizes him and shoots him on the street? Canon must get that money back to the Confederacy. Alert everyone. We find him and we see to his safety." The men hurried from the room.

Relief and embarrassment flooded through Canon. Well, he had always wondered what it felt like to be small, and now he ought to know. He felt as if he were a foot tall. He had been suspicious about the mission, about Mack Orbi, about everything.

There was no way Orbi could have known Canon was eavesdropping. Everything else might go to hell, but the benefactor was clearly what Canon and the Confederacy hoped he would be. It was up to Canon to live up to his own reputation. Chagrinned, Canon carefully negotiated his way back along the limbs. What an ass he would have seemed had he been caught.

No, he reconsidered, probably not. A man careful as the benefactor would understand Canon's desire to make sure everything was square, just as Canon had understood the searching of his luggage. Regardless of his own prejudice against Trask, Canon now felt confident of the mission's success.

In one of his few talks with Carolina about Adam Trask, he asked her which side the man was for in the war. Her answer gave him hope.

Trask cared only about power and money, she assured him. Trask would come down on the winning side, she said, because Trask would not choose sides until the war was over. Carrie, to Canon's surprise, had not pressed him once about the mission. He guessed she not only knew Canon would tell her nothing, but she really had no choice about coming along.

Three minutes after Canon retrieved his coat from the bar, he knocked at the door of Room 213. He had picked up quite an entourage coming through the lobby. Four people followed him up the stairs, and two more were waiting in the hall.

"Yes?" came the reply to his knock.

"Robert Johnston here," said Canon, feeling silly about the appellation in spite of himself. He heard a muttered, "Thank God," in response and berated himself again for his unwarranted suspicions. "One moment, sir," said the thin voice. It was more like a couple of minutes, but finally the door opened and Mack Orbi greeted Canon with undisguised relief. "Welcome, Mr. Johnston, welcome," said the man, shaking Canon's hand and drawing him into the room.

Immediately, Canon saw the reason for the delay at the door. Orbi had changed into suit coat and patent leather shoes. Idly, he also noticed that Mr. Orbi appeared taller than he had thought, and that his hair, brown dappled with gray, had reddish highlights Canon had not picked up in the dim light outside the window.

As they walked into the sitting room, Canon saw that Orbi had a strangely rolling gait. After a quick glance at the man's feet, he knew why the man appeared taller and was amused by the reason. The man was wearing lifts in his shoes. Well, thought Canon, remembering P. G. T. Beauregard's extra large desk, small men sometimes do go to extremes.

They sat in overstuffed chairs, and when Canon admitted that he had not eaten since morning, Orbi nodded at one of the three men standing near the doorway. He hurried from the room.

"Please try this excellent bourbon, sir," said the host, "and here is branch water to mix or chase." The bourbon was excellent indeed, but Canon watered it liberally and drank sparingly. When he and the money were safely on the way home, he would drink deeply to celebrate. Until then, he would be moderate.

At least in drinking. For thoughts of moderation vanished when the large platters of food arrived, so quickly that Orbi must have ordered them as soon as he heard Canon was in hotel. Canon had a beefsteak at least three inches thick and actually hanging over the sides of the large serving platter. With it were oriental dishes of rice mixed with seafood and poultry. Canon ate greedily while his host entertained in his whispery way.

"You are without doubt the largest man I have ever seen," he said, "yet my men say you literally disappeared in the bar crowd. I had set them to wait for you, as they have done for the past week, for your protection." Orbi laughed quietly, deprecatingly. "They saw you and then they did not. I've been worried sick about you."

Any vestiges of doubt about the man's honesty immediately vanished from Canon's mind. If there had been a clandestine reason for having him watched, Orbi would never have been so open about it.

"It is a strain to take a foot off one's stature," Canon said, "but I thought it best not to attract attention. I guess when I was in the bar, I finally realized I was in San Francisco and wanted to have a quick look at the town."

Canon hated to lie so shamelessly, but he was too embarrassed to tell the truth.

"Quite right, sir," said Orbi, admiringly. "Quite, and well done. Anyway, it is a great relief and a great honor to have you here. You cannot know how good it is to see you, my dear General.

"Don't worry about speaking freely in here. All is precaution, I promise you. You are one of the South's great heroes, General." Canon felt a fleeting sadness as he recalled Stonewall Jackson saying the same words to him.

"To know that it is you," continued Orbi, "the leader of the Black Horse Cavalry, and the Stonewall Brigade, who will act as my agent in allowing me to do for the Confederacy what I have so much wanted to do—it is almost too much."

Canon raised his glass in a toast. "Then you are George McClavel. I wondered. But it is the Confederacy who thanks you," he said. "Your name will live forever in the south."

"Do you think so? How wonderful. Now, here, Rabe—it is all right for me to call you so, when we are alone? Good, thank you. Please listen carefully, Rabe. I have a number of men throughout the city, all sniffing day and night for any hint of interference with our plans. We have found none, but we must remain vigilant. There are those who would stop us if they knew what we are about.

"You are a known man, Rabe. I must ask you to stay close by until we have you on your way home on the stage, guarded by my men. They will get you safely through to Texas, do not fear differently, and put you on a train. Then they will join the nearest Confederate regiment to fight for Dixie. But nothing must prevent the money's getting to Richmond."

Canon was impressed by the man's earnestness. He made a silent vow that nothing would stop the money from getting to the Confederacy.

Orbi said Canon would receive the money the following afternoon. It would be Wednesday and the bank closed on Wednesday afternoon, so there would be no observers. On Thursday morning, Canon would take the morning stage eastward, flanked by Orbi's riders.

With that happy thought, a nightcap toast to the success of the mission and a last handshake, Canon retired to his room. Canon's own plans for the return trip, if the *Star* was not available, should come to fruition within a very few days.

In bed, too excited to sleep, Canon wondered if he ought to let his host in on those plans. Extra men might come in handy. But no, they might also slow him down. Canon wanted free movement if he had to resort to his own maneuvering. He remembered Stonewall Jackson's admonition: If no one but himself knew his plans, there could be no interference with them. Canon could tell Orbi, if it became necessary, in his own good time.

He thought of the lush Carolina Lee lying only a short ride away, and wished he could go to her. She would be happy to see him, too, he thought. But it was all right. A night apart would make their next night together all the better. Tomorrow, he would get the money. By tomorrow night, he would have five million dollars and Carolina Lee with him. Not bad for war time, thought Canon, as sleep finally enfolded him.

The next morning seemed endless. No, he was told, he could not see Mr. Orbi, who was out "seeing to things." Canon admired the man's thoroughness, but he was left to sit through the day, with only short distractions by an excellent breakfast and lunch, which he was too nervous to fully enjoy. He dressed in broadcloth suit, four-in-hand tie and cowboy boots he bought at one of the shops downstairs.

At two p.m., a nattily attired Orbi knocked on his door and Canon followed him out into the corridor. Orbi gave a short, sharp whistle. Doors to each of the eight rooms on the second floor sprang open and sixteen men stepped into the hallway. They split into two groups, eight preceding and eight following Canon and Orbi. Some were dressed as cowboys, some as dandies. All were wearing guns, either in gunbelts or under their coats in shoulder harness.

"As I said," smiled Orbi, "I have tried to take every precaution." Canon was impressed, and said so. He had rarely seen such meticulous care. The group went down the stairs and walked out onto the boardwalk beside the muddy street. It had not rained and the mud puzzled Canon. Orbi noticed Canon's puzzlement and pointed down the street to a wagon pulling a large wheeled cylindrical tank. "Water wagon," he said. "Often dusty here this time of year. The streets are watered each morning and afternoon."

Two blocks of shops and saloons beckoned to them before they reached a squat, two-story brick building built more like a fort than a downtown business. The facade bore a gaudy sign, Bank of San Francisco. One of the men in the lead group knocked twice on the door, paused, and knocked twice more. The door swung open and Canon found the inside of the bank as different from the outside as two things could be different. All was silk and pink marble. Persian rugs and rich tapestries lent an air of opulence unsurpassed even by the Carlton. Mahogany gleamed blackly in the muted light.

Two bank employees, dressed in red uniforms of spangles and gleaming brass, fawned over the group as they led the way down a marbled hallway bedecked with paintings and etchings to a door marked, with a solid gold plaque, "Adam Trask, president and owner."

Canon anticipated the meeting with a mixture of distaste and delight. He was about to make the acquaintance of a man who had tortured Carrie, but who was willing, regardless of what Carrie had said, to risk his obviously healthy economic well being to save the South. Carrie could not have an inkling of the awesome economic power of the North, and Trask risked facing that power. Canon decided he could forgive the man practically anything for that.

He found himself standing next to the door, the others obviously waiting for him to do the honors. Canon gave an inward shrug, knocked twice, and was bid enter by a rich rolling bass voice. He opened the door and walked inside.

Orbi entered behind him and closed the door, leaving the guards outside. "Mr. Johnston, what a pleasure to meet you," said the man walking toward him. Canon eyed him dispassionately. He was tall, scarcely three inches shorter than Canon. His thick shock of black hair contradicted Canon's own blond locks, which Canon had freed from the hat when he entered the room.

Trask was dressed in frock coat and brocaded vest, the obligatory western four-in-hand dangled toward the middle of his wide chest. The dark black hair was slicked back, the tiny moustache was well tended, the black eyes gleamed. Trask looked the epitome of the western card sharp as pictured in dime novels of the period. Canon wondered whether the man cultivated such a look. Then he considered that Trask had been a westerner for years. It would not be beyond reason that tinhorn gamblers had copied their look from Trask, a man doubtlessly much admired by would-be men of wealth.

Trask's grip was as firm as his swarthy features were powerful. Powerful was the correct word for Adam Trask. Here was a man who had power and knew how to use it to get what he wanted. What men like Trask usually wanted was more power.

A formidable foe, thought Canon, the word slipping unbidden into his mind. Yes. Definitely a foe. Canon knew right away that, though he could forgive this man anything, he could never like him.

Trask may have been forty years old, maybe fifty. It hardly mattered, for the Trasks of the world were seemingly immune to the aging process. Their muscles somehow tighten with age, rather than slacken, the wit gets keener and the ego grows by leaps as lesser beings are trampled underfoot. Here is misery incarnate for the poor and the innocent, thought Canon. Thick black hair, black moustache, dark coloring. No wonder a seventeen-year-old girl fell quickly under the spell of such a man. Canon wondered if Trask had Indian blood. He did not subscribe to the theory that red men could not hold liquor, and became cruel when they drank, but he could believe it of Trask.

Canon only smiled at the man and shook his hand. "Glad to meet you," said Rabe Canon.

"Oh, you'll be gladder still, soon," said Trask, with a snorting sneer of a laugh that was supposed to express some sort of comradely good humor, Canon thought, but which fell distressingly short.

A macabre thought slipped into Canon's mind as Trask laughed his braying laugh. I wonder how many men he has killed, thought Canon. Suddenly Canon was laughing, too, drowning Trask's. Perhaps it was not a pleasant laugh, for Trask's suddenly ceased. He and Orbi looked strangely at Canon. Another thought had come to Canon, hard on the heels of the first. Regardless of how many he has killed, thought Canon, still laughing, it is not so many as I have killed. Not nearly so many.

The peculiar interlude ended with Trask leading Canon and Orbi, with purposeful steps, through a door that led from the office into a smaller adjoining room. This one, in contrast to the other, was windowless and well lit. A full wet bar filled one corner, a couple of cushiony recliners were the only furniture. Canon reckoned the room had seen interesting sights.

"Could I get you something from behind the bar, Mr., uh, Johnston?" said Trask with an enigmatic smile.

"Not now, thanks," said Canon.

"Are you sure you wouldn't care for anything I have here?" Trask said with a sweeping gesture toward the paneled wall. Canon noticed a tiny imperfection in the joints of the veneered planking. The wall was hinged, he guessed. But he decided to allow Trask his moment.

"I think not," said Canon, pleasantly, and Trask again let go his irritating bray of laughter.

"Oh, you think not, do you," said Trask. "Why, General Canon, what will the Confederacy say to your turning down . . ." Trask touched the wall and it slid silently back to reveal the heavy iron door of a small vault ". . . ten million dollars." Canon had planned a gesture of surprise. Now he had no need to act it.

"Ten million?" he said. "I was told it would be five."

"Quite right, quite right," said Orbi, rubbing his hands together briskly as Trask bent to the door, fiddled with it and swung it open. He reached in and removed a thick belt, which he handed to Orbi.

"But what is five million to a war?" said the benefactor. "Hardly anything. A drop. A pittance. A month. So I contacted certain friends who feel as I do about the Confederacy, and who have so much of this," he opened the belt, "that you'd think they print the stuff themselves." He handed Canon a bill bearing the likeness of Salmon P. Chase, secretary of the Federal treasury. The bill's denomination was ten thousand dollars. "There are one thousand of those bills in this belt," he said. "They are yours to take to the Confederate government in Richmond." He handed the belt to Canon.

The rich leather, and the unspeakable wealth inside it, felt like glory in Canon's hand. He looked inside the belt at the rows of bills, then up at the two men who now stood side by side.

"Gentlemen," he said, "I will get this money to the Confederacy if I have to kill every Yankee between here and Richmond." Orbi and Trask looked at each other and nodded.

Solemnly, Canon lifted his shirt and tied the belt around his waist. It wasn't heavy, but Canon knew the weight, perhaps the fate, of the world now circled his body.

There was little to fear for Rabe Canon on the short trip back to the hotel, surrounded by armed guards, but Canon vowed never to take another step while wearing the moneybelt without having the Krupp fifties strapped on top of it.

Back in his room, under Orbi's watchful eyes, Canon placed the moneybelt in a sturdy rolltop desk which Orbi, no doubt, had caused to be placed there. Orbi took a key from the pocket of his vest, locked the desk and gave the key to Canon.

"I was not prepared, I have to admit," said Orbi, "for you to arrive quite this early. It will take two, perhaps three days to make everything ready for your departure. I want you to enjoy yourself during that time. Go out and see the sights, but I must ask you not to leave without my men to protect you.

"It is not without possibility that you will be recognized, and perhaps assaulted by some Yankee fool in the streets. Stay close by at night, and walk warily during the day."

Later, they went to the dining hall for dinner, enjoyed a leisurely meal of shellfish and shark, which Canon found delicious, and retired to Orbi's room for brandy and cigars.

After several snifters of brandy, Orbi questioned Canon closely about the Confederacy and its remaining defenses. Did the fall of Atlanta, he asked, end any hope of outright victory?

"It was a great coup for the North, no doubt, sir," answered Canon, "and a shocking defeat for us. But the government is in Richmond and Lee is in the field. Frankly, we could lose Richmond and, with Lee in the field and supplied by your ten million dollars, we could continue to prosecute the war to a successful end.

"I am not sure we can still conquer the North, but, so long as our armies continue to have the means to fight, the North will not conquer us."

Orbi seemed gratified by the answer. "Please do not be worried or offended by my questions, Rabe," he said. "I am somewhat of a student of military history, and newspaper reports are often conflicting or misleading. I would like to know where we really stand."

Remembering Beauregard's injunction to not let the benefactor know of the South's imperiled situation, and to bolster Orbi's confidence, Canon freely exaggerated the South's resources. He doubled, sometimes tripled the strength of various units. It was all right, he decided, to let Orbi believe he was equipping a formidable force rather than maintaining with his money a desperately dwindling army.

Canon finally shifted the topic around to gold fields, but the hour was growing late and Orbi yawned mightily. "Let us speak tomorrow of my adventures in California," he said, "if you will forgive my lack of manners. And day after tomorrow, I hope, we will send you homeward with at least five hundred men, perhaps as many as a thousand."

Dismissed, Canon rose, bowed and retired to his room.

He had made up his mind. He would fetch Carrie tonight, place her in a nearby hotel, and give her two days of San Francisco. Two wonderful days together and then, if his plans worked out, they would make the trip home.

Canon wondered how difficult it was going to be to get loose from the hotel and Orbi's men. He found out by walking out the door of his room. Four men immediately fell in beside him. He had expected two.

"Need something, sir?" one asked. "You tell me what you want, and I'll see that it is sent up." The man winked. "It will be delivered by a most beautiful young lady who would be happy to share your bottle and your time."

"No, no thanks," said Canon, with an answering grin. "I had thought to stretch my legs, but I can see the wisdom of keeping to my room. Perhaps I'll look into the, uh, offer later on. Goodnight."

"Goodnight, Mr. Johnston."

Canon stepped back into his room, annoyed despite himself. Now he was determined.

He undressed, noisily as possible, clumping the heavy boots on the floor, blew out the lantern. Then he quietly pulled on his moccasins and the leather pants he wore for night hunting. He rolled up his deerskin shirt and stashed it under his pillow. He climbed heavily into bed, bouncing the mattress and emitting the great sighs of one who looks forward to dreamland.

Five minutes later, he began a deep, rhythmic snore. He snored loudly for ten minutes, then he heard the doorknob unlatch. The door opened only half-way when Canon gave a yell and threw the long-bladed bone handled knife he had taken from Carrie in Richmond. The man in the door yelled louder than Canon, for the knifepoint had whacked into the doorframe six inches from his head.

"My God, man," Canon shouted, "don't you know better than to walk in on someone who's lived at war for two years?"

"Do now, sir," said the man, on his third try. He glanced at the clothing piled on top of the boots, closed the door. Canon threw back the covers, retrieved the knife and pulled on his shirt. He put rolled up quilts under the covers and placed the knife next to the pillow. It would draw more attention, now, should another sentry try the door.

Taking his gunbelt from his luggage, Canon strapped it on as he paced softly to the window. Dammit, he thought, the moon would be full tonight, but it wouldn't rise for another hour. Plenty of time. The trees effectively blocked the streetlamp glow from his room. Canon knelt by the window and waited.

Ten minutes later, he had the pattern of the outside sentries. One lapped the courtyard, another circled the hotel. Quietly, Canon crawled back in bed, snored loudly for a while, then gradually eased it back until the room took on the aura of a tired man in deep sleep.

Back at the window, it took another ten minutes for the sentries to reach the positions he wanted. The wind was up, as in every seaport. Occasional gusts shook the tree leaves, rustling like ghosts in the night, and scudded clouds across the sky. Canon slipped the window up, waited until a large gust of wind began to ripple through the oaks across the courtyard. When it reached the oak outside his window, he launched himself for the nearest large limb.

It took fifteen minutes for him to work his way over the alley. When the sentry turned the corner, Canon dropped lightly to the pavement. In less than five minutes, he was outside the barn where Old Scratch was stabled.

He moved quietly and quickly toward the stable, and almost blundered into two more sentries stationed at the front door. Thoroughness indeed, grinned Canon to himself. Even his arrival in town had not gone unnoticed, or Orbi had made his men investigate the surrounding stables to see how Canon was traveling. Still, he could understand sentries to protect him at the hotel, but he had not given thought to the possibility that his horse would be protected, too.

The sentries didn't think much of the idea, either, he learned as he crept closer, under the covering shadows of side buildings. They were sitting in front of the padlocked barn door, playing cards and bitching. Canon backtracked and circled, coming up behind the barn from downwind. The wind brought him snatches of conversation.

One man complained about "this damned Operation Turchino" and was immediately shushed by the other. Nettled, the complainer whined that he would like "to kill the stupid bastard" who was making them miss the nightlife of the town.

That will be either me or Mack Orbi, thought Canon, commiserating with the sentries. Whiskey and whores all over the place, and these two get stuck guarding a horse. Keeping an ear alert for changes in location of the voices, Canon duckwalked to the back of the barn.

There was a corral, and the barn was probably latched on the inside. Above the wide twin barn doors, however, was the smaller hayloft door which allowed easier access for the storage and removal of hay. It, too, was latched, but on the outside.

Barn entry by hayloft was a skill Southern men learned as adolescents and perfected as teenagers. Canon was up and in within seconds, and sat until his eyesight adjusted. The musty smell of stored hay and aged horse droppings filled the barn, but Scratch soon sniffed him and gave a low questioning whinny. Canon called an almost inaudible code word. The big horse quieted immediately. Not so the others, which whickered and stamped at the intruder.

The sentries cursed the noise and were quickly inside, flashing their lanterns around into the darkness.

"I told you, dammit," said the complainer. "Nothing but a rat or a snake or something. Come on." He stopped in front of Scratch. "Sure is a fine animal," he said. "Biggest horse I ever saw. Just like Canon's the biggest man."

Again, his companion turned on him. "Johnston. His name's Johnston," the man hissed. "Major hears you say that, and you are busted for sure."

"All right, all right. Johnston. Big, stupid Johnston."

Laughing, they left the barn, and Canon smiled ruefully. At least they had cleared up the identity of the stupid bastard.

The horses were quiet now as Canon inched down the ladder and slipped among them. Scratch, too, stood silent as the bit and saddle were put in place. Canon led him to the back door, inched it open in tune with the moaning wind, eased it closed and scotched it with a rock. The gate was simple. He led Scratch for several hundred yards to warm them both up, then mounted and walked him for a half-mile.

As they walked, the sentries' conversation replayed in his mind. It was very likely Orbi the man meant when he said "major." Innocuous in itself. Many Southern planters took the title of colonel or major, earned or not. But none of Orbi's other men had called him so. And they had referred to "Operation Turchino." What in hell is Turchino? he wondered.

Orbi had said he was a student of military history, and he was certainly running this thing as well as any operation Canon had known. Whatever the hell was going on, Canon decided, he wanted to check on Carolina. And he wanted to get back to collect the money. Once he had Carolina and the money, Mack Orbi could play military all he wanted.

Scratch was straining to run. Canon gave him the reins.

Half-way there, under a now bright full moon, Canon was forced off the narrow rutted road by a black carriage heading toward him in full roll. He paid it little heed.

20

# He Just Didn't Like Him

It was almost midnight when Canon leaped off Scratch's back in front of Carrie's hotel. The stallion had halved the time of his first leisurely trip along the route. Lamplight shone bright through the downstairs windows of the hotel. Canon didn't like it. Rural folks normally would have been long in their beds.

Canon beat his knuckles against the locked door until a Mexican servingmaid cautiously opened it. She bunched together with both hands the red shawl draped over her frayed white cotton nightgown, and her large dark eyes shone wide with fright in the bright moonlight.

Canon could not recall her name, but remembered her. She had shown him and Carrie to the hotel room.

She said in broken English, "Senor! The man come, say you are *muerto*—murdered—and take woman away."

Canon felt his heart shrink. "Jesus! Who was it?" he said.

But the girl knew little. A black carriage, followed by three horsemen, had come an hour ago. One of the horsemen had told Mrs. Johnston that her husband had been shot and killed, and had led her, sobbing, away to the carriage.

An hour! Canon knew that no horse could catch the carriage before it reached San Francisco, but Scratch was a horse to try. He was on the black and away without a word, calling up a mental picture of the expensive carriage and the two black horses that pulled it.

There couldn't be many rigs like that in Frisco. Canon thought he knew where to look first. Adam Trask had come to reclaim Carrie. That he had resorted to a ruse to accomplish it filled Canon with hope and dread. He wanted to believe Carolina would reject Trask, but he feared that Trask wouldn't accept a no.

If Scratch had sailed on the way to Carolina Lee, he flew on the way back.

It had been long since Canon had killed in reckless battle, but the three men had been as good as dead when they set the ambush. They needed only to go through the process of dying.

When he had forced the last outlaw to gasp out Trask's name, most of the puzzle clicked into place like the joining of the exquisitely machined pieces of the Krupp pistols, still warm in their holsters from their bloody work.

Canon almost rode Scratch to death the remaining miles of pursuit. He knew it, but so great was his rage that he pulled back only when he felt the proud stride falter. White foam flew back from the Arabian's muzzle, splattering Canon's face. The horse would have run itself into the ground had Canon allowed it, and it was this thought that brought out Canon's pity.

The renowned Frisco fog had set in with a will by the time Canon reached the city, obscuring the bright moonlight, making hazy shadows of buildings and trees. It was on a foggy morning he had met Stonewall Jackson, it was on a night of smokefog in Chancellorsville when Jackson had been shot.

This foggy night, Canon would wrest out the avenues to complete his revenge. He stopped at the first all night saloon he happened upon. Such places don't feature wallclocks, theirs being a business where time is best forgot. But the reed thin, pale bartender pulled out a large turnip-shaped timepiece at request and told Canon it was a quarter until three o'clock in the morning.

Raucous men listened to a jagtime piano, plinking along in tune to the clinking of glasses and shouts of laughter. Canon ordered bourbon and was served. He made a desultory remark about the fog, how it shrouded the new buildings in town he had come to see. Canon's Southern accent was hardly rare. If the barman noticed it, he gave no sign.

Rather, as Canon hoped, the man took up the building boom, speaking of inside knowledge of new stores and hotels. When he paused to pour more bourbon, Canon said, "I've heard banker Trask is building a fine new home."

"Not so's I've heard," came the laconic reply, the barman testy at the prospect of someone overshadowing his own knowledge.

"Well," said Canon easily, "I heard this afternoon he is moving to the east side of town and will build a house big as a palace."

The answer restored the bartender's good humor and sarcasm. "Mister, you don't know beans. Adam Trask already lives on the east side of town in a house bigger than a palace. His house almost *is* the east side of town. You can see it up on the hill from anywhere on the east side."

Taking no chances on missing it, Canon said, "You sure? My companion told me earlier this evening the new house being built near the wharf was Trask's."

The bartender, drying one glass and filling another, smirked. "Your companion knows little of San Francisco, my friend. That was the Higgins house. Trask's sits right on top of Nob Hill."

"Well," said Canon, placing a silver dollar on the bar, "what does it matter to poor folks like us, anyway." It was a statement rather than a question, and the barman nodded in agreement as Canon headed for the door.

Scratch was trembling from exertion, but Canon could not spare him. He allowed the black to drink deeply from a trough in front of an Italian restaurant. A ragged organ grinder with a grubby monkey stood on the street, twirling out a twinkling tune. Canon dug a coin out of his pocket. The monkey spotted it before the half-drunk grinder did and jumped out with his tin cup, rattling the thin chain attached to his foot.

The grinder, lulled by drink and his own music, came to life, whirling the handle of the instrument more quickly. He broke into an inebriated shuffle.

"This is for you," said Canon, pulling back on the reins to raise Scratch's head from the trough, "if you happen to know the meaning of the word 'turchino.'"

"At's a easy," grinned the man, "turchino is color, color of sky, color of deep sea. Torchino mean blue." Canon flipped the coin high and the monkey adroitly moved the cup under it. It went in with a rattling clang that was lost amid the sound of the tired Scratch's again thundering hoofbeats.

The passage of ten minutes brought Canon to the bottom of Nob Hill. Though dimmed to outline by the fog, the mansion a hundred yards away could be seen rising into the air. It seemed all dark. Canon left Scratch with a command to remain and graze. Using Indian stealth, Canon moved up the hill.

As he neared the house, Canon saw weak light shining from the corners of the drawn shades on the bottom floor. It was a half hour before Canon allowed himself to believe there were no guards posted.

But then why would Trask feel the need for guards when he thought the only possible threat to him lay dead on the road to Mendocino? Considering the unstinted arrogance of the man, Canon doubted that Trask even entertained the notion that his plans would fail. He would be willing to wager a hefty sum that Trask had probably even told his men to wait until morning to report Canon's death. Trask would want the night with Carolina uninterrupted.

Canon strode boldly to the front porch. One window was slightly open. Kneeling, Canon reached through and drew aside the curtain.

Adam Trask was in glory. Carolina Lee lay gagged and spread naked before him, tied to a billiard table. Trask, too, was nude. And very drunk. He weaved his way around the table, brandy snifter in one hand, large cigar smoking in the other. A quirt protruded phallic-like from one of the table pockets.

Carolina, covered with cuts and burns, wiggled and moaned. Her body, pointed directly toward Canon, was covered with the sweat of pain, her thick patch of butterscotch pubic hair was matted and mussed.

How wonderfully she whimpered, Trask thought, how magnificently she cringed and begged. He wished her big boyfriend were tied beside her, dead, riddled with bullet holes from the guns of his hirelings.

How dare she leave Adam Trask!

"How dare you leave me, bitch," he said in the most pleasant of voices. "Bitch, cunt, slut, whore. I own San Francisco and I own you, little puss. Didn't you know it? Well, you shall know it soon enough, and remember it always. If I decide to let you live."

Snorting his sneering laugh, Trask reached the glowing cigar tip toward the nipple of her right breast. Canon could see the fascinated leer on Trask's face. Carrie shrank from the cigar, screaming into the gag. So intent was Trask that he did not hear the whisper of sound made by the window as it raised. But the sound of twin hammers locking froze Trask still as death. He looked up, cigar still poised at Carrie's breast.

"If you make even a tiny move toward her," Canon said icily, "you will have two very large bullets in you very quickly indeed. Now take two slow steps back." Trask complied, still grotesquely maintaining the posture of his cigar.

Canon holstered his right pistol and pulled the bowie knife from its sheath. Carrie sobbed when he removed the gag and again as he moved around the table, cutting the knots and massaging blood into the deep creases in her skin where the ropes had held her. She struggled to a sitting position, controlling her sobs, and wrapped both arms around him. Gently, he pushed her away and walked over to Trask.

Both men were trembling, one with rage, one with fear. Then Trask made a pitiful attempt to rally, though a drunken naked sadist has little power in the way of persuasion.

"See here, Canon," he said in a strained voice. "This is between Carolina and I. I am her legal guardian, you know. And there is the matter of ten million dollars that you and the confederacy can forget unless you leave right . . . Arrrrrr!" Canon had jabbed the pistol barrel right into Trask's mouth. Splinters of teeth flew and blood burst from the man's gums.

Trask fell moaning to his knees, pulling away from the pistol barrel, now slimed with bloody spittle. The snifter and cigar dropped to the carpet as Trask grabbed his torn mouth, bending low his head as he deepened the kneeling crouch. Then he lunged up, one hand locked around the other, driving them toward Canon's groin.

Canon had hoped Trask would try something. He drove down the bowie as Trask thrust up his hands. The big blade stabbed deep into the joined hands, just where the fingers locked. Trask screamed, and the primal sound unleashed total fury within Canon. He holstered the pistol and grabbed the banker around the throat, digging his thumbs in deep. Canon jerked the man off the floor, took three steps and slammed him hard into the wall, tightening his grasp on the neck.

Trask had great pride in his own strength. In younger days, he wrestled for the joy of beating other men. His arms were corded with muscle, his hands were covered with bulging blue veins. He had killed with his hands more than once. He had slowly strangled the life from Carolina Lee's father, and put his own secret front man in charge of the gold mine. But he had never felt a grip like this.

Drunk and weak, bloody and hurt, Trask wondered dimly what miraculous rescue lay in store for him. His own efforts to dislodge the huge hands around his neck felt puny to him, futile. He fought for breath and life, blowing bloody spit into Canon's face.

Twice, he viciously kicked Canon's shin. Canon did not feel them, but he knew the kicks had to be hard because he heard Trask's toes snap. Trask suddenly realized that he was dying, that his sight was dimming, that the pounding and roaring in his head was the desperate attempt by his heart to keep pumping. He had to think of something masterful, something unexpected, something to save his fleeting life.

He could not. His struggles lessened, became shudders. His feet drummed the beat of death on the wall behind him. At last, his wounded tongue poked obscenely through his broken teeth.

With a growl, Canon flung the dead thing aside. It rolled over twice on the carpet like a sack blown by the wind, and was still.

Carolina, who had sat mute on the table, suddenly screamed, "You bastard! You killed him, didn't you!" Canon nodded grimly. "Goddammit," she yelled, senses still in shock, "I'm the one he hurt. Why didn't you let me kill him?" For a moment, she buried her face in her hands and sobbed. Then she gingerly rolled off the table and limped into Canon's waiting arms.

Her legs and back were welted from the quirt cuts, and Trask had burned a dotted cross into her abdomen. It started between her breasts and went down to the top of her pubic hair. The arms of the cross were under her breasts. The burns had created big water blisters, she said, then he had burned through the blisters.

She had been numb with shock, watching Canon kill, but now the pain of her wounds was turning to agony. She went upstairs to find salve for the burns. Canon went outside and whistled up Scratch. He made a brief ride around the grounds to make sure no one had come around. He found only that the blessed fog had thickened to the consistency of milk gravy.

When he re-entered the house, he collected all the oil lamps he could find on the first floor and began to shake the liquid onto the carpet, walls and drapes. Carolina, dressed in a loose shift and shawl, came downstairs and watched for a moment. She carried a dampened cloth with which she cleaned Trask's bloody spittle from Canon.

"Rabe, there's probably a fifty-gallon tank of that stuff in the basement," she said. "There used to be, anyway."

Canon smiled at her. "I knew there was some reason I wanted to keep you around, lovey," he said. "That's marvelous. Since you know where everything is, find everything of value that we can carry easily. The bastard promised the confederacy money and by God he's going to keep that promise."

Carrie blushed prettily through her burns and bruises. "Carrie," said Canon, in a teasing, soothing tone, "you are a wicked girl. Now what have you done?"

She pointed to a stuffed pillow case tucked by the staircase. Canon found it was filled with jewelry, cash, stocks, bonds, deeds and at the bottom were five packets of ten thousand dollar bills in greenbacks, like the bills given to Canon.

"He hadn't changed the combination to the safe," she said. Canon kissed her gently, took her hand, led her outside. Then he hurried back inside to the cellar. Minutes later, he carried the last burning lantern as far as the doorway, turned and tossed it inside. The kerosene began its slow flickering blue dance to conflagration.

"Darling," he said, when Carrie came up to him, "I know you are in awful pain, but you have to be brave a little while longer. I have to go pick up more of these," he held up the greenbacks. "Do you understand?"

"Yes, Rabe. I'll get along. But before you go there is something important I need to tell you," she said.

"All right, lovey, but please listen to me first," said Canon. "We'll ride double until I find a carriage for hire, then I'll get you to a hotel and you wait there until I come for you." He whistled for Scratch.

"Yes, darling, I understand, but please listen a moment . . ."

Canon lifted her gently to the saddle. "Carrie," he said, "we have to get out of here." He grabbed the saddlehorn, started to swing up behind her.

"Dammit, Rabe, I know where Mrs. Jackson is."

The news was so unexpected, so shocking, that Canon simply stood speechless for a moment. Then the flickering blaze inside the house mushroomed with a soft giant sigh. Window panes blew outward with a rain of tinkle. They were washed with light, and Carrie was delighted with the astonished look Canon wore.

He quickly swung up behind her and spoke Scratch into a smooth canter.

"She's here, Rabe, in San Francisco, and I think she's all right, at least for now."

"How did you learn about her?" said Canon.

"When they kidnapped me. When the man came in and told me you were killed, I thought it was my worst nightmare come true. Until I climbed in the carriage and saw Adam.

"Adam told me about the money you had come for—I thought you were out here to raise an army—and that he had killed you in a fair fight over me. That scared me. I knew Adam could never kill you in a fight that was really fair, but his idea of a fair fight is when the other man dies and he doesn't.

"Then I saw you ride by, trying to get to me, and I laughed in Adam's face. I knew you would come for me, darling." Canon listened intently, though Scratch's gait was so smooth their conversation was in near normal tone.

"Oh, Rabe, he'd gone mad. I knew he was going to kill me when he let me hear about Mrs. Jackson. We stopped by the wharf, and two men came out of a little bar. They all talked as if I weren't there.

"Adam told them he was tired of having his little shack—that's his place on the waterfront—being used as a hideout and jail for the most famous widow in the South. Then he said he wanted Mrs. Jackson out of there. When he said it, I knew he was going to kill me.

"Rabe, he wanted to rape me but he couldn't, wasn't able to, uh, do it."

"Don't think about it, Carrie. You'll be all right soon and we can talk about it then, if you want to."

"All right, darling. Well, anyway, the men told Adam they were reliably informed he was being amply rewarded for the shack, and that they would move when they damn well wanted to move. And then they went back in the bar."

"Where is this shack?"

"It's not really a shack. That was part of Adam's humor. It's an eight-room house out from town about five miles. There aren't any other houses around. I'll have to show you how to get there." They were nearing downtown. Canon twice directed Scratch into an alley to hide from passing buggies.

"Rabe," Carrie continued, "let me take us to a house I know where we can both stay and be safe. But I have some bad news for you about the money. You don't have to go get it. It's not worth anything."

"It's counterfeit, isn't it."

"Rabe! How did you know?"

"Several unpleasant truths have come to light recently, lovey, which I plan to deal with directly. But I have to go back to the hotel.

"Listen, Carolina. I plan to get in and out quickly, and I don't think anything will go wrong, but if I don't get back, you get to another city and telegraph Beauregard. Tell him everything. Mail a letter, too, to make sure. Then you take the stuff from Trask and get the hell to England or France. Jenson will take you if the *Star* is still around. But I doubt that it is."

"Rabe, tell me what's happening."

"I will, I promise, but there is no time now. And where is this house you know?

"We're coming up on the turn, soon. Three or four more blocks."

A few late drunks and ladies of the evening owned the town at this early hour, otherwise the streets were empty. Carrie strained to see through the ever congealing fog, directing Canon this way and that through steep, twisting roadways. Canon, too, strained to see landmarks for the trip back to town.

It was four A.M. when Carrie directed him to stop in front of a two-story brick house. Lights blazed from the windows.

"They're up early," Canon said, dismounting and carefully easing Carrie from the saddle, "or haven't they been to bed?"

Carrie smiled. "They've been to bed, all right," she said. "They just haven't slept." Canon understood, and laughed.

She knocked at the door, waited, knocked again. From inside, a distinctly Southern female voice said, "Weah closed. Come back tomorra night."

"It's me, Miz Sutcliffe. Carolina Lee."

The door was opened immediately by a smallish, roundish creature, holding a silk wrapper to her ample bosom. Long, blonde finger curls fringed an aging, painted face.

"Well, chile, what a surprise," said the smiling woman. "Come in. Come in heah and let me look atcha. It's been a coon's age." She took Carrie in; Canon followed. Miz Sutcliffe gasped when Carrie removed her shawl and the vivid welts on her shoulders stood out in the foyer's light. The little woman turned venomously on Canon. "Who's Goliath, heah? He hurt you, chile," she said.

"No, ma'am. He saved me," Carrie said. "Miz Sutcliffe, I'd like you to meet General Rabe Canon of the Confederate Army, leader of the Black Horse Cavalry and commander of the Stonewall Brigade.

"Don't worry, honey," Carrie said to Canon, "Miz Sutcliffe is Southern to her toenails. General, Miz Mamie Sutcliffe."

Canon bowed, and the woman dropped into the most elegant, graceful curtsy he had seen. She walked up and peered myopically at him, then squeaked.

"It *is* you," she said, breathlessly. "Oh, my. What an honuh and a joyful day foah me and mah house. I have yoah photograph from the newspapuh hanging on the wall of mah room, right next to Robuht Lee. Welcome to my house. I am at yoah disposal, suh."

"Ma'am, I have to warn you that I might bring trouble to you."

"Nossuh. No such of a thing."

"Then I would like to stay long enough to write a couple of letters, and then I have pressing business," Canon said. "If you are certain you will risk me, I will return shortly."

Mamie Sutcliffe again gave her elegant curtsy, and led Carrie and Canon into the dimly lit plushness of the finest little bawdy house Canon could think existed. She hurried him into her office, produced quill, ink and paper. Miz Sutcliffe examined Carrie's wounds with gasps of dismay while Canon swiftly scratched out his messages.

Carrie was naked when Canon turned back to them. Miz Sutcliffe was gently washing Carrie's wounds. He sealed the letters, handed them to

Carolina. "Mail them, Carrie, far from here if I don't return. Then go to another city and telegraph, then to another city and send another letter.

"Perhaps Miz Sutcliffe will get word to Jenson in the unlikely event that he is still available, and he will meet you at another port. I will leave it to you to explain to Miz Sutcliffe what she should know."

Carrie walked Canon to the door. Miz Sutcliffe delicately remained in her office, curtsying her goodbye to Canon. In the foyer, Canon said, "Carrie, tell Miz Sutcliffe little as possible, for her own protection. If she knows little, it is little trouble that can come to her." He kissed her gently. "I expect to return soon," he said, "but if something goes wrong, I want you to have Scratch." He told her what to do, then he walked out the door into the night and fog.

He was afraid he would find Scratch foundered or dead, so hard had he been used and so little care given him. But the light ride from Trask's house in the cooling fog had evidently been the best thing for the big horse. Though bedraggled, Scratch felt like a coiled spring under Canon when he sat the saddle. Canon knew the hour was late and each passing minute increased the danger for him. After leaving Sutcliffe House, Canon had but two friends he could count on: Scratch and the fog. He pushed Scratch, hard as he dared, toward the Carlton, fifteen blocks away.

The fog was a living thing, its snaky tendrils weaving around him. Birds were a-twitter. A horse or carriage occasionally could be heard in the streets.

This is going to be close, thought Canon, nearing the hotel. He left Scratch back near the stable, with orders to stay until called for. With trepidation, Canon approached the hotel.

All was still around the Carlton, save the lone sentry in the alley still lapping the block. Canon waited restlessly, senses alert, and watched the man appear, disappear, appear, disappear. Canon sprang to the courtyard wall, gained the top, flattened on it.

Finally, through the glowing mist, Canon made out the phantom form of the inside sentry. He was sitting in a chair, wrapped in a poncho against the cold, head back. Asleep. Canon hoped it wasn't feigned. No matter. He had to go in, though he sensed danger all around.

Canon sprang up into the tree like a panther, and like a panther he perched, casting his senses this way and that. Without audible sound, he began to climb. Outside the still open window of his room, he peered in, straining his eyes until he made out the bed. It appeared undisturbed, but he knew that once he committed himself to leaping for the sill, there could be no chance to change his mind.

With a deep breath, he jumped, caught the sill with his hands and braced his feet into the brick wall to lessen the sound of impact.

It was lightly done, and the slight noise of his landing was lost in the fog. Again he blessed the roiling mist, and pulled himself into the room. He turned immediately, ready to dive back for the tree limb, but nothing moved. The bed cover was rounded up as he had left it, the knife, barely visible in the dark, still lay beside the pillow.

He stepped gently to the desk, inserted the key and opened the roll top. The money belt was there. He opened it and gazed in admiration at the packets of bills. Canon tied the belt around his waist. He would put it underneath his shirt when he was far from the Carlton and safe.

Canon heard the rustle of the bed cover as it was thrown back on itself, and Mack Orbi's voice was smooth. "I have a shotgun trained on your back, General," said Orbi. "Stand as you are or I shall send you straight to Rebel heaven." He vented his sharp whistle and men with lanterns poured in through both doors, pistols at the ready.

"Now please sit down, General Canon," said Orbi. "No. Right where you are. On the floor. So much more difficult for a person to move quickly while sitting."

Orbi rose from the bed and held the shotgun muzzle to the back of Canon's head while the men took Canon's pistols from the holsters and bowie knife from its sheath, and the money belt. He was thoroughly searched, the hideaway gun and his other knife were placed in the pile made by the Krupps and the moneybelt. The pile was carried from the room. Orbi returned to the bed, sat.

"Why, Mr. Orbi," said Canon. "I am shocked. I only stepped out for a stroll on the town. Your men prevented me earlier, so I sneaked out so as not to cause a row."

"Please, General, give me some small credit," said Orbi. "It simply won't do, you know, although you almost got away with it. One of my men awakened me an hour ago to report a tragic fire at the Trask residence. Still burning, in fact."

"And so is Mr. Trask," said Canon. "In hell."

"Tsk, tsk," clucked Orbi. "A pity."

"Perhaps," said Canon. "The bastard couldn't stand the heat, and he couldn't get out of the kitchen."

Orbi let the remark pass. "You are a most persuasive man, I understand," he said. "I assume Trask told you everything before his unfortunate demise."

"He told me nothing."

"I wish I could believe you, Canon. But I am afraid I can no longer allow you to be part of my little plan for the Confederacy."

"Your plan is ruined already. I telegraphed Richmond last night."

"No," said Orbi, with a laugh. "It will not wash. You don't know my full plans or you would not have returned. At least Trask could keep some secrets. And you could not have telegraphed. I have had each telegraph office in the city covered for two days, looking for anything you might send over the wires.

"But you will telegraph Richmond today to say that all is well but that you have fallen ill and the money will be delivered by other hands."

"I don't think so."

"Perhaps not. But other arrangements can be made. My plans are only a bit disrupted, not thwarted. We will find your lovely companion. Then you will negotiate. You see, there are many things Mr. Trask does not, ur, did not know, including my true identity.

"Even the president knows little about the operation, save the code name, Operation . . ."

"Torchino," said Canon, pleasantly. "Your president may know little about Torchino, but mine will soon know it quite thoroughly. Letters are being taken to other cities right now to be sent through the United States mail to several people in the Southern states.

"Probably, you can stop none of them. Certainly, you cannot stop them all. The letters outline the details of your Operation Blue, including the counterfeit bills and the fact that you are the bumbling head of the Federal secret service, Allan Pinkerton."

Pinkerton, his face a picture of contorted fury, sprang from the bed, eyes wide and wild, teeth and fists clenched. "You're lying, you Rebel bastard. You better pray that you're lying," he hissed.

"Not a bit," said Canon pleasantly.

Pinkerton mindlessly placed the shotgun beside him on the bed and, elbows on knees, dropped his head into his hands. For long moments he was silent, but the half dozen agents in the room muttered darkly.

When the detective looked up, Canon could see that his face had paled.

"How did you find out?" said Pinkerton. "How could you have known?"

"I will tell you what I know if you will tell me what I do not know," said Canon. "That I know about the operation is evident, and I will tell you how I came to learn of it. But there are some other questions I have that you must answer for me as well."

"Agreed," said Pinkerton wearily, "so long as there is no breach of security involved."

"Well, then," said Canon, "I'll start the session. Trask, acting on his own, I suspect, kidnapped my, uh, companion tonight and tried to have me killed."

"The fool!"

"Precisely. If he was a bad one, it followed that you, too, must be suspect and therefore the entire scheme. But, without Trask's interference, there were several things that caused me to doubt you.

"The rash on your neck, for example," said Canon, and Pinkerton absently scratched the angry red flesh. "It likely stemmed from shaving sensitive skin unused to a razor. So it was probably that you were used to wearing a beard. You wear lifts in your shoes. Now we have a man who is trying to alter his appearance so he won't be recognized.

"But recognized by whom? Not Trask. Your identity would be of no importance to him, or to anyone else in San Francisco. So you altered your appearance just for me.

"And not only do you exhibit a military air, I overheard you use words like 'posts' and 'being busted,' and I also overheard you say 'surveil.'

"So we have here a small military detective who has the resources to offer ten million dollars, and to order fifty men around. We have a Yankee who doesn't want to be recognized by an easygoing Confederate like me.

"Why would a Yankee want to give the Confederacy ten million dollars? Not to help it, surely. And how could ten million dollars hurt? If it is counterfeit. It would destroy the Confederacy's credit if it used ten million dollars to secure loans, and the money turned out to be counterfeit."

Pinkerton sighed deeply. "Where did you overhear my conversation?" he said. Canon pointed outside, where dim dawn colored the fog, to the tree. "While your men were searching for me after my arrival, I was doing my own surveillance.

"But I must say, Major Pinkerton, that it was arrogance on your part to risk the scheme by using a couple of easily traced foreign words that mean 'blue.' It took me a little while to go through the variations of Orbi, but even someone as little versed in Spanish as I am would notice 'brio' sooner or later. And your Mack, I suppose, comes from your erstwhile benefactor, General McClellan."

"Just so, General. Just so. But if you knew the money is counterfeit, why did you return here this morning. Why did you not flee?"

Canon took a shot in the dark.

"I came here to kill you for the murder of Stonewall Jackson, the taking of Mary Anna Jackson, and I could use the money to escape," said Canon.

The detective's face flushed with sudden anger. He sat up straight on the bed.

"I am not an assassin, sir," he said with dignity, "nor a despoiler of women. I am an agent provocateur and a damned good detective. That your Jackson was killed and his wife kidnapped is regrettable. Those were not my plans.

"It is true that I wanted Stonewall Jackson kidnapped, and I wanted the counterfeit money in your hands. Those *were* my plans. We knew you had recovered your health enough to travel, but not enough to return to war.

So you were chosen to receive the money. We'd have liked to have had the money closer to the Confederacy, but Trask was the only believable banker greedy enough to cooperate with counterfeit bills.

"We needed you, General, to legitimize the money. If it came too easily to the confederacy, suspicions might have been raised. The money is almost perfectly printed. It was prepared by the same engravers who produce legitimate Federal greenbacks, and printed on the same paper.

"But three flaws were placed in the bills. Experts, even without prior knowledge, could locate them if they were sufficiently diligent. We needed you to come here, to this free city, to be impressed by the Bank of San Francisco.

"When it was learned that you had discovered that Jackson was assassinated, but had not yet reported it, the men responsible for it decided without my knowledge to kill you, too.

"I tell you sincerely that I am glad the attempt failed, and when you made the facts known about Jackson, it was in the best interest of the Union to keep you alive so you could courier the greenbacks. We knew you were aboard the *Southern Star*, and could have had a warm welcome waiting for you if we had chosen. The *Star*, by the way, is being hounded by our fleet even as we speak.

"As to Mrs. Jackson, that is the doing of three of the same men, my former agents, who are now out for themselves. They brought her here, without my knowledge, to use her to influence you should you find out the plans. But I will have no part of something so despicable. I am sending men this afternoon to take her from those who have her. She will be transported safely home.

"Miss Lee will also be relocated safely to a Northern city, where she may visit you in prison. I have for years had Union dealings in the west, and met Miss Lee when she was with Trask. I did not know she had left him until she showed up in Nashville, working for the Union. Someone out here had recruited her. I could not allow her to see me, though she might not have discovered me as you seem so easily to have done.

"One of my men, who followed you to Mendocino, must have described her to Trask, or perhaps let her real name slip to him. I don't know how he knew about her. But he insisted she be given to him. I refused. He took her anyway, and he paid for it."

"He tortured her, Pinkerton, with a burning cigar," said Canon, grimly.

"My God, the fiend!" said Pinkerton, genuinely aghast. "Well, if it is true that you murdered him, then the authorities will likely want to keep you in San Francisco. But I give you my word, General, that you will be taken back to Washington and treated decently as a prisoner of war.

"You won't be taking back my ten million tainted greenbacks, but you will get about ten million years in Federal prison. All in all, the capture of the leader of the Black Horse Cavalry will make the mission worthwhile and successful. I will return with you in triumph."

"If that is the case," said Canon, "you won't mind telling me who it was in our government that ordered the death of Stonewall Jackson."

Pinkerton was silent for a moment. "I will tell you," he said. "I suspect they have rooted out the rat by now, anyway. I certainly would have. Even if they have not, you will be in no position to expose him. And I despise the little beast. It was your assistant undersecretary of war."

"Hillary?!" cried Canon. Pinkerton nodded.

"That little worm," said Canon. "*He* ordered the death of a man like Stonewall Jackson." Canon paused a moment, then said, "Why?"

"I have wondered about it myself," said Pinkerton, thoughtfully. "I think he just didn't like him."

It was Canon's turn to sink his head into his hands.

The room was silent for a while, then Pinkerton rose from the bed with a yawn. "I must ask you to excuse me, General," he said. "It has been a hectic few hours, and a busy day is dawning. A few hours sleep will do us both good.

"We will turn you over to the Federal garrison here while we make plans for your return voyage in a Union vessel. Newspaper coverage must be arranged for the announcement of your arrest. I will put my men on it. We will leave for the garrison at noon, I think, so please get some sleep. Good morning."

As Pinkerton left, he placed an agent on each side of the open window, and two men at each door. Canon figured at least a half dozen would be outside in the hallway.

Heat from the several lamps in the room refused entrance to the fog, pressing eagerly against the raised window pane.

Outside, the sun was up. But the fog remained so thick the sun only changed it to a paler shade of gray. It rolled against the window like a spirit seeking entrance. It beckoned to Canon, teasing him with a perfect cloak if he could only get outside to wear it.

Canon grabbed a carafe of water from a table near the bed and drained the quart. He removed his gunbelt and dropped it on the bed, then fell beside it. He didn't take time to remove his moccasins. He yawned, pulled the down filled comforter over his head, stuck it back out. "Put out some of those goddamn lanterns," he ordered gruffly. The men looked at each other, then the one by the door looked at Canon and shook his head. "Look, I need some sleep. Leave one burning, if you're afraid of the dark, but put out the others," he said. The one man shrugged, then did as Canon requested. Canon poked his head back under the cover. He was asleep within a minute.

The water he drank woke him an hour later, as he had planned, but he did not open his eyes. Indians called the water trick "nature's wake-up." But this call would have to wait. Canon's four inside keepers were talking in muted tones. Good. They were no longer giving him their full attention. He rolled over, facing the wall, opened his eyes. It was dark in the room, though Canon thought it must be past eight. The fog would burn away by noon.

Canon tossed in bed a bit, not enough to draw much attention; just enough to allow him to slip the pillow case from the pillow. He pulled his gunbelt closer to him.

On board the *Star*, Canon copied the style Jenson had told him was commonplace in San Francisco since the perfection of the self contained cartridge. Using a narrow strip of leather, he had fashioned bullet loops and attached it to his gunbelt. It carried almost a half box of bullets. He set to work.

Slowly, ever so slowly, he used his teeth to worry the lead from its brass casing and dumped the powder into the pillow case.

An hour later, Canon sat up and sleepily asked to be allowed to use the privy. He was told to use the chamber pot. He asked for privacy. He was told to go to hell. Canon got up and urinated noisily, with sighs of satisfaction, into the ornate porcelain pot. Then he looked around, distressed.

"Uh, I haven't finished," he said.

"So finish, already," said one of the men at the hall door.

"Look here, now," said Canon in an offended tone, "some things are not done in the company of others."

"This will be, if it gets done," the guard said.

"Goddammit, get Pinkerton in here right now," Canon said hotly. "A goddam bird couldn't get out of this room. Even Pinkerton would allow me five minutes of decency."

The men at the hall door looked at each other, then at the men at the window and the connecting door. The man at the hall door finally nodded.

"All right," he said. "Five minutes. And not a second longer. You try the smallest move, we'll truss you up, if we don't shoot you."

"Thank you," said Canon with dignity.

"Come on, boys," said the leader. "The hard-assed general of the Black Horse don't want us to know he's human." Laughing, the men left the room, closing the hall door behind them.

Quickly, Canon knotted most of the gunpowder into a corner of the pillowcase. From under the bed, he pulled out his heavy cowboy boots. He took dried mud from them that had been picked up the day before from the watered street and, using his own urine from the chamber pot, worked it into thick clay.

He took a wick from one of the lamps and rolled it in gunpowder. It made a serviceable fuse that fit well the hole Canon tore in the knotted part of the pillowcase, first spilling out a palmful of powder. Canon sealed around the fuse with clay. He shoved the little bomb into the empty carafe, leaving a few inches of fuse protruding. Then he packed clay around it.

Canon piled the remaining powder in front of the hallway door. Then he emptied lantern oil on the bed. Removing the chimney from the single burning lamp, Canon lit the bed. He quietly tore a square of cloth from the sheet, fired it on the glowing pyre of mattress, and tossed it gently onto the pile of gunpowder at the door.

The black powder whooshed up, releasing great clouds of oily black smoke. In seconds, the room was black dark as the bottom of a coal mine. He dropped to the floor behind the desk, holding the carafe and the burning lamp.

One of the guards noticed the smoke streaming blackly from under the door. "Jesus," he yelled, "look at that!" Shouts began to sound in the hallway.

When the door opened, Canon lit the fuse and rolled the carafe into the hall. He threw the lamp after it. Canon figured that four guards got into the room before the bomb exploded, rocking the floor nicely. The four men in the room with him began firing their pistols wildly, blindly. He heard two of them yelp in pain as each took a bullet.

Canon crawled back toward the open window, from which black smoke poured out to mingle with the fog. A booted foot stepped down close to him. He grabbed it, jerked, and a body fell heavily down next to him. Canon stood, picked the man up bodily and threw him through the window into the tree limbs.

"There he goes!" shouted a man in the courtyard, and shooting opened up outside. Another man rushed to the window. Canon hit him over the head with the heavy chamber pot, caught the slumping figure, dragged him to the doorway and threw him against the far wall in the hall.

"There he is!" shouted one of the men in the hall. More shots rang out.

Pinkerton rushed from his room into the smoke filled hallway, dressed in nightshirt and brandishing a pistol. "What the hell . . ." he yelled, and strode into the melee. There was screaming, shouting, cursing, yelling. And more shooting.

It was a half hour before enough smoke cleared from the hall to allow visibility. Order finally restored, Pinkerton found six men wounded by gunfire and splinters of glass, four overcome by smoke and burns, thousands of dollars in damages done to the hotel and an empty room where his prisoner had been.

"You damned fools!" raged Pinkerton. "What happened?!"

"I reckon he must've snuck in a mortar and one of them new Gatling guns," ventured one, haltingly. Pinkerton raised his eyes toward heaven, then turned on the man. "What are you standing here like an idiot for, you idiot. He can't have gone far.

"Listen, all you men. Fan out in a circle around the hotel. Each man is to walk for five minutes in straight a line as possible from the hotel, fast as he can, asking people if they've seen him. If he hasn't been seen, start moving back toward the hotel in a tightening, clockwise circle. He'll be somewhere within it.

"Now hit the street. He can't have gone far and he'll be hiding nearby. Let's go!" The men rushed from the room and Pinkerton followed them out.

Well, that man is smarter than I thought, said Canon to himself as he rolled out from under Pinkerton's bed. Carefully, he opened the door and checked the hallway. Empty. He collected his weapons and moneybelt from Pinkerton's dresser, and grabbed one of the fat cigars he found there.

Canon walked back into his room, pulled the gunbelt from where he had stashed it under the bed. He lifted his shirt, strapped on the moneybelt, then buckled on his guns. He noticed that one corner of the bed matting still smoldered. Canon blew on it gently. It burst into weak, blue fluttering flame. He lit his cigar from it, turned and went through the window into the tree.

He had to hurry. Clumsy as they were, fifty men weren't going to be easy to get through. The fog sure helped, but it would burn away soon. Canon crept along a wide limb until he was over the alley. He took a deep puff off the cigar. He dropped down.

21

# A Coffin for Canon

Allan Pinkerton was growing nervous. He had thought quickly, had moved quickly. The net was skillfully thrown. But three hours had passed and the Rebel general was still free.

Pinkerton, standing outside the Carlton, tried not to think about how much this operation had cost his government in time, money and manpower. Worse, he had kept most of it secret from The Ape—he had come to think of Lincoln in McClellan's terms—because he was so sure of the plan's success. He wanted to share the glory with no one. Now he wished he had someone who could share the blame.

But he must not be negative, Pinkerton reminded himself. It was nearing noon. The fog had finally dissipated. Canon was likely hiding in bushes or trash close to the hotel. Every shopkeeper and passerby had been questioned intensely. No one had seen Canon. No matter, Pinkerton assured himself. Canon had gone to ground, was perhaps even still inside the hotel, but he could never get through the ring of agents. And now the fog was gone. Every inch of territory inside the ring would be searched and doublechecked. He would recapture the Rebel and this time Pinkerton would not be so courteous. Canon would wear chains until he was safely stowed in the stockade in Washington.

One of Pinkerton's agents walked up.

"Any word?" said Pinkerton.

"Found his horse, sir, by the stable, but some little colored boy stole it."

"Stole it?!"

"Yes, sir. The horse looked like it was used up. We tried to get it inside to unsaddle it and rub it down, but it was all teeth and hooves when anyone got close. Then we brought oats and water to it, but it wouldn't eat or drink.

"We sent for cowboys to rope and throw the evil bastard, then this little nigger that was hanging around the stable hollered 'scratch four,' or something like that, and before anybody could blink, the nigger was on the horse and gone. We never even had a chance to shoot."

Pinkerton fumed for a moment in silence. "So the general has some help, does he? Organize some men and search all the stables in the city."

"Yes, sir."

"Anything else?"

"It's the wagon, sir. The one that waters the streets. Driver wants to know if he can get on with it. Says it'll get dusty here in a hurry with the fog gone."

"Just where is this wagon?"

"Near the stable, too, sir. We stopped it there when it came through in the fog. We've searched it."

"Let's have a look," said Pinkerton.

The cylindrical tank sat squat and ugly behind a wagon on the seat of which was an aging Irishman, whose body resembled that of the tank, except that the tank had four wheels. Whether from anger, drink or the heat of the day, the Irishman's face was florid and he railed at the grinning detectives around him for holding up his work.

When he observed the deference shown to Pinkerton by the men, he slid off the seat and spryly advanced on the little detective, shouting to be let alone. Pinkerton waved him aside and stepped close to the iron tank. A cistern shaped neck sat atop and amid the tank. It allowed the tank to be filled to the top without water being sloshed away.

Ignoring the ranting man, Pinkerton climbed up on the small sideboard of the tank and peered down into the lidless cistern. Murky water, topped by a brownish foam, came almost level to the bottom of the cistern. The tank was full.

Pinkerton took out his pistol and with its butt rapped sharply on the cistern. It rang hollowly. He crawled down, walked to and fro, clanging the sides of the tank with the pistol butt. He crawled back up and again checked the water level. The tank was full as ever.

"He ain't around here, sir," said one of the men. "The tank has been full since last night, and the driver says he ain't seen nothing. There ain't nobody alive inside the tank, unless he's got gills. We've been here fifteen minutes.

A man can't hold his breath no fifteen minutes, can he, Major?"

"Not that I've heard," said Pinkerton, turning away from the tank. "Not even five. But with that bastard, you can't be sure. Give it another ten minutes, then let it go."

"Yes, sir, Major Pinkerton."

"It's Major Allan, you goddamn fool."

"Yes, sir."

Pinkerton nodded. "I'm going back to the hotel," he said, striking the tank a last, frustrated, ringing blow. One of the wooden pistol grips broke in half, the pieces landing at the feet of the detective. Pinkerton stared at the pieces for a moment. "Goddamn it," he said. He turned and offered the pistol's broken butt to his man. The man didn't understand for a moment, then resignedly reached under his coat, produced his own pistol from the shoulder holster, and swapped with Pinkerton.

"Bring him to me at once when you find him," said Pinkerton, "and in one piece. No playing with him." He turned and walked away.

"Yes, sir," said the man to Pinkerton's retreating back. The man stared at the pistol Pinkerton had left him.

"Goddamn it," he said, and struck the tank with the broken butt.

"I wish the son of a bitch *was* in there," he said to the driver, who had given up his tirade and was leaning against the wagon bed. "He sure wouldn't be thirsty."

And I wish you'd stop that godawful clanging, Canon thought.

Pinkerton walked into his room and found the hotel manager there, staring through the open connecting door into the ruined room and shaking his head. He turned when Pinkerton approached and handed him a newspaper story in which General W. T. Sherman had announced from Atlanta his forthcoming plan to "march to the sea."

"This prisoner of yours . . .," began the manager as Pinkerton scanned the paper. Pinkerton looked up. "Yes?" he said. "He any relation to General Sherman?" said the manager.

Pinkerton glanced up from the paper at the manager, ready to chew him. The glance took in the dresser in the room. Pinkerton stared for a moment, then ran to the window and began to shout. Not only was Canon gone, so were his guns and the moneybelt.

At the stable, the Irishman had calmed down. "Can I get on with me work, now?" said the driver in a thick brogue. "'Tis going on half an hour now that you've caused me to delay."

The agent gave permission. Then he saw the commotion begin at the Carlton as agents within hearing distance began to run toward the hotel in response to Pinkerton's shout. Other agents, seeing their comrades running toward the hotel, thought either than Pinkerton was in trouble or that Canon had been caught. The circling net of Federal agents collapsed on itself, pulling in toward the hotel like the sides of a deflating balloon.

Inside the tank, his head in the empty cistern, Canon heard the shouts and retreating footsteps. He had heard everything, even under water. The iron tank and the water were good conductors of sound. He had again put his head up into the cistern soon as Pinkerton had left. But Canon certainly was not thirsty. Twice he had swallowed huge gulps of stagnant, greasy water.

The street was on a very shallow incline. There was enough of an angle to make the tank appear full, which it almost was, while leaving an inch of space between the water and the top of the tank at the tank's uphill end.

That one inch allowed Canon to press his nose and mouth against the rusty top of the tank and carefully suck in some air. The driver evidently had been in a nearby saloon when Canon spotted the wagon through the fog and climbed cautiously in. On his knees, his head had reached up into the hollow, empty cistern. Water came up to his neck.

When he first crawled into the tank, he had been ready to get back out and run some water from the spigots, then he found the inch of air near the tank's front. He had thought himself home free when the tank rumbled away, until it was stopped at the stable. Then he had thought he was a dead duck. Now, he only hoped the powder in his cartridges wasn't too wet to fire if he was discovered.

Canon heard a mumbled, tuneless Irish ditty and the seat spring creaked as the driver climbed aboard. Soon the water was sloshing inside the tank as the Irishman set off at pace.

What's the hurry? thought Canon, getting another unwelcome mouthful of the oily water. But the water level began to drop as the driver worked the spigot lever from his seat, wetting the dusty streets of San Francisco. The water had dropped to Canon's chest by the time the wagon drew to a halt. Canon cautiously raised his head above the open cistern rim in time to see the Irishman disappear inside a saloon.

No wonder he was in such a hurry, Canon thought. "Well," he said aloud, "if he's getting off the water wagon, I guess I will, too." He slid over the side and slinked to the alley. The saloon, he realized delightedly, was on Miz Sutcliffe's side of town. He was less than six blocks away. About time something went right, Canon thought to himself, taking to the backstreets.

Miz Sutcliffe answered his knock at the back door and pulled him inside. She eyed his sopping condition.

"Wheah on earth you been, General?" she said. "Me and Carolinuh been worried sick about you."

"I'll tell you about it, Miz Sutcliffe, but first I need something dry to wear and something hot to eat."

"Certainly, anything else I can get you?"

"You might not believe this, Miz Sutcliffe, but I'm dying for a drink."

"Of cose. Bourbon and branch water be all right?"

Canon winced. "Just bourbon," he said.

He was in Mamie Sutcliffe's room, using a huge fluffy towel to dry himself while he sipped his third bourbon. His clothes were drying on the roof. The moneybelt and his gunbelt were stretched out to dry in a stream of sunlight that came through the open window.

Carrie Lee walked in. She wore a short thin negligee of blue silk and carried a platter of steaming steak and scrambled eggs. Canon eyed her appreciatively.

"I'm not sure which to taste first," he said. Carrie smiled. Her wounds were carefully dressed, the white cotton bandages plain under the filmy silk. She seemed in less pain than when he left. Canon wanted her badly, but there was no time for making love. There was work to be done.

"Rabe, darling, we were so worried," she said, placing the platter on a sidetable. "We thought they caught you."

"So they did. But I fired them."

Thirty minutes later, Canon, wrapped in a sheet, pushed the empty platter away and lit a cigar. He sent Carrie for Miz Sutcliffe and explained what he wanted her to do. He ended the conference by asking Carolina to draw a map to Trask's other house. Mamie left on her errand.

"Can Scratch be ridden, lovey?" said Canon, turning his attention to cleaning and oiling his pistols and sharpening the bowie knife.

"I don't think it would be a good idea, Rabe. He's about blown. But he's now the prettiest white Arabian you ever saw. Miz Sutcliffe's groom did a wonderful job with the dye."

"He did a wonderful job taking Scratch, too, and he earned a twenty-dollar gold piece doing it. Now please go see if my clothes are dry enough to bring down from the roof while I try to figure a way to get out of town.

"Pinkerton said he would send his men to get Mary Anna at noon. I expect my escape slowed his plans, but once he realizes I slipped them, he'll realize I'll go there. I have to get there first."

"Miz Sutcliffe and I knew you'd go there, too, Rabe. We've got a plan, and she's been working on it half the night. I didn't tell her it is Mrs. Jackson we're going after, only that a Confederate woman was being held prisoner by some Yankees. Miz Sutcliffe insists on helping. So do I."

"Now, Carrie . . ." Canon began, but was cut off.

"Just listen a moment, dear," said Carolina. Canon listened. He began to smile.

When she showed him into the special room in the house, Canon shuddered in spite of himself. It was a funeral parlor. The draperies were black silk, the few benches were mahogany. In the middle of the room, so much like the one in his dream that he shuddered again, was a black casket. He tried to make light of it.

"Are you trying to tell me that some of the boys like to stop by after work for a cold one?" he said.

"Don't be silly," said Carrie. "The girls who entertain in here aren't really dead. They wear lots of white powder and darken their lips and they, uh, lie in ice for a while before they get in the casket.

"Some of the really weird men pay lots of money for specialties like this," said Carrie. "Wouldn't you like to try it once"?"

"No, thanks. I like women who move, lovey."

The hearse was a converted wagon, pulled by a newly white Arabian. Black cloth, almost to the ground, swathed the wagon bed on which lay the coffin. Wreaths of flowers surrounded it.

Miz Sutcliffe and Carrie, veiled and dressed in black, pressed handkerchiefs soaked in camphor to their eyes as they drove out of town. By the time they reached a roadblock, their eyes and noses were red and swollen, and tears flowed dramatically down their cheeks.

Three men from the Union garrison blocked their way. One held up his hand and ordered the hearse to halt.

"Trouble, ma'am?" he said to Carrie, who burst into sobs.

Miz Sutcliffe nodded and answered. Carrie, and Canon in the coffin, were taken aback when she spoke. The Southern accent was gone and in its place was the voice of a high tone western lady.

"The last wish of our dear departed was to be buried in a grave overlooking the bay," she said. "We sent a servant out this morning to dig the grave. He is waiting for us now. This is the least we can do for our darling. Is something wrong?"

"It'll be in the papers this evening, ma'am. Confederate general name of Rabe Canon—you've probably heard of him—is loose in San Francisco. He's a desperado, sure enough. He robbed a bank, killed the banker and near about burned the Carlton Hotel to the ground. A bad man, ma'am.

"I don't suppose you've seen him? About eight foot tall, blonde hair? No, I reckoned not, but orders are orders. I have to look inside."

"Inside! But there is death inside," said Miz Sutcliffe.

"Sorry. Got to. Orders."

"Captain," cooed Carolina.

"An unfortunate sergeant, ma'am," said the man, saluting, "but at your service all the same."

"We will do you a service," said Carrie gently. "It is death itself inside that coffin, perhaps your own. It is the smallpox." She resumed her sobs. "See my marks?" She lifted her veil to show the tiny pocks Mamie had drilled into thick rouge.

"Lord!" said the soldier, stepping back involuntarily. He looked at the other soldiers doubtfully.

"Did you not say the madman you want is eight feet tall, sir?" she said.

"Nearer seven, actually, but he looks eight when he has a gun in his hand, so I am told."

"Please look at the coffin. It is six feet, and there was room in there for my darling little daughter as well as my husband, who was slight," said Miz Sutcliffe, herself bursting into sobs and moans.

"Well and all," said the sergeant. "Exactly. My apologies and sympathies, ladies. Please and do pass on through."

If the soldiers had looked at the wagon's tracks as it rolled away, they perhaps would have noticed the twin furrows left by Canon's dragging feet. The holes cut in the bottom of the coffin perfectly matched the holes cut in the wagon bed. Inside, Canon lay with pistols at the ready.

The large house stood on Trask's peninsula, the next nearest dwelling a mile or more away. The wagon stopped at the turn into the road, a quarter-mile from the house.

Canon made a close study of the road and pronounced himself satisfied.

"No indication of any recent riders," he said. "Four sets of hoofprints and marks of carriage wheels. No one has been in there today. But Pinkerton's men will be along soon.

"Here's what we do: There will be a lookout or two on the road, so you will drive me to the water and I'll swim so I can come up behind the house. You will stay at the water until I come for you. If someone comes up, you are here to look at property.

"There will probably be shooting at the house, but it won't last long. Now let's go, please."

"How will you get back here with the lady?" said Miz Sutcliffe.

"There will be plenty of extra horses," said Canon grimly. Miz Sutcliffe, who had never seen Canon angry, felt of a stab of fear lance her heart. The soldier at the roadblock was right, she thought; here is a man who can be very bad indeed.

Canon ran to the water's edge and stripped. He placed his clothes and gear into the waterproof bag he had brought and tied it to his back. He stepped into the icy water of San Francisco Bay.

Two long baths in one day? Canon thought. The Black Horse would call me a sissy. Long swimming strokes took him closer to the point of the peninsula, several hundred yards away. He stayed near the rocky shoreline.

Canon beached near a copse of eucalyptus which bordered the shore near the house. Unpacking his gear, he dressed quickly and quietly, checked his pistols to make sure they were dry and buckled on the gunbelt.

The first guard was about where Canon expected, from Carolina's description of the layout, kneeling in the midst of a thicket of shrub sixty feet from the house. The man expected trouble from the look of things. A shotgun, no, two shotguns lay on the ground in front of him.

Canon, sixty feet behind the guard, crept closer. His moccasins made no sound in the sandy vetch. For a moment, from twenty feet, he debated on whether to throw the knife. Too many dry leaves covered the ground. He did not have the time he needed to move through them without noise.

Dammit! He had no time at all. He ducked quietly to the ground as he picked up the sound of approaching riders. Pinkerton was almost there. It was almost a minute later when the guard perked up. No wonder our cavalry rides over their pickets, Canon thought. These people are deaf.

Nine armed horsemen rode at a trot into the clearing. Pinkerton was not among them. There was some very wet work to be done here, Canon guessed. Nine riders against three in the house, if Canon figured correctly. He suspected the nine were badly outmatched. There would be another man with two shotguns on the far side of the clearing. It would be a savage crossfire.

The lead horseman stopped near the front steps.

"Come out, Field," he shouted. "Bring Sherer and Wallace. No need for guns here. We've come to make you rich."

A man stepped out under the shadow of the porch, which was railed by a low wood wall. Canon could not see his features clearly, but he could see the shotgun the man held at present arms.

"I see you got guns," drawled Field, "but I don't see money."

"It's in the saddlebags. Pinkerton said he'll pay a hundred thousand for the lady, but not two. You'd never get that much out of the South."

"I hear Canon got away," said Field. "Figured you'd be coming out for the lady. What does Pinkerton figure? He think he can make Canon come back in by offering Widow Jackson in trade?"

"Just bring her out," said the Pinkerton man. "There's nine of us against your three. Bring her out, we'll take her back, and you boys get the money and your freedom. We brought the money."

"Whether you did or not is all the same," said Field. As he spoke the word, Field leveled the shotgun and emptied both barrels into the agent, cartwheeling him backwards off the horse.

The man in front of Canon stood and loosed both barrels into the riders, the roar of his shotgun echoed by the other from the far side of the clearing. Six saddles were emptied by the crossfire.

The three remaining riders each got off a desperate, futile shot while the three kidnappers reached for their back-up shotguns. Field dropped to a knee behind the wooden railing and brought up his other shotgun. The three riders were cut down as they turned their horses to flee.

The man in front of Canon knelt, broke open the shotgun to reload. Canon had moved right behind him during the firing. With one quick move, Canon encircled the man's neck with his left arm, pulled him up and bowed him backwards. "This is for Stonewall Jackson, you bastard," he said, and stuck the heavy blade through the man's spine. An "oooff" whooshed out of the man. His legs kicked once, reflexively, as the spinal cord parted. Then his muscles relaxed and the foul smell of sudden death was in the air. Canon eased him noiselessly to the ground.

Field walked down the steps from the porch into the carnage in the yard. A couple of the agents, dying but not dead, were groaning. Field pulled a pistol from the gunbelt on his hip and shot each man once in the head. "Sherer? Wallace?" he called. "Come on out. There aren't any more." A man stepped from the opposite edge of the clearing, shotgun dangling from the crook of each arm. He, too, wore a pistol. Both looked toward the thicket where Canon knelt.

We better check Wallace," said Field. "He must've took a stray bullet." They started toward the thicket. Field replaced his pistol and broke open the shotgun. Canon figured Sherer had already reloaded. When they were within fifteen feet, Canon stepped out, cocking the drawn Krupps. Field and Sherer stopped, staring at Canon and considering the situation. Each wanted to try, each hoped the other would try first and draw the fire. Canon hoped they would do it.

"Hello, Canon," said Field. "Figured you'd be coming to visit but I didn't figure on it being this quick. We just saved Mrs. Jackson for you. You seen it. They wanted to take her and make you give yourself up. I figure you owe us for saving you and Mrs. Jackson."

"You mean Widow Jackson, don't you, Field?" said Canon. "I owe you all right, and I always repay every debt I owe."

"Where's Wallace?" said Sherer.

"In hell. I already paid him."

Sherer moaned. "We got any options a'tall, General?" said Field.

"Yeah. You can decide what kind of knot you want in the noose, if you answer a question for me."

"And what might that be?" said Field.

"What part did Frank Lawson take in the murder of Stonewall Jackson?"

"Don't say nothing, Field," said Sherer. "He gonna hang us nohow."

"True," said Canon, "but I can hang you with a knot that strangles or a knot that snaps. Your choice if you answer, mine if you don't."

Sherer started to weep quietly. Field looked at him with contempt.

"Lawson didn't do no shooting," said Field, "just put us on picket duty. We was told by Pinkerton to kidnap Jackson, but your man Hillary is the one who told us Pinkerton changed his mind.

"It didn't really sound like Pinkerton to me, and then we each got ten thousand dollars from a pick-up point outside Richmond, and that didn't feel like Pinkerton, neither. Pinkerton never paid that much for nothing. Say, do one thing for me."

"I might, if you'll answer another question for me," said Canon.

"Shoot," said Field, and Sherer moaned at the terminology.

"Did A. P. Hill have anything to do with Jackson's death?"

"I don't know. Not that I heard of. But I ain't often privy to that type information. One thing I would like to know is whether Pinkerton actually sent the money to me. Mind if I check the saddlebags?"

"No time," said Canon.

"Hell, I never had no luck," said Field, flipping up the shotgun barrel. Canon shot him in the throat with his left pistol and in the heart with his right, hoping Sherer would draw, also.

Field flopped straight back, dead. His heavy brown boots kicked high, hit the ground. He was still.

Sherer, instead of trying for a shot, thew down the shotgun, fell sobbing to his knees, looked to his left at Field, then buried his face in his hands. "Please don't hang me," he sobbed.

The display of cowardice from a man who shot Stonewall Jackson from ambush disgusted Canon, and got Sherer his wish. Canon shot him through the top of his head. Sherer's arms flew out straight at his sides as his body rocked back, then he fell face first into the dirt.

Mary Anna Jackson was in the back bedroom of the house. The room overlooked the bay. She was tied to the chair on which she sat. A red kerchief was in her mouth. Already petite, she had lost much weight. Lines of strain and worry creased her face and there were dark circles under her eyes. But there were no marks of physical abuse that Canon could see. She wore a plain brown dress.

When Canon freed her, she tore the gag from her mouth. "Oh, Rabe, I can't believe it is really you!" she cried in a strangled voice, then rushed weeping into his arms. He hugged her for a moment, then pushed her away.

"We have to get out of here quickly, Mary Anna," he said. "Can you ride?"

She nodded. "Those awful men . . ." she said, half in question.

"They are dead," said Canon, "but that much shooting will likely have been heard by someone around here, even deserted as the place is. Are you sure you are all right?"

"They didn't . . . do anything bad to me, Rabe. I tried to refuse to eat but they threatened to rape me if I didn't. I thought I would never be free of them."

"Everything is all right," soothed Canon. The words had barely been spoken when he heard hoofbeats coming into the yard. Drawing his pistol, he ran for the front door, and broke into laughter. Mamie Sutcliffe and Carolina Lee, brandishing their hideaway guns, rode bareback into the yard on Scratch.

"It's all right," Canon shouted back to Mary Anna. "It is only the western version of Southern cavalry arriving." He yelled out the door for the two women to wait.

Canon gathered the few pitiful clothes the gang had allowed Mary Anna, stuck them in a battered valise he found, and led her outside. She walked past the dozen dead men without halt or falter.

Canon helped Carrie and Mamie to other horses, took a saddle off a third and put it on Scratch.

He helped Mary Anna onto Scratch. She looked down at the horse.

"I believe Scratch and I have something in common," she said. "We both are turning prematurely white in the hair." Canon checked all the saddlebags before climbing on a horse. They were empty. As he rode past Field's body, he looked down. "No time, no luck, no money," he said. Field only stared.

They rode at a brisk pace back to the carriage. The ripe red sun, big as forever, dipped its toes into San Francisco Bay, turning the water blood-gold. Canon quickly stripped the saddle off Scratch and hitched him to the carriage.

Before he clambered back into the coffin, he saw Mamie, Carrie and Mary Anna sitting on the carriage seat quietly looking at each other.

Carrie did not know whether she should introduce the women, so she stayed quiet. Mary Anna did not know whether she was supposed to show she knew Carolina, so she also stayed quiet. Mamie, confused and sitting between the two, tried with spectacular unsuccess to make herself small.

"I am genuinely sorry, ladies, for my inexcusable rudeness," he said. "I can only plead that other pressing matters have conspired to make me forget my manners. Introductions are certainly in order.

"Miz Sutcliffe, these two ladies have met on a previous occasion. I would like for you to meet Mrs. Mary Anna Jackson. Mrs. Jackson, Miz Mamie Sutcliffe."

Unable to curtsy sitting down, Mamie nodded nicely and took the hand offered by Mary Anna. "How do you do?" said each lady, as if a dozen men had not been slaughtered almost in front of them fifteen minutes earlier.

Canon was about to crawl in the coffin when understanding lit Mamie Sutcliffe's face until it glowed red as the lowering sun itself. Canon saw her lips quiver.

"Fahgive me foah my being inquisitive, but are you perchance the wife of the late Generul Jackson?" said Mamie, hope and fear plain in her natural southern voice. Mary Anna nodded politely.

The bedazzled Mamie vaulted from the wagon seat lightly as a svelte teenager. She curtsied, bowed, curtsied again. "Mrs. Jackson," she said, southern as a honeydew melon, "it is a great honuh in mah life to meet you and invite you to mah humble abode."

"Miz Sutcliffe, I look forward to it very much," replied Mary Anna.

Canon controlled his laughter. He resaddled the riders' horses and shooed them toward the house.

Again in the coffin, Canon considered whether it might be best not to return to San Francisco; whether he should simply flee with Carolina and Mary Anna. No. Pinkerton would have the entire Federal garrison out when he learned that Mary Anna was gone. He would know she was with Canon and that they were outside the city. They could run but they could not hide.

The money, too, was in the city, locked in Mamie's safe. He trusted that Mamie would take care of it, but he had placed her in enough danger. The money would go back home with him, as would Carolina, as would Mary Anna, as would Miz Sutcliffe if she wished.

Canon thought his plans to return home should reach fruition soon if he could make his connections. In the meantime, much had to be done and it was best done in the city. He would check out the *Southern Star* somehow, but he was sure Pinkerton told the truth about the Union fleet being after her.

Besides, Pinkerton would not think that Canon, once outside the city, would return to it. It would be one helluva lot easier going in than it would be getting out. Sooner or later, though, they would have to get back out.

Canon was too tired to think on it. He had not slept in nearly thirty-six hours. Whatever else occurred, sleep was his number one priority. Like Mountain Eagle, Canon had taught himself not to snore, so he had no fear of tipping off a roadblock.

This coffin is damned comfortable, thought Canon. As the carriage jounced along, he drifted into a dreamless sleep.

# Part III

## 22

# *Three Eagles*

The Great San Francisco Exposition began its six-week run November 16, 1864. For weeks, the newspapers had been full of wonders that would be exhibited and demonstrated. Marvelous modern mechanical miracles would be shown, scientific discoveries announced, medical breakthroughs heralded. The exposition was a repository of hints that the industrial age was around the chronological corner.

No mystery on earth was safe any longer from the questing humans who were possessed with a compulsive will to seek, to find, to know. What the mind of man could conceive and believe, it could achieve, said pamphlets for the fair. And the proof was right here.

Steam driven machines that would harvest and gin cotton, and make slavery unnecessary, were there. So were devices that could dig deeper, plow further, cut quicker and even fly.

Many of the mechanical marvels dealt in death. Death had been big business for the past three years. Money was to be made by anyone who could produce a machine capable of killing on a larger scale. One such machine was perfected by an American, Richard Gatling. It was a machine gun. A Gatling gun. The prototype was displayed and demonstrated at the fair. Repeating rifles were displayed. Many of them were already in the hands of union soldiers outside Petersburg, Virginia. They could fire sixty rounds a minute in seven-shot increments. Rebels disdainfully called them "Sunday" guns, saying they could be loaded on Sunday and fired for the rest of the week. But they killed Confederates by the thousands.

Bullets were no longer cap-and-ball, with paper cartridges of powder. Bullets, like the ones Canon used, were self-contained and cut loading time to a fraction of what it had been.

Not even the depths of the sea nor the heights of the air were safe from the makers of war. Submersible ships were on display, as were high flying hot air balloons. Balloons were now being routinely used by both sides to observe battle and direct artillery fire.

A highlight of the exposition would be an attempt on opening day by Messieur Devereaux of Belgium to break the world altitude record in a "stratospheric" balloon named *Eagle*. It would reach the breathtaking height of five miles, the dark little man predicted dramatically.

At that height, he announced, he expected to be driven by winds blowing in from the ocean, "westerlies" he called them, at speeds approaching one hundred miles per hour. Yes, he said, he would defy death. Women positively mobbed the brave little fellow.

Steel was well on its way to reshaping the world. Herr Krupp, whose German company had tooled Canon's pistols, displayed a single cast block of steel that weighed one ton. It had already broken through the floor of the warehouse twice.

Herr Krupp's pistols, at the moment, were being meticulously checked by their owner. Canon was cleaning them as he read the day's paper in Miz Sutcliffe's parlor. He was sitting beneath the huge Rebel flag that had graced the wall since 1861.

Miz Sutcliffe's sympathy for the South was well known. One of every two California households that cared about the war were on the Southern side. That meant a lot of houses for Pinkerton to search, for that was what the little bulldog was doing.

For his failings, Pinkerton was also tenacious and methodical as the bulldog he so resembled. Sooner or later, the knock would come at Mamie's door. Canon knew they had to get out soon.

It had been four days since the killings at Trask's shack. Not a word had been said in the papers during that time. Pinkerton had evidently effectively gagged the press while he scoured the countryside.

In the meantime, Canon and the Sutcliffe household had been busy within the city. They had time, for a change. For Pinkerton had sent out the garrison and his men, as Canon expected, to check every hotel, roadside inn, house and hiding place. This had left San Francisco virtually free for

Canon to roam at will. He had been out every night, scouting and search-ing. The *Southern Star* was indeed gone, but safe, Canon had heard. And from adjoining rooftops, he had watched the daily forays of Pinkerton search parties.

But it was time to go. Although the exposition was set to open next day, it had suddenly, after two weeks, been replaced in the headlines.

The front pages today were full of articles about two things, the burning of Atlanta by Sherman, and the Confederate killer, Rabe Canon.

Canon's photograph took up a quarter of the *Chronicle's* front page. His description was given. Headlines told of terror and random violence perpetrated by the crazed Rebel. Included were claims that Canon had singlehandedly massacred a dozen peaceful secret service agents and had kidnapped a woman they were trying to protect from him.

He had bombed the Carlton Hotel, wounding many civilians. He had murdered in cold blood the city's much beloved banker, Adam Trask, then robbed and burned his home. Editorial writers screamed for his blood. The *Chronicle* had posted a reward of ten thousand dollars in gold.

Canon could not escape, the *Chronicle* assured its readers, and no panic should be felt. Two thousand men from the Federal garrison were institut-ing a house to house search. The citizenry should not fear, but should be wary of the huge blond-headed fiend, who was probably in the company of two outlaw women. Descriptions were given of Carolina Lee and Mary Anna Jackson.

From the rooftops that morning, Canon had seen the house-to-house search begin. A large force had begun on the fringe of the city, a smaller force concentrated on the houses and businesses around the Carlton in the center of town. Canon estimated it would take two days for the search to reach Miz Sutcliffe. He intended to be gone by then.

The only thing that had held him this long was the money. Pinkerton had delayed spreading word of the counterfeit bills because he thought Canon was outside the city. Now the word would spread. Because during that time, Mamie's girls had quietly used the fake bills to purchase every piece of expensive jewelry in San Francisco. A few gold bars and some dust had been bought, but it was too bulky and too heavy. The gold had been cached.

Instead, Canon probably owned more diamonds than any individual in America. Rare stamps, coins and paintings were at a premium also. Canon guessed he had spent more than half the ten million dollars.

Late last night, he had ridden to the most out-of-the-way telegraph office he could find. It closed at midnight and Canon watched the Pinkerton agents depart. Canon waited an hour, then broke in easily.

One of Stonewall Jackson's favorite ruses had been to cut in on telegraph lines and send false messages to Yankee generals, saying that the Stonewall Army had been spotted at a town fifty miles from its real location. Canon learned to operate the telegraph and had employed the same trick for the Black Horse. Last night, he had sent one message fleeting over the wires to Richmond: Black Horse to Beau. Arrest Hillary. Dollars were trap. All well so far.

Canon hoped it got there.

Leaving the office, he rode to the edge of the badlands bordering San Francisco to the east. Anyone watching would have agreed with the *Chronicle* that Canon was quite mad. He stood there with Scratch and howled at the moon like a hungry coyote. For two nights past, he had done the same. Last night, the coyote he had listened for finally answered.

Canon threw down the newspaper and poured another bourbon. His plans were made now, for good or ill. He figured the odds at fifty-fifty. Luck would have to take a hand for Canon.

Miz Sutcliffe called her girls "soiled doves," as did they themselves and most of their patrons. It was a peculiar and whimsical appellation for "whore," Canon thought. But most of the girls were honest, and trustworthy, if not tempted beyond reason.

Just the day before, three of the doves booked boat passage for Texas, paying in gold. It was risky, but necessary. The ship was scheduled to depart tomorrow evening. Pinkerton's men would be watching.

There were a dozen doves in the house. All had loudly proclaimed when they were hired to be full fledged Rebels. Miz Sutcliffe would not have hired them otherwise. Canon thought most of them really were Southern patriots. But he was unsure of three and suspicious of one. Still, each had been given one of the ten thousand dollar bills for their own, and had taken checking accounts at distant banks. But the reward, another ten thousand in gold, would make them rich for life. No doubt about it, Canon thought, time to go.

Mrs. Jackson had been introduced to the girls as Mrs. Johnston, the sister to Mr. Johnston, who was ill and had to spend so much time upstairs. Carolina, recognized by some of the girls, said she had married the suffering Johnston. He had a rare disease called elephantiasis. If any of the girls saw him, they were not to wonder at his size.

Canon doubted any believed it to begin with, and certainly none would after they saw the paper today. Time to go.

He heard a burst of laughter downstairs. Sutcliffe House was open for business. Mamie had at first insisted on shutting down for a while, but Canon convinced her it would be a sure way to draw attention.

He recalled with a smile how Mary Anna had swallowed hard, twice, when she learned the kind of establishment that had welcomed her. But she soon recovered and was, as always, gracious to one and all. She spent her days sewing for the girls and her nights reading.

Miz Sutcliffe buzzed happily through days of delight. The Confederate hero had come to her house, had included her in a daring rescue of a great Southern lady, and said lady now resided under the Sutcliffe roof. She could not have been happier.

Carrie healed well. The burns had crusted; welts from the quirt were beginning to disappear. They had spent their nights in a room, making love for hours. As she spent great amounts of time with Mary Anna, a real friendship growing between them.

She walked into the room, as Canon thought about her. She smelled of lilacs and wore the finest dress at Miz Sutcliffe's disposal.

"Miz Sutcliffe will close at midnight, darling," she said, "and we will proceed with our plans. Scratch has been given double rations of oats and water. The groom has been rubbing him down twice a day. He says Scratch is ready. I hope so," she said, with a little catch in her throat.

"Now, lovey, I told you everything is going to be fine."

"Please, please don't get yourself killed. I love you."

"You're a darling girl. And I won't get killed. I will live to see a rope around Hubert Hillary's scrawny neck. I promise you that. But, Carrie darling, it is still three hours until we have to get ready for Miz Sutcliffe's midnight soiree. How do you think we might be able to while away that much time?"

Carolina grinned, and reached for the buttons of her dress.

At eleven-thirty, Canon shook Carrie awake. The house was oddly quiet. Canon realized there was no tinkling piano or raucous laughter coming from downstairs. Mamie must have shooed the guests out early, he decided. He and Carrie dressed, collected Mary Anna from her room, and walked downstairs.

Most of the girls were assembled, as were the outdoor men. A startling array of clothing, bottled emollients and tools filled the parlor. Miz Sutcliffe was happy as a bird.

"Let us begin, General" she chirped.

"In a moment, Miz Sutcliffe."

"But, suh, we must hurry."

"We will, ma'am, but first there is a presentation to be made."

"I don't unduhstand."

"Please sit right there," said Canon, indicating a strange, wheeled chair. She sat.

"Ladies and gentlemen, I thank you on behalf of the three of us who have received the generous hospitality of this house." He noticed that Mary Anna colored only slightly at the mention of the word "house." "For your sacrifices and loyalty, I thank you. Foremost in this has been Miz Mamie Sutcliffe." A smattering of applause.

"I give the floor over to another great Southern lady, Mrs. Mary Anna Jackson." More applause. The doves who had not learned Mary Anna's identity seemed confused but applauded anyway.

Mary Anna walked over and took Miz Sutcliffe's plump, pink little hand.

"Mamie," she said, "I have been a guest in many fine homes, where many fine people live. But I have never known anyone finer than you. I will remember this house, this home, as a place of joy and safety. I will remember it as the home of truly great woman. Quality is as quality does, and Mamie Sutcliffe is beyond doubt a lady of quality.

"I have asked you in to return with us, and you have said that you must stay here. Here is something for you that I hope you will remember us by. I hope you will wear it proudly, as it was worn. It is second hand, I'm afraid, but more the valuable to me because of it." She opened her hand. In it lay a tiny brass star.

"This little metal star was worn by my husband, a man who loved his country and his countrymen. He lived his life according to duty and honor. You are the same type of person, Mamie Sutcliffe, so allow me to present one of the stars which was pinned on my husband's collar by General Lee and President Davis. My husband was a man I'll remember, always, as Tom Jackson, but the world remembers him as Stonewall. He'd want you to have this."

Mamie Sutcliffe was too shocked to move, amidst the applause. Gently, Mary Anna took her hand, opened it, placed the star on the palm, and closed the little hand over it. Then she kissed Mamie on the cheek. Little coos of approval came from the circled doves.

Miz Sutcliffe drank in the applause for a moment, beamed in it. Then she rose, dropped into her elegant curtsy, and fled the room in tears. She was back within moments, composed. With a shy grin, she resumed her job of overseer of preparations. It was a long night for her and Mary Anna Jackson.

It seemed too brief a sleep for Canon, up at dawn and checking his gear for the third time. Outside, Scratch waited patiently in the stable, saddled and ready. The groom had already exercised him.

Canon made brief farewells to the ladies, kissed Carrie and climbed on Scratch. He rode into the street at six forty-five. It seemed quiet, though the city was beginning to come to life in the listening morning mist. Canon had wished for fog. Well, he thought, can't have everything. He rode toward the docks.

They trotted a couple of blocks toward the steamship lines when Canon felt an unpleasant tingling at the nape of his neck. Company, he thought. Two blocks up the street was an almost hidden alley. If they were after him, the alley was his only hope.

He put Scratch into a lope, then a canter as riders appeared at each end of the street. Many riders. Canon gave Scratch the word to run as the riders began to dismount and unsling carbines. Canon reached the alley just as Pinkerton yelled for him to halt. He turned in as the rifles fired. Bullets burned the bricks behind him, but Scratch was running full tilt toward the fence at the alley end. He flew it easily. They turned into another narrow way. If Pinkerton had cordoned the entire area, he was caught. The alley was empty.

Behind him came the view halloa. He swiveled in the saddle, saw riders swelling into sight. He couldn't tell how many, but it looked to Canon like Sherman's entire army had suddenly materialized in San Francisco. The chase was decidedly on. Canon's life, and perhaps the life of the Confederate nation, now depended on the heart and hooves of Old Scratch.

City structures thinned quickly in the direction of the badlands. Within two minutes there were no more two story buildings to be seen. Within five minutes, there were only warehouses and occasional shops.

Canon glanced at his reflection in the final shop's window as Scratch carried him flying past it, a white blur. Canon's own long blond hair trailed out as he lay low over the saddle. The momentary glimpse in the mirrored window filled Canon with joy. What a magnificent creature was Old Scratch, back from the dead. White mane whipping with the wind created by his own speed, tail straight out and streaming, ears back and belly to the ground, Scratch bobbed his great head in time to the drumming hoofbeats. The horse was straining every nerve.

Hell, he wished now that he'd put Scratch back to his true midnight color, if it had taken all night. Let the Black Horse run!

Canon took a quick glimpse over his shoulder. The riders were falling far behind. They had not come close enough even for another shot. But he knew they were also cutting off the side avenues. No matter. He had no intention of changing direction. Soon, though, the pursuit would recognize where he was heading.

A loaded wagon pulled out in front of him from the last warehouse on the edge of town. Scratch flew it without breaking stride.

He again glanced at his followers. Jesus, there must be fifty of them, he said to himself. And they would be riding top line cavalry mounts. Fifty to one. The dirt under Scratch's flying hooves turned to loam, then sand. Canon reined the big horse back a bit, though Scratch tossed his head, wanting more rein. But Canon said no. Even Scratch couldn't outrun a wasteland.

Scratch fought like his namesake to be allowed to run, but Canon continued to rein him back. They slowed to a canter, then a lope, finally a trot. The pack would gain swiftly on them, but something had to be saved for the final sprint. Timing would be more than crucial. It would mean life or death.

Scrub brush and treacherous tall grass stretched to the horizon. Silhouetted in the distance by the rising sun stood a sandstone hill. It was the landmark he sought, the place of refuge he must gain. In the prairie air, the hill looked like it was a mile away. Canon knew it to be five.

Shouting, then shooting, cranked up behind him. Had to be warning shots, thought Canon. The Pinkertons were still a half-mile behind him. A furrow appeared in a stubbed pine tree ten yards to Canon's right. Make that a quarter-mile, he thought, fooled by the prairie perspective. And make tracks.

They gained distance for two miles, then began to lose it as he again slowed Scratch, saving him for the last dash. The next three miles would tell all. Thick, oppressive humidity surrounded them. Its heaviness reminded Canon of the Swedish steam baths of intense heat that he once so enjoyed.

He was not enjoying the heat now. It drained the muscles and the will of even the most stubborn and well kept horses. And men. The heat was becoming tortuous. Canon could feel the vitality being burned out of Scratch at every stride. He knew that behind him, horses were dropping like fleas off a dying dog.

He threw another quick glance behind him. The gap had closed to less than five hundred yards. Puffs of smoke marked the shots fired, but no bullets came near. Canon faced front again. He had to give the bulldog, Pinkerton, his due. He was riding at the forefront of his men.

Scratch was tiring quickly. Flecks of streaming froth flew from his muzzle. Canon could hear the breathing grow more labored.

He thought the hill was no more than a mile away, now, but he couldn't be sure. He had already misjudged the distance once. But there was no longer a choice. If there was anything left in Scratch, it was time for it.

Canon pulled out his bowie knife. He grabbed tight to Scratch's sweat soaked mane. Leaning down, he cut the saddle cinches, making sure the cuts were clean through. He must not entangle the horse's legs.

"Now, Scratch," he yelled, and thrust the saddle from him. Scratch shot forward like the arrow from a bow.

Canon reached the hollow in the middle of the hill a quarter-mile ahead of his pursuers. There was water there, in a natural tank. Scratch had blown, drank, rested and was receiving a special Canon rubdown when Pinkerton rode up.

With satisfaction, Canon counted twenty-three weary riders on twenty-three spent horses. Scratch had done in more than half the horses racing after him.

Pinkerton's three-piece suit, his hat, his face, were covered with grit, but the stump of a cigar was clamped doggedly between the detective's teeth. Canon looked up and smiled as the pack surrounded him. He was sure he had not heard so many hammers being drawn and locked at one time since the Battle of Antietam.

"Hello, Pinkerton," said Canon, continuing the rubdown. "A morning gallop is so refreshing, don't you think."

Pinkerton slid off his horse and walked wincingly to Canon. He looked up at him. Canon stared back impassively. Pinkerton threw his cigar savagely into the dirt.

"I ought to hang you right here," he said.

"Sorry," said Canon. "No trees."

"Very funny, General. I am going to put you in chains, Canon, and then I am going to put you behind bars for so long that you won't remember what it was to be free."

"I don't think so," said Canon, calmly.

"What do you mean? You're my prisoner."

"Maybe."

"Maybe?"

"Maybe. And, as I like to point out, wherever there's a maybe, there has to be a maybe not."

Pinkerton exploded. "Here's a maybe for you, Canon. If you climb on that locomotive you call a horse within fifteen seconds, maybe I won't shoot you in the ass as we travel back to the garrison. Do you surrender or don't you?"

"I'm not really sure, Pinkerton. Let's find out. Are you here, my uncle?" called Canon. There was a very intense silence, then a low voice rumbled down from the hill.

"I am here, my brother's son."

"Well, then, there you are, Major," said Canon, then, formally, "Major Allan Pinkerton, I would like to introduce you to Two Eagles, war chief of the Ogallala Sioux, and my uncle, though I have not yet had the honor to meet him myself."

"Where is he?"

"In due time, Major. First, please tell your men to pile their guns on the ground here next to me."

"Go to hell, Canon."

"Listen carefully to me, Pinkerton. I need you alive or you and your men would be dead right now. You are surrounded and outnumbered. If one of your men fires a shot, I won't be able to stop the Sioux."

Pinkerton rubbed the rash on his face. "You're bluffing," he said. "No reports of Indians for miles and miles."

Canon sighed. "If you will order your men to hold their fire, I will show you what you're up against," he said.

Pinkerton turned to his muttering men, who were still on their horses and staring at the walls of the natural bowl that surrounded them.

"Nobody fires a shot until I give the word," Pinkerton yelled to them. "Everybody understand?" There were grunts of assent from the men.

"Uncle, please have half your men show themselves," called Canon.

"I will show half of half," rumbled the answer.

"All right."

From the rim on the left, twenty yards away, there slowly rose twenty-eight Indians. All had their backs to the sun, all had new repeating rifles at the ready. They lowered themselves out of sight, except for one, who spoke.

"I am Two Eagles, once of the Cherokee and now of the Ogallala. For the son of my brother, Mountain Eagle, I have brought men. When I told our village we would get new rifles and meet white men in battle, the price of war ponies rose three times; all wanted to come.

"Now the hearts of my men howl for blood. Their rifles are thirsty for blood. We wear the paint. We will kill these puny men."

Pinkerton did some quick mental calculations, then said, "It's another of your damned tricks. It would be impossible for more than a hundred Indians to move from Sioux territory here without the movement being seen and reported by our troops."

Two Eagles raised his right arm. Another group of braves rose from behind another section of the hill. Canon counted twenty-five.

"Nephew, I see you today for the first time," said Two Eagles. "But I have heard of your great size and skills. The newspaper tells us how you and your men of the Black Horse fight with daring and honor.

"Mountain Eagle, too, has sent word that you and the great warrior Wall of Stone were brothers in battle, and feared by your enemies. He told me your heart matches your great size. I wondered if it could be true that a man be so big, and now I see my brother spoke rightly.

"These men who chase you are dogs. We will kill them like dogs. They do not hear the words of Two Eagles, who holds their miserable lives in his hand. Let us show the little pink one, then."

Again, the chief raised his hand, and from the far side of the bowl, more warriors rose, whooping and brandishing their guns.

Pinkerton looked sick, looked around. "Throw down your goddamn guns," he said bitterly.

"Just slowly dismount, one by one, and stack your weapons here by me," Canon countermanded pleasantly. "And don't try to hide one. You'll be searched very thoroughly, and if one of the Sioux learns you've tried to cheat him . . . well, just take my word that you don't want it to happen."

The mound of rifles, pistols, knives and saps grew quickly.

"Now, all of you go over by the water and sit down," said Canon. "A great man once told me that if you make a prisoner sit, it is much more difficult for him to cause mischief. Or something like that."

Canon personally removed Pinkerton's weapons.

"All right, Chief, please come down," he called.

Two Eagles and his band came yipping down the hillside, grabbing horses, and guns off the pile. They were painted for war, but most were lean to the point of being gaunt. They wore ragged breechclouts and moccasins. They reminded Canon of Rebel infantry.

Pinkerton watched sourly as the band went through the stack of weapons, haggling and wraggling over the best pieces.

"That's less than thirty of them," said Pinkerton. "Tell the rest to come down. We're not going to hurt them."

Two Eagles walked up to Canon. The two men embraced.

"I think my Uncle is as wise and bold as I have been told by my father, Mountain Eagle," said Canon. "Am I correct, Two Eagles?"

Two Eagle's face lit up with a toothy white grin. "You are wise, Hawk, as my brother named you," he said.

"What the hell are you two talking about?" demanded Pinkerton.

Canon reached inside Pinkerton's coat, took three cigars from an inside pocket. He handed one to Two Eagles, poked one in Pinkerton's mouth, and bit the end off his own cigar and spit it into the sand. Pinkerton shrugged, brought out matches, and lit the cigars.

"It's an old Stonewall trick," said Canon. "You show your numbers, then keep the enemy occupied while you move them to another place and show them again, and again if necessary. Two Eagles had you outnumbered by a total of six."

Pinkerton's face, already red from the rash and the sun, flushed a deeper color of crimson.

"Two hundred more be here by dark," said Two Eagles. "Your ship arrive sooner than we think. We only half way here when we learn you in trouble, then we move fast. This many outrun rest of war party."

Canon and Two Eagles spent the afternoon talking while the Sioux set up a temporary camp and secured the prisoners. Buck and Mountain Eagle were well, Two Eagles said, but there was sad news. A Yankee raiding party had tried to reach Montgomery but were routed at the outskirts. They pushed around the city, burning the countryside.

Canon knew what was coming next, but did not interrupt. Mulberry had been burned. When the Yankees learned it was the home of Rabe Canon, they made sure that not a board was left of the plantation. Buck and Mountain Eagle had fought, had killed many Yankees, then slipped away when the fight became useless. They were now scouting for the cavalry of General Nathan Bedford Forrest.

Canon had hoped he would be able to show Mulberry to Carrie. She would have loved it, would have perhaps made it her home. But Canon refused to dwell on it. He would worry about rebuilding the plantation when he, Mary Anna and Carolina were safe in Richmond.

That night, sitting around a campfire with Two Eagles and Pinkerton, Canon began to work toward that end.

"Major," he said pleasantly, "I believe that, although you are a bluebellied Yankee dog, you are a man of your word. May I be assured of that?"

"General, you are without doubt a worthless bit of Rebel scum," returned Pinkerton, just as genially, "but I tell you that I have never in my life broken my word of honor. What is it to you?"

"It has been fun playing with you, Pinkerton," said Canon, "but I must get back to the war. I have, as you know, a rat to catch. When I go, I wish to have a clean slate and a head start."

"Please continue."

"When I leave San Francisco, you will give me a week's grace before you start after me. And you will give me your word, tonight, that no reprisal or punishment of any sort will be visited on those who have helped me, including Two Feathers and the Sioux."

"If I agree?"

"You will be held here for two days and released unharmed. You'll get back neither your weapons nor your horses, but you will get plenty of water for you and your men to make it back to town."

"I will be a laughingstock."

"Not a bit. Before morning, the rest of the war party will be here. Only you, I and Two Eagles know of the ruse. The rest of your men can believe the other Indians they think they saw went back to meet the main body of the tribe. You will be a hero for not losing a single life against fearful odds."

"And if I refuse?"

"I will be earnest with you, Pinkerton. Full grown white men are of little use in a Sioux village. They are instead a nuisance. Whether you and your men live or die is of extreme unimportance to the Sioux. If you remain their prisoners, you will be driven as slaves across the miles to their village.

"This means you don't get horses and you'll be lucky to get a mouthful of water a day, which is usually all the Sioux allow themselves. Half of you, maybe all of you, will die on the way and will be left where you fall. The Sioux will make sure you're dead before they leave you, of course.

"If any of you do make it to the village, you will be lower than slaves. You will be treated worse than their dogs, far worse than their horses, which they cherish. If someone in the tribe decides he wants to mutilate or kill you for sport or spite, not a finger of protest is likely to be lifted on your behalf. And there is always the possibility of torture."

"You are telling me the truth, Canon?"

"My word of honor, and I don't give it lightly, either. What I have described to you is the way of life for Indians. It sounds cruel. It is cruel. But it is the way they treat prisoners from other tribes and the way they expect to be treated themselves if captured."

"Then I not only find your terms agreeable, but damned generous. May I also have the word of Two Eagles?"

"It shall be as my nephew wishes," said the Indian. "What bargain you make with Rabe Canon, Two Eagles and the Sioux will honor it. You have the word of Two Eagles."

"Very well," said Pinkerton. "You have my word that no reprisals or punishment of any kind will be meted out to any who have helped you in California, including Two Eagles and his Sioux, and including Mamie Sutcliffe."

"Pinkerton," said Canon, "you astonish me."

"I think not," said Pinkerton. "Was dear little Kate in on this? She told us exactly where to wait for you this morning."

"Not intentionally. She overheard what was intended for her to hear."

"Just so," said Pinkerton. "Let's see, where was I . . . oh, yes. You have my word that you, General, and those traveling with you will not be pursued nor even mentioned by me or my men for one week, beginning on my return to San Francisco. Canon?"

"Yes, Major?"

"Are you certain about the week? You can bind me to it longer, you know. I shall make it two weeks. For you, Mrs. Jackson and Miss Lee."

"That's damned generous of you. I gladly accept."

"Here's my hand on it," said Pinkerton.

"And willingly taken," said Canon, shaking hands.

"My Uncle, I must leave you," said Canon, turning to Two Eagles. They rose and embraced. Canon removed something from his pocket. It was fifty thousand dollars in Yankee greenbacks. "Spend it quickly, Uncle. There are many rifles in town."

"Damn you, Canon," said Pinkerton.

"Now, now, Major. Your word of honor. Remember?"

"I'll get you, Canon. Two weeks isn't much time, unless you plan to sprout wings and fly back to Richmond."

"I'll keep that in mind. Goodbye, Major. Uncle, a word with you, please."

Canon's leisurely ride back across the grassland took better than an hour. Old Scratch crowhopped occasionally, wanting to run. But Canon wanted to enjoy what might be his last night of freedom. There was no telling what might be waiting for him at Sutcliffe House. He wanted a slow, beautiful ride through the prairie on Scratch, and finally Scratch realized it and settled down.

The house was dark when Canon reached it at ten o'clock. It was shuttered. No outside lamps shone at the time when the house was usually opening for business. A black wreath of mourning hung from the door.

Canon's gentle knock was answered immediately by two men he had never seen before. Both were slight, but tall. One was older. His beard and moustache were gray. The other had jet black hair, shorn short, with a tiny black moustache. The smaller, dark man leaped in Canon's arm and kissed him full on the mouth.

"Why, lovey," he said to Carrie, "those things really do tickle." She smiled through the moustache.

## 23

# The Wind from the West

M. Georges Deavereaux rubbed his tiny, artistic hands enthusiastically as he considered the coming delights of this day.

It was going on eight A.M., and the sun and the winds were perfect for his ascension in the *Eagle* at nine. He checked the weather once more through the window of his little rented house next to launch site.

The big red balloon towered above the ground, swaying with the breeze, straining the heavy rope that bound her to earth.

Deavereaux checked himself in the full length mirror he had bought for the house. Ah! he thought, the wind is but perfect, and Deavereaux is its match. His red linen duster and beret, his thick black goggles—these items were not truly necessary, but how they made American women pant for him. Like the one yesterday.

She arrived with a sightseeing group being given the pre-opening tour of the finer exhibits. He did not notice her at first. She was shy, and stayed at the back of the small crowd. And he had not noticed her, clad as she had been in the black hooded cape that covered her body. Ah, that body!

He had finished his demonstration of the balloon's mechanics, and the rest of the crowd had left. She stayed behind, mesmerized by the little balloonist and dazzled by his disregard of danger. Timidly, she had come to him, asking to be shown more.

The silly girl. The great Deavereaux would show her all. When she had opened her cape and thrown back the hood, M. Deavereaux was transfixed by her beauty. Her tawny hair, blown by the exquisite wind, her full breasts straining the tight fabric that hid them from him.

He allowed her inside the gondola, shown her the working mechanism and the alcohol tins which would provide the flame to make his *Eagle* soar to untold heights. She melted as he stroked her, but the beautiful one had unfortunately mastered her heated senses and refused him.

Virgin that she was, she had promised to be waiting for him when he returned to ground. Two, three days at the most to find a returning wind, and Deavereaux would convert her virginity in the most perfect Belgian manner. She would be here this morning to see him off. He had promised a special place for her, and for her brother and her sick sister, behind the gondola.

Deavereaux ran to the window again, seeking in the growing crowd any sign of her. He found none, but saw that his handlers had fixed the little bandbox behind the balloon so she could send him to the sky with a farewell kiss.

Oh, happy day for M. Deavereaux!

Carolina enjoyed most of the afternoon she spent with Deavereaux. She had oohed and ahhhed for an hour and joined him inside the roomy gondola. He would sleep here, he manfully said, warmed against the chill, cruel winds only by the thought of her beauty. She learned to work the mechanism. Child's play, he told her, but no place for a child, he added, trying to get his hand up her dress.

She amusedly allowed him to stroke her, but had deftly avoided his more persistent advances. He was a dear little man, was M. Deavereaux.

Fifteen minutes before the Belgian was to gain the dais for his farewell speech, two tall, spare men pushed an invalid lady in a large wheeled chair through the gates of the exposition and were engulfed by the roiling crowd.

The crone in the chair was afforded some leeway by sightseers, but none took much notice. There were too many wonderful sights to see. Legs protected by a large lap robe, she kept her gray head down. Canon, kneeling in the chair, felt he was frying under the heavy make-up, the wig and the robe. The seat had been lowered almost to ground level. He appeared no taller than average female height. All three of Miz Sutcliffe's stable boys had accompanied the wagon to load and unload the chair containing Canon's bulk. It had pulled away amidst waves and cheers from most of the doves.

Only Miz Sutcliffe and the little dove, Kate, wept. Miz Sutcliffe wept from sadness, Kate wept from the bruises the other girls had inflicted on her when they learned of her treachery.

When Mary Anna, Carolina and Canon passed out of sight in the wagon,

Mamie turned and gave Kate one more furious pinch before ordering her back in the house. To one of the houseboys, Mamie said, "It's the rough trade for that one, from now on."

At the fair, Mary Anna and Carolina, stumbling now and again because of the ungainly cowboy boots with the lifts inside them, strained and muscled the wheelchair into the pavilion next to the balloon site.

It was the armory pavilion, a huge barn structure with rolling doors at each end. The Carlton, laid flat, could fit inside with space left at each end.

Canon was awed by the spectacle of weaponry. They were such stately seeming toys of destruction. Gleaming steel and giant muzzles appeared to be arcane works of art. Shells big as tree trunks stood beside them.

He stopped the chair in front of the Gatling gun. This one was not beautiful. It looked like what it was. Here was death personified and multiplied. Canon thought it the most lethal thing he had seen.

The Gatling, as if it recognized its status, sat apart from the other weaponry, near the open door. Canon saw the reason. This section of the barn wall was hinged. It would be opened like a door and the Gatling gun, from its pedestal, would be demonstrated this morning. A placard in front of the piece said it was to be fired following the balloon lift.

Canon wished he could watch it. The machine gun, weighing only eighty pounds, according to the card, was capable of firing five hundred rounds per minute with accuracy. The small steel tubes around the barrel looked obscene. Canon reckoned one man with a gun like this could stop a cavalry charge. Stop it dead.

Passing again into bright sunlight as they exited the pavilion, Canon beheld the highlight of the exposition. M. Deavereaux was inside the gondola of the *Eagle*, topping it off with flames from the burner. It skittered and bounced on the ground, begging to be allowed its leap to the sky.

Canon looked back into the now empty pavilion. Everyone had come out to watch Deavereaux begin his dance with the wind. Canon thought it best to wait inside, in shadow, until the moment of departure was at hand.

Deavereaux was in his glory. He had moved up to the dais for his farewell oration. Hundreds of people, perhaps a thousand, stood expectantly in front of the raised dais, hanging on his every word. In a moment, he would finish his fiery speech, leap back into the gondola and set sail for the stratosphere.

He glanced unhappily back at the empty bandbox behind him. Surely the mademoiselle would come. Surely she would not disappoint the Great Deavereaux at his moment of triumph. Why, he did not even know her name! Ah, this must be she, or at least her party. There was the brother, no, two brothers, and the pitiable specter of her mother, head bowed, her back humped with age.

Deavereaux finished his farewell as he heard them push the dear mother onto the bandbox. To ringing cheers, Deavereaux bowed with great flourish, turned and leaped into the gondola. Immediately, he turned to one of his amour's brothers on the bandbox.

"The mademoiselle," he said in heavy accent, "she is not ill, I hope."

"No, messieur," replied the gray bearded man, in a voice that, while gruff, would have seemed surprisingly feminine to Deavereaux had his mind been on such things. "My sister is overcome with fear for your safety, and asked us here to wish you well and to tell you that she anticipates your swift and happy return."

"Ah!" said the mollified Belgian.

"But," continued graybeard, "she asks that you please bestow your farewell kiss on our darling mother."

"Uh," said the reluctant Belgian, then, gallantly, "But of course." They wheeled the crone close, and Deavereaux puckered and reached for her.

And suddenly was staring down the bore of the biggest pistol he had seen.

"You will stay very still, and not say a word," Canon ordered, pressing the hidden muzzle against the Belgian's side. The little man stood as ordered.

"Hurry, now!" said Canon to his companions. He helped Mary Anna and Carolina into the gondola, then clambered in beside them, dragging his bulky shawl in afterward.

A few of the crowd, and all the balloon handlers, began to wonder what was going on as people joined the little man in the gondola. It was advertised as a solo flight.

"Take us up, messieur," said Mary Anna in perfect French, "or I am afraid you will become shot in very short order."

Canon did not wait, as he saw the handlers move toward the tie line. The line was very thick, but Canon's bowie knife was very sharp. It parted beneath the blade with magical speed. When the handlers reached the rope, it lay in coils and the balloon was slowly, then swiftly, seeking the sky.

The large crowd, unaware of what happened, burst into applause as the *Eagle* raced to the wind and clouds. When Canon unfurled Mamie's over-sized Confederate flag, draped it over the side and loosed a terrific Rebel yell, the crowd returned the yell wildly.

Not a word passed inside the crowded gondola as the balloon slipped the bonds of gravity. Here was beauty on a scale of magnificence none of the three knew. Even M. Deavereaux, though taken aback by his passengers and no stranger to the air, watched in wonder as the crowd, the buildings, the fair and then the city dwindled away to toys beneath them.

Behind them lay the blue pacific, white capped and infinite, below them the city was miniaturized, ahead of them the panorama widened into an azure horizon with hues of green and gold.

They were free. Nothing could touch them except sunshine, bright and pure, and sweet-scented air. Strangely, they felt no breeze, though Canon could see they were moving at great speed over the land. He asked the Belgian about it.

Evidently the man was a fatalist. He displayed not the slightest qualm about his predicament, though he was sad at what he was certain was his own imminent demise.

"You are the monster, Canon, of whom I have read," he said, with a lot less Frenchness than he had formerly employed.

"He is not a monster," said Carolina. "You will be well treated and set down safely to earth."

"You will be well compensated," said Canon, removing five ten-thousand dollar bills from his pocket. "I will tell you how to spend this wisely." He handed the money to Deavereaux, who brightened considerably at the news and at the money.

Harking to Canon's question, the Belgian took the bills from Canon and laid them in a line on the gondola rail. Carrie gasped and reached for them, but the little man imperiously held up a hand to stop her. Not a single bill even rippled.

"We move with the wind," he said, "at exactly its speed and direction. Viola! There is no wind." But he gathered up the bills as Canon explained what they were and put them inside his red duster. "With this," the balloonist said, "the great Deavereaux will build a real balloon." He patted the pocket and broke into laughter.

Over valleys, across checkerboarding fields, the balloon flew. Now at ease, Deavereaux became a gallant host. Each of the three guests took lessons from Deavereaux on how to work the mechanism, how to load the canisters of fuel. He gave basic instructions on the ballistics of flight.

Grasping the cord of the burner, Deavereaux spewed a sheet of flame into the gaping maw of the balloon. The corresponding rise into the sky gave a jolt to their stomachs. He explained the basics of the westerlies, the dangers of the mountains, the vagaries of rising masses of warm air he termed "thermals."

After three hours of travel, he coached as Canon brought the balloon to a slow descent. They were coming down over a lush green valley many miles east of where they set out. So quickly had the trip been made that Canon thought there could be no one expecting them below.

They were two hundred feet off the ground when rifle shots rang out. Deavereaux was frightened, but Canon quieted him. Beneath them, pouring from a cut in the hillside, rode Two Eagles and his band.

The balloon was ten feet off the ground when Indians, standing on their full-striding ponies, began to leap for the lines Deavereaux lowered from the gondola. Six of the braves hung on until the gondola struck the earth and tumbled on to its side. Canon threw out the iron anchor that roped the balloon to its landing site. The balloon's occupants, forewarned by the Belgian, were tossed about but unhurt.

"We'll have to work on the landing," said Canon to Two Eagles, after they had embraced. "How is friend Pinkerton?"

"Your Uncle is happy to be away from the little whisperer," said Two Eagles. "He offered many horses and much money for Two Eagles to join the bluecoats. He is a man of determination, that one. He will not quit."

"Will he keep his word, Uncle?"

"His word is good. He will do as he promised. He hates you and admires you for you bested him. But there is no fear. The pink one is a warrior.

"As is your great horse," continued Two Eagles, pointing behind him to Old Scratch. The Indians had removed the paint from Scratch. He was midnight black and beautiful. "Without the words you gave, even I, Two Eagles, maybe could not have ridden horse." Canon suppressed a grin. He would wager the old Indian tried very hard indeed to ride Scratch without using the code words. He noticed that Two Eagles limped as they walked over to Scratch.

"Nor will I ride him again," said Two Eagles. "He is a great horse, but he is your horse. I will not form a friendship with him. When the young buffalo man of dark skin brought him to me, I felt a great bonding of spirits with this devil horse. But a man's horse is a man's horse. Today, Two Eagles rode the black one. From now, the horse will be led when we travel.

"And when we return to our valley, he will roam free with our mares. It will be a great life for the big one, and he will make many colts for us."

"My Uncle is well named," said Canon, "for like two eagles, he has twice the heart and soul of any other. You are right that the black is a man's horse. He needs the company and friendship of men, and I must go into great danger, unknowing of whether I return.

"Let my Uncle become friend to this horse. Just as I have two fathers, let the horse have two brothers. Was he not gifted to me by the man of stone, I would pass him to you in return for your kindness to me. Treat him as your own, and if I do not return one day to claim him, he is yours."

"Aieee," said Two Eagles in surprise and delight. "So the black one is gifted to you by Jackson. A great gift, nephew, and a great gift from you to me. It will be as you say. Come, now. I have supplies for you."

Deavereaux showed them how to tie the four drums of alcohol onto the edges of the gondola, adding to the two already in place. He deflated the balloon to lessen the chances of its being spotted. They needed to learn how to reinflate it, anyway, he said, just in case.

Buffalo robes, blankets and canned goods were loaded into the gondola to augment the scanty supplies the Belgian had loaded for his planned two-day trip. Two Eagles also gave Canon all the ammunition he could spare. Canon paid him twenty thousand dollars for it. Word about the counterfeit money would spread slowly to outposts.

Canon removed his make up, again donning his frontier garments. Carrie and Mary Anna removed their make up and donned dresses. Even with their short hair, the two women were more than nice to see. Mary Anna was handsome, Carrie was beautiful. Canon expected to be challenged a time or two for her, but evidently Two Eagles exercised iron control over the band.

The Sioux were mannerly and educated, for the most part. Many, like Two Eagles, had attended white schools and could read and write to some degree. After dancing and feasting, they all talked long into the night. Two Eagles posted scouts for miles in every direction so there was no chance of being surprised.

Next morning, Deavereaux begged to be allowed to continue the trip, promising he would give the Confederacy a regular air army. Canon could see, too, the man was pining over Carrie. But there was too much danger and too little room. Though Canon would have liked to have him along, he refused to consider it.

They left the little Belgian happy. After he had reinflated the balloon, and goodbyes were handed around, Carrie gave M. Deavereaux a kiss at lift off that had the Indians firing their rifles in celebration. Deavereaux and the tribe gave passable attempts at the Rebel yell as *Eagle* gently climbed astride the wind from the west.

Canon almost relented, just before they lifted away, when Deavereaux had called him aside. Canon could scarcely believe how little time Deavereaux estimated the trip home would take. A week, said Deavereaux, at most.

It was beyond Canon's comprehension. The two thousand miles across country was at best a six-month journey, and about the same in any passenger ship. *Southern Star* was hardly a passenger ship.

But Deavereaux had taken them up, up, up to where the westerlies raged. There, far above the clouds, five miles above the earth, they had ridden buffeting roaring winds, freezing and getting barely enough oxygen to breath.

They had stayed there perhaps five minutes before Deavereaux returned them within sight of the earth. Then he showed Canon on the map how much territory they passed over in that brief span. It left Canon incredulous.

Before the new crew departed, Deavereaux warned Canon only to gain that much altitude in case of emergency. He gave one other warning. It was the one that almost changed Canon's mind. The place of danger would be the Rocky Mountains. The winds there blew in crosscurrents miles above the earth. Small test balloons had been launched. Few had been recovered. All that were found were shredded.

As the balloon gained altitude, Canon thought of the Belgian's warning about the mountains and a shudder ran through him. He wished he had taken Deavereaux with them. The man clearly relished thoughts of the dangerous encounter. But they were airborne now. No turning back. They flew into the glare of the morning sun.

North and east they flew, over Indian territories where a different war was being fought. Over great deserts and a great inland sea that Canon had heard was more salty than the ocean. Over forests they flew, over mountain and dell. Deavereaux told them they would near the Rockies by nightfall and that nothing, literally nothing, should cause them to attempt a night crossing. It was as much as their lives were worth to try, he said.

Late in the afternoon, a blue haze in the distance began to take shape. It appeared first to be a monstrous bank of clouds, and white could soon be made out against the blue. Then, on a sudden, there was a peak poking against the sky. Blue mountain, snowcapped peak, blue sky. No. No sky. The blue beyond was another mountain. Canon took his first look at the Rocky Mountains and swallowed hard. Twice.

Not so Mary Anna and Carolina. They thought the mountains the most beautiful things on earth. They laughed and clapped their hands, hugged each other in their joy. Canon didn't have the heart to tell them. Not just yet.

It was time for them to practice with the balloon, he said. They would get a little closer, see if there were any playful air currents they could ride, and do a couple of landings just for fun. They would cross the beautiful mountains next day. Canon made sure his voice didn't waver when he said, "beautiful."

They skimmed low over brownish grasslands twice, then Canon had slammed open the lever, let the flame fill the balloon and rush it skyward. What they had seen as they neared the ground was a sight that left them agog with wonderment. Mountain Eagle had told Canon of the endless buffalo herds which freely roamed the grassy western plains, but it was a sight that had to be beheld for belief.

What Canon and his companions had taken for brown prairie grass, where he was going to land, became as they lowered one vast herd of the strange looking animals. For miles and miles they overflew the herd. Then they gained altitude, passing through a cloud cover, and rode the whipping wind for two hours. When they again dipped through the cold clouds, bespattered with rain until they emerged beneath them, Canon was sure the brown they now saw had to be earth.

But it was buffalo, still. Hundreds of thousands of the beasts, going unconcernedly about their business of graze, graze, graze. They again ascended above the cloud cover, testing winds until they found one blowing parallel to the mountains. This time when they descended, they found grassy plain, dropped down for the night and deflated the balloon.

"Were they real, Rabe?" asked Carolina as he prepared pallets for the ladies from fresh pine boughs and buffalo robes.

"They were real, all right." he said. "I only wish everything in the world could be as real as that buffalo herd. Millions of them, maybe, living together in peace. One of these days, maybe the white man will take a lesson from the buffalo herds."

So far as crossing the Rockies, Deavereaux admitted it was a guess.

"Try the crossing at ten in the morning," he said. "The balloons released at that time of day have come down less shredded than the others." Canon thought the man was kidding at first. He wasn't.

There was no going around the Rockies, either. Go north and the winds would push you into them, said Deavereaux, try south and you hit the Sierras. Up and over. Quick as you can.

At nine o'clock next morning, the balloon was reinflated. Then Canon took out a lariat and began to weave a lattice across the top of the gondola. Carrie and Mary Anna stopped breaking camp to watch. When Canon finished most of it, he stowed the camping gear and called the ladies to him.

"Both of you have been very brave," he said. "Now I have to tell you there is one more obstacle, then we will be riding free to Richmond."

"The winds up in the mountains," said Mary Anna in a very low voice, "I, uh, take it they are not tame." She grabbed Carrie's hand.

"No," said Canon. "No one has ever crossed the mountains in a balloon. Test balloons which have been sent up, well, some have never been recovered so they probably made it. A lot of them didn't make it.

"But none of those balloons were nearly this big or this strong. I have no doubt we will make it. But we can't go around, and I can't leave you here alone.

"I waited to tell you because it would do no good to worry about it until we had it to do. We have it to do now, and it is time to go."

Mary Anna and Carrie looked at each other, smiled, hugged and then hugged Canon. They got inside, Canon pulled the lever, the flame roared. Up went the *Eagle*.

November is a nasty time in the Rockies. Blizzards sweep out of nowhere. Temperatures can plummet forty degrees in as many minutes. Snow can blind you in the morning and the sun can burn you in the afternoon. Or vice versa. Winds scream with incredible force. They swirl, they cross, they quiet, they surge. Air pressure bounces like a ball.

Canon dropped the balloon back, fed it flame, and caught a light wind pushing toward what appeared to be a pass. It was a light cool morning. He thought they would gain altitude as they neared the pass, hoped they would pass high over the snowy peaks.

The downdraft hit them at what he guessed was two thousand feet. It blasted the warm air down on them from out of the balloon. Canon envisioned that the top of the balloon must look like it had been stepped on. He opened the throttle to full and the balloon careered sideways, throwing them into a muddled heap. The throttle cord was ripped from Canon's grip, tearing open his hand.

The balloon righted momentarily, and was hit by a crosscurrent that twirled the gondola like a toy top. Canon grabbed the cord, jammed the throttle open and tied the cord to the gondola.

All or none, he thought. All or none.

They were out of control. Any attempt to steer was useless. The wind whipped them between two small peaks, the gondola brushed tree tops, then an upsurge caught the little airboat and shook it like a baby shakes its rattle. It was snowing, and then a minute later, they were in sunlight.

Mary Anna was retching. Carrie tried to get to her to hold her head when they were blown sideways and down into a blizzard. Canon had no idea where they were in regard to the mountain, but the burner mechanism was beginning to glow red. Canon took no time to think. He took out the bowie knife to cut the throttle cord. As he reached up, a howling wind twisted the gondola, flipped it up and over. For a heartbeat, the three occupants were pressed face down on the rope lattice. Canon cut the throttle. The flame withered away to almost nothing, then they were falling.

The gondola hit the mountain with a teeth jarring crash. Shooting stars and exploding suns went off in Canon's head. Everything was rolling sideways, over and over. Then the blackness swirled through the suns and stars, and the night took him.

He came awake with a start, and with a smile. He smelled coffee brewing. A fire was popping and crackling close to him. More, and better, the smell of lilacs surrounded him. He looked up from her lap at Carolina Lee. She was smiling, too. She helped him to a sitting position. After a brief spell of dizziness, he looked around. And down.

They were on the downhill side of a mountain, in a couple of inches of snow. Away below them stretched a sunlit plain of green forest. Hell, it wasn't even very steep down to the foot of the mountain. Smallish pine trees were growing here and there. They were at the treeline, on the homeward side of the Rockies.

By God, thought Canon, we can walk to Texas from here. He looked behind him and groaned. Walk they damn sure would. One corner of the gondola floor was broken open. Its lines were tangled like hibernating snakes. The empty balloon lay like a red puddle on the snow. Mary Anna Jackson stood beside it, or rather knelt beside it next to a small fire. Seeing him, she rose and brought him a cup of coffee.

The dark liquid scalded his lips, his tongue, his throat. He blew on it, then drank deeply again.

"It is not nearly so bad as it looks, General," said Mary Anna. "The gondola ropes look like plow lines after the mule got into a hornet's nest, but only one is broken. There's one bad tear in the balloon, and the burner mechanism got knocked a bit awry. But it is fixable, Rabe, it shouldn't take more than a day."

Underneath the full coffee aroma, Canon could detect a sharp pinetar scent. He remembered that Deavereaux had given them a canister of mixture to repair any holes that might get torn in the balloon fabric.

"Quick, Mary Anna," said Canon, "check the sack I brought with us. The mission may depend on it." Mary Anna reached inside the gondola and found the cotton bank sack in which Canon had put diamonds and greenbacks. She sat on a log next to the fire and took the sack in her lap, thrust her hand inside. A smile lit her features.

"Never fear, Rabe," she said. "The South is saved." From the sack, she pulled a quart of bourbon.

While they worked repairs to the balloon, lines and gondola, all three tried to reconstruct what must have occurred. The passage of the mountains took little more than an hour, but what an hour.

They could not agree whether they made it through the pass or over the peaks. The wind curled over the mountains like a breaking wave and smacked them into the side of one of the mountains buttressing Rabbit Ear's Pass, or so it was called on the map.

The balloon had burst. They could see the mark in the snow, at least a quarter-mile up the mountain, where the gondola smashed down. They rolled, then the deflated balloon acted as an anchor, pulling them slowly to a halt. It had been narrow, and harrowing.

Canon, laughing, poured a large dollop of bourbon in his coffee and went to help Mary Anna. Carrie took out the frying pan. Everything, and everyone, was well at Rabbit Ear's Pass.

The women praised Canon for his foresight in creating the lattice for the gondola. Without that canopy, the gondola would have been far less crowded when it crashed. Maybe empty.

Canon worked on the gondola while Carolina unsnarled the lines. Mary

Anna, readying the gluey mixture to seal the four-foot gash in the balloon fabric, shouted out a discovery.

"This mixture," she called down the hill to Carrie and Canon, "it is blue."

The meaning was lost on them for a moment, then it struck Canon.

"Is it, now," he called back in statement. "Is it, indeed."

The balloon was repaired by mid-afternoon. The trio lugged it downhill, past the snow line. They found a green grass meadow, only slightly tainted brown by the coming winter. A rippling stream, almost cold as the snow from which it sprang, ran musically over rocks.

He and Carolina gamboled like puppies while Mary Anna laughed at them. Canon had a secret cache of snowballs, and he pelted Carrie with them until she was gasping from laughter. A brush with death brings out the kid in people.

Canon and Carrie took a long hike, getting back their ground legs, while the wise Mary Anna took a long nap to give the lovers time to find a quiet soft spot. Canon took her amidst late blooming wildflowers of blue and white.

As Carrie slept, he decided on a night flight over the flat lands of Kansas and Missouri. Thanks to the triple knots of M. Deavereaux, the gondola lost only one of their canisters of alcohol. There was plenty of fuel.

Part of Canon's decision to fly at night was made in regret at the affectation the trio had agreed to add to the balloon. It had been childish, but he had felt like a child, and he wouldn't change it.

But he also wanted to fly at night. To see more closely the same stars he had seen from the ground on hunts in Kansas. Canon thought it was likely that by morning they would be across the flat lands and in the border state of Kentucky.

Kentucky had in a close vote, with more than a little union manipulation involved, chosen to remain in the Union. One of Abe Lincoln's most famous quotes was his reply to a Union general who had said that, "Regardless of Kentucky, God is on our side." "We certainly need God on our side," Lincoln is said to have replied, "but we must have Kentucky."

Some of the South's best troops had come out of the state. Still, it would be best not to have to land in that land of the bluegrass. Forty-eight hours more, thought Canon, and they would be in Richmond, and no one the wiser.

He had no way to know that their daring escape by balloon had been chronicled internationally, as had the carnage accredited to him by Pinkerton.

The detective had kept his word, refusing to speak about Canon or anything that happened in the badlands, except that he and his men had been captured by Indians, and had escaped unharmed.

Nor did Deavereaux talk. The Belgian suddenly forgot all the English he knew, and much of the French. Reporters could get nothing from him but gibberish.

But some of the onlookers at the fair had seen how tall was the female figure in the gondola, and the Rebel flag had made it certain. Canon, the monster, was in the balloon and headed for home. The news screamed over the telegraph.

A Yankee reception was planned in Missouri for General Canon. It was spoiled by Canon's decision to fly at night. The balloon was last spotted at dusk by a Yankee raiding party chasing the guerrilla Quantrell at the Colorado-Kansas border.

Its course was plotted and units alerted at spots where Canon might land for the night. Artillery was placed on heights along the plotted route.

Four miles high, blissfully counting shooting stars, Canon, Carolina and Mary Anna flew over the waiting guns without a thought.

The Yankee cavalry sergeant who had spotted the balloon had done so by chance. He was scanning, from a valley, surrounding hills. He hoped the lowering sun might glint off a saber or horse harness. Instead of Quantrell, though, the crusty old soldier saw something huge in the dusky sky. He got out his field glasses and zeroed in. The waning light was just sufficient to allow him one clear view of the balloon, which the crew, since the mountains, had renamed *Dixie*.

"There's a bold son-of-a-bitch," said the sergeant, handing his glasses over to the lieutenant. The lieutenant had to agree.

Mary Anna Jackson had put the blue glue to patriotic use. Fully a third of the red balloon had been painted with stars and bars. It had become the largest Rebel flag in the world.

# 24

# *Black Boots*

Dawn breaks early at high altitude. It was still dark when Canon awoke, but the stars were beginning to dim and a faint radiance touched the night. Canon woke, senses a-tingle. Carolina was already up, standing at a corner of the gondola where he had loosened the lattice. She heard him stir.

"Rabe, come look!" she said. "There's a herd of fireflies down below us. Look how lovely!"

Canon did not try to puzzle any sense out of the statement, for he thought he had heard a more ominous sound. There it was again. A pop and a hiss.

He grabbed Carrie by a slender ankle and pulled her down on top of him. She laughed and started to kiss him, until she saw the look on his face.

"First, lovey," he said, "fireflies don't come in herds, and they aren't around in November. And I don't think they fly quite this high."

He crawled over to the gondola's side, peered over. Below, he saw winks of light he recognized as muzzle flashes. In the lightening sky, he finally made out vague outlines of six balloons rising swiftly toward them. They must have spotted the *Dixie*'s outline against the canopy of stars. There was no sound of rifle fire, it being borne away on the wind.

A bullet tore through the gondola next to his arm. Canon said a foul word, grabbed the throttle cord and gave the burner a long blast. The *Dixie* lurched upward. He shouted to Carolina that she and Mary Anna should huddle in the far corner and place all the buffalo robes underneath them.

The Yankees knew there were women on board and were aiming for the balloon rather than the gondola. There were far more pops and hisses signaling hits on the balloon than bullets which occasionally ripped through the gondola. Canon gave them credit for that.

He wondered how many rifle bullets the balloon could take. He reached for the shawl he had worn at the fair, and unwrapped the thing inside.

It was still ugly. Its eighty pounds had been good ballast, though a bulky problem within the tight gondola. Canon had determined to get it back to Richmond. The Confederacy had nothing like it.

The thing had come with six long metal tubes full of standard .50 caliber bullets. Canon had set it up on the mountain meadow, inserted one of the loading tubes which held one hundred-fifty bullets, and had torn pine trees apart from five hundred yards. The Gatling gun had reduced a grove of defenseless pine trees to toothpicks in less than a minute.

Dozens of bullets now pierced the balloon without discernible effect. One thing in favor of the thin fabric was that bullets didn't flatten and mushroom when they struck it, as they did when they struck flesh and bone. They still ripped a hole going in and out, but the exit wound was no larger than the entrance wound.

The *Dixie*, much larger and better built than the Union observation balloons, was beginning to pull away. The Yankee riflemen stopped being gentlemen. Bullets began plowing through the gondola. Canon had stacked all the rope around and under the women, there was little chance of their being hit. But it sent Canon into a rage.

He cut free two of the three remaining containers of alcohol and the balloon leaped. When it leveled, he tied the anchor line to the Gatling and lowered the heavy trident thirty feet to steady the basket against recoil. He hoisted the tubed snout of the machine gun over the top of the railing. There were no women in the other gondolas. Just "those people," as Robert Lee referred to Yankees.

Canon's first burst of thirty rounds rocked his gondola but only scared the hell out of the three Yankees pursuing in the lead balloon. It also gave Canon the range. The second burst of thirty shot the hell out of them. All three slumped over the railing. With no one to feed the flame, the balloon began to fall away.

Then Canon turned the ugly muzzle on one of the other balloons. He raked it with forty rounds. Whether the bullets took effect or whether the fliers were scared, the balloon dropped back.

In fact, all the balloons were dropping back. Their pilots were gauging back the flame on their burners. Canon, battle blood singing through him, would have liked to drop down with them. He wanted to cut the flame on his own balloon and get down to business with the remaining five. But he had women to consider and a rat to catch in Richmond.

The Yankee balloons were distant specks now. There should be no more problem. He was wondering why he still carried a deep feeling of dread when the first artillery shell burst no more than twenty yards to his right. Seconds later, they were rocked by another blast to his left.

That's one hell of a note, thought Canon, reaching for the emergency flow lever. The first damned shot and they get the range perfectly. He pulled the lever and hot air whooshed out of the balloon. They could descend much quicker than rise, and they had to change locations. The balloon started to drop just as the sky exploded.

Canon wished perdition on whatever Union gun crew was firing at them. The bastards were too good. They had quickly bracketed their shots. The third shell burst directly over the balloon, slashing a wide cut in the fabric. But for the emergency descent, it would have blown them to debris.

The balloon skin was tougher than it looked. One long blast of the burner and the *Dixie* leveled, caught an air current and began spanking along with it. They could still make it, Canon thought, if they took no more hits. The bursts were all around, but too high now. The gunners would not have time to depress the gun elevations before the balloon drifted out of range of anything but a lucky shot.

Then Canon saw the damn thing coming. A cannonball, of all things, from an old smoothbore that could never have touched them at higher altitude. Mesmerized, Canon watched the twenty-pound shot describe a long parabola. He knew it could not miss.

Inertia inherent in a cannonball was a caution. Canon had seen men reach out a foot to stop an apparently spent cannonball barely bobbing along the ground and, with a yowl of pain, lose half a leg to it.

The ball got larger. Then there was a great ripping flat noise and two large holes were speared in the middle of the *Dixie*. They were out of range now, but beginning to sink. Canon opened the burner to full blast, held it until the fabric began to smolder. Their rate of descent lessened, but it was over for the balloon.

Regretfully, Canon hoisted the Gatling gun over the side. He followed it with the things of greatest weight and smallest value. Canon thought bitterly that he could probably fit that category. If he had been awake and alert, he figured, he would have seen the muzzle flashes in plenty of time to escape. Mary Anna and Carrie had sat wide-eyed but quiet through the barrage. Now Carrie made only one small mewling groan when he hoisted the chest containing fifty pounds of gold and threw it over the side.

Canon did not have the time nor inclination to compute the worth of the gold he deepsixed. He reckoned now only in mileage. Gazing at the map as the *Dixie* lost altitude, Canon calculated they had crossed the Kentucky border and would make twenty more miles at their rate of descent. The nearest town with a railroad would be Bardstown. From there it would be three hundred more miles of dangerous travel to the Virginia border.

The balloon would have made it in a day. Now, if they had to go by horseback, it would take a month. A train ride would be dangerous, but it would cut traveling time to three or four days. Scowling, Canon put the map in his pocket and the thought from his mind. Whatever it took, he would make it to Richmond. Whatever happened, he would see a noose around Hubert Hillary's neck.

The balloon, as if in apology for dying, touched the gondola to earth gently, lifted a bit, bumped it again and turned it lightly over on its side. There was no ground wind at all. The balloon lay where it fell, expelling its final breaths like a dying whale, wounded and beached.

"Listen, ladies," said Canon, as they crawled from the gondola and began to collect gear. "We must not waste any time, but I don't think we have to worry about any Yankees being right on our heels. The balloons will probably be along in a while, but we left them far behind. They won't know for sure we were forced down.

"I didn't see any cavalry, but the telegraph wires will be singing. We have to get horses first, and we'll make plans as we ride."

Canon rolled up the balloon and they covered it and the gondola with branches. He put on a brave face for the women. Looking at the balloon, Canon said, "Well, dear, at least you let us down gently." Carrie and Mary Anna laughed ruefully, dutifully.

Each chose a change of clothes from their gear, then stashed the rest in the gondola. They were dressed in plain fashion. Canon carried a small valise that contained their clothing, some food and the Krupp fifties. He wore a black cloth coat and his moccasins, and the money belt that contained four million dollars worth of gems and rarities and two million in cash. They wrapped paintings worth a million dollars in a waterproof and buried the package next to a tree. They began to walk.

Border states were dangerous places for Rebels and Yankees alike. Either uniform could get its wearer ambushed and killed, on the same stretch of road.

They walked three miles, Canon estimated, when they saw the farm-house. Leaving Carrie and Mary Anna in a thicket of pines, he approached the house openly but carefully, senses alert. His gunbelt and pistols were left with Carrie and Mary Anna. In one of his thigh high moccasins, under his pants leg, he carried the bowie knife. A little pistol was tucked in the other. Another hideaway pistol was tucked in his waistband at the small of his back. The two long-bladed bonehandle knives were in his coat pockets. If it came to a fight, he was prepared.

The farmhouse sat on a neat knoll, overlooking a rutted road. Pastures full of cows and horses fanned out behind the white frame house. A couple of wandering streams ran through the rich land. They had been laboriously dammed to make two picturesque ponds. It was an idyllic spot. The word "neat" kept entering Canon's mind. Here were farm people who cared about their land.

He passed a barn. All appeared to be in repair, tools and harness were stacked and shelved. The yard was well tended, the home newly whitewashed. This was a place where war seemed unreal, and stupid. At least, war had not touched this place. Not yet. No, Canon, cried his guilty conscience, not until you walked up.

He stepped to the door, but his knock brought no response. Quietly, he opened the door and put his head inside. A muffled keening came from

the back room, and he followed the sound. In a small blue bedroom lay
a woman in a blue nightgown, face down on the bed, her face to the pillow. As Canon watched, uncertain what to do, her crying stopped and her
breathing regulated in sleep.

It was closing on nine A.M. The sputtering lamp on the bedside table
indicated low fuel, its wick almost burned away. She had probably been
weeping all night. Softly, he approached the bed. He saw that the sleeping
woman held a daguerreotype in each hand. They were pictures of soldiers,
one old and one young. There were two letters on the bedside table, the
ink on each stained with tears. Canon could not help it. He picked them
up. He saw from the dateline that each had been written at nearly the same
time. Probably, each had arrived here within minutes of the other.

The husband, Lemuel, Canon read, had died a hero's death defending
Miller Hill near here from a rebel attack. Lemuel Atkins was stationed at
a window of Union headquarters when a determined Confederate cavalry
attack broke through the Union lines. He and a young rebel cavalryman
fired on each other. Lemuel died with a bullet through his throat. He did
not suffer, Mrs. Atkins, and his own return fire killed the Rebel.

The other letter completed the horror. Young Lem died a hero, Mrs.
Atkins, it said. He was mortally wounded, shot to the heart, when his cav-
alry unit broke through Union lines and attacked a well defended, strategic
Yankee headquarters in a house on Miller Hill, near here.

An eyewitness saw the Yankee who shot him pitch backward from the
bullet Lem fired. Lem killed the man who killed him, Mrs. Atkins. He died
a hero. His last words were of you and your husband.

Canon went through the house until he found quill, ink and paper.
"Ma'am," he wrote, "I had urgent need of horses but would not wake you.
These will not compensate your loss nor erase your grief; I only hope they
help." Canon took two small diamonds from the moneybelt and placed
them on the note, which he put beside the letters on the table.

Outside, he took a bag of oats from the barn, used it to entice and
capture three horses. There were only three sets of harness in the barn. He
took them.

When he returned to Carrie and Mary Anna, leading the two horses behind the one he rode, he did not tell them what he found at the farm. Except that he met an honest woman who this day understood war better than any general in the world. He helped the women onto the horses and they rode away. Keeping to off road trails and side roads, they finally saw, from a hill, Bardstown at sundown. There were Yankees everywhere.

It took an hour to skirt the town, and another to follow the railroad tracks going east until they found a steep incline. Canon rode south hard for a half hour and released the horses. It was past ten o'clock when he returned, breathing hard from his run. They ate cold canned food and settled in to wait.

A train passed, laboring up the steep hill. Canon let it go. The second one rumbled up at midnight. They chose a stock car in the middle of the train. Canon slid back the door of the slow moving car. When no one shouted or shot at them, he lifted the women aboard and climbed in behind them.

A half dozen cattle and a like number of horses were in the car, had been in it for a while, judging by the smell. Canon found some clean hay and spread it in an empty corner. He heard snorts from Carolina, could picture her wrinkling her nose at the smell. He started to joke that he apologized for the sleeping quarters, but that he was prepared at the moment to sleep in a latrine. Then he realized she was not snorting. She was snoring, gently. He joined her.

He wakened as the train slowed, and slid out the door. The locomotive was taking on water at a little depot on the line. Sidling up close, he heard the conductor say it was almost five o'clock. Canon was about to go back to the cattle car when an authoritative voice, on the far side of the locomotive, said, "You will stop at a point ten miles up the road and we will conduct a full search of the train."

Canon dropped back to the coal car behind the locomotive, crawled under it and up the track. All he could see were two tall black cavalry boots, polished to a mirror sheen. The firelight from the coal box gleamed on them. Canon could see himself in the reflection.

The engineer was arguing that the train had been thoroughly searched in Bardstown. Another search would put him badly behind schedule.

"Listen," said Black Boots, "three horses were found this side of town.

The people we want are on this train, and I mean to have them.

"There is a curve ten miles up the track. I have blocked the rails just past that point with crossties, and newspaper reporters are on hand for the capture. As you approach the curve, you will give a long blast of the train whistle, and you will slow to ten miles per hour. We will be ready. Do you understand?"

"Yes, sir."

Black Boots walked away.

The train was beginning to move when Canon crawled back into the cattle car. Mary Anna and Carrie looked questioningly at him. "Get ready, ladies, they are on to us," he said. Neither woman spoke, but packed gear with a will. "Now here's what we'll do," Canon said. He had their full attention for two minutes, then he buckled on his gunbelt, checked the Krupps as the train swayed into speed. Then he swung out the door.

The training Canon got in the rigging of the *Southern Star* served him in good stead. He quickly made his way up the open wood rails of the cattle car, knelt on top of the swinging crib for a few moments to atune himself to the sway. He moved forward.

Eight coaches separated Canon from the half-car full of coal behind the locomotive. A cold misty drizzle had begun to fall, wetting the greasy soot that accumulated on top of the cars from the engine's smoke stack. It made the footing even more treacherous. Canon, hatless, used the gooey soot to blacken his face, hands and hair.

He low-crawled the last coach, and was looking down on the black, greasy fireman who swept shovels of coal into the relentless flaming maw of the furnace firebox. Canon reached under the coach overhang, found a handhold, flipped over and down.

The fireman must have caught the movement out of the corner of his eye and looked up at Canon descending. The fireman was made of stern stuff. Canon must have looked like an apparition straight out of hell, big and black. Almost against his will, the fireman drew the shovel back like a bat, gripping the handle, ready to swing. In the glow from the furnace, the fireman saw the giant slowly shake his head. No.

Then the fireman saw something else. Canon lifted the Krupp from his right holster, cocked it, and stuck the muzzle almost against the fireman's nose. Again, Canon shook his head. This time the fireman nodded. He dropped the shovel and, with a yell, leaped off the train.

The engineer, amidst the roar of the locomotive and intent on the rails, did not hear. Canon picked up the shovel and jacked in a few scoops of coal. The engineer turned to see what had so inspired his fireman. The bottom of the shovel sounded a flat gong when it met the engineer's forehead. The man dropped like a mail sack. Canon took a twenty dollar gold piece from his pocket and placed it in the pocket of the engineer's overalls.

"Not bad pay for sleeping on the job," Canon said to him as he helped him off the train.

Canon fiddled with the controls until he learned the rudiments and soon slowed the train to a very respectable stop. He hopped off, thought he could dimly make out the form of Carolina and Mary Anna pulling the ramp down out of the stock car, and set to work.

It took a couple of minutes to uncouple the locomotive from the rest of the train. Within two more, Carolina and Mary Anna rode up, bareback, leading extra horses. Again inside the cabin, Canon pushed the train to full throttle and eased out the clutch. The engine sneezed achoo, achoo, achoo as it pushed the drivers attached to the eight iron wheels. They spun on the wet rails, frictioned them dry, grinding sprays of sparks as iron caught iron and the huffing engine shot away with a scream of tortured metal.

Canon gave one long pull on the whistle cord and detrained.

A away, the Yankee lieutenant stood atop the pile of oil soaked crossties. He was confident he would soon be a Yankee colonel. Rabe Canon was as good as captured. At the sound of the train whistle, his sergeant ignited the crossties. The lieutenant had told the corps photographer to make one shot of him standing on the crossties, stopping the train. The flames would be good effect. Then there would be more pictures with the captured Rebel. It would be glorious.

But where in hell was the damned train? He had told the fool engineer not to blow the whistle until he hit the curve. The lieutenant waited, cursing underneath his breath. The damned fire was almost up to his ass already. His bootsoles were starting to smoke.

He was trying to think of a way to gracefully dismount the conflagration, and how he would barbecue the engineer's butt when, ah, he heard the train coming. He struck his pose, head up, arms back, chest out, hands clasped majestically behind him. And . . . sweet Jesus! The locomotive thundered around the bend, two hundred yards away, wide open.

Two things dawned simultaneously on the puzzled cavalry man: He was about to be struck by a runaway locomotive, and he was on fire. With a magnificent oath, the lieutenant abandoned the pyre, and for the moment his burning desire and his plans for blazing glory.

He took time only to have a long drink of water while an orderly polished the cavalry boots to their former sheen. The shaken fireman was brought to him. He had seen the man, and two women, ride bareback into the woods leading a string of horses. They had ridden eastward.

Day was breaking, though gray and drear. The Rebel did not have much of a head start. Canon was riding bareback with two women, and the lieutenant knew the terrain. He could still have a colonel's rank.

Canon knew the terrain, too. Had hunted the area, years ago. And the women with him were expert equestriennes. He knew tricks the Yankee lieutenant would never even hear about. But he had never seen so many Yankee patrols. Canon used all the tricks he knew. He laid false trails, he doubled back, he covered the horse's hooves so they would leave no prints. The three riders exhausted the first set of horses, then sent them careering off in a different direction, brush tied to their tails.

All day and night, in a pouring rain, Canon and company eluded roving patrols of Yankees. But there were just too damned many patrols. Knowing they were chasing one man and two women, the union cavalry split into groups of ten and covered the territory. Canon ducked one patrol only to be spotted by another.

They had ridden bareback for nearly twelve hours. In that time, they had probably gotten a total of two hours rest, and no sleep. Canon and the horses were exhausted, the women were nearly dead from fatigue. They had come up against a river, too deep, swift and wide to ford. They would drown if they tried.

Then, as the rain slacked a bit, Canon saw the bridge. They were still ahead of the Yankee patrols, though barely. If they could reach the bridge they might still have a chance. On the other side, he could hold off a dozen Yankees while Mary Anna and Carrie fled with the moneybelt. Canon led them back from the river until they intersected the road that ran to it.

They entered the roadway almost at the instant a group of Yankee horsemen rode out on it from the other side of the forest, five hundred yards down the road from them.

Desperately, the trio drew the last ounce of energy from their horses and rode like hell for the bridge. A volley of shots rang out behind them. As they neared the bridge, Canon feared that a patrol might be lying in wait for them there, though he could see no sign in the muddy road. No matter. It was their only avenue of escape.

Canon looked behind him. The Yankee scouting party, on fresher horses, was gaining ground quickly. He figured the Yankees would reach the hundred-yard span about the time his company got across it. Then he would wheel and charge them. He untied the moneybelt, slipped it from around his waist. Carrie shook her head when he, riding next to her, tried to hand it over. She knew what he intended. "You have to, darling," he shouted. She took it, and they were on the bridge.

They were almost to the far side when dozens of rifles poked their long snouts out of the dense growth at the sides of the far bridgehead and opened fire. Canon reined his horse so hard that Carolina, then Mary Anna, rammed into him.

Unseated for the first time in years, Canon desperately tried to hold on to the reins as he flew helplessly over the horse's head. In that, too, he failed. He landed on his neck, rolled over and over. He saw the bridge boards under him the first two flips he turned, and the dirt of the roadway the last two flips. And then he slammed very hard into a pair of tall black cavalry boots. With woozy head and sinking heart, Canon realized he could see his reflection in the mirror-like sheen of those boots.

The cold muzzle of a pistol pressed against his ear, and a smooth voice enquired, "You are General Rabe Canon of the Black Horse Cavalry?" Weary, dazed, sick at heart, Canon did not even look up. He nodded. Almost made it, he thought. Almost, almost made it. "And who might you be?" said Canon dully, still staring at the ground.

"Well, I might be U. S. Grant, and I might be the Lord of Hosts. In fact, many say those are the same entity. But it so happens that I am confederate Major John Mosby, ranger, and I am at your service, General."

"Yeeehaawwww," said Canon quietly.

Mosby wanted very much to hear of Canon's California escapades, but Canon was too exhausted to go into detail and Mosby was too polite to push. The Gray Ghost was astonished that Mary Anna Jackson, a woman he knew but slightly and greatly admired, was in his camp. The three refugees ate a hurried hot meal, then slept away the day. Mosby's rangers spent the day ambushing and chasing the still scattered Yankee patrols.

That night, around a campfire, Canon recounted the events of his clash with Pinkerton for Mosby and his officers. Later, he took Mosby aside to get inside news of the war.

"We are in desperate straits, General," said Mosby. "Every Rebel soldier knows it, yet somehow all remain in good heart. Our troops are hungry. Many have been known to boil and eat their shoe leather, and joke that it is a real tongue in cheek.

"There is a running battle in the Shenandoah Valley, their Phillip Sheridan against our Jubal Early. Early does his best, but he has not the men, and he is not Stonewall Jackson. If the war continues in this fashion, the Confederacy cannot last another year.

"As for me, I will fight until they kill me." The statement was simply and honestly made. There was no boast in it. Canon was humbled before such bravery. Then Canon asked the question that burned inside him.

"There is something I wish to know that I did not want the men to hear, Mosby," he said. "What do you know of Hubert Hillary?"

A look of distaste crossed Mosby's features.

"Hillary is implicated in the Pinkerton scheme," continued Canon. "Have you any word of him?"

"I have a word *for* him," said Mosby. "Yes, I know of him. The scum fled Richmond a week ago. Word has it that he is with Quantrell, or at least with some of his men."

"I thought Quantrell was in Kansas."

"He is," said Mosby, "but a group of his outlaws split from him. Rumor has it that they are somewhere in the Shenandoah."

Back at the campfire, Canon asked Mosby how his band of two hundred happened to be here at the right place and right time.

"Why, General, you and your balloon escapade have been headlines. All Southern troops have been alerted to search for you and assist you. This area is a little out of our territory, but the Yankees have been making pretty free with Southern sympathizers here.

"We like to let them get to feeling they are the cocks of the walk. Makes them careless. When they get cocky and careless, we fall on them and kick their collective ass.

"My men were getting ready to start teasing and separating them. I was dug in, about to send some troops out to lure some patrols to the bridge when you did it for us. I didn't know who you were until you rolled up at my boots, but I figured anybody with that many Yankees after him can't be all bad. We waited until you were close, then shot the hell out of those Yankees that were chasing you.

"The boys will mop up in the morning, shouldn't take long. We'll have you safe in Richmond within a week."

The Gray Ghost was good as his word. As Canon parted from the ranger, just outside Richmond, he gave Mosby fifty thousand dollars worth of the counterfeit greenbacks.

"Word may be already out in the banks, but Yankee horse dealers and store owners may not have heard," said Canon. "Just in case, though, here's something that will work anywhere, anytime." He handed Mosby one of the largest of the diamonds. "Keep safe," Canon said, and rode on to Richmond.

25

# *Behold, a Black Horse*

The first day of December, 1864, brought the season's first killing frost to Virginia. It was an omen sufficient to the evils of the day.

Save for weather, the Confederacy's capital city did not look a great deal different the morning Rabe Canon returned to it from the way it looked when Canon left. But it felt different. Winter had replaced fall in the heart of the city, and in the hearts of its residents. The chill of impending doom lay on the Rebel nation.

The morning Canon, Carrie and Mary Anna rode in, tragic headlines bannered the freshly printed newspapers. Five confederate generals had died November 30, at the Battle of Franklin just south of Nashville.

Only a heroic rear guard action by Nathan Bedford Forrest saved the South's western army. Canon wondered what part Buck and Mountain Eagle played in that action. He wondered if they were still alive.

Canon left Mary Anna and Carrie at his house and rode straight to Beauregard's headquarters. Mosby had telegraphed that he was bringing Canon home, and Beauregard was waiting anxiously.

As glad as the little Frenchman was to see Canon, it was plain that he was in shock. Beauregard had commanded the Western Army. All the slain generals were his friends.

When Beauregard had cleared his office of subordinates, Canon removed his moneybelt and emptied it on Beauregard's massive desk. The glittering gems brought a genuine smile to the commanding general's face. Beauregard whistled thinly.

"Well," he said, "give me a tall hat and call me Honest Abe," he said. "When your telegram arrived, we gave up hope that anything worthwhile could come of the mission. I thought only that we were about to lose another of our best generals." His own words caused him pain. He was silent for a moment.

"Forgive me, Rabe," he said. "We should have bands playing and the president here to welcome you home. But we are too much in grief and disarray. I hope that soon you will get the recognition and reward you have earned."

"Thank you, sir," said Canon, touched. "But, if I may, I would like to return to the field quickly as possible. Let me ask, first, if you have any knowledge of my people who are with Forrest."

"I am sorry, General. I do not. General Forrest has stopped the Yankees from capturing our army, but they are still fighting every day. As soon as I hear anything, I will let you know immediately. As to your request, it is gladly granted."

The words sent a thrill through Canon. Beauregard sat down, and indicated a chair next to him. Canon took it, waiting expectantly.

"Your written report can wait, General Canon. You are to rest today, and assume another special assignment at earliest in the morning." Canon realized he was holding his breath, hoping he knew what was coming.

"The traitor Hillary has been seen in the Shenandoah Valley with a band of perhaps one hundred men, formerly with Quantrell. Captain Lawson is with him. We believe they are trying to connect with Sheridan so they can turn themselves in and request asylum.

"Jubal Early has fought two encounters with Sheridan in the valley, and was bested each time. A third and decisive battle is looming.

"General Canon, you are ordered to resume command of a portion of the Black Horse Cavalry. The unit is here in Richmond, being refitted and reinforced. You will run the traitors Hillary and Lawson to earth. You are authorized to execute them immediately on their capture, in whatever manner is best suited and available.

"After you have carried out your priority orders, you will join Early, also. Is everything clear?"

"Very clear, sir, and very satisfactory."

"Hillary apparently got word of your telegram from California, damn his rotten soul to hell," said Beauregard, "and went to ground until he could make contact with Lawson. It is cat and mouse in the valley now. Hillary is running from Early, who is aware of him and has the same orders of summary execution as you. But if Hillary makes it to Sheridan, he will be safe."

"He will not, sir."

Beauregard smiled grimly.

"No," he said. "I don't think he will. Good hunting, General Canon."

"Thank you, sir."

From headquarters, Canon went straight to the stable behind his house. "Hammer, old boy!" he cried, going to the stall where the big palomino rested.

Hammer pealed out a long whinny, tossing his head in recognition. The horse was healed and healthy. Canon could see he had been exercised regularly, the muscles appearing in top tone.

Though Canon had resolved no more than three days earlier to never ride bareback again, he would not take time to saddle the stallion. He drew him out of the stall and into the corral, leaped on and put Hammer through his paces, sans bridle, sans saddle. It was if they were never apart.

An hour later, Carolina came to the little corral. "Rabe Canon," she called, "you get in here and get some rest. I don't know what you'll be doing tomorrow, but I'll bet you won't be here. I sent Mary Anna to my place where she will stay for a few days. Now get in here and go to bed."

"Why, lovey," said Canon, "I thought you wanted me to rest." He dismounted and chased her inside.

Next morning at five o'clock, Canon, in full uniform, rode Hammer into the confederate garrison to the welcoming cheers of one hundred men sitting on stamping black horses.

He carried the Rebel flag, staffed, given him by Mamie Sutcliffe. Mary Anna had worn it under her dress since they landed the balloon in Kentucky. He had also gotten a telegram the previous evening from Mountain Eagle. The Eagle and Buck had read of Canon's escape by balloon, and the Eagle had managed to get a Rebel courier to send news.

He and Buck were safe, were scouting and were killing Yankees. They were having a great time, said the Eagle, and planned to see him soon as they whipped back the Yankees. Then they would join the Black Horse, if Old First With The Most Forrest would let them. The Confederacy might be crumbling around him, but Canon was happy.

A milky light announced the coming day as Canon rode to the front of the gathered horsemen, ordered them to close ranks. They did so in admirable fashion.

Canon waited until not a jingle was heard from horse harness. "Men of the Black Horse," he called, "I am proud to be with you again." His words brought shouts of approval. Again, Canon waited for quiet.

"Now I am going to tell you something that has been kept secret," he said, "and that you will keep secret. Signal that you so swear by raising your right hands." One hundred hands raised.

"Many of you served under General Jackson, a great leader and a great man." More shouts. "I am going to tell you our mission. I am going to tell you something that only a few have come to know since the night at Chancellorsville." The silence was total. "I tell you of my own certain knowledge that Stonewall Jackson was murdered at Chancellorsville through a Yankee plot, helped by traitors then in our midst." An ominous rumbling went through the troops. It grew into a roar of rage.

Canon held up his hand for silence. It was quickly given him. "Of the ten men responsible, eight have died at my hand." Shouts. "Today, we ride after the two men responsible for the plan. We ride after Hillary and Lawson, traitors to the cause, and the murderers of Jackson." The roar began again, but Canon quelled it.

"The very day Jackson earned his nickname at First Manassas, he drew a pledge from his Virginians. They promised that day to a man that they would do their duty, or die in the attempt. Today, I promise you that I will avenge Stonewall Jackson, or I will die in the attempt. Will you so pledge?" The answer rang the rooftops of Richmond.

"Then follow me," yelled Canon, "for Jackson."

"For Jackson," screamed the troops, and the Rebel yell rent the already breaking light of dawn.

Fifty miles away, inside the command tent, Frank Lawson shook Hubert Hillary awake for the third time of the morning. It was cold on the plain of the Shenandoah. Hillary whimpered in his plagued sleep and burrowed deeper into the blankets of his cot. Well, thought Lawson to himself, let the little pig sleep. They had evidently shaken Jubal Early off their trail.

Lawson walked outside to see that preparations were under way to move out. They had camped here two nights. That was all the time Lawson considered safe. If he had trustworthy scouts or pickets, he would not have to worry so, he thought. But this band of border trash was nothing more than cowards and cutthroats. Only fear and greed kept them together.

Then he laughed scornfully at himself. And what else is it that keeps you with them, Frankie, my boy, he thought. Well, maybe this would be the day they found Sheridan and safety. He walked over to one of the sentries. The man was asleep on the ground. Lawson, overcome with rage, kicked the man in the head as hard as he could. The man rolled over from the force of the blow, his snore ceased and his breathing took on a different cadence of unconsciousness.

"If you want to sleep, then sleep," said Lawson. He had given orders the previous evening to ride at daybreak. It was mid-afternoon before he could get the outlaws together.

Some days there were seventy-five men in the band, some days there were twice that many. There was no order, no discipline. The scum came and went as they pleased. He knew that many simply went off and hid in order to escape work and the possibility of having to fight Early. Then they would ride in and join the group as it rode to a new campsite.

Disgusted, Lawson spat, then moved out. God help us if Early does catch us, he thought. There was even a worse thought, but he did not permit it to linger in his mind.

Day after day, for a week, Lawson tried to run the camp and also do the scouting. The scouts he sent out usually did not return for two, three days and then had little to report.

Night after night he had to listen to Hillary whine. Two more grinding days passed. Then, finally, incredibly, one of the scruffy scouts returned with good news. He had run across a drummer on one of the roads who had seen Sheridan breaking camp, not thirty miles away. The drummer didn't know which way the Union Army was heading, but at least Lawson had the vicinity. He would find the trail next day and follow it. Two days, three at the most, and he would be safe. Lawson considered whether to move camp, but knew he could not do it and also search out Sheridan. He would leave the camp in place until he located the Federals.

Next morning, two hours before daylight, Lawson walked out of his tent into the thickest ground fog he could remember. Goddamn, he thought to himself. Have to wait for this to clear. Feeling mean, Lawson decided to hand out a little discipline.

He found the brutish oaf who passed for one of his officers, sitting by the fire, drinking coffee. "What are you doing up this early, Sergeant?" Lawson asked gently.

"Took a chill, Colonel." Lawson had also promoted himself. "Had to have some fire and some coffee."

"Did you check the horses for loose shoes and sores yesterday, as ordered, Sergeant? Did you see to their feed?"

"Ain't had no time, Colonel, and today the fog be too thick," whined the oaf. Lawson kicked the man in the side. The fellow rolled off the log he sat on, oooffffing and clawing the dirt. Fear and pain were the only things these animals understood, Lawson felt.

"Your head's too thick, you fool. You'll wish you had time when Jubal Early comes riding down on your ignorant ass. Now you do what I tell you," menaced Lawson, "or I'll make you walk." Scowling, the sergeant pulled himself to his feet and scurried away. Lawson walked back into the tent.

"Excuse me, your Excellency," he said to Hillary with exaggerated politeness as he shook the sleeping form. "I hate to trouble your Excellency, but we must be up and about." Hillary only groaned.

What a whiner, thought Lawson. All he had heard since he picked up Hillary at his hidey hole outside Richmond was complaint and fear. He listened patiently as he could, most of the time. Hillary would be useful in Washington. Once, though, when Hillary had particularly grated on him, Lawson had snapped that perhaps the undersecretary would prefer to be back in Richmond with Rabe Canon and the Black Horse.

Lawson did not know that Hillary feared Canon more than anything in the world. It had become a phobia with him. Hillary was so horrified by the thought of Canon that he would hardly speak his name. He had seen the Pinkerton men in Richmond that Canon had killed. Seen gaping knife wounds, obscenely large bullet holes. He had read and believed the stories printed in the California papers about Canon. When Lawson threatened to give him to Canon, Hillary had blanched and fell silent. He didn't complain again for hours.

But Hillary would move well in Washington circles. They would be heroes. If I thought he wouldn't be of use, Lawson said to himself as Hillary opened his eyes, the little pig eyes would open and stay open.

In a fit of pique, Lawson said, "Word is that Canon is in the valley, looking for us." He had heard no such word, but the effect on Hillary was electrifying. The little turd was extraordinarily quick when he wanted to be. He was out of the bunk and in his boots in an instant. He grabbed his walking stick, a new affectation for his Washington appearance, and hugged it to him. His eyes were wide.

"Where is the bastard?" Hillary said, voice shaking. "Where shall we run? Where is he?" Hillary was so terrified that Lawson was shamed. The man is pitiful, he thought. "Calm down and go back to sleep," Lawson said. "It is just a rumor. Last I heard, Canon was trying to get away from California in a balloon." Lawson laughed at the mental image he conjured. "Still," he said, musingly, "I wonder where he is." Lawson took off his boots and crawled back in his own bunk.

"Yes," echoed Hillary softly. "Where?"

Two hundred yards away, up the hill, Canon rose to one knee. He listened to the clink of the camp coming awake. The fog was beginning to thin a bit, he thought. He could make out spectral silhouettes of tents. He lifted a hand and motioned for the Black Horse to move up slowly. The motion was relayed from man to man.

It had taken Canon four days to locate signs of the outlaws and another three to track them down. He had pushed the Black Horse unmercifully. They ate in the saddle, even slept in the saddle, always moving. Canon pushed too hard. Trying to track the outlaws at night, Canon's scouts had confused their trail with tracks left by one of Sheridan's units.

They had come up on Sheridan's rear guard and fought a sharp skirmish. Then Canon backtracked. All day and into the night, Canon searched. Late yesterday, he thought he saw wisps of smoke eastward. He was afraid it would be another false scent, another chimney smoke from some small cabin tucked among the blue hills of the Shenandoah. He sent out two weary riders, who soon came riding back at full tilt. It was the outlaw camp, five miles away. One of them had seen Lawson.

Canon rode out to make sure. There was no doubt about it. Through his field glasses, he had seen Hubert Hillary entering a tent. Canon watched the camp long into the night, counting men, making sure they weren't getting ready to move out.

Everything he saw in the camp gave him confidence. Their numbers were equal or above his own, but discipline was lax, the men seemingly unconcerned. Pickets stayed barely out of range of the firelight. Their eyes would be useless in the dark. He saw that almost all of them slept on duty.

At midnight, ground fog came rolling in. Canon rode back to the Black Horse. He called his two captains, discussed tactics, listened to their advice. They would attack from the east, out of the sun. It was the direction that Lawson, himself heading east, would least expect attack. He had the men check their gear.

When they moved out at one A.M., Canon personally checked every horse to see that string and sacking had been correctly applied. Each horse muzzle was wrapped, each hoof covered. When the ninety-nine rode out into the fog, it was if they were ghosts. Not a snort nor footfall was heard from the horses, not a jingle from the harness. They could have passed within fifty yards of a sentry in the fog. He would have heard nothing.

By two A.M., they were set up on the ridge of a low hill two hundred yards above camp. The horses remained saddled and muzzled, and would stay muzzled until the minute of attack. The troopers slept on the ground, holding onto the reins of their mounts.

Before the Black Horse had broken camp, Canon had called the men around him. He did not want to give Lawson and Hillary any more chance than they had given Stonewall Jackson, but he wanted them to know what was about to happen to them. He wanted to trade the element of surprise for the element of fear. To a man, the Black Horse agreed to the plan.

Canon had known there could be no sleep for him this night. In the dark and fog, he checked his gear, every strap and ring and tie. He checked his pistols, quietly sharpened his saber and bowie knife. When he had finished, it was only three thirty A.M. He did everything again.

Now he waited in the fog, listening, thinking. Canon thought he would always love fog. It would always bring special memories to him. He watched it swirl chillingly around him, Confederate gray.

He watched the half-dozen campfires burn low, then some of them would burn more brightly when one of the raiders would rise and throw on more wood. Some burned away to embers. Occasionally, he caught the hint of a snore or snort from one of the men in the camp, rolling in their sleep. A couple of times he caught smothered snatches of conversation. But as the dawn came limping in behind him, the camp was as quiet as Stonewall Jackson's tomb.

When he began to glimpse the camp through the fog, he knew it was time. Canon had often wondered how he would feel at this moment, when he would confront the managers of Stonewall Jackson's assassination. To his surprise, he felt neither rage nor fear. It was as if he had come to the end of a long, difficult journey. He felt good.

The fog would begin to go now. He was familiar with Shenandoah fog, had learned its ways along with Jackson. He walked the few yards to the top of the hill. The Black Horse was awake, waiting his orders, twenty yards down the far side. He pulled the sacking off Hammer, climbed on. It was just daylight enough for the horsemen to see him and they did as he had done. He waved them up. Silent as death, they fanned out to either side.

Canon pulled his saber from its sheath, held it high in his left hand, and let it drop. One hundred men responded as one to the signal.

"Stonewall," they said in a whisper. Canon again gave the signal.

"Stonewall," said his men, louder this time, and again, "Stonewall."

Lawson had come awake at the first whisper, Hillary at the second. Hillary looked at Lawson in the twilight inside the tent.

"What in God's name is that?" said Hillary in a hushed voice.

"It is not God," Lawson replied, reaching for his pistol. "It is the devil, Hillary, and he is come for you and me."

At that moment, Canon whirled the saber around his head.

"STONEWALL," screamed the Black Horse, and with a rolling Rebel yell followed Canon through the ragged remnants of fog, out of the sun, down the hill into the outlaw camp.

"Jesus God!" yelled a sentry, leveling his rifle as the riders bore down on him. He crumpled as Canon's bullet struck him in the chest. A sleepy raider stumbled out of a tent, rubbing his eyes with one hand and clutching a pistol with the other. Canon fired across his own body. The man clutched his stomach and fell.

Behind him, Canon heard sporadic firing, then it grew more frequent as the Black Horse swept into the camp. There were few tents, most of this rabble being too lazy to bother with one. He hoped most of them would surrender, but he doubted they would. They knew they would hang.

He was nearing the cluster of tents in the middle of camp, keeping his eye on them. The fog and fast moving horses would hinder hidden fire from the tents, but they still posed a threat. The tents of Hillary and Lawson would be among them.

A man leaped up from beside one of the campfires, swinging a bayoneted rifle around toward Canon's left side. Canon stood in the stirrups, above the compass of the bayonet swing, and brought down his saber. The blade sliced through the back of the man's head, flipping the back part of the balding crown through the air.

Canon reined Hammer in, hard, on the far side of the tents. The horse's hooves gouged furrows as they dug, throwing dirt and dead grass. Canon was out of the saddle before the sliding horse came to full stop. He threw a quick look behind him. The injured man was on the ground, his legs still churning crazily.

The guerrillas formed a cluster out in the camp, and the Black Horse ringed it, slamming into it, sending the defenders shocked and reeling.

Canon strode recklessly through the camp toward the tent he had seen Hillary enter. He felt buoyant, confidant now. The fight belonged to the Black Horse. He would come through this alive, and take Hillary and Lawson back to hang.

Out of the corner of his eye, Canon saw the man he had sabered. Incredibly, the horribly wounded man, brains leaking, still made the grotesque running movement with his legs, spinning his body in a bloody circle. Canon aimed, ready to put the man of misery. In front of him, a tent flap jerked back and Frank Lawson emerged, gun in hand.

Without thinking, Canon yelled, "Lawson." Lawson half-turned toward the sound, saw Canon and brought up his pistol. Canon's shot was quicker. It took Lawson in the middle of his chest, slamming him to his back and throwing his own shot wide and low.

Many of the guerrillas had been casting glances back to the tent, looking for their leader, needing order and organization. When they saw him fall, they threw down their guns and begged for mercy. The firing began bleeding down.

Off to one side, Canon saw a small cluster of outlaws make a break for horses. Some of the Black Horse harried them, firing and calling for them to surrender. Two made it to horseback, sans saddle, and were shot down as they tried to flee.

Canon dropped as firing opened up behind him, and scuttled crablike to where Lawson lay. Other members of the Black Horse rode toward the firing.

Lawson's eyes were closed but he was breathing, deeply and irregularly. His eyes opened when Canon pulled the pistol from his grasp. Lawson looked curiously at his hand.

"Can't feel a thing," he said. "Didn't know I still had that pistol. Don't matter, anyhow."

Canon checked inside the tent, found it empty and pulled Lawson inside. He picked Lawson up and placed him on the bunk. Then he saw the reason Lawson could not move. The bullet had passed through his body, tearing a fist-sized hole in his back, shattering his spine. Lawson was already beginning to take on the death pall, though the wound bled little.

There was a bottle of brandy on the table. Canon gave Lawson a swallow. He drank it greedily.

"Thanks, Rabe," he said, then he tried to laugh and made an awful retching, choking sound.

"You big bastard," he said, "you are absolutely the best I have ever seen. You must have scared this ragtag outfit so bad with that 'Stonewall' trick that you won't find a clean pair of drawers among them. I bet they were shaking so much they couldn't aim if they fired. Doubt your casualties will be two percent. Hope they ain't, anyway."

"Why did you set up Jackson, Frank?" said Canon.

"Didn't know they was gonna kill him. Well, hell, that's a lie. Thought they might, though Hillary said they wouldn't. Told me it was an abduction. Told me he'd see I got rank and favors when Jackson got took and nobody would get hurt. Said all I had to do was put eight men on picket duty during the confusion of battle.

"When it was over, I felt so damn dirty that I figured nothing was too bad for me to do, then. So I throwed in with Hillary, the pig. And look what it got me. Got me blowed to smithers by the leader of the Black Horse." Canon sat back on his heels.

"One thing, Rabe," muttered Lawson, "and if no one else believes it, I hope you will. If I could the next day have traded my life for Jackson's, I'd have done it gratefully. Those are the words of a dying man."

"I believe you, Frank," said Canon. "Frank, did Hill have anything to do with it?"

"He didn't know the set up. But . . . I told him to hang back on the reconnaissance that night. Whispered it through the wall of his tent. Don't know that he heard me. Couldn't say.

"Listen, Rabe. Get Hillary. You know he's trying to reach Sheridan. Go get him. And give me one more pull off that bottle, then leave me or finish me. Don't matter which."

Canon tilted the bottle for him. Lawson swallowed once, coughed chokingly, shuddered. His head fell over and brandy washed out of his mouth.

Canon stood. He took a long, slow swallow of the fiery liquid, a silent toast to his dead friend gone bad.

There was a long slit in the right rear corner of the tent. Canon flapped it back, emerged slowly with gun in hand. He heard, from the front of the camp, much more shouting now than shooting. The Black Horse was mopping up.

Canon bent to his knees. The small bootmarks with pointed toe must have been made by Hillary. He followed them to a rope strung between two trees. Lawson would have kept his horse back here. Hillary, on the other hand, would have had to be catered. The little prima donna would have insisted on having someone care for his horse. Have it saddled for him and brought to him.

The bootprints danced around and around the hoofmarks. Of course! Canon looked back inside the tent. Lawson's saddle and saddleblanket were under his cot, but no bridle. Hillary was riding bareback. Canon grinned a vicious grin, whistled sharply for Hammer. He would deal with this one alone. Hammer came trotting around the tent. Canon urged him into a run even as he put foot to stirrup.

Only the most experienced rider can stand to ride bareback for any length of time. Canon was still sore from his own barebacked ride. Hillary would be in considerable pain by now. But it was nothing, thought Canon, to the pain that was coming.

Hillary's track started due east. The damp fog, now dissipated, made the hoofmarks into easy reading for any experienced tracker. Still, in his hurry, Canon almost missed the prints when they veered sharply north. Hillary was trying to throw off pursuit.

Canon knew the territory and Hillary did not. There was a dense thicket of scrub and brambles due north that was practically impenetrable. It would take Hillary at least ten minutes to reach them, then he would have to turn. It was almost certain that Hillary would again turn east.

Canon plotted in his mind Hillary's speed and the distance. He figured the angle he would need to intercept, then he put Hammer to full gallop. Even if I'm wrong, Canon thought, I won't be much off. Even if he had to traverse the trail, he'd have the little bastard within an hour.

He had ridden no more than ten minutes when he cut Hillary's trail. It appeared that Hillary must be moving the horse at fast trot. The little man must be frightened, indeed, thought Canon, to withstand a trot this long. But Hillary would never be able to hang on bareback to a running horse.

Canon approached the crest of a low rise, topped it and stopped Hammer. Halfway across the rolling plain, five hundred yards away, bobbed the ridiculous figure of Hubert Hillary. Even as Canon watched, the fat little man turned and looked. Canon had wanted that. He wanted the murdering bastard to see vengeance riding down on him.

Hillary did. It was the worst thing he had seen. Worse than he had imagined. Hillary had used his coat and waistcoat to create a softer seat. He had been making, he thought, a reasonable pace.

But now he saw Canon's saber flash as it unsheathed, saw the horse rise into a pawing stand and give an awful war cry, heard Canon's Rebel yell as it bounced across the plains. Hillary kicked the horse into a lope.

Canon moved Hammer into a gallop. Fifty yards behind the fleeing figure, Canon replaced his weapons, unhitched the rope from the saddle, tied the back end to his saddle horn and shook a loop in the front end. Canon was twirling the rope around his head, about to throw it, when Hillary gave a cry and pitched headlong to the turf, rolling over and over.

Canon rode over him with pleasure. Then he swung Hammer around, stopped over the inert body and dismounted, gun drawn. He dropped the rope next to Hillary.

The man lay quiet. Canon prodded him with a boot toe, but drew no response. Hillary was apparently senseless, breathing shallowly but regularly.

Placing the muzzle of the pistol at the fallen man's temple, Canon said, "One of the most clever of all animals is the pig, Hillary, and a pig is what you are. One sudden move, conscious or unconscious, and I will turn you into a pork chop."

He found one hideaway gun in Hillary's left pocket and another in his right boot. Hillary still clutched an expensive looking cane with his left hand. And from the looks of the pig's right ankle and right arm, he would need the walking stick. Arm and ankle were certainly broken, skewed out at angles. Well, thought Canon satisfactorily, those ought to be very painful.

They were. Hillary regained consciousness with a sharp intake of breath, let the breath out in a whimper of pain. He looked up at Canon with fear and hate.

"I'll give you twenty thousand dollars in gold to let me go," Hillary said through clenched teeth.

Canon stood back, pocketing the hideaways, keeping his pistol pointed at Hillary's head. "And where would you, a humble public servant, get that much gold?" said Canon.

Hillary brightened. "In England," he said. "A account. My speculations during the war have been very successful."

"What was it that caused you to speculate on the murder of Stonewall Jackson?" said Canon tightly. Hillary, a hope blossoming in his head that he could possibly buy Canon off, failed to note the dangerous tone of voice.

"I? I? My dear sir, I had nothing to do with it," he said. "My word as a Southern gentleman."

The roar of the .50 caliber broke Hillary's ear drum, the powder blackened and blistered his face, set the thin fringe of hair smoldering. The bullet took away most of Hillary's right ear. Hillary screamed, writhing on the ground. He finally realized he wasn't killed.

"Oh, you brute," he moaned, features contorted. "All my life I have been victimized by great hulking lummoxes like you and by the sneering back-stabbers like Jackson." Hillary almost died then and there, and he realized it. He whimpered. Canon with an effort brought himself under control. He cocked the pistol and pointed it at Hillary's left ear.

"Why did you have Jackson killed?" he said.

"All right, all right," said Hillary, sniffling. "A cretin like you will never understand, but I will tell you. Jackson was ruining our chances for peace, don't you see? We were winning too many victories with Jackson and Lee. The North was ready to talk peace, but the high and mighty Southern aristocracy would not have any as long as Jackson and Lee kept winning.

"The Confederacy was being slowly strangled, but everyone was willing to put up with it for Lee and Jackson. It was only I who saw what must be done for the good of both sides. The Union was bound to win, sooner or later. We were being outgunned, outmanned, outprovisioned. It would have meant total surrender."

"You mean like now," said Canon evenly.

"Yes, but it wasn't planned this way. With Jackson out of the way, we would lose a battle and gain peace. Jackson was to be kidnapped, but how could you hold a Jackson prisoner for blackmail? Women and children would have taken up arms. No, no, no. I am sure of it. Jackson had to die, for the good of the South. But the fool Lee went on without Jackson and now the war is lost. I did it for the Confederacy."

Canon shook his head. The man was insane. An insane, second-rate government lackey had almost singlehandedly lost the war. Canon was almost as tempted to send Hillary on to Washington as he was to hang him. It might not be too late for Hillary to lose the war for the Yankees. But Canon had sworn to see a noose around the man's neck, and he would make good his word.

Hillary tried to sit up. The numbing shock of his broken bones wore off as he realized they wouldn't move and he howled with pain.

"My God, you have broken my arm and my leg," he said, amazement in his voice. "You unspeakable ruffian." Canon moved to help Hillary to his feet. "No. Pray do not touch me. I require no help from the likes of you. I will rise on my own."

Hillary rolled onto his stomach, keened with pain as he drew himself up to his knees. Leaning heavily on his stick, he drew himself up to his one foot. "Poor Hillary," he moaned to himself, "poor man. But it is all right. You should have expected no less."

Canon turned, disgusted, to Hammer. He would lash Hillary onto the other horse. If he fell off a lot, he would put him on Hammer. But first he would give Hillary the opportunity to fall off a lot.

Again holstering his pistol, Canon pulled out the bone handled blade he had taken from another of Jackson's assassins. Reaching for the rope, Canon sensed danger, immediate, imminent and he whirled. The goddamn stick! But Hillary was too far away to do any harm with a cane sword.

Canon turned back, dropped to a knee, scanned the horizon. Perhaps one of Lawson's men had escaped, had him in his sights. He saw nothing. He stood and turned to face Hillary.

"You," said Hillary, "are a great fool." He pointed the stick at Canon. There was a click, and Canon finally understood. Too late, thought Canon, throwing the knife and flinging himself backwards as the walking stick roared. He felt the bullet go deep in his chest. Blood, breath and consciousness flew from his body.

HE WAS BEING STUNG. Over and over. Ants covered his face, stinging him again and again. Canon forced his eyes open. He was so tired, so tired. And there was terrible pain in his chest. His breath was wet. Out of the darkness, Hillary's face appeared. Hillary was leaning over him, slapping him. Canon tried to move. Could not. He felt as helpless as he had in the dream of Jackson.

"Good! Good!" giggled Hillary, using the cane to hobble back. "I was afraid you would die before I could get you conscious. But I knew you wouldn't die so easily, not the master of the Black Horse. No, you will not deprive little Hillary of his glory. Oh, but you are dying all right." The demented creature attempted a limping dance.

"Oh, what a glorious shot I made," Hillary continued. "You hulking fool. You big cow. Oh, what a grand shot I made. Right to the heart. The blood is simply pouring from your mouth. You are dead, General Canon. Dead at the hands of Hillary. Is it not delicious? What was that charming term you used? Ah, yes. Pork chop. You are a pork chop, mighty leader of the Stonewall Brigade. Mighty horseman. One shot from little Hillary's little gun, and Goliath is turned into a pork chop."

Seething anger erupted inside Canon, giving him strength. He moved his left hand to his holster.

"No, no, no," chided Hillary. "I have your pistols." He came closer, leering at Canon. Canon saw the handle of the knife protruding from Hillary's left arm, near the shoulder, just where Jackson was hit by the fatal bullet.

Hillary followed Canon's gaze. He laughed. "Yes. Yes," he said. "You hurt me again, you swine."

He used the cane to poke Canon in the chest. Canon coughed a volume of blood and the world went gray. "But it is nothing serious, General. Nothing little Hillary can't handle. Little Hillary is used to pain. Oh, yes." He giggled.

Hammer, standing over Canon, began to toss his head and stamp.

"Keep that animal away from me," Hillary warned, struggling to lift the cane higher. "I have reloaded and I will be happy to shoot the beast."

Canon shook his head at Hammer. "Back," he said. "Be still." The palomino quieted, moved back two steps.

"Time will heal my wounds," Hillary said. "My poor ear, of course, is disfigured. But long hair is still very fashionable. A wig should do nicely. I will be the rage in Washington, and show my poor ear to tenderhearted ladies and tell them I how I earned the wound as I laid waste to the rogue leader of the Black Horse Cavalry.

"Perhaps I will take your ear, after you take that last bubbling breath. Yes, I shall. Both your ears. And I will show them to the hoi polloi of Washington, and tell how I made you pay. Pay and beg." He poked the stick viciously into Canon's chest. Canon willed himself to hang onto consciousness.

"Won't you beg me, General Canon, before I go? I really must be getting along, you know. No, I don't suppose you will beg, will you."

Canon summoned his strength. "Maybe," he whispered.

"What?" said Hillary. "What did you say?"

"I said I'll beg."

"What a delight," said Hillary. "What is it you want? Water? Or perhaps you are in such pain you want me to finish you. Is that it? Tell me what you want. If you beg nicely, I will do it."

Canon tried to talk. It hurt like hell to breathe.

"I made a promise . . ."

"Yes?" said Hillary.

"I swore I would not die until I saw a noose around your neck."

"Oh, you did? Is that all that is keeping you alive? How bizarre. How delightful." He took up the loop lying next to Canon and with difficulty raised it high as his head.

"And you will beg, my dear General?" said Hillary coquettishly.

"Please," said Canon.

"Again."

"Please," said Canon.

"Once more, louder."

"Please, damn your soul to hell," said Canon, with all the voice he could muster.

"Tut, tut. You forget yourself. But very well. Your last wish and all." Hillary slipped the loop over his head. It dangled in front of his chest.

"Tighter."

"Tighter? You fool. Here, have it." Hillary managed to get his wounded arm up and drew the loop up. Then the man began to dance again, waltzing around Canon, hobbling on his cane, trailing the rope.

He hobbled his wild waltz close to Canon, leaned over him, propping on the cane. "I think I will kill you, now, Canon," he said, "since you seem so unwilling to die from my first marvelous shot. Anything to say?"

"Actually, I'm beginning to feel better, Hillary. You hit me in the lung, not the heart. And I know lots of people living with one lung."

"Well, la de da," said Hillary. "What do you plan to do to me, Mister One Lung."

"Hell, Hillary. I'm going to do just what I said I would do. I'm going to hang you. Hammer! Three!"

The palomino took off at a gallop. With a gasp of horror, Hillary saw the rope begin to uncoil. He hesitated for a second, trying to decide whether to use his almost-paralyzed arm to aim the cane or loosen the loop. With a look of utter despair, he realized neither would help him. Even he could hit the fleeing horse, one bullet would not stop the palomino.

He looked Canon in the eye. "For God's sake, no," he said softly.

"For Stonewall Jackson's sake, yes," said Canon.

Watching the rope uncoil, Hillary tried to raise the cane. Whether he was trying to shoot Canon or Hammer, he never got close. The last coil uncurled.

With a hopeless gurgling cry, Hillary was yanked off his feet as if taken by a mighty gust of wind. The cane went flying through the air. Hillary went tumbling after Hammer.

The little man was still alive when Hammer raced back by in the huge circle Canon had ordered him to run. Hillary was kicking and trying to get his legs under him, and pulling at the rope with all the strength in his wounded arm.

He was still alive when Hammer pulled him past for the second time. Canon could hear gurgled breathing. And Canon thought Hillary still lived on the third pass, from the look of terror in the man's eyes. Canon believed him dead by the fourth pass and was relatively sure by the sixth. By the tenth pass, Canon could hardly stand to look at the faceless thing anymore and allowed Hammer to stop.

Too weak to worry about freeing Hillary's remains, Canon called Hammer to him, had the big horse lie down, and he rolled into the saddle.

Hammer stood slowly. On the ride back, leaning over the saddle, Canon occasionally glanced behind him to see how much of Hillary was left in the rope. Then he passed out.

He woke up when one of his captains pulled him out of the saddle. The loop at the end of the rope was empty.

"Where is the bastard?" said the captain, thinking Hillary had somehow ambushed Canon and gotten away.

"Oh, I caught him," said Canon weakly. "He was so broken up about it that he went all to pieces." Then the fog, which Canon claimed for friend, rolled gently over him.

It was a long night for Canon, in which scenes spun like a twirling crazy quilt through his delirium dreams. He saw himself cut down by Hillary's bullet, saw Jackson take the mortal wound, saw Carolina cry and cringe as Trask reached his cigar down to her.

He saw the bulldog face of Pinkerton, chomping on a cigar, and saw the elegant little curtsey of Mamie Sutcliffe and the smiling Mary Anna. Time and again he saw the pouting lips and sultry smile of Carolina Lee. And, finally, he smelled lilacs and knew when he opened his eyes that this Carrie Lee was real.

He was back in the hospital at Richmond, but this time the doctors smiled when they came in to check him.

Beauregard came by, with President Jeff Davis. They looked grim, but had glad tidings. Buck and Mountain Eagle had joined John Mosby, fighting in Texas. They were fine.

The New Year, 1865, turned into a new world. Canon finally regained his feet, was up and around, tottering like the Confederacy. The millions he brought back from California had helped, but a hundred million could not have saved the Confederacy.

One day in early spring, he moved back to his house in Richmond. He got there just before the Yankees. On April 2, the Confederate congress abandoned Richmond and the Yankees moved in.

Canon was placed under house arrest, but was treated with the greatest respect. Lee surrendered a week later, and five days after that, Lincoln was killed.

By summer, Canon was saddling Hammer unassisted and taking short rides with Carrie, Mary Anna and a dozen Yankee guards. Doctors felt he would eventually recover complete use of his lung.

The Confederacy wound down.

On May 10, the second anniversary of the death of Stonewall Jackson, three days before the final battle of the war was fought near Brownsville, Texas, Canon got word that Buck and Mountain Eagle had gone west to join the Indians. And he had his last and best dream about Stonewall Jackson.

He saw a smiling Jackson, a whole Jackson, sitting in his turkey hunting clothes under tall green shade trees. A pleasant river rolled peacefully past.

Canon wasn't sure, but as the dream faded, he thought Jackson looked his way. And smiled.

# *Epilogue*

It is a park near New Orleans. Away from the wharf and the roiling brown Mississippi River where steamboats make their lonesome, booming whistles scream at all hours.

It doesn't matter. New Orleans, at least in the district of the park, doesn't sleep. It is a city of lights. The city is full, raw, teeming and straining.

The Civil War was over quickly for New Orleans. She was captured early, occupied and then released to go on her merry way. And if ever there was a whirlagig, brash and laughing city, prism colored and thrashing, it is she.

But today, there is a hush here, in the park. It is the closing ceremonies of a dedication. Gray-haired men pull the tattered remnants of their Rebel uniforms tighter. Heads are bowed as the statue is dedicated to the memory of a hero for the world.

The aging chaplain of a brigade called the Louisiana Tigers is called on to render the final prayer. It is a remarkable prayer, and here is how it ends:

"And, when, oh Lord, in thy inscrutable wisdom, it was decreed the Confederacy must fail, it became necessary for thee to remove thy servant, Stonewall Jackson.

"Amen."

Confederate General A. P. Hill died, shot through the heart, at the Battle of Petersberg near the end of the war. He and an aide, reconnoitering the woods following one of the frays, rode up on four Union soldiers who had them immediately under their guns.

Hill charged, trying to draw his gun. It was a suicidal charge, said the aide.

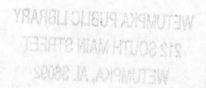